PRAISE FOR
SASHA PLOTKIN'S DECEIT

"*Sasha Plotkin's Deceit* is smart, gripping, and captivating. Vaughn Sherman writes with a depth and authenticity that remind me of John le Carré. I was lured into the story from the first page. Fantastic!"

—Carla Neggers, *New York Times* bestselling author of *Saint's Gate*

"In *Sasha Plotkin's Deceit*, Vaughn Sherman weaves a Cold War tale of love, mystery and betrayal. Sherman pulls no punches describing the life of a CIA operative called to one final game of cat and mouse with a KGB counterpart from his past. The mission could destroy his marriage, his family and his career. Written from an insider's perspective, this poignant look inside the world of spies kept me wondering until the very end."

—Robert Dugoni, *New York Times* bestselling author of *Murder One*

"It's the early 1970s. The Cuban Missile Crisis is over. The CIA still smarts from the Bay of Pigs fiasco. American soldiers are still slogging through the quagmire of Vietnam. The Russian tanks are gone from the streets of Prague, but the shadow of Mother Russia lays heavy on the fragile geopolitical landscape. In a war of clandestine operations, America needs her best agents on the job. The only problem: there's a Mole in the CIA . . . Th~ ~ ~nger the Mole is a KGB officer, Sasha Plo   officer, Chris Holbeck, a reluctant hero w.   m his family for taking on the quest for   he action shifts from a peaceful sailing d.   ~as Viking roots) to CIA headquarters at L~ ~ ~,, ~~~~es into a flashback about the first contact between protagonist and antagonist, zips to Stockholm—Sweden is a geopolitical buffer between Russia and the U.S.—for some clever spycraft, including a Swedish damosel and part-time agent, who opens her heart to our hero. He's having trouble with his wife, but will he surrender to the damosel? Problem: the only way out of Sweden is a submarine. The only way to the sub is a small boat—and the KGB guy gets seasick in the bathtub .... An unpredictable spy novel with a big heart and a resounding ring of authenticity."

—Robert J. Ray, author of the Matt Murdock mystery series, including *Murdock Cracks Ice*

"*Sasha* is a must-read for fans of the spy genre. It delivers an intriguing and creative premise that quickly draws the reader in, while avoiding the chronic faults that spoil most spy novels—over-complicated, hokey or synthetic plot-twists, long wallows in tradecraft, and over-the-top traitors or heroes. All the players are very credible and resemble those of my own experience. Sherman portrays the human interactions and scenes involving 'company business' extraordinarily well. He also weaves the practical tradecraft delicately and naturally into the story line, showing how subject it is to Murphy's Law. The overall effect is enhanced by a smooth and comfortable literary style."

—Howard Ellis, retired CIA

SASHA PLOTKIN'S DECEIT

SASHA PLOTKIN'S DECEIT

A NOVEL

Vaughn Sherman

Seattle, WA

CAMEL PRESS

Published by Camel Press
PO Box 70515
Seattle, WA 98127

For more information go to: www.camelpress.com
www.vaughnsherman.com

This is a work of fiction. Names, characters, places, brands, media, and incidents are either the product of the author's imagination or are used fictitiously.

Cover design by Sabrina Sun

Sasha Plotkin's Deceit
Copyright © 2012 by Vaughn Sherman

ISBN: 978-1-60381-811-7 (Trade Paper)
ISBN: 978-1-60381-880-3 (eBook)

Library of Congress Control Number: 2012931965

10 9 8 7 6 5 4 3 2 1

Printed in the United States of America

PROLOGUE

April 2, 1972

Hans checked his wristwatch, a non-descript Timex worn especially for the occasion. Seven ten in the evening, the published time of sunset in Moscow on this gloomy, early spring day. So gloomy that a casual observer unaware of the statistical time the sun was to go down would know only that the day was almost over. Beyond the time of sunset, Hans knew also that official twilight's end was 7:47 p.m.

That and a thousand other details were needed to carry out the task successfully. He stood at the hotel window, watching the gray sky slowly darken, trying to calm his nerves with a mantra learned from a Buddhist monk. The monk had moved him spiritually more than the Russian Orthodox Church had ever done during his childhood in Germany, where he'd been raised by well-to-do Russian émigré parents. Tonight, though, he couldn't find the center, the quiet place he needed to be.

The telephone jangled him out of those thoughts. "Herr Weiner?" the voice said.

"Yes?" Hans replied. The assistant manager of the hotel was calling.

"Will Herr Weiner be wanting his supper served at ten-thirty?"

"Yes, Pyotr, that will be fine." This was the signal that Pyotr was still in the game for tonight. It irritated him that the fellow was speaking in grossly accented German. Pyotr knew very well that Hans's Russian language ability was native.

For a couple of years Pyotr, recruited by Hans using ideological motivation, had carried out simple intelligence tasks in Moscow. Pyotr thought he was working on behalf of a German intelligence agency; in fact his recruiter was a long-time CIA agent. Pyotr would be sorely disappointed to learn that fact, for he was fascinated with all things Germanic—having come into the world through the one-time union of a Russian mother and a German soldier during the final days of the Nazi occupation during World War II.

Hans and his controllers feared Pyotr was the weakest link in the chain of events planned for later that night. But there was nothing to be done. Hans had to get out of the hotel unseen by the KGB minder assigned to him during these trips, and Pyotr was the only one who could help.

Hans opened the hidden compartment in his suitcase, taking out documentation that proved him to be a Russian telephone technician living in Moscow. He placed his true documentation in the concealment device. A consulting engineer employed by a German telephone firm, Hans could talk the lingo indicated by these papers. But that and the supposed telephone equipment in his briefcase would get him past only the most casual observer. If apprehended by the authorities while carrying this package, he would be finished.

Supper was brought to his room by a member of the wait staff. The food in this small hotel, an establishment catering more to Russian than to foreign businessmen, was surprisingly good. He enjoyed an array of dishes much like those served on his family table before the war: borscht, a cucumber and radish salad, black bread and the one glass of beer he allowed himself before an operation.

Hans took his long black coat and fur hat from the closet, put the briefcase on the bed, and settled down in the one easy chair in the room. He tried to read a novel, saw the words on the page, but they made no impression.

There came a gentle tap on the door. He donned the coat and hat, took the briefcase in hand and joined Pyotr in the hall. As always he noticed the pervading odor of hotel hallways in Russia, a mixture of smoke from the god-awful cigarettes, colognes and perfumes, and—strangely—mothballs.

Pyotr was pushing a waiter's cart loaded with dishes. He made no attempt to get the dinner dishes from Hans's room, indicating by his expression and a nod of the head that they must hurry. Entering a service elevator, he used a key to send the car to the basement. As they had worked out during a quick hallway meeting the day before, Pyotr gave a copy of the key to Hans while letting him out at the bottom level. Hans would use that key to go back to his room when he returned from the operation. *If* he returned from the operation.

Everything had worked out as planned up until this point. Following Pyotr's directions, Hans walked through a storeroom to find a large sliding door that opened to a loading dock. It was closed. A smaller door to the side was also closed, but it was unlocked. Now he was walking on a deserted street, looking—he hoped—like a Russian official or businessman returning from an evening meeting. Only seven blocks to go. The blocks ticked off one by one as he trudged along with his briefcase, sighting only two people in the mostly residential area. Neither paid any attention to Hans as they turned onto perpendicular streets. After five blocks of travel he was in a mixed-use neighborhood, combining business offices with light industry.

Now he was at the target street with only one hundred meters to go. Sweat trickled down from his armpits; his heart pounded. The operation would be a 'go' if nobody was in sight. He turned the corner. The street was deserted.

Hans walked quickly to a manhole cover located between the sidewalk and the middle of the street. It took a surprising effort to shift the cover far enough away from the hole for him to enter. He dropped down and slid the cover back into position, more frightened than at any other time in his life.

But now the dozen training sessions in preparation for the mission took hold. He turned on a tiny flashlight that was part of the kit in his briefcase and proceeded with the automated responses learned from his training. Equipment was taken from the briefcase, simple preparations were made to the communications conduit running through the tunnel, and the equipment was attached. Hans worked up such a nervous sweat from the pressure of this work that he unbuttoned his overcoat. He could smell his own fear. Nevertheless his hand remained steady, and the work was accomplished in less than half an hour. Once the device was attached and tested, he made sure that all other materials had been returned to the briefcase. He positioned himself directly below the manhole cover, turned off the light, and pushed up the cover just far enough to scan the street. Nobody in sight.

Anxiety gave Hans a jolt of adrenaline, making it easy to push and slide the cover open. He hauled himself and the briefcase onto the street. Just as he was about to drop the cover into place, he was startled by the noise of a speeding car. He froze. Hans Weiner's last thought on earth was that he recognized that sound. He knew it from riding in Zil limousines while conducting business in the Soviet Union.

The Zil had parked around the corner on the same street Hans traveled from the hotel, its arrival timed by an observer in an office building facing the target street. Word had been passed by radio when Hans emerged from the manhole. The KGB driver found an easy target as he sped up before crushing Hans beneath the heavy machine.

The device Hans had installed so successfully worked for about ten minutes before being disconnected by KGB technicians.

For two days following the incident, nothing was heard from or about

Hans. Then a brief article appeared in *Izvestia*, reporting that a German telephone engineer by the name of Hans Weiner had been struck and killed by a car late at night in Moscow. His blood alcohol level at autopsy showed that he had been extremely inebriated, making it probable that he had wandered into the roadway in front of the moving vehicle.

Pyotr disappeared from the hotel where Hans had stayed. Months later, the Soviet Government had still not protested the incident, either to the Germans or the Americans.

PART ONE

CHAPTER ONE

Tuesday, November 7, 1972—7:30 a.m.
Edmonds, Washington

Perfect! Damn perfect!

It hadn't been perfect when he steered his dad's twenty-eight-foot Tollycraft cruiser out of the Edmonds Marina. A thick fog bank snuggled against the eastern shore of Puget Sound, fog so thick at dawn that he had to follow close to the ends of the lighted piers before reaching the harbor entrance. Once through the opening in the breakwater, he'd sounded the horn and picked up speed to six knots. Turning on course to Possession Point, setting the automatic pilot, he was expecting another five minutes in fog when suddenly it was gone.

Mount Baker, almost one hundred miles to the north, was visible and snowcapped. The Cascades and Mount Rainier were still hidden by the bank of fog behind him, but to the west the Olympics were clear, dusted by a recent snowfall. A tug with log rafts in tow was moving with the end of a flood tide, entering Possession Sound on its way to a mill. While in the fog Chris felt and smelled only dampness, but now the salt air reached him in a breeze created by cruising speed, bringing an almost visceral sense of peace. His grip on the steering wheel relaxed as he was overcome by memories of working on his family's tugboats in these same waters, a youngster starting to find his way in the world.

Now in his mid-forties, Chris stood at the helm located on the boat's open after-deck, feeling like a man of the sea, like he had re-discovered the place he belonged. Long johns under sturdy wool pants and a Norwegian sweater kept out the cold and damp. His almost-blond hair, wide-set blue eyes and six-foot frame attested to his Swedish ancestry.

He was getting fishing gear ready for action when the marine radio squawked with a call. "This is the Seattle Marine Operator calling the *Mor*. The *Mor*. Please switch and answer Channel Twenty-Six."

Damn. What could that be about? Chris took the microphone from its hook alongside the radio, switched frequencies and replied, "This is the *Mor* to the Seattle Marine Operator."

She said there was a personal call; that meant the caller could only be Lisa or one of his parents.

"Chris?" It was Lisa, his wife.

"Yes, Honey. What's the matter?"

"There might be a lot the matter. Mike just called from Washington and made me tell him how to reach you. He wouldn't tell me what it was about, but I'm letting you know that it better not mean you're traveling without the family again."

Mike Mitchell, head of European operations for the Central Intelligence Agency, would be Chris Holbeck's boss when he reported back to Headquarters after a two-year tour in Vietnam without his family. Now he was staying in Edmonds, nearing the end of a home leave shared with his wife and children.

"You know I wouldn't leave you here with the kids unless it was absolutely necessary."

An angry voice: "You're not going to leave me and the kids here for any reason, Chris. I love you very much, but if you and your damned outfit do that to me again ..." The thought was left hanging.

"Come on, Honey."

"Come on yourself. If this changes our plans to leave for Washington next week in any way, then you better start looking for another wife and kids."

The connection broke. Signing off with the marine operator, Chris felt a throb in his temple. He had looked forward to this day for two years—needed the quiet contemplation of fishing by himself—and wasn't going to give it up for anyone. Waiting for a call from the Agency, he returned to the preparations for his day on the water, baiting crab pots with salmon heads and backs and getting fishing rods ready. The contemplation had turned to a slow burn, to fuming over yet another phone-call interruption of time he should be able to call his own.

With more than twenty years of experience as an operations officer with the CIA, Chris counted the number of interruptions as beyond reckoning. Four of them would always be in his memory. Three were calls that came while he and Lisa were making love. He remembered those with a smile on his lips and warmth in his heart—fond recollections of a married life close to perfection in the early years.

And then there was the fourth time. That one happened during a tour in Sweden, where he recruited a young Swedish-American woman as a support agent for the Station. During Bisan's first year in this role they spent a lot of time together in training and operations. While working on a case in Copenhagen, Chris and his agent stayed in the same hotel for two nights. Letting down from the stresses of the second day, they shared a bottle of wine during dinner in a wonderful restaurant alongside the harbor. Then a cognac with coffee in their hotel bar. Returning to their adjoining rooms they were relaxed, content with a good day's work, and just a bit fuzzed up by the drinks. A goodnight kiss in the hall outside their adjoining rooms seemed only natural. What seemed only natural turned into a sudden urge, a mutual understanding communicated by eye contact as they pulled back from a deep kiss. And then they heard the phone ringing in Chris's room. They were needed out on the street in fifteen minutes. Quickly sobered, they completed an operation that brought kudos for both. It was a close escape for Chris, whose record of marital fidelity remained unbroken. It was the nearest he ever came to being unfaithful to Lisa.

The radio squawked again. It was Mike this time.

"How's the fishing, Chris?"

"Thanks for asking." He hoped the sarcasm in his voice would come through. "I haven't wet a line yet. It isn't even eight o'clock in the morning here, and I don't much appreciate your waking Lisa so early."

"I'm sorry, but it seems one of your really important guys from our last days together is out in Western Europe again. He's signaled for a meeting with you. Gary wants you in his office tomorrow morning, and we've booked reservations out of Dulles Airport on tomorrow night's flight to Stockholm."

"Stand by one. I've got some maneuvering to do with the boat." Putting the *Mor* out of gear before going back on the air, he took a moment to calm down and consider his situation. Any way he looked at it, the situation was lousy.

"Sorry, Mike, I've got it under control now. There is absolutely no way I'm going to be in Washington by tomorrow morning. You know damn well what that would do to my family after already being separated for two years. Let someone else see my friend. Tell him I'm dead!"

"He won't see anyone else, Chris. And you of all people know how important this is. What do you want me to tell Gary?"

"I'll call him, but not before I get me some salmon."

"Okay. Listen, Chris, I hope things go well with Lisa. I can imagine how she's going to feel about this change in plans. I'll pass that on to Gary and hope to see you tomorrow myself."

"I'm making no promises until I've talked with Lisa, but I'll see you before long anyway."

"Oh, and one more thing," Mike said.

"What's that?"

"Remember your friend Bob visiting you in Saigon a couple of months ago? He asked me to remind you of a story he told. He thinks the fellow who wants to see you might know something about that."

Signing off, Chris let the *Mor* drift for a while longer. Yes, he remembered the story. He didn't want to, because that memory just put another stone on the side of the balance saying he must travel to make the contact. Now he was forced to revisit the past.

In September, just two months earlier, while still posted in Vietnam, Chris was visited by one of his best friends. Bob Brewer was Deputy Chief of the CIA's Soviet Division. The visit was a complete surprise, Brewer showing up unannounced at Chris's Saigon apartment just before dinner ....

※ ※ ※

A big man, taller than Chris by three inches and heavier by a good seventy-five pounds, Brewer wrapped his friend in a bear hug.

"What in hell are you doing here, Bob? You could at least have let me know you were coming."

"That would have spoiled the surprise."

They were still standing in the doorway of the apartment. Chris suddenly remembered his manners. "Sorry, Bob. Come on in. Can you stay for dinner?"

"I can stay longer than that. Maybe you didn't notice." Chris in fact had not noticed the small suitcase alongside Bob in the entry. "Or maybe you have a sweet young Vietnamese girl living with you. That could be awkward."

"No, no. No young thing here. I do have an old Chinese lady who takes care of me. She's a great cook. Come on in. We'll get you set up in the spare bedroom. Sue Mai! Sue Mai!"

When Sue Mai appeared, Brewer found that she was indeed old, stooped with age, wearing a gap-toothed smile that didn't add to her looks. Her graying black hair was pulled back severely, and she was dressed in a long, blue-and green-patterned robe and wearing bright red slippers. She pushed him aside to heft his suitcase and take it to the spare room. His protests that he could carry it himself brought a stern look and wagging finger. Very quickly she had set out a tray of drinks in the living room. While the men were helping themselves to drinks in the small living room, they could hear the old lady singing in Chinese as she cooked their dinner.

With drinks in hand, the two colleagues began a conversation that would last until one o'clock in the morning. More than just colleagues or mere friends, these two were comrades-in-arms who had traveled to several places in the world on operations to gather information or recruit Soviet and East Bloc officials.

"So why the visit just now, Bob?" Chris fired the opening shot. "I can't imagine that you traveled halfway around the world just to visit me."

"You're right, Chris. My mission this time was in Bangkok, but I decided to hop over here for a recruitment operation."

Chris was startled that his old friend would be here in Saigon on a recruitment mission. His own responsibilities would require that he know of any operation related to Bob's area of expertise. "Now I'm really surprised, Bob. I haven't heard anything like that. Who's the target?"

"You are, my friend."

"Get serious."

"I'm perfectly serious. But before we talk of such things, how secure are we? This is pretty sensitive stuff. Does Sue Mai understand English? Can she hear us while she's cooking out there in the kitchen?"

"She understands only a few words having to do with running a household. You can feel quite secure while she's singing out there. She'll be going home after dinner. And now, while she's singing, tell me."

"I'll begin by telling you that my boss, Gary Llonis, agrees that you would be the best man to head an effort in our division to ferret out a mole. There's always been counter-intelligence activity on this problem, but now we have solid evidence that the mole exists. We want you to find the son-of-a-bitch."

"I'm sure you know that I'm slated to work with Mike Mitchell as Deputy Chief of the European Division."

"We know all about that. Gary and I have been talking about it with Mike. He's agreed to work out something. You won't lose that opportunity. This is very serious, Chris. I'm authorized to tell you about a failed case that proves the existence of a mole in our own office."

They were interrupted by Sue Mai calling them to dinner. Chris got to his feet immediately, motioning Bob to do the same.

His guest was amused. "She's got you obeying like a trained seal!"

"You bet. Just wait until you taste the dinner she's put together. You'll be another one of her slaves." It was a typical Chinese dinner—sweet and sour pork, two chicken dishes, bean sprouts and rice, washed down with tea—yet more delicious than meals Brewer had enjoyed in scores of Chinese restaurants.

Sue Mai left for her home immediately after cleaning up the kitchen, allowing the two men to get back to discussing the sensitive operation.

"The loss of that operation," Bob continued from the conversation before dinner, "was a tremendous blow. The device had huge potential, but it was only a success for a few minutes and the agent who placed the device was brutally killed by the KGB."

"Was he an American?" Chris interrupted.

"No, a European, but a long-time, highly dedicated agent who had done great work for us. This operation was conducted on a need-to-know basis tighter than any I've seen. Only a handful of officers were aware of it, and even fewer staff. They—and that includes Gary and me—are all being looked at as possible security risks, but nothing's turned up."

"How about on site, where the operation took place? Did any local asset know about it?"

"Just one. Unless our agent who was killed clued him in, and we believe there's zero chance of that. He knew nothing of the target or the device. Besides that, he disappeared from the hotel where he worked immediately after the incident. We're certain he was arrested, and it's likely he was executed."

* * *

Chris's memory of Brewer's visit ended with that thought, leaving him still more puzzled. It didn't seem likely that the Soviet officer who wanted to contact him could have knowledge of the operation Bob described.

A couple of seagulls screeching close overhead brought Chris back to the here and now. With slack tide approaching, *Mor* had drifted little during the conversation with Mike. He ran to Cultis Bay to drop the crab pots and get ready to fish for salmon.

After taking rough bearings on Possession Point and Skatchet Head to mark the position of the pots, Chris gunned *Mor* out to the edge of the bar. Satisfied that he'd found the right place, he throttled back to the slowest possible trolling speed and dropped the salmon gear overboard. Forty-five minutes later there was a hard hit on the port fishing rig. Chris put the engine into neutral, grabbed the rod and set the hook, managing to stop a strong run that used up much of the line on his reel. A couple more runs with still enough energy to call for cautious handling and the fish was in the net—a twelve-pound blackmouth salmon. This was what life was all about.

An hour went by and the ebb tide had begun to run before another fish hit, this time a smaller blackmouth. A third fish about the same size was netted ten minutes later. He reeled in the lines, stowed the poles and ran back toward Cultis Bay to pick up the crab traps. Among several undersized and female Dungeness crabs were six large male "keepers." Were it not for the call from Headquarters, the day would have been a dream come true.

It was only mid-morning. Success had come too quickly. Beautifully realized as it was, the dream ended too soon. If he hurried he could get back to Edmonds and downtown to Seattle in time to join the family for lunch at the Space Needle. His parents had invited Lisa and the children to a farewell meal, followed by a visit to the company boatyard and an outing on the latest towboat in the fleet. But, under the circumstances, he didn't want to see Lisa together with all the others. He knew there would be a showdown. It would be better for the two of them to face off someplace without the family around.

He throttled *Mor* to a slow cruising speed, deliberately following a long route that would get him back to Edmonds in the early afternoon. Now he'd have time to think out the situation created by the call from Mike, time to consider the best strategy to use in his talk with Lisa. What a way to end a dream.

CHAPTER TWO

Tuesday, November 7, 1972—1:00 p.m.

"I am!"

"No you aren't. I am!"

Girlish voices, pitched higher than usual, were spoiling the atmosphere for lunchtime patrons at Seattle's SkyCity Restaurant. Five-hundred feet above Seattle Center, the rotating restaurant is popular with tourists visiting the iconic Space Needle, a principal attraction of the 1962 Seattle World's Fair.

The place is also popular with Seattle families celebrating special occasions. For the older Holbecks the celebration was to be a combination of saying bon voyage to the younger Holbecks and their children, and later introducing them to a new vessel in their fleet of towboats. Son Chris had opted out in favor of a solo fishing excursion. It should have been a pleasant affair even though they were sad to part with their son's family. But the little party had been spoiled for Chris's mother, Gunborg, known to the family as "Mor." It just wasn't right for her granddaughters to be arguing this way. Still worse was the fact that their mother, Mor's daughter-in-law Lisa, was doing nothing about it. Ever since Mor and Lisa had first seen each other that morning, Lisa had been moping about.

"Tell her, Farmor." Melissa, her eight-year-old granddaughter, was turning to a higher authority to settle the argument, using the Swedish term for grandmother on her father's side. "Tell Lisbet that I'm the smartest one."

Since Melissa was usually kind to Lisbet, her three-year-old sister, Mor believed the girl was reacting to the tension exhibited by her mother. "I don't think I said you were smarter, Missy, I said you know more than Lisbet because you're older. Both of you girls are very smart." Not to neglect her teenage twin grandsons, she added, "All my grandchildren are very, very smart."

The group was close to finishing dessert and Herman had already called for the check. The girls' bad temper and Lisa's sad mood were just too much for Mor. She decided not to accompany the rest of the family to see the new boat, but rather to go home by bus now.

When she turned to Herman to announce her plan, she saw he was immersed in the world of boats, sketching a hull on a napkin for the twin boys, who sat on either side of him. He had the full attention of Matthew and Mark, strapping young lads in their last year of high school.

"Herman!" Ignored by the men at the table, she waited a bit before repeating, "Herman!" More sharply this time. When he looked up she said, "I've decided not to go on your boat ride this afternoon. There's some downtown shopping I need to do."

Herman was disappointed. "But you promised!"

"I know. I know, and I'm sorry, but this just has to be done." With that she rose to her full height of six feet, kissed Lisa on the cheek, kissed the girls on the top of their heads, waggled her fingers at the male contingent across the table, and headed for the elevators.

Down at ground level she walked to the Monorail platform. Another holdover from the Seattle World's Fair, the Monorail whisks passengers on its mile-long track to downtown Seattle, taking only two minutes for a journey scheduled every ten minutes.

Hissing as it braked into the Seattle Center terminal, the Monorail brought a dozen passengers from downtown. A like number waited to board, Mor among them. With her height and regal bearing, she drew curious stares from the others waiting on the platform. She swept by them to take the front seat. This was Mor at her loftiest, for she was embarking on one of her periodic missions to right the wrongs of her world.

Mor had no intention of shopping downtown. She preferred going to Edmonds by bus rather than spending more hours in company she couldn't enjoy. Something had gone seriously wrong, and when that happened she needed solitude, time for reflection.

To see that something had gone wrong, you only had to look at Lisa. Lisa, who had been so happy these past weeks with her husband home from that dreadful Vietnam. Lisa, so happy last night, but so withdrawn today, with nothing to explain the long face, the monosyllables, the lifeless eyes.

As she left the Monorail's downtown terminal to transfer to an Edmonds bus, Mor saw herself in a glass storefront and reflected on her aging face. She had never come to terms with the fact that her face was more round than oval, falling short of classic Swedish beauty.

Born of Swedish parents on the beach of Nome, Alaska, where her father was mining gold out of the sand, Mor was an American citizen. After entering the United States, her parents had become citizens at the first opportunity. They told everyone who would listen that their daughter was American-born. This accident of birth was not a matter of pride for Mor. From her earliest memories of visits to Sweden—from Sunday school friendships in the Swedish church with children who had been born in Sweden—she wished she had been born there herself. Never mind, she had kept all the traditions, retained the language, given it to her children, and assumed the role of the matriarchal Swedish mother in her family. It was for this she was known to all as "Mor"—pronounced "Moor"—the Swedish word for mother.

By most standards her life was a story of success. She and her husband owned Tows, Inc., the Puget Sound tugboat company founded by her father using the gold dug out at Nome. Mor married a Swedish marine engineer imported by her father, and as everyone knew—for Mor had told them many times—it was a marriage made in heaven.

She had thought of herself as still young until two-and-a-half years ago, when she lost Björn. A Marine Corps major, her oldest son was killed just two weeks after volunteering for a second tour of duty in the Vietnam jungle.

Only five other passengers rode the bus to Edmonds; most read or gazed out the windows. The quiet of the early-afternoon ride gave Mor a place and time to reflect on another tragedy brewing, this with her youngest son, Chris. She thought bitterly about this new disappointment. From his toddling years Chris had acted more Swedish than his older brother, had gone along with her "Swedish act," as the others called it behind her back. He played his father's game, too, working on the tugs as a deckhand from his early teens. Herman wanted him to enroll in marine engineering at the University of Washington, but Chris excelled at languages, demonstrating a genius for linguistics beyond the Swedish he had learned at home. He ended up as a Russian linguist and left the Seattle area two days after finishing his master's degree to join what his parents had thought was the Foreign Service but now knew was the Central Intelligence Agency. She missed him deeply, painfully, not only at first but through all the years when he married, had children, and kept his family from her by spending most of their time in Europe. She was grateful that his last European assignment was in Sweden, giving her an excuse to visit and satisfying her longing to be with Chris's family while spending time in the country she loved.

Her bus arrived in Edmonds. Now Mor walked briskly up the hill to their comfortable, sprawling, country-style house. After hanging up her coat and hat, she went to the kitchen to make a pot of coffee and take a packet of spritz cookies out of the freezer. Her doctor had told her to lay off the sweets, but Mor was in a mood to indulge herself.

Settled in the living room with her coffee and her cookies—a sweeping view of Puget Sound framed in the picture window—she saw one of the Tows' tugs pulling two barges loaded impossibly high with equipment probably destined for a port in Southeast Alaska. She had to smile at the company name painted in huge letters on the sides of the tug: TOWS. Her father had painted this on the first little tug he built after returning from Alaska, thinking to advertise that he was available for towing. Tows it was then, and Tows still. Now the company had expanded far beyond the reaches of Puget Sound, with ocean-going tugs towing to Alaska. They also had a large contract for towing in Vietnam. That damned Vietnam.

She shuddered. Vietnam—the place that had bedeviled her so much in recent years. Mor could still recall the panic that welled up in her on learning that Chris was to be sent to Vietnam, all too soon after Björn died there. Chris's assignment to Vietnam, following the awful news about Björn, was a blow that deepened the hurt. His assurances that he would be working in Saigon at the American Embassy did little to relieve her awful anxiety and foreboding.

Living nearby in a rented home while her husband was away those two years, Lisa and her children spent much of their time with Mor and Herman. They had all been overjoyed when Chris returned safely and moved his family into her home for a few weeks of leave before going back to the other Washington for an assignment there. And now? Tears sprang to her eyes. She stood up and helped herself to more coffee and just a few more spritz.

Looking out the kitchen window she was surprised to see Lisa drive up in the Volvo sedan she and Chris had brought back from Sweden. As Lisa came into the kitchen, Mor saw she had been crying. They were surprised to see each other.

"Mor! What are you doing here? I thought you were going shopping." Lisa frowned at the sight of her mother-in-law.

"And what are you doing here?" Mor retorted. "I thought you and Herman were going out on the new boat with the children. Nothing's wrong with any of them, is there?"

"No, Mor, they're fine. I just wanted time to myself to think things out."

Mor took another cup out of the cupboard, filled it, put more cookies on the plate and ushered Lisa into the living room. "That's why I came home, too. Do you want to talk about it? I know it has to be something serious for my happy Lisa to be so sad."

"Oh, Mor." Lisa sobbed and snuggled her head against Mor's ample bosom. The difference in their heights was pronounced. At five feet, three inches, Lisa was petite and blond, with "girl-next-door" looks admired by men and envied by women. Mor, who had just barely rescued the coffee cups and cookies from being crushed in the embrace, gently pried Lisa loose and sat her down.

"Now, what is it? Something to do with Chris, I'm sure."

"More to do with that damn agency he works for. I answered a call from Washington early this morning while you were still asleep. It was so urgent that they insisted I tell them how to get hold of Chris by ship-to-shore radio while he was out on the boat. I know all too well that this means he's going to leave us again. He's already been in Vietnam for two years, and we planned to go back to Washington next week ... This is just too much. After that time he left us for six weeks over Christmas, I warned him that I'd never accept anything like that again. Then came the Vietnam tour, which was close to the last straw. I'm afraid this time if he leaves, it will be the last straw."

"What are you going to do?" Mor swiveled her chair around to look at Puget Sound through the picture window, not wishing Lisa to see her tears.

"I called Chris on the boat before they could get through to him from Washington. I told him that I'd leave him and take the children with me if he did this to us again."

"And what did he have to say when you told him that?"

"I didn't give him a chance to say anything. I just hung up."

Mor was tempted to ask if that was a wise thing to do, but before the words came out she felt a slow fuse of anger burning. Anger at a son who was acting so stupidly, endangering his marriage to this wonderful girl, risking the loss of his children. And all this in the name of the CIA, that agency she knew in her heart was responsible for starting the war in Vietnam and might now be the cause of the dissolution of her youngest son's marriage. *Kaere Gud*, she thought to herself, is there no end to the evils the CIA does in the world? All those things people said in Sweden about America and the agency were true. No wonder Swedes were always demonstrating against the American Embassy.

"Yah, Lisa, we shall see." Those blue eyes she had passed on to Chris were snapping. Mor was about to set the world right again.

CHAPTER THREE

Tuesday, November 7, 1972—6:00 p.m.

A s his taxi left the freeway for the entrance to SeaTac Airport on this early November evening, Chris saw from the reader sign that the temperature was thirty-seven degrees. Approaching the season of joy, Thanksgiving and Christmas. The airport was all but deserted, the spreading darkness settling its gloom and mist over the area.

He checked into the Northwest Airlines counter in the main terminal then rode the automated subway out to the satellite, where he'd be boarding the Red Eye Special, a flight used by many businessmen, congressmen and federal workers. You could put in a full day's work in Seattle and still be at work in Washington the next day—as long as you didn't mind getting by on four hours' sleep. Chris didn't mind much of anything at this point.

It was hard to believe everything that had happened on just this one day—fishing for salmon and crab, receiving the order to fly overseas, carrying on a monumental argument with Lisa that might result in divorce and the loss of his children. The scene at the old house in Edmonds had drained him. He'd hoped that assuming a cheerful air would defuse the pending argument with Lisa. He hadn't expected to find her home when he arrived, but he'd known she was there when he saw the Volvo. To his surprise he found Mor there, too. Their grim expressions made it clear what was to come.

The lines were quickly drawn, the battle brief. Chris was thrown off balance when he found himself opposed by his mother as well as Lisa. Uncharacteristically, he lost his temper early in the fight. Chris was angered by the sight of Lisa hiding behind his mother's skirts, and irritated at his mother for interfering, even though she couldn't possibly understand his situation. He made it clear that he was being called away to Sweden to work on an old case—Lisa certainly knew which one. But she'd clung to Mor, crying, and he had stalked out of the room—white-faced and tight-lipped—to pack. Damn her. Damn her!

Just before six o'clock DC time, he caught Gary by phone in the office to let him know he'd be coming in the morning.

As he washed up, changed into a suit, and gathered clothes for the trip, he rationalized his decision to obey the Agency's call. If Lisa had been more reasonable, he told himself, he might have been persuaded not to leave. But he knew in his heart that Lisa could not really oppose his leaving; knew, too, that Lisa was just as aware that refusing to make this meeting could have serious consequences for both of them and their family. His only farewell to the two women he loved most in the world had been, "I'm leaving now." Holding one suitcase, he slipped out the back door and walked to downtown Edmonds, regretting most of all that he would not have a chance to say goodbye to the children and his dad.

First Chris stopped at the bank, where he withdrew five hundred dollars from the account kept separate from Lisa's while in Vietnam. Next he took a taxi to the airport, a costly ride that would be on his expense account. He'd had no problem buying a ticket at the Northwest Airlines counter, although it was a long wait for the flight. He passed time with drinks and dinner, then browsed through the bookstore. After a half-hour of staring blankly at the racks, he decided not to buy a book. Now he boarded the jet through a covered ramp, escaping the cold rain that followed the evening buildup of clouds. Chris found he had a three-seat row all to himself. The flight was only about a quarter full, its passengers tired-looking men in suits rumpled by a long day's work. After takeoff the no-smoking light had turned off, and the stewardesses were taking drink orders even before the plane lifted above the Western Washington cloud cover. A wave of nostalgia drifted over Chris as they broke through the cloud layer and he saw Mount Rainier bathed in moonlight some twenty miles off to the right.

"Would you like a drink, sir?" The stewardess was good-looking, though the makeup and helmet hair were a bit too much. "Yes, thanks, a double vodka on the rocks." After this day he needed the double.

There would be lots of time on the flight tonight to reflect. He needed to think through the case history before seeing Gary in the morning. Emotion is the best driver for creating un-erasable memories. Among all the friends he had met while in the CIA, Aleksandr Elyovitch Plotkin was most unforgettable. Their relationship was so emotionally tangled that it was exhausting just to think about it.

He must have drifted off. When he woke, his tray table was in an upright position and someone had covered him with a blanket.

CHAPTER FOUR

Wednesday, November 8th, 1972—8:30 a.m.

Gary Llonis, Chief of the Soviet Division, had an office on one of the upper floors of CIA Headquarters at Langley, Virginia. Relatively sumptuous compared to those of lesser officers, its main feature was a large executive desk. A high-backed simulated leather chair faced away from tall, narrow windows overlooking parking lots and the now bleak Virginia countryside. Two couches and an easy chair, a coffee table and some indifferent prints elaborately framed were supposed to give the office a relaxed and homey feeling, but in the end it came off like the rest of the building—cold and functional. The architects' whimsical touch of painting interior doors in assorted bright colors did nothing to dispel the impression that the building was just another large monument to bureaucracy.

The wall clock in the outer office showed exactly eight thirty in the morning when Llonis opened the door. Llonis was famed for his punctuality, also for his industry, laboring ten hours a day, six days a week, no more, no less. Outside those hours he brooked no interference with his private life, leaving all but the most critical night calls on urgent cables to a trusted deputy who was empowered to answer them.

"Good morning, Mr. Llonis," his two secretaries said in unison.

"Morning, ladies." Tall and imposing, Llonis was distinguished by his totally bald head. The overall impression had earned him the nickname of Daddy Warbucks, which seemed appropriate to the officers he chewed out for one sin or another. Llonis, who left the FBI to join the Agency when it was formed in 1947, was a master of tradecraft—that mysterious set of skills needed to recruit, train and run intelligence agents. He was known for scrawling fierce criticism on field dispatches that offended his sense of professionalism as well as outgoing messages prepared by officers in his own division. Those in the field felt the sting of his wrath in replies from Headquarters. His own officers experienced it more directly when their messages were returned without approval for transmission—the dreaded notation signaling a meeting with the boss.

Entering his own office, he hung up his coat and sat down at a desk cleared of all documents save one—a sealed envelope marked "Eyes Only." Bob Brewer, his deputy, had prepared it and placed it there before Llonis' arrival. It analyzed some twenty hours of Plotkin files and others relating to the case. The deputy had gone home to shower and shave before returning to the Agency for another day's work.

A secretary came in with a cup of coffee, the first of many he would consume throughout the day. "Call the branch chiefs and tell them this morning's staff meeting is cancelled." Explaining that he would be tied up in a meeting with Chris Holbeck and Mike Mitchell, Llonis asked her to bring them to him as soon as they showed up. Next he took the lengthy document from the envelope and began to scan it quickly.

Brewer's report was a model review, a sterling example of why he'd brought Bob into the division as deputy. Bob was also willing to handle night calls and stay all night at the office when the job required it.

A summary heading the body of the report opened with:

> The Plotkin case began strangely and ended the same way. Agency contact with Plotkin was established after his arrival in Sweden on an assignment as a member of the KGB residency, under consular cover. The contact was made by a highly respected case officer, Chris Holbeck, a successful recruiter and Russian speaker who shares an unusual ability with Plotkin: they are both gifted in the Swedish language to the point of native fluency. With this uncommon common interest, Holbeck and Plotkin became involved in what seemed to be a clandestine relationship of sorts, beginning with a meeting at Holbeck's home instigated by Plotkin. Although nothing substantive was discussed, Plotkin indicated his people were unaware of this meeting and agreed to a safety signal before coming to another meeting at Holbeck's home. Holbeck felt they had established a friendship that would require a long period of nurturing before hitting him with a recruitment pitch.

The phone rang. It was Mike, announcing that Holbeck had arrived, and that the two of them would come up to Llonis' office in thirty minutes. He went back to the summary:

This new relationship caused great excitement at Headquarters and exerted pressure on Stockholm Station and Holbeck to make a solid recruitment pitch to the target. Atypical for this usually aggressive officer, Holbeck at first refused to attempt a blunt recruitment pitch, reasoning that his relationship with the target was one of friendship. He felt that, under the circumstances, a careful nurturing of the case over a long period was essential to success, pointing out that time was on our side because contact had been made so early in both his and Plotkin's assignments.

In March 1969, Headquarters sent a flat-out order that a direct recruitment pitch should be made, citing interest at the very highest levels of Government as the reason for this timing. Stockholm's reply was predictable. They agreed to make the pitch but warned that it was premature and would probably backfire, resulting in the target being recalled to Moscow. They were both right and wrong, as will be seen below. However, the door was left open after a bizarre series of events, never explained to Headquarters' satisfaction.

Just prior to a scheduled meeting with Plotkin, Holbeck had a skiing accident and was unable to carry it out. Plotkin traveled to Moscow, then, upon his return, signaled for a truly clandestine meeting in a town north of Stockholm. The results of that meeting and a failed defection attempt left us knowing a great deal about this disaffected Soviet KGB officer; however, because Plotkin left Stockholm days after his last meeting with Holbeck, we have had little information on his whereabouts and activities.

Plotkin accepted a mail drop address but never used it until sending the letter that prompted this review.

As far as we know, Plotkin has remained in Moscow ever since leaving Stockholm suddenly in the spring of 1969. At first we thought he had been forced back home under a cloud. However, recently he's been seen in diplomatic circles, claiming to be with the Ministry of Foreign Affairs and once again focusing on Scandinavian interests.

Whatever the case, the letter signaling Plotkin's desire for a meeting with Holbeck was mailed in West Germany. The letter proposes November 12th, this coming Sunday as a meeting date. The only apparent problem is the site. Our translators (the letter is in Swedish) give us this: 'I hope we can get together at that old place during my visit. I'll come by a bit after 2:00 p.m. on 12 November.' The problem here is 'the old place.' It's probably the park where they were supposed to meet for the defection, when Plotkin didn't show. Holbeck will have to fill us in on that.

This case is of the highest interest because Plotkin's career has included many years as an illegal agent in Canada and England. It seems likely that he has been working on support of illegals while in Moscow. Even though we're not sure who's directing our 'problem,' there's a chance that Plotkin has information to help us solve that.

So ended the summary. Llonis put the document in his lap and pushed back his chair, away from the desk, to take better advantage of light from the windows. He was reading the body of the report carefully when Bob Brewer opened the office door, eyebrows raised in an unspoken request for permission to enter.

✳ ✳ ✳

"Come on in, Bob. I've got a few pages to go. Excellent job. Excellent!"

Brewer was pleased. He was proud of his ability to get along well with this man others found so difficult. Dropping his large bulk into the easy chair, he took the *Washington Post* from the coffee table and leafed through it while his boss read through the report.

Finished, Llonis rolled himself back to the desk and placed the report on the blotter, carefully aligning the document with the leather trim. "You're looking fresh, Bob, considering you missed a night's sleep. It's a fine job. I must say, though, that there are holes in this case I don't understand."

Brewer shifted uncomfortably in his chair, which looked as if it might succumb to his 250-pound weight. He and Chris Holbeck were good friends, so he had forced himself to be as objective as possible. It was hard not to take sides. Hard, too, for him to understand what was behind some of the strange things that happened in Stockholm during that early part of 1969.

"Well, Gary, I can only repeat what I told you when we first discussed it yesterday morning. I have total faith in Chris, and I think people here have just read too much into some of the events. To tell you the truth, I think it's a pretty straightforward case that was muddled by Chris's accident and some wild hair that got the Soviets to pull Plotkin back. We'll never know until he's recruited or he defects. Sure, Plotkin acted strangely at the end. I don't know why that surprises anybody. It takes an aberrant personality to defect, and Lord knows it takes an even more aberrant personality to accept recruitment in place. When you're out in the field dealing with these people you know that, but somehow when you're at Headquarters there's a tendency to deal with the field as if their targets marched to everybody's drummer. They don't."

Llonis drummed his fingers on the desk. "I respect your opinion, Bob, but you know the reasons for that pressure, the same as you know why we're meeting with Holbeck today." Brewer nodded, eyebrows knit in a frown, while Llonis continued. "Sometimes I feel like I'm not really running this division, but acting as a buffer between the top brass and the field. The pressure comes down from the White House and the NSC, and every manager all the way down the command chain gets it from both ends."

There was another tap on the door, and a secretary ushered in Chris Holbeck and Mike Mitchell.

✳ ✳ ✳

Chris was delighted to see that Bob Brewer would be included in the meeting. Bob was a Headquarters type, unable to take lengthy overseas assignments because his wife was an invalid. Nevertheless, he was one of the Agency's top recruiters and was often sent on temporary duty assignments to pitch Soviet and East Bloc targets. Chris had been with him on cases that lasted for weeks, and they'd come to know and respect each other during the short periods of meetings and much longer periods of waiting in hotel rooms and wandering various cities. Bob's visit in Saigon was one of the high points of Chris's last months in Vietnam.

Five minutes passed in the usual small talk, while Llonis's secretary brought in coffee. How did Chris like Vietnam? He didn't. What was he going to do about a house when the family moved back here? He already had one, and had given notice to the renters. Llonis and Mitchell commented on the weekly meeting of division directors, giving the other two a chance to chat about their families. Coffee was poured. The secretary closed the door.

"I want to tell you, Chris," Llonis began, "that we are truly sorry to drag you away from your home leave, but circumstances make it imperative that we re-establish contact with Plotkin. I know that while you were still in Saigon Bob gave you a light briefing on our problem here."

There followed a pregnant pause, forcing Chris to ask, "The mole?"

"As I'm sure Bob told you, we're keeping the highest possible restrictions on information concerning the actions taken to ferret out this son-of-a-bitch. To get to the point, we have hard information that the infamous mole—the spook in our midst everybody has speculated about through the years—not only exists, but is probably here in one of my offices."

"In the Soviet Division?" Chris was startled that the penetration could be so close.

Llonis was thoughtful as he picked up the document on his desk, looked absently at the top page and lined it up again with the blotter trim. "We don't know for sure, but the Soviets definitely have a read on our operations right here in Langley. We've lost a number of assets in the Soviet Union, valuable people who have disappeared or are known to have been executed. That's not speculation; it's hard fact. There are also signs that the Soviets have acted on information they shouldn't have available to them. We have a source—still viable, thank God—who has seen some of that. The situation is so serious that Bob and I are running that source as a "vest pocket" operation reported only to the top floor, keeping even our own Soviet ops people out of the loop. Very, very few people in the field know about it. We're going to run your Plotkin operation the same way. The West German desk knows that letter came into the mail drop, but they simply forwarded it here. Fortunately, Bob got hold of it before our desk officers learned of its significance."

Llonis now had Chris's full attention, the worry about his own situation dissipating as the excitement of the game revived. "I can't see where this fits into the Plotkin case," Chris said. "I don't know where he's been since I last saw him, but I assumed he was and always would be an Illegals body. Of course, the mole could be an Illegal. Do you have anything solid about Plotkin being tied into this one?"

"We don't know that he is, but we can't pass up any opportunity to get a handle on the situation." Llonis paused, toying with the pen in a holder on his desk. "You know, Chris, that we're not oversupplied with sources in the Illegals Directorate. We're hoping that if you can hook Plotkin this time he may at least know something about this case even if he's not directly involved."

"Okay," Mike looked at his watch. "I don't know about the rest of you, but I don't have much time. Where do we go from here?"

Chris responded. "I guess the first thing is Plotkin's letter. What does it say?"

"Sorry, Chris, I forgot that you haven't seen it yet." Llonis pulled the letter and translation from the document prepared by Brewer, handing it across the desk to Chris. The text was so short that it took only a moment for Chris to review both.

Brewer asked "Is the translation accurate? What do you think? Does it seem genuine?"

"Seems to be. It's so simple that it's not hard to translate."

"But what about the meeting in the 'old place'? Which one is that?"

"It must be the park at Drottningholm where we were supposed to have met on that first defection attempt. That's a pretty good spot for a pickup with lots of cover in trees and some small buildings."

"Good." Llonis was back in the conversation. "I'm sure you're going to want to review the file as much as possible before leaving. We've got you scheduled to go to Stockholm this evening on the SAS flight out of Dulles. That'll give you most of the afternoon here. You and Bob can work out the operational details after you finish the review."

"I'm not comfortable with that," Chris objected. He had been standing at attention, but now shifted about restlessly. "Not Stockholm. If we're going to run this case without the Swedes knowing about it, you don't want my entry into Sweden coming to their attention. The Swedish passport control people would certainly get a hit on my name in their watch books, showing me as a CIA officer, and they would alert the Foreign Office and Police."

"What do you suggest, then?"

"That flight transits Copenhagen. Let's ask our travel people to make that my destination. I'll take the airport bus to the ferries and go across to Malmö. There's no passport control inside Scandinavia now. I can take a train from there to Stockholm."

Llonis was giving him a sidelong look. "Don't you have to show your passport to register at a hotel?"

"Yes indeed, but the last thing in the world I want to do is stay at a hotel. I'll figure out something on my own. I don't need any help for the first meeting, at least. Any counter-surveillance, and I mean *any* counter-surveillance, would chase Plotkin off. But if he's decided to defect or has information of immediate importance, I'm going to need to contact the Station. If he's defecting because he's in trouble, I'll want a hell of a lot of support in a big hurry."

Llonis turned to Mitchell. "That's your territory, Mike."

"Yeah, I'm afraid so. That's a tough one. With Sweden neutral and our relations pretty stiff because of Vietnam, there's no way we could call on the Swedes to help us get Plotkin out of there if he's decided to defect. Norm Wykowski is still Chief of Station in Stockholm. Good man. He should be your point of contact."

"Right on, Mike," Llonis said. "I've got a lot of respect for Norm."

"We have to let him know what's going on, of course," Mitchell continued, "I think our best bet is to send him an Eyes Only cable that Chris is coming, give him a short rundown on the case, and ask for contact instructions. If I get a cable off to Norm right now, we might have an answer back before Chris leaves tonight. Norm will be unhappy about the short notice on something like this being done on his territory, but I can smooth that out later."

Llonis shook his head. "That's good so far as it goes, but there are loose ends here. If Chris doesn't stay in a hotel, where's he going to stay?"

Brewer drummed his fingers on his cheek. To Mike Mitchell, he said, "In a safe house, I suppose, but I'm concerned that Norm won't have exclusive access to a safe house without his staff knowing about it. Do you think Norm could arrange something on his own to keep knowledge of the case buried?"

"Hell if I know, Bob," Mike said, throwing up his hands. "Our information isn't that detailed. We'll just have to ask him in the cable."

"Aren't you afraid, Chris, that someone will recognize you on the street in Stockholm?" Llonis was still worrying the tradecraft bone.

"It's been more than two years, Gary, and I wasn't that well known outside our Embassy people and diplomatic contacts, or in the neighborhood where we lived. I do worry a bit about being seen in that area if the meeting with Plotkin comes off, but I'll be careful. I'm sure I can work out a place to stay when I meet with Norm."

Llonis stood up behind his desk and gave the surface a slap. "Well, gentlemen, I'm not sure we can do much more here. Bob, why don't you take Mike and Chris to your office and work out the rest of the details?"

Already at the door, Mitchell spoke before Brewer could reply. "I'll go on down to my office and draft a cable to Wykowski. I've got a lunch meeting to get to after that, but I'll be around later this afternoon if you need me for anything. Be sure and stop in to see me before you leave, Chris." As Mitchell walked out it was agreed that Chris would use Brewer's office to review the case files, giving the deputy a chance for some much-needed rest.

Brewer escorted Chris to his office. Opening the safe next to his desk, he pulled out several inches of files covering the Plotkin case.

"One thing, Chris. I'm sure you'll remember from your Headquarters days the notes put on dispatches and cables as they're routed around. Some of them are going to hurt your feelings. They're very complimentary in the early stages of the case, then get pretty nasty during the last months. Should I have one of the girls bring you something from the cafeteria?"

"Yes, that'll be fine. Will you be back before I leave?"

"I'm not leaving. I'll just stretch out on the couch here for a couple of hours. Your travel docs should be ready by one o'clock. Mike will be back from his lunch about the time we get those and then the three of us can talk about operational details. We'll have you say goodbye to Gary, then I'll drive you out to Dulles Airport. Maybe we'll have time for dinner together before your flight leaves."

"I'd enjoy that. My bag is down at the guards' desk, so we wouldn't have to stop off anywhere. But what about the interrogation brief for Plotkin? The only thing we covered in there was setting up the meeting."

"Gary told me yesterday that he wanted responsibility for that. I forgot to ask him, but I'm sure he'll be working on it this afternoon and will get it to you before you leave." Brewer stretched and yawned. "I'm fading fast. Tell my secretary what you want to eat." With that he dropped his big body onto the couch and closed his eyes.

Chris stepped out of the office and asked Brewer's secretary to bring him a hamburger and coffee. Back in the office he stared at the small mountain of files in front of him. How to begin? He slipped the bottom-most file out of the stack, leafing through to the first document on the case. It was a dispatch reporting Plotkin's 1968 arrival in Stockholm, stapled to the background information available to Headquarters at that time. Someone on the Swedish desk had scribbled "could be interesting" on the routing slip before it was sent to the Soviet Division.

He had a few hours ahead of him to try and put everything together, put it into perspective. But whose perspective? His? Headquarters? Lisa's? How about Plotkin's perspective? No matter how he got it down by the end of the day, he knew that everything would be different after the meeting with Plotkin. Dragging himself away from those thoughts, he realized success would depend on how he handled the case and conducted himself when he and Plotkin confronted each other. Continuing upward through the file, forward in time, he came to a dispatch written in November, 1968. His first lunch with Plotkin—the first one-on-one meeting. Now he started reading more carefully, putting the pieces together, forming in his mind the case as it actually developed from that rainy November day when they lunched at Stockholm's Stalmästaregarden Restaurant, to the last session with Plotkin only five months later.

Those few months of his life had been reduced incompletely into a half-foot of files, about an inch a month. He wondered how much his life would have been worth in inches of files if he had reported the whole story.

PART TWO

CHAPTER FIVE

Fall, 1968: Four Years Earlier
Stockholm

One of the personal theories Chris had developed during his career concerned the task of recruiting Soviet and East Bloc intelligence agents. Experience at that game had taught him to believe that successful spotting, development and recruitment depended about equally on luck and skill, much like the card game of cribbage—so popular with the boat crews on his family's tugs. The crewmembers who won at cribbage invariably bragged about their skill; those who lost just as invariably complained about their bad luck. The Plotkin case had involved a mixture of good and bad luck, while challenging his skill set to the limit.

The good luck factor began in the early fall of 1968. William Alfred Broom III asked Chris into his office to inquire if he and Lisa would like to attend a dinner party at the Broom home. The guests would include Peter Palmstjerna, the newly appointed Swedish Foreign Office's Chief of Protocol, who had received his appointment after a long tour in Moscow.

It was unusual for the American Embassy's First Secretary to include CIA people in his dinner parties. Bill Broom was an Ivy League type from a wealthy family, driven by ambition. With the help of an equally ambitious and wealthy wife, he had already risen further and faster than most of his Foreign Service classmates. Determined to continue this progress, he took care not to have too much social contact with the spooks in the CIA Station. But he and his wife had taken a liking to Chris and Lisa, who had arrived a few months earlier on a direct transfer from Madrid. Chris believed that the invitation wouldn't have come if he and Lisa hadn't been so socially skilled, so in his mind that put it into the 50-

50, luck vs. skill category. With this invitation Broom unknowingly started the spotting process in the Plotkin case.

On the evening of the dinner, four other couples, Swedes all, were visibly embarrassed when Palmstjerna arrived a half-hour late without apologies— something that simply was not done in punctual Sweden and certainly not by a protocol officer. He was unaccompanied, as Chris later learned from Bill, because of a separation from his wife.

Other than the Brooms, the only person at the party who was known previously to Chris was Nils Schmidt, a Swedish maritime shipping man and sailing friend. When Palmstjerna joined a small conversation group conversing in Swedish—an all male collection that included both Chris and Schmidt—he made disparaging remarks about the United States involvement in Vietnam. Schmidt tried to tell him that Chris was with the American Embassy, but the protocol chief ignored him. It was not until Bill Broom called the group to dinner, pairing the protocol officer with Lisa, that Palmstjerna realized the folly of pegging Chris as a Swede.

Palmstjerna experienced another blow to his ego during dessert, when he began talking about Scandinavian names. He made the mistake of saying that he didn't like the name Jensen.

"Why not?" Lisa asked, actually batting her eyes at him with intentional coyness that Chris thought would surely be obvious to all. Chris peered around his dinner partner to look directly at Palmstjerna. "I think, sir, you should be warned that my wife is trying to trap you." Lisa and her partner ignored him; Lisa was having too much fun and Palmstjerna was too self-absorbed to pay attention.

"Why is it that you don't like the name of Jensen?" she asked again.

"Well, it sounds bundisk to me. Do you know what that means?"

"Farmer-like? Peasant-ish?"

"You know more Swedish than you admit. That's just about it. But why do you force me to give a reason for disliking the name?"

"Because that was my maiden name." Lisa smiled sweetly and batted her eyes at him once again. Palmstjerna's heavily jowled face turned red with embarrassment. To his credit, he recovered with grace. Seated to the left of the hostess as the honored guest, he was required by Swedish custom to give the tak för maten speech, a "thanks for the food."

After finishing his gracious speech, Palmstjerna stood up, gallantly kissed Angela's hand, walked around the table to shake hands with Bill, and walked out.

As the evening came to a close, the guests gossiped about what had gotten into Palmstjerna to make him act so rudely. Nils Schmidt and others who already knew him agreed that he was usually quite proper in his dealing with people at all levels.

Whatever the reasons for Palmstjerna's actions, the evening was successful for Chris. Bill and Angela Broom became fast friends; they often included the Holbecks in their parties and arranged many interesting introductions. Later the Blooms told Chris the reason for Palmstjerna's strange actions that night. His estranged wife had filed divorce papers the day of the party. He had come directly to dinner at the Brooms from a final, failed attempt at reconciliation.

Chris never expected to hear from him again, so he was surprised a few weeks later when Palmstjerna phoned, calling him "Chris" and himself, "Peter." Peter said he was hosting a cocktail party in honor of the new Spanish Ambassador. Because Chris was fluent in Spanish and had recently served in Spain, Peter thought he and Lisa would fit in well at the party. He'd send an invitation if Chris thought he might be interested in accepting, which he was.

Lisa, on the other hand, had not been so quick as the others to accept Palmstjerna's apologies for his actions at the Broom's dinner party. "Maybe I'm just smarting over what he said about my name, but I suspect he's got something up his sleeve to invite us out of the blue like that." Chris thought that was ridiculous and told her so, though he had to admit to himself that she was an instinctive people-reader. She wasn't always right, but her first impressions were often more accurate than his own.

The party was held in what Palmstjerna called his "bachelor digs"—a beautiful older apartment the size of an American tract home—on the third floor of a building on Strandvägen overlooking Stockholm's inner harbor. Cocktail hours require less punctuality than a dinner party, so Chris and Lisa arrived a bit later than the appointed time in order to avoid being the first guests. Peter met them at the door. Holding each firmly by the arm, he escorted them into the living room and steered Lisa into a group of women, introducing her as the wife of an American Embassy political officer. Left on his own for a moment, Chris was just helping himself to a drink from an offered tray when Peter took him by the elbow. From the ladies' group Lisa gave him her "What did I tell you?" look, as he found himself maneuvered into a circle of men speaking Swedish. Peter didn't interrupt the conversation to introduce him.

Soon Chris joined in their talk about the raising of an old warship, the Vasa, now in a floating museum. The group could see the ship as they stood by windows overlooking the harbor. The others, apparently Swedes, seemed to accept him as the same. The conversation dragged on with the usual inanities that made Chris dislike cocktail parties.

As the conversation turned to the best cheap restaurants in town, Chris began to focus on one of the other men in the group, a light-haired fellow who seemed a little older than he. There was something different about him. It was the way he stood, his general appearance, the same kind of thing Chris tried to avoid when he was trying to pass himself off as a Swede. Then it came to him. This was no Swede. This was a Russian. Not just any Russian, but a member of the KGB residency at the Soviet Embassy in Stockholm—Aleksandr Elyovitch Plotkin.

Plotkin's arrival in Stockholm in early 1968 had been documented in Station records. Chris had read about him while reviewing the material, and now he recognized the face from the photographs on file. One of the dispatches had mentioned that Plotkin had spent a year in Sweden as an exchange student at Stockholm University in the late forties—though even that would make it hard to explain his remarkable fluency in the Swedish language. As good as he himself was, Chris knew that his own Swedish would not be at this level if it weren't for his parents keeping up the language at home while he was a child.

Chris had sensed it was time to move on to another group, but now he caught the attention of the Russian and saw a communication of sorts—a brightness of the eyes that combined with a slight smile to suggest that he, too, had recognized a counterpart in the intelligence business.

Pushing across the circle to ease himself and Plotkin out of earshot of the others, Chris said "It's interesting that our host invited the two of us to the same party. I think I know who you are, and I assume you know who I am."

The Russian had such a friendly, disarming grin that Chris felt some warmth toward this man who was by political definition part of the enemy camp. He was slightly shorter than Chris, with hair a darker shade of blond and worn longer than the American's. A pleasant face appeared somewhat stern by virtue of a constantly furrowed forehead and heavy eyebrows. Most noticeably, he stood always erect, like a military man at attention. Chris remembered that the background information on Plotkin included some citations for bravery as a tank commander during World War II.

"You must be the officer at the Soviet Embassy who speaks such fluent Swedish," he continued. Somebody at the Diplomatic Club luncheon told me about you the other day. You're a second secretary, aren't you?"

"Right, and you're Chris Holbeck, Political Attaché at the American Embassy. I'm Aleksandr Plotkin. They've given me a consular job here, though frankly I'd rather be in the political business. But why are we speaking Swedish? I understand you're something of a Russian linguist." A short exchange in Russian was followed by a few thoughts in English, which Plotkin spoke exceptionally well—albeit with a slight accent that Chris was unable to identify on short acquaintance. After testing each other's language abilities, they lapsed back into Swedish.

"Tell you what, Mr. Plotkin," Chris said, "I think I'd better start circulating. Peter's reason for inviting me was supposed to be my ability to speak Spanish, so I should start using it if I want another invitation. He's bound to ask each of us about the other."

"Call me Sasha." As Peter looked over the Spanish Ambassador's shoulder at them, they exchanged a warm handshake. After insisting that they might see each other before long, they parted. Chris thought this brief encounter had created one of those rare bonds that goes beyond age, gender or our other usual measurements of human interaction.

CHAPTER SIX

November 1968—New Year 1969

There's a price to be paid for meeting significant contacts in the world of spydom. It takes patience and energy to withstand the rigors of the diplomatic cocktail/dinner social circuit and maintain a cheerful attitude no matter how one feels. Occasionally it pays off. In the Plotkin case, the social ball was passed from the Brooms to Palmstjerna, then from Palmstjerna to Plotkin—an unusually small price for meeting an unusually significant contact. Now it was Chris's turn to pick up the ball and run with it.

He still had that aim in the back of his mind when, much to his surprise, Plotkin made the next social move. In early November he phoned Chris at the Embassy to extend an invitation for lunch on November 15th. It would be just the two of them at a popular and rather expensive Stockholm restaurant, the Stalmästaregården. Headquarters—cautiously pleased with the news of this meeting—awaited a follow-up report before making any judgment about its significance.

The caution was well-placed, as it turned out. The invitation was exciting; the event was not. While Chris enjoyed the opportunity to exchange information and political views with his Soviet counterpart, Plotkin was not very forthcoming with personal information. Chris learned that he was married—with a wife who was an obstetrician in Moscow—and sad to have no children. His wife wasn't interested in offspring, due to the suffering of children she had witnessed during the war.

"Your wife is lovely," Plotkin had said of their meeting at Palmstjerna's party. He showed more interest in Chris's family life and children than in politics. He went through a rote list of questions concerning U.S. policies and the war in Vietnam, while appearing to pay little attention to the answers.

Chris reported these disappointing results to Headquarters, adding that for form's sake he should invite Plotkin to some kind of social event in response to the Russian's hosting their lunch. If the results of that exchange were not more promising, he would probably drop the effort to develop a close relationship—a disappointment in light of his enthusiasm over their introduction at Palmstjerna's party.

It was in the back of his mind to call Plotkin once again to arrange a contact when an idea struck him. He and Lisa were spending a rare evening at home— she writing invitations for a buffet supper at their home, an unusual affair that he wasn't very keen on. With less than two weeks until Christmas, Lisa and some of her friends were lamenting the combined social and family pressures of the season. For some reason he was never able to divine, they had decided it would be fun to add one more party only three nights before Christmas Eve—a let-your-hair-down affair, giving everybody a chance to relax before the onslaught of Christmas itself. He had even more trouble understanding why Lisa had agreed they would host the party, with some of her friends bringing food dishes. At least it would be on a Saturday night, allowing for one day of rest.

The guest list was a mishmash of Lisa's friends from the International Women's Club and the American Embassy, a few diplomat couples from other embassies, and two Swedish Foreign Office people who were married to Americans. Lisa was writing out the "regrets only" invitations as Chris reviewed the list. If everybody came, there would be about thirty-five people.

"Honey, do you really think anybody's going to show up for this?"

Lisa gave him her exasperated look. "Of course they will. I know at least fifteen women who will drag their husbands here. It's our turn to have the kind of party we like."

"That's what I mean. *Dragging* their husbands here. That doesn't sound like much fun to me." When Lisa didn't reply, he added, "If we have to have the party, may I add a couple of people to the list?"

She put down her pen, looking at him suspiciously. "Work again. It must be somebody who means something to your work."

This woman really annoyed him at times. "Of course, what's wrong with that? You knew when we married that you'd be involved in my career. For some reason it seems to be bothering you more here than it did anywhere else we've been."

She let that pass. "Who is it this time?"

"I was thinking of inviting Peter Palmstjerna and Sasha Plotkin."

"My God, what a pair! Peter's one of the oddest people I've ever met, and Plotkin's a Soviet hood. Great additions to a party that's supposed to be relaxing."

"Sasha is not a hood. You know that very well. He's a high level KGB type, one of the most important I've ever dealt with. And just because Peter acted so strangely when we first met doesn't mean he isn't a nice guy. He had some personal problems."

"I don't like it. This was supposed to be *our* party, me and my friends."

"Neither do I." His temper was rising. "I think you owe it to me after arranging a weird party like this. Make out your own goddamned list!" He stalked out of the room, throwing the list down on the desk where she was working.

They didn't discuss it further. The next night he was writing letters at the same desk, long after Lisa had gone to bed. Opening the drawer where she kept her things, he found a guest list. The last two names on it were Plotkin and Palmstjerna.

Lisa was right in almost every way about the party. The main element she had misjudged was the number of guests. Not only did almost everyone accept, but many brought house guests visiting during the Christmas holidays. Instead of the expected thirty-five friends, there were some fifty people jammed into their home. The dancing going on in the living room shook the house to its foundations. Since starting to pour drinks after dinner, he'd hardly had a chance to leave the bar.

Palmstjerna came up to the bar and ordered a plain tonic with a twist of lime.

"Not drinking tonight, Peter?" Chris hadn't served him anything stronger than tonic since dinner.

"I no longer have a wife to drive me home. If you lived closer to the city I'd have taken a taxi, but as an impoverished servant of the crown I can't afford it. Drove my own car, you know."

"Pity." Chris mimicked his language. "Should think your government would provide a chauffeur to one in such an exalted position."

Palmstjerna laughed. "You don't know my government as well as you should." They were interrupted by a tipsy American business couple in a hurry to get back to the dance, both ordering bourbon on the rocks.

"What do you think happened to Plotkin?" Palmstjerna had a comical way of arching his eyebrows when asking a question.

"What do you mean, 'What happened to him'?"

Strange question, Chris thought.

"He was invited to the party, but I don't see him."

"What gave you that idea?"

"Well, he was, wasn't he?"

"As a matter of fact, he was. He didn't send his regrets, but as you've seen he didn't show up, either. How did you know he was invited?"

"He told me. We had lunch together a couple of days ago, and you and Lisa came up in the conversation. He said you'd lunched together and that you sent him an invitation to this party."

"What'd he have to say about us?"

"Better not say. I don't want to swell your head."

"I'll take that as a compliment, Peter. What do you make of Plotkin? As far as I can tell, you know him better than any other western diplomat."

"Which is to say, not very well." Palmstjerna reached across the bar for a bottle of vodka, adding a few drops to his glass before he refilled it with tonic. "For taste, you know. No, I don't really know him well. The last year I was in Moscow he turned up at a couple of parties we gave at the Embassy, and I lunched with him two, maybe three times. He was supposed to be in the Scandinavian section of the Foreign Ministry, though I never saw him there or on any official business. For a time I wondered if the Soviets might be aiming something at me, but nothing ever developed. Truth is, he even went through the 'questions of the day' as if he didn't much care. On the whole, Chris, I got the impression that he likes me. Like he likes you. And Lisa."

Chris was going to ask him about this mention of Lisa when more dancers crowded into the room where the bar was set up to replenish their spirits, keeping Chris too busy to talk further with Palmstjerna.

It was nearly three o'clock in the morning by the time the last guests had left, the main clutter of the party was swept up, and he and Lisa were getting ready for bed. "What do you think now, Mr. Smarty Pants?" she asked from inside the dress she was pulling over her head.

"You were right as usual, Honey. I do think a lot of people are going to be sorry tomorrow, though. We've never gone through so much booze at one party."

"Like I told you, it was a time to let down from all the pressures."

"Yes, I suppose you're right." Still in her slip, she was bending over to pull off her stockings. He leaned down to kiss her on the nape of the neck. She straightened, turned, and threw her arms around him. "If I haven't told you so before," he muttered, finding it difficult to talk because she was squeezing him so hard, "I do appreciate your adding the two 'P's' to the guest list."

"Show me how much you appreciate it."

He did.

If the party ended on a happy note, the days from Christmas to New Year were even happier. While most of the other party guests were presumably sleeping it off the next morning, Chris and Lisa had to get up early in order to meet their twin boys at the airport. On the way they collected four-year-old Melissa, the apple of her father's eye. Missy had spent the night at the home of her Swedish girlfriend from the play school they attended, a Swedish *lekskola*. By now she was as fluent in Swedish at her age level as her father was at his.

It was September when the boys left for school in Switzerland, and then they had been with the family in Stockholm for only a couple of weeks. Mor and Herman had the boys with them for several weeks each summer ever since Matthew and Mark were not much older than Missy. There was some family strain over this, but the twins enjoyed such fine summers with their grandparents that Chris and Lisa were reluctant to change the routine. Now, though, with their spending the school year in Switzerland, the parents would have to figure out what to do next summer in order to have more time with them. Matthew and Mark had turned fourteen a few weeks earlier. Time would fly and soon they would be in college.

The SAS flight from Geneva was crowded with travelers arriving for Christmas. The boys, joking with a stewardess, were among the last of the passengers to leave the plane. Both parents were amazed by how much they had matured in those few months since they left home. They filled the car with merriment on the way home, teasing Melissa, telling school jokes, teasing their parents about the freedoms they claimed to enjoy at school. Soon they were talking about food. They were starved. It was beginning to feel like Christmas.

It felt like Christmas all the following week. The Embassy practically shut down between Christmas and New Year. The Holbecks enjoyed being a whole family again. They visited friends, sang together in the evenings, skied near the summer palace at Drottningholm and ice-skated almost every day.

The last day of the year was a lazy one. Chris and Lisa worked together to fix a huge breakfast of the kind Chris remembered from the days on his dad's tugboats. When he was able to sit down to his own meal—basking in the warm family atmosphere—he listened as the boys talked about their plans for the day. They were going to the Bill Brooms' in the afternoon, to help decorate and then attend a teenage party that evening. They promised to be home no later than 1:30 a.m. Chris and Lisa were invited to a Swedish neighbors' for a black tie dinner followed by some serious bridge.

"Sounds stuffy," Matthew remarked as he went to the refrigerator for more milk, "black tie just to play bridge?"

"Not stuffy at all." Lisa was miffed. "The Stenbergs are lovely people who are hanging on to the old traditions. With what you've told us about schools nowadays and what they let you get away with, I think more people should do it. Besides, they've even set a place for Missy at the table. That's why I made her that long dress I showed you. She's going to sleep over there while we play cards."

After engaging in a minor skirmish with Missy about not being old enough to stay up until midnight, they all worked together to clean up the breakfast dishes before going about their activities. Lisa would drive the boys over to the Brooms. Chris was looking forward to changing the oil and lubricating both their cars. With most of his days spent in a suit and tie, he liked getting into grubby clothes and working on machinery. It was his only real hobby, an opportunity to relax without constantly having to relate to other people.

The afternoon went as planned until four o'clock. Finished with the service work on both cars in the garage that was part of the basement, Chris had just started to polish the Volvo. "Christian. Oh Christian!" It was Lisa, calling him from the basement stairs. He knew there was some problem. She never used his full name unless she was unhappy with him.

"Yes, Honey?"

"Telephone," was her only answer before going back upstairs and slamming the door.

He guessed what it was before he'd wiped his hands and gone upstairs to answer. The Embassy communicator was calling. A message had arrived. He must come down to read it right away. They received far too many calls of this kind to suit Lisa.

"What are you so unhappy about?" Chris asked as he hung up the phone. "It shouldn't take long."

"*Shouldn't* is one thing. What usually happens is another." He could see that she was more than just annoyed. The quiet, relaxed tempo of the past week had been broken. "Don't forget that the Stenbergs are expecting us at seven o'clock, and we can't be even a second late without bothering them. How are you going to get down to the Embassy, do whatever you do down there, get back, shower and into a tux by then? You're filthy. And look! You've tracked in dirt from the garage." She fetched a broom and dust pan and swept up the few specks of dirt, her movements jerky with her anger.

Chris walked out of the room and upstairs without answering. After putting on a clean shirt and slacks, he went back downstairs to get his overcoat from the front closet. "See you in an hour," he called out to Lisa. She didn't answer.

The message could have waited until the office opened again, but that wasn't the communicator's fault. He was just following his orders by precedence of the cable. While he was there, Chris read the other messages that had come since he was last in the office. It was 6:30 p.m. when he wheeled into their driveway, leaving just time enough to shower and dress for the party.

Missy met him on the stairway, already in her party dress. "How beautiful you look, Sweetheart!" She did a little curtsy that inspired him to pick her up and swirl her around.

"There was a man here to see you, Daddy," she said, as he set her down carefully.

"What man?"

"I don't know. Mommy said, 'He's a friend of your father's.'"

"I'll ask her. Don't get that dress wrinkled, now. I'll be ready in two shakes."

Lisa was seated at her dressing table in the bedroom, putting on her earrings and looking not at all happy. "Were you in the living room?"

"No, I came up the back stairs. Why?"

"Your friend Sasha was here. On the table down there there's a bottle of vodka and some tinned caviar that he left for you."

"Sasha Plotkin?"

"You have some other friend named Sasha who'd bring you vodka and caviar?"

Chris tried to ignore the sarcasm, keeping his voice even. "No, but I certainly didn't expect that." He paused, adding, "Our Soviet friends do have a habit of delivering gifts to their contacts at New Year. I'm just surprised that he would bring one to me. I kind of thought the thread was broken when he didn't show up at our party. What did he have to say?"

Finished with her earrings, Lisa turned around to stare at him as he was hurriedly pulling off his clothes to get into the shower. "I'm not sure I should tell you right now. It will take your mind off the bridge game tonight."

"So don't tell me."

His attempt to look casual, to suppress his eager anticipation about what Plotkin had said, was so transparent that Lisa laughed. For the sake of his work he could (in her mind) lie, cheat and steal from other people with perfect equanimity, but he could never fool her. He was so much like a little boy at times like this that she couldn't stay mad at him.

"You know I'm going to tell you. He invited himself to lunch here on Wednesday, the eighth of January. Said he wanted a completely private lunch with just the two of us, and that we shouldn't mention it to anybody else."

"Now that is interesting. What else did he have to say? How long did he stay?" Chris was standing by the tub in the bathroom, afraid he'd miss the answer if he turned on the shower.

"You get showered. I'll tell you while you're dressing."

Immediately upon finishing the shower, he was pumping her with questions. Plotkin, she told him, had arrived unannounced, alone and on foot. He didn't seem at all put out when she told him Chris wasn't home, easily accepting her invitation to come in for a cup of coffee and cookies. He seemed friendly. A little nervous, perhaps, but she didn't really know him well enough to judge.

There wasn't time for any more conversation about this strange turn of events. It was 6:55 p.m.—five minutes left to get themselves and Missy into their coats and run over to the neighbors. With the knowledge of Plotkin's visit swirling in his head, Chris had to struggle to keep up with the conversation over dinner, to concentrate on the duplicate bridge hands afterwards. Considering the circumstances and competition, he was pleased with himself and Lisa when the scores were tallied just before midnight. They had come in third.

"Thanks for trying so hard," she whispered as they exchanged a champagne-laced kiss at midnight. "You were a good sport."

"Thanks yourself, sport." He put down his glass to give her a proper New Year's kiss and hug, not caring what their conservative Swedish neighbors might think about this demonstration of affection.

CHAPTER SEVEN

Friday, January 2, 1969

On the second day of the New Year, Chris drove the twins to Stockholm Central train station before going back to work. He and Lisa had decided before Christmas vacation to let them experience traveling by rail in Europe on their return to school. Chris had believed that parting with his sons would be less emotional with no women present, their mother and sister in particular. So why, he wondered, did he have tears in his eyes as he left the station and headed for the Embassy?

Headquarters was ecstatic over Plotkin's cable requesting a private meeting. Their first response congratulated him for moving the case to this point. Detailed comments and suggestions would follow.

As many times as he'd been involved in operations abroad, Chris should have been prepared for the onslaught of advice in the next few days. There were cabled particulars on communications systems if it proved that Plotkin would accept recruitment in place, and on subjects to be covered in debriefings. There was a lot of agonizing over how to move Plotkin out of Sweden if he were to refuse recruitment but wanted to defect. Given the current state of relations with Sweden, it was thought to be unlikely that the Swedish Government would cooperate in such a venture. (Smart, those people at Headquarters! Chances of that kind of cooperation ranged from none to a snowball's in Hell.) Endless speculation about the man's psychological makeup was meant to assist Chris in handling the meeting.

"All this because the guy wants to have lunch with me and my wife," Chris complained to the Chief of Station, Mike Mitchell. "We've got to slow them down." He prepared a politely worded cable suggesting that Headquarters was jumping the gun. Before sending it, Mike edited his draft to make it still more polite. The only response from Headquarters was to refer to the Stockholm cable in their continuing stream of advice. Technicians in various parts of Europe were put on standby, ready to travel immediately to Sweden if the need should arise.

Lisa had correctly predicted the effect on Chris of Plotkin's New Year's Eve visit. He had managed to struggle through the dinner and evening of bridge, but from then on he was totally distracted. Before going to sleep and upon waking, at every meal, during the office routine, at home and on social outings with Lisa, he seemed to think of nothing else. Other than Lisa, nobody noticed a difference; only she saw the way his eyes wandered, his inability to concentrate on a book he was supposedly reading during their few evenings at home. She found it more and more irritating that Chris, who was usually so attentive and loving toward her and the family, was simply going through the motions. When he read to Missy before tucking her into bed and saying prayers, his heart wasn't in it. He kissed Lisa goodnight, turning out the light and rolling over with his back to her, without their usual five minutes of soft talk about their days, without any interest in making love. She said nothing to him. He had acted this way in the past when important cases were on the horizon and was probably like this on those long trips he made. She hoped it would all be resolved during the lunch with Plotkin, just a few days away. Determined to serve the best lunch she'd ever put on the table, to be her most gracious and attractive self, she bit her tongue and waited.

Plotkin arrived on foot a few minutes before half-past noon on the appointed day. Through the slats of Venetian blinds in Missy's room, Chris watched him turn the corner a block away. An elderly woman, bundled against the cold, was hurrying away in the next block down, headed toward the shopping square. No cars traveled the snow-covered road. Plotkin glanced down the street in both directions before entering the path to the Holbeck front door.

Lisa was at her best on this occasion. She had never seemed more genuinely sweet and gracious when she met Plotkin at the door, taking his coat and fur hat for Chris to put away in the closet. Steering their guest gently by the arm, she led the way into the living room and excused herself for a moment. The two men only had time to exchange a few words before she was back with a tray that carried a plate of thin crackers and another with the lumpy gray caviar Plotkin had brought on New Year's Eve, surrounded by thin lemon slices. Putting that down, she hurried into the kitchen again to return with another tray holding the gift bottle of vodka and three frosted glasses.

Plotkin laughed. "Dear lady, I intended these things for you, not to be saved for me."

Lisa looked stricken. "Don't you like caviar? I thought it would be a special treat for us to share together."

"Of course. I didn't mean to hurt your feelings. Let's share it. But I can't drink much vodka today. Maybe one very small glass, and then nothing with lunch."

"I have a very nice wine to go with the lunch. You must drink at least one glass to appreciate the meal."

"All right, all right," Plotkin laughed again, "one glass. But no more. I think your wife is trying to ply me with drink," he said, turning to Chris.

"I doubt it. That would take an ulterior motive, and I don't think Lisa has had one in all her life. She's the most open person you'll ever meet."

Plotkin helped himself to caviar, then unceremoniously downed the vodka Lisa had poured. Chris and Lisa followed suit, feeling uncomfortable that no toast had been made with the drink. There was an awkward silence. It was finally broken by Plotkin.

"To tell you the truth, Lisa—may I call you that?—I'm eating the caviar out of obligation. I don't really like it much. My tastes are quite simple. I like the Swedish custom of *husmanskost*, a given menu for every day of the week. You know. Everyday food."

"I understand the custom, but that's for supper. You'll be getting something much better for lunch." She stood up to go into the kitchen for their meal. "And yes, you may call me Lisa if I may call you Sasha." With a swish of the swinging door she was gone.

The sounds of Lisa moving about the kitchen seemed loud in the silence that followed. Chris and his guest each had another cracker, Plotkin taking his without caviar. Chris resisted the temptation to take another glass of vodka. Somebody had to break the silence. It was beginning to feel like the lunch they had at Stalmästaregården. He tried talking about the Russian and American space programs. The war situation in Vietnam. Plotkin responded politely but without much interest and few comments. It was not until Chris mentioned his brother fighting in Vietnam that the Russian showed much animation. He sat up attentively and seemed about to add his thoughts on the subject when Lisa came in to announce that lunch was ready. Plotkin leaped to his feet, taking her by the arm as they led the way to the dining room, Chris following.

Their dining room table was so long that Lisa had set three places at one end, sitting at the head of the table herself. "I hope you understand why you're sitting on my right, Sasha," she said as he held the chair for her. "In Sweden the guest of honor is seated to the left of the hostess, but we follow the American custom and seat him on the right."

"As long as it has nothing to do with politics, it's fine by me." It looked as if he was beginning to relax.

And relax he did. Lisa served a crab soufflé that she rarely made because it took so much preparation. She had been right about the dish demanding the wine, which went so beautifully with it that Plotkin violated his own rule and had two glasses. Whether it was the food, the wine or the topics of conversation, he became lively and friendly, remaining so throughout their time at the table. The main topic—children—broadened out to family life in general. Plotkin showed a keen interest in his hosts' family, asking many questions about the children, their schooling, what sports they enjoyed. Having heard about Chris's family already, he asked Lisa about hers. Chris and Lisa were struck by the depth of his sympathy when she told him she'd been orphaned as a teenager, her parents killed in an airplane accident. Relaxed as he seemed, he still would not talk much about his own family other than to repeat what he had told Chris about his childless marriage. After dessert Lisa moved the coffee service into the living room and excused herself, saying that she had a weaving class. Both men refused her offer of a brandy. Plotkin seemed disappointed that she must leave.

Now it's time to get serious, Chris thought.

"I was really pleased when Lisa told me you wanted to have a private lunch with us, Sasha. It's good to get together just as friends, with no complications."

"Just what I had hoped," Plotkin replied. "I've enjoyed this a lot. You have such a beautiful family. I'm sorry I didn't have a chance to meet your twin boys. Or to see Missy again. What a pretty little girl!"

"Well, maybe someday you can meet the twins. And perhaps Missy will be here next time you come. You will come again, won't you?"

"Of course."

"Doesn't this pose a problem for you, though? I assume your people at the Embassy don't know you're seeing us today."

"No, they don't. As far as I'm concerned, it's none of their business."

"What time do you have to be back?"

"Not for a long time. But I have to leave here no later than two fifteen. That gives me about five minutes more." He looked at his watch as he said it.

"When do you think we might do this again?"

Plotkin reached into the breast pocket of his suit jacket, pulling out a small memo book and leafing through it slowly, thoughtfully. "Do you think Lisa would mind having me here again on Wednesday, the twenty-second? I have some time free that day."

Chris in turn pulled out his pocket calendar. "Just a minute. I'd better check her calendar," he said, walking into the den. "That looks fine. What time do you want to make it?"

"About the same as today," Plotkin called from the living room. Chris made a notation on Lisa's calendar before going back to join his guest.

"Look, Sasha," he said as he sat down again and took a sip of coffee, "it can't be very safe for you, seeing us this way. Let's be frank. I know your position at your embassy, and you know mine, I'm sure. If there's any help I can offer ..."

Plotkin seemed to be expecting this probe, showing little reaction. "No. No help. I just enjoy having a relaxed lunch with friends, away from the pressures."

"How about these meetings, though? There must be some risk in your coming here this way. Something could always happen between the time we make a date and the time we meet. Shouldn't we have some kind of signal that everything is all right before we meet?"

"That's an idea." Plotkin poured himself some more coffee and glanced at his watch, a little nervously this time. They both were quiet for moment, then he asked "Do you always drive that Volvo you had at Stalmästaregården?"

"Usually."

"You know the NK department store, alongside Kungssträdgården?" Nordiska Kompaniet was *the* department store of Stockholm. Everybody knew it. Chris nodded.

"There's a passenger loading zone at the entrance on the park side. Why don't you pull up in that zone with the Volvo a couple of hours before I'm due here on the day of the lunch, say, between ten and ten fifteen? Let's make it as close to ten o'clock as you can manage. Wait for a couple of minutes as if you were going to pick up a passenger and then leave. I'll consider that a signal that the lunch is on. And it will still be on if your car is parked outside the house here. If you don't show up at NK I won't come out here, and if your car isn't parked outside I'll just keep walking by."

"That sounds fine. But what if I have to cancel for some reason? How do we get in touch?"

"I'm sure you'll think of something. Many thanks, Chris. I'll look forward to seeing you again on the twenty-second." He jumped up, retrieved his coat and hat, and left so quickly that they hardly exchanged another word. From the living room window, Chris watched him glance up and down the street before stepping beyond their hedge-bordered gateway.

Headquarters was less ecstatic over Chris's long, detailed report of this meeting than they had been over the announcement about the lunch. Their expectations were too high, as Chris had feared. There was the usual double-think about Plotkin's motives, and concern that this might be part of a KGB operation aimed at Chris, but some enthusiasm remained. Again they were full of advice on the upcoming meeting, pushing Chris in a series of messages to be more aggressive with this Soviet, more explicit in explaining the ways Chris could "help" him and what Plotkin could do for the western cause. And again, in messages still more heavily edited by Mike, Chris tried without much success to slow down the speculation and enthusiasm.

The night after the lunch, Lisa was fairly glowing with excitement when

Chris came home from the Embassy. He had missed dinner because of the long messages exchanged with Headquarters. "Did I do good today?" she asked, bringing a drink for him into the den. "I thought it went wonderfully."

"Honey, you've never done better," he told her sincerely. "The lunch was delicious. Perfect."

"How was your talk afterwards? Did you make any headway?"

"Not really. Have you looked at your calendar? I made a note that he wants to come again on the twenty-second. Is that okay?"

"I suppose so. I don't know that I can top today's performance, though. You really didn't get anywhere with him?" Her look of disappointment was lost on Chris, who was deep in his own thoughts.

"Without really saying so, we talked with the understanding that he's KGB and I'm CIA. And he did set up some safety signals for our next meeting. But that was with my pushing. He didn't volunteer a thing."

Lisa was truly disappointed. She had hoped that today's lunch would resolve the case and end the distraction that was keeping a barrier between her and Chris. Her disappointment was all the greater because she had tried so hard. She swallowed it, though, keeping up a lively chatter through what remained of their evening together. And throughout that time she could see her husband retreating into himself again, the barrier growing still thicker. Later on, in bed, her hopes for lovemaking were dashed when he once again kissed her, turned out the light and rolled over, away from her.

They went out the next two evenings, attending dinner parties that Lisa found a relief compared to staying home with her distant husband. The third evening they were at home again, with no change in their relationship. She was so disappointed by now that Chris was at last beginning to feel it, through all his vagueness. To *feel* it, but unable to do anything about it. The case had such a hold on him that he couldn't respond to his wife, no matter how much he loved her. Bedtime was a repeat of previous nights.

Now more aware of her mood, Chris sensed after the light was out that Lisa was not going to sleep. She was a sweet, gentle sleeper, usually drifting off quickly into a soft breathing that touched him. Not tonight. From his side of the bed he could sense her tension, hear the carefully controlled breathing that was not part of her sleep. Suddenly she sat up, reaching across him to turn on the light.

"I don't mind having Sasha once in a while for lunch. What I do mind is having him here every day for breakfast and dinner, too, in your mind. And I absolutely detest his being in bed with us every night. It's obscene!" She got out of bed, stalking angrily to the closet for her robe and slippers.

"What are you doing, for God's sake?" Chris was getting alarmed.

"I'm moving into the guest room." She was already at the bedroom door.

"You can't do that." He was shouting now. "What will Missy think?"

"Stop shouting. I know what she'll think if you wake her. In the morning I'm going to tell Missy that you're sick, and I don't want to catch it." She was gone, closing the bedroom door quietly despite her anger.

Making no attempt to follow or change her mind, Chris lay awake much of the night with his bitter thoughts. When he awoke in the morning, both Lisa and Missy were already up preparing breakfast. While Missy was in her room after breakfast, getting ready for *lekskola*, Chris asked Lisa if Missy had noticed that she had slept in the guest room. She had.

"What did you tell her? That I was sick?"

"No, Dear, I told her that you were sleeping poorly and keeping me awake."

"What happens next?"

"That, my dear Christian, depends on you."

CHAPTER EIGHT

Monday, January 20, 1969

For Chris, this was a time of waiting. Waiting for Plotkin's second visit to his home. Waiting for a break in the situation with Lisa, who continued to sleep in the guest room. He was less distracted now by the Plotkin case than by Lisa's new-found independence. Always the dutiful wife, usually accepting and helping with both his personal desires and career needs, she was making it clear that there were new rules in their relationship. He could have dealt with these new rules better if she was willing to talk about them. She was not.

It was as if she had turned the tables on him. Chris had rarely been able to discuss his work with her, excepting cases where she was involved socially, such as these beginning stages of the relationship with Plotkin. Now she avoided discussing her activities with him. When going out she neither told him in advance nor discussed later who she had been with. Some nights he would arrive home for dinner to find her gone. In these cases she would leave a note. "Over at Millie's for dinner. There's food in the fridge." When she took Missy with her on these evenings he was able to learn from his daughter that they were perfectly innocent outings with friends. On a couple of occasions, though, he would find a babysitter home with Missy, who informed him that Mrs. Holbeck was "out." Asking a babysitter about his wife's activities would have been too embarrassing. Lisa returned at reasonable hours from these outings. The first time he asked where she had been, she said she'd been at Millie's for dinner again. The next time he did not ask her, nor did she tell him anything about her evening.

Lisa was not unfriendly toward her husband during this time. She continued to prepare most of the meals at home, did the household chores, entertained twice at their home and went with him to a number of cocktail parties and a dinner. Nobody else, Missy included, seemed to notice any difference in Lisa or Chris. She simply would not sleep with him, declined to speak of her own activities, and refused to discuss their relationship. Whenever Chris tried to raise the subject, the only thing she would say was, "I told you before. It's all up to you."

A wife out of control, as Chris thought of this situation, posed a danger both to his personal security and that of the Station. He worried increasingly about it, imagined that she had fallen into some Machiavellian scheme orchestrated by the Soviets, that she had a lover, maybe even one of his friends in the business community. Two days before the next meeting with Plotkin, he and Lisa attended a buffet supper at the home of one of these friends. Chris found himself talking with Millie Jones over drinks after dinner. Millie commented on how tired he looked, saying she understood from Lisa that he was working long hours and seldom home for dinner. "But that at least gives us more time with Lisa. She's a lovely person, Chris. You're lucky to have her as a wife."

Thanks, Millie.

* * *

He got drunk that night. Not enough to disgrace himself, but Lisa was embarrassed at his losing control and had to drive him home. Once they were upstairs she accepted a boozy goodnight kiss, watched him walk slowly and carefully to the bedroom they now called his, trying to show he was in full control despite the drinks. Worried, she got into her nightgown and walked down the hall to listen at the closed bedroom door, hoping to hear his usual snoring. Nothing. After standing there for a few minutes, feeling chilled in her thin nightie, she still heard no sound. She opened the door. Her normally over-neat husband had scattered his clothes on the floor and fallen into bed in his underwear. He was still wide awake, staring at her with hands behind his head, elbows akimbo.

"I'm sorry for everything, Honey," he said. "Why don't you come to bed where you belong." She closed the door, walked softly back to the guestroom and cried herself to sleep.

* * *

Chris attended the Ambassador's weekly staff meeting on the twenty-second, a nine o'clock review of activities in the various Embassy offices. When the Ambassador asked for comments from his section, he passed, mentioning that he was only present because Mike was out of the city on a skiing vacation. Normally a short meeting, this one dragged on because of a long presentation by Bill Broom about the ramifications of Sweden's position regarding American involvement in Vietnam. At nine forty-five, Chris asked to be excused for a meeting he must attend. The Ambassador, looking bored with Bill's long discourse, waved him out of the conference room.

Chris had not needed to hurry as much as he thought. It was not yet ten o'clock when he arrived at NK, the Stockholm department store where Plotkin would observe his safety signal, so he circled the block before returning to pull into the passenger loading zone across from the park A Stockholm policeman was strolling slowly down the block toward him. Chris watched the NK entrance intently, hoping he appeared to be waiting for someone. He resisted temptation to look over toward the park, where he hoped Plotkin was checking his safety signal. The policeman walked by, peering in at Chris and then continuing his slow walk. In his rear vision mirror, Chris saw the uniform turn the corner, out of sight. He stole a glance at the park. No Plotkin.

What if Plotkin hadn't arrived in the park yet? He decided to wait a minute longer. A loud tap on the driver's window startled him. It was the policeman who had walked by earlier.

"You can't stay here." Close up, Chris could see that the policeman was very young, hardly a man yet. Or was Chris just getting old?

"I'm waiting for my wife."

"You've waited long enough. Move on." The voice was rougher than the face. Chris drove off.

It was a brilliant, sunlit day. Fresh snow contrasted sharply with the dark old stone in many of Stockholm's buildings, giving the city an unreal, Christmas-card beauty. Chris thought about going directly home, where he might be able to chat with Lisa while she was preparing their lunch, to begin mending their relationship. He returned to the Embassy instead, to work on reports and handle other paperwork that was his responsibility while the COS was absent. It was exactly noon when he got home. He had checked carefully for surveillance, sure there was none.

Lisa seemed in good spirits when he arrived, bustling about the kitchen, humming softly to herself. He perched on a kitchen stool, watching in admiration. She was an excellent cook and hostess. Her abilities and personality, to say nothing of her good looks, had been real assets to his career. He was touched that she would still help him this way, despite the difficulties between them.

"I love you, you know." Chris watched carefully for her reaction.

"I love you too, you know." She smiled slightly as she said it.

"Then why do we have these problems?"

"You know why. When you come back to the real world we'll talk about them. Not before."

"Meaning what? What do you want me to do? Quit my career? Go home and run tug boats around Puget Sound?"

Now she was irritated, trying to remain patient. "Meaning you have a guest coming for lunch in a few minutes. Go wash up. Then put the sherry decanter and glasses in the living room. After the other night I'm going to keep you off hard liquor for a while." He obeyed meekly, feeling a mixture of guilt and chagrin over the thoughts that had led up to that evening of drinking.

Standing once again at Missy's window, Chris watched Plotkin come down the street—from the other direction this time—and turn quickly into their gateway. Lisa was as sweet as before in greeting her guest at the door. His arrival and welcome were such a repeat of the first time that it seemed a ritual had already been established. Except for a switch from vodka to sherry.

"What, no vodka today?" Plotkin asked.

When Lisa didn't answer right away, Chris said, "I tried to crawl inside a bottle of liquor the other night. Lisa is slowing me down. I'll get something stronger if you like."

"No, thanks. Sherry will be fine. I do that myself sometimes. Usually when I'm alone in my apartment. You know, I really miss my wife and our times together. That's why I enjoy being with you. I can feel the closeness between you."

Lisa and Chris exchanged glances, feeling some embarrassment in light of their personal situation. It seemed fakery that others should continue to see them this way.

"A very nice compliment." Chris poured a glass of the sherry for each of them, raising his quickly this time before the Russian could drink without a toast. "Skål, and may you enjoy your wife's company again soon."

"Skål." Plotkin met their eyes as he took a sip of sherry. "I shall. That's one of the things I was going to tell you today. I'm going home to Moscow soon."

"No! Not so soon. You haven't been here that long." Lisa acted so sincerely disappointed that Chris was surprised. This news should be the best she'd heard in a long time, considering her feelings about his involvement in the case.

"Not to stay, Lisa." Plotkin laughed at her reaction. "I'll be back in a month's time."

Chris was puzzled. It was unusual for any diplomat, intelligence type or not, to return home for such a long stay while still so early in his posting. "It couldn't be home leave so soon, could it?"

"We don't get home leave that often. It's what you might call 'consultation.'"

"No problems for you, I hope."

"Nothing like that, Chris. I'll be back, and we can continue our lunches then."

"When will you be going?"

"In a couple of weeks. I don't much like flying Aeroflot, so I'm taking the night boat to Helsinki and rail from there."

"Then we won't be seeing you until you come back?" Lisa was on her feet and ready to put their lunch on the table as she asked the question. Plotkin, as though his mind were already home in Moscow, looked at her blankly. He said nothing, his head moving slightly in a curious nod that could have meant "yes" or "no." Rather than press for an answer, Lisa left the room.

"Is this for general publication, Sasha?" Chris was finding this whole situation more curious all the time.

"Of course not!" Plotkin snapped at him. "I thought I made it clear from the beginning that these are private meetings."

This was the lead that Chris had been looking for. "I understand that part of it. But I have to tell you, Sasha, that I'm having a lot of trouble with the ground rules here. I think it's time we talk about them. This isn't the normal way an officer from your service and one from my service meet."

"What's the 'normal' way?" Plotkin's expression was a mixture of annoyance and apprehension.

"They either meet socially, as we did at a restaurant lunch, or—let's be frank here—they meet clandestinely. This is neither the one nor the other. You've put clandestine rules on a social relationship—having lunch with me and my wife at our home, not wanting anybody to know about it. It seems to me you want 'to have your cake and eat it, too,' as we say."

"I don't understand that. Explain it to me."

Chris paused before he answered. "I'm not sure I know enough even to ask the right questions, to say nothing of giving you an answer. I suppose what I'm trying to get at is that you seem to want a friendship with me and Lisa, yet you don't want us to talk about it because it would get you in trouble. I like you, Sasha. I really do. I feel we have a friendship, but I don't understand it. No matter who we are as people, we can't live the same kind of lives as those who aren't in our kind of work. What I'm trying to say, what I'm trying to ask is: are you disaffected? Do you want to defect? Do you want to work for my service? Are you playing games, enjoying our hospitality, setting the rules? Or maybe you're just genuinely lonely and tired of playing by your service's rules." Pausing to take a drink of his sherry, Chris concluded lamely, "That's what I meant."

With impeccable bad timing, Lisa opened the doors to the dining room. "Come on, you two. Time to eat." As Chris stood, Plotkin remained seated. He was deep in thought again, making no move to join his hosts.

"You're as bad as my kids. I said 'Come on.' " Lisa stamped her foot in mock impatience. "Lunch will be ruined if you don't come right away. What have you two been up to while I was gone?" She directed the question at Chris. Plotkin came to life again, rising and taking Lisa's arm as they went into the dining room. "Nothing to concern yourself about, dear lady. We can talk about it when you go to your weaving class."

"My weaving class was cancelled for today."

She doesn't take hints very well, Chris thought.

"Isn't there something you could be doing after lunch?"

"Well, I suppose if you two want to be left alone I could go down to the *lekskola* and walk back with Missy. It's a beautiful day."

"I'm sure Missy would love to have you walk her home on such a nice day." The glance Chris gave her along with the remark did the trick. She decided to go for Missy.

Their conversation over lunch returned to the mundane at first. The weather, the Holbeck family, life in Stockholm. Somehow they got onto American films. Plotkin had seen two films in Stockholm theaters that he thought were useful guides to American life. *Bonnie and Clyde* and *Guess Who's Coming to Dinner?* Both fit the stereotypes he'd been taught about American life, the one dealing with crime and the Great Depression and the other with racial problems. Lisa was as interested as Chris in setting him straight. They sent words tumbling over one another and their guest, trying to explain what they saw as the real meanings in these films. Lunch was over before Chris realized that—while they'd been busy justifying some very real problems in their homeland—Plotkin hadn't much chance to talk.

Lisa drew them back into the living room with their coffee before she left to get Missy. "I guess I won't be seeing you again before you go home, Sasha. Have a wonderful trip, and be sure to call us when you get back."

Plotkin bowed and kissed her hand. "Thank you, Lisa. But we don't have to say goodbye now. Perhaps we'll see each other again before I leave."

"How's that?" Chris and Lisa, both surprised, spoke at the same time.

"I'll talk to Chris about it while you're gone." The two men walked her to the door, then returned to the living room. Plotkin seemed nervous and in a hurry now, sipping hastily at coffee too hot to drink comfortably.

"Before you start asking questions again, I'll tell you that I can't answer many of those you asked before we ate."

"I think we'll both be a long way ahead if you can answer even one."

"Right. I'll answer one. No, I'm not playing games with you and Lisa, Chris. What was that expression of yours? I guess I want to have my cake and eat it, too. Whatever you might think, my Embassy does not know about these lunches."

"Then you're disaffected. You've answered another question."

"Perhaps, but that doesn't really answer the question." Plotkin's expression was grave.

"Disaffected from what? You didn't ask that. You're assuming that I'm disaffected from my government. I won't say I am or that I'm not. I think I'm more disaffected from all the power centers in the world. From America, when I see the films we were talking about at lunch and listen to my favorite Americans rationalizing them. From Sweden, when I see the slums of south Stockholm in this so-called welfare state. Although I love her, I'm disaffected from my wife because she refuses to give me children. I'm depressed. I can't tell you all the answers because I don't know them myself."

"You're going to have to answer them some day."

"Of course. I won't promise you answers, but we could talk more about it next week. I could come by again for lunch on Friday. The same, ah, situation won't exist then and it will be a little more risky, but I want to get a few things straight in my mind before I return to Moscow."

Chris could feel excitement welling. Maybe Headquarters' optimism was justified after all. "I can just about guess what that situation might be. I'll respect your reservations for now, but I hope we can talk about it later."

"Everyone's entitled to make guesses."

"Any guesses about where all this will lead?"

"Not really. I've known since we first made plans that it couldn't go on indefinitely, even though I wish it could. Your offer to help me is useless. The only thing I'd want from you is a United Nations passport, so that I could be a citizen of the world. I'd like my allegiance to be to my family and friends, and the rest of it to be my choice."

"We all wish sometimes that we could drop our responsibilities and go to some paradise," Chris said, "but that doesn't work in this world. Why don't we start talking about real issues? There are things I could do for you if you were willing to work with us or defect, but there's not much point in talking about them until I know where you stand."

"No, I don't have time. My situation calls. Anyway, Chris, you can say nothing now that would sway me one way or the other. You've been in the business a long time, just as I have. You know as well as I that this kind of decision is very personal and doesn't hang on issues as much as it does on background, and how that background has affected a person. I'll tell you another thing. I've lived in the west longer than you realize, and I've had more of a chance to make comparisons than you know. Your side doesn't come out as well as you think in those comparisons. That makes the choice harder."

"We can offer—"

"Don't try to tempt me with your offers," Plotkin cut him off, his voice rising in anger. "I have a good idea what they are. They mean nothing. Nothing! You know what's happened to some of your agents, like Penkovsky. Your history of handling defectors isn't much prettier. No, don't give me any of your materialism."

"You didn't let me finish. You don't know that what I was going to say had anything to do with that."

Plotkin rose to his feet and said in a friendlier tone, "I really have to go, Chris. I don't want to argue with you. I respect your position and you must respect mine. We'll talk more about it next Friday. Same time, same place, same signals?"

Chris sighed. "Okay, Sasha, if that's the way you want it. I'd like to have a lot more time to discuss things with you, but as you say, I have to respect your position." He shook hands with his guest, giving him a big grin. "But come back with some right answers."

Plotkin said his goodbyes and left quickly. Chris paced the living room for fifteen minutes, giving the man time to get away before he returned to the Embassy to write a report.

CHAPTER NINE

January 23-31, 1969

It was a difficult report to write.

He rolled a piece of paper into an old manual typewriter he used for drafts. With the Plotkin file open on his desk he typed the classification, the address line, and identifying code words that would limit distribution and get the cable into the right hands at Headquarters. Riffling through the file, he added references; then he sat back and stared at the page.

The report went slowly. It was close to quitting time when he finished and gave it to his secretary to put in final form, then called the communicator to stand by. Both secretary and communicator were unhappy about having to stay late. They should complain. He'd also have to stay late to sign approval for the transmission since Mike was still on vacation. Reading it page by page as it came out of the secretary's typewriter, he was satisfied. It was honest, it was direct, and the more he reviewed the situation the more he felt there wasn't much more he could have done to influence Plotkin. Their next meeting should put some finishing touches on this operation, one way or the other.

Time between this meeting and the next would normally drag, but there was no chance for that. A cable arrived the next morning announcing the death at Headquarters of the European Division chief. That afternoon another message came, asking for Mike Mitchell's emergency contact instructions while on vacation. He was wanted at Headquarters immediately, as a candidate for the vacant position. Chris was kept busy reaching Mike at the lodge in Norway, meeting the Mitchell couple when they flew in from Oslo, and going over Station business with Mike for several hours before driving him back to the airport for the flight to Washington.

Mike was confirmed as the new Division Chief the following Tuesday. One of the Stockholm case officers, Bill Broxton, was involved in a serious car accident on the highway to Uppsala on Wednesday. By good fortune he was not carrying any sensitive documents, but he was taken to a hospital and would be laid up for at least two weeks. Besides having to portion out this officer's work and carry part of it himself, Chris had to monitor his condition in cable exchanges with Headquarters.

Plotkin was on the back burner. Headquarters was so preoccupied with the other events that their responses to his cables about the last meeting were muted. There was a brief flurry of cable traffic on technical aspects of the meeting, Headquarters wanting a follow-up surveillance of Plotkin after the meeting and a confirmation of his departure from Sweden. Chris managed to convince them that it would be foolhardy to attempt surveillance, given the limited assets at the station's disposal. He did agree to prepare an agent to go along on the night boat to Helsinki when Plotkin traveled, if they could nail down his date of departure through their travel agency sources. He'd use Bisan, a Swedish girl who was being developed as a support asset. That meant still another meeting. He saw her Thursday night, showed her a photo of Plotkin and briefed her on the mission.

Lisa wasn't home when he returned from that meeting. Well after midnight, from his bedroom, he heard the stairs creak as she went directly to her bedroom and quietly closed the door. The babysitter told him Lisa was at Millie's house. He wondered.

Friday dawned much like the day of his last meeting with Plotkin, cold and clear with new snow. Such a pretty day that this time he resolved not to return to the Embassy after signaling Plotkin at NK that the meeting was on. After the safety signal at ten o'clock, he'd go directly home, maybe have a chance to chat with Lisa before lunch.

Upon leaving the Embassy, he noted that the sun hadn't warmed the air at all. The squeaking snow under his feet confirmed how cold it was as he walked toward his car. The shadows from the trees along Strandvägen weren't quite as long as they had been last week at this time. Stockholm was on the downhill ride toward spring. In the scant hour he'd been at the Embassy the car had cooled off completely. He let it warm up before driving downtown to wait the few minutes at NK for Plotkin's safety signal. No policeman this time, and no Plotkin visible in the park. But then he hadn't seen Plotkin last time, either.

Next he headed west from the city, toward home. Chris enjoyed the drive and was feeling good as he slid to a stop in front of his house. Lisa didn't reply to his cheery "Hello" when he let himself in through the front door. Now what? Her actions were so strange these days he was afraid she might have taken off without preparing the lunch for Plotkin. A walk through the dining room to the kitchen put his mind at ease. The table was set, and soup was simmering on the stove. She must have walked down to the shopping square for some last minute items. It wasn't yet ten thirty, and she had no reason to expect him. He went back to the front windows to look down the street, on the chance that he might see her walking back. No Lisa, only a skier heading toward Drottningholm. This castle was located not much more than a mile from their home across Drottningholm Bridge. It was a favorite residence of the royal family and surrounded by a park open to the public. He and Lisa had skied there several times with the children during the Christmas holidays.

An idea struck. Chris went quickly to his bedroom to change into long johns and ski pants, then to the front hall for his ski parka, hat and mittens. Next he went to the garage for his skis. He'd ski down to the square to pick up Lisa and come back with her. Outside the garage door, he slapped his skis down on the new snow and fastened the cable bindings.

Out on the street Chris looked in the direction of the square. Still no Lisa. Nobody, in fact, on the street. In the other direction the skier had long since disappeared. An hour skiing at Drottningholm would probably do him more good than trying to talk with Lisa.

Few people were outdoors on this work and school day. It was terribly cold, but the atmosphere brought some needed peace to Chris. He felt good. The children in their neighborhood were on skis most every afternoon. As he used his poles to push himself along and keep his balance, he thought about how Missy and her friends skied merrily along with no poles. Ah, to be young again!

There was a knoll off the beaten path in the park where somebody had built a small ski jump, maybe a couple of feet high. Probably some of the older boys who lived nearby. Chris thought about trying it.

He'd do it.

Climbing the knoll took more out of him than he'd expected. Wheezing at the top, he made his weekly resolve to start an exercise program. The knoll wasn't high, but looking down the run to the jump, it appeared a lot more impressive than from the bottom. Well, he had been a pretty good skier during college days. There wasn't anybody in sight to embarrass him if he botched the little jump. He poled hard and headed downhill.

Two things surprised Chris. First, his skis were much faster than expected. When he started out he almost lost his balance backwards. Then, when he dug in the poles and launched himself on the jump, he went much higher than he thought he would. In the few seconds he was in the air he realized that he had overcompensated for the first mistake. Now he was leaning too far forward. He tried to bring up the tips of his skis and failed, hitting the snow with the tip of one ski. He somersaulted, bounced on his shoulders, made a half-roll and came to a stop with his right ski buried in the snow. His leg must be badly twisted, he thought. He moved to untangle himself and came close to fainting. It was more than a twist, for sure. The pain was awful when he tried to move.

Chris lay back, chilled, and felt the panic start. Nobody was in sight. What if he couldn't get back in time for Plotkin's arrival? He realized with a groan that his Volvo was parked in front of the house, the final signal that lunch was on. He tried again to move but almost fainted from pain. He called for help several times, then just lay there, losing hope. It was about ten minutes before he lost consciousness, a victim of shock and hypothermia.

CHAPTER TEN

Friday, January 31, 1969

Astrid Svensson was a nurse at *Karolinska Sjukhuset*, the largest hospital in greater Stockholm. Her parents' home was in Bromma and a long way from the hospital, but she still lived with them as a matter of practicality. Apartments on rent control were notoriously hard to get, and she couldn't afford key money to avoid the waiting time.

Living with her parents had an additional advantage: Astrid was engaged to a grounds keeper at Drottningholm castle. As the number two grounds man at the castle, Lasse was building a reputation they both hoped would translate into a good job with a landscaping firm in Stockholm. Then they could be married.

Being so close to Drottningholm gave the couple occasional opportunities to visit in Lasse's cottage on the castle grounds. She was on a night shift at Karolinska, and he pretty much made his own schedule. After some satisfying time together, she was on her way back home from the cottage. There were a few foot prints along the trail through the park but no ski tracks other than hers until she came close to the edge of the park. There she saw another set of tracks that veered off toward a little ski jump. Having played in these woods many times as a child, she knew that the jump was built there every winter. Reminiscing, she followed the tracks to see who might be using it now. It was not long before she saw the still form below the jump, realizing at once what had happened. At first she thought the man was dead. On his back, face bluish with white spots of frostbite on the cheeks, he did not stir or indicate in any way that he was aware of her presence. His right leg was broken, judging from the odd angle.

Kicking out of her skis, Astrid kneeled alongside and shouted at him, "What have you done?" No response. Hands trembling now, she put her ear alongside his mouth and felt for the carotid artery in his neck. He was alive! Breathing was shallow and pulse slow and weak, but he was alive! Now what to do? She couldn't move him by herself with that broken leg. There was no apparent head trauma. The jump was so small it qualified as child's play, so it was unlikely he'd knocked himself out. He must be unconscious from exposure.

Astrid took off her jacket and tucked it around the man's torso, then slapped her feet back into the ski bindings. She raced out of the park and to the first home she found. It took forever before the door was answered by an elderly lady, who held it open just a few inches.

"Quickly! A man has had a serious accident in the park. I need blankets and an ambulance at once!"

The old lady remained suspicious. "Do I know you? I don't seem to recall seeing you around here."

"I'm Astrid Svensson. I live across the bridge in Nockeby. I'm a nurse."

"Astrid Svensson. I don't remember that name, but I do know there's a Svensson family over that way. I think the man's name is Carl Erik."

"That's my father." Astrid was hopping about with excitement and frustration. "Really, this is an emergency. The man could die if he doesn't get help right away. He may die while we're standing here talking. Please give me some blankets right now and call an ambulance to come to the park."

"But ..."

Astrid was a big girl. A very big girl. She stood tall and had an imposing figure for which the word "buxom" would be inadequate. The lady was no match for her as Astrid pushed the door open, took the lady by the arm and firmly led her into her own house. Her frustration was too great to wait longer.

"Telephone." It was a command, not a question.

"Over there." The phone was on a desk in the entry hall. Astrid saw the ambulance number posted on the telephone, dialed, and gave clear instructions. The ambulance drivers were to go about 200 meters inside the park from the street end, then up a trail to the left another 100 meters to find the victim. She'd be with him. Hanging up, she gave another order.

"Blankets."

"Upstairs in the linen closet." The woman understood by now that there would be no further argument or questions. She followed Astrid upstairs and helped her locate three warm blankets. Astrid draped them over her shoulders as she ran quickly downstairs again, thanking the lady and promising to return them. In a minute she was back on her skis and poling madly into the park.

When she returned the man was lying as before, looking about the same except that the white patches of frostbite on his cheeks had grown. Quickly out of her skis she unfolded the blankets and laid them over the victim's body, then slid under them and as gently as possible took Chris in her arms. She had read in a study on hypothermia that body heat was the best possible source of warmth.

Waiting for the ambulance, Astrid finally had a chance to think about what was happening and what she'd done. Here she was, lying with another man in her arms not more than a half-hour after she'd lain with Lasse. She didn't even know the man … had never seen him in fact. It struck her so funny that she started giggling, was still giggling when she heard the two-toned blare of the ambulance's warning signal. She heard the vehicle stop at the street end, expecting to hear doors slam, but then it came right down the trail to the cutoff for the knoll.

❊ ❊ ❊

When Chris regained consciousness he was wholly disoriented. There was no pain, only an awful weariness and sadness. He struggled to open his eyes, wondering at the sight before him. He was apparently in some kind of hospital, lying on a gurney, covered with blankets except for his right leg. That, he saw, was in the process of being wrapped with tape and plaster. A couple of doctors and a nurse were chatting in Swedish as they worked on his leg. He groaned. It suddenly came back to him what he had done to himself.

"So. We are back with the living, are we?" The nurse, an older woman with a brusque manner, came to the head of the gurney and slipped the thermometer out from under his tongue. "And who might we be?" She had to be a Swedish Army nurse.

"Where am I?" He asked the question in English.

"You are in Bromma Hospital, in much better condition than you deserve for that bit of foolishness out in the park. But who are you?" She continued speaking Swedish.

As awareness returned so did Chris's professional wariness. *What was really going on here?* He knew he'd fallen and hurt his leg, but he had no way of knowing for certain that he was in Bromma Hospital, couldn't remember a thing after lying injured in the snow. "Who are you?" he parried, trying to clear his mind, adding more confusion for the nurse and doctors since this time he asked in Swedish.

"I'm nurse Sjöberg. But that's not important. We don't know who you are." She turned to the doctors in mock exasperation, trying to add a light note to the situation. "Here we have a fully grown man who hurts himself while trying to act like a ten-year-old boy. We don't know who he is because he doesn't have any identification, and now he doesn't know whether he's an American or a Swede. I think—" She broke off and rushed to the door as it started to open. "You can't come in here!" She started to push the door shut again.

"My husband is in there." It was Lisa's frightened voice.

Nurse Sjöberg looked at the doctors. The older one nodded. Lisa came in the room. "Thank God, you're all right!" She ran to the gurney and practically threw herself on Chris. The younger doctor pulled her away. "Please, Missus, please. Your husband is hurt. You'll hurt him more."

"What happened to you?" Lisa stood back to survey her husband on the gurney, noted his leg in the cast, now being given finishing touches.

The older doctor answered her question. "Your husband apparently tried out a little ski jump near Drottningholm. He succeeded in breaking his leg. But worse, he lay there for a long time without help and is suffering a bad case of hypothermia. We've got his leg patched up. Now we have to get him warmed up to a human temperature."

"How bad is it?" Lisa asked.

"The leg has a simple but painful fracture. He has only just now come back to consciousness." The doctor reached out to nurse Sjöberg for the thermometer she'd taken from Chris's mouth, looked at it and handed it back. "Yes, he is still a long ways from normal, but now that he's conscious he should be all right. We'll keep him here for a couple of days. But who is he? He had no identification when the ambulance picked him up."

"He's a diplomat at the American Embassy in Stockholm, Chris Holbeck. I'm his wife, Lisa."

"What was a diplomat doing on a cold work day in Drottningholm, throwing himself off a tiny mountain with nothing at all in his pockets?"

"I wish I knew." Lisa's worry and sympathy were turning to anger, much like a mother who has found a lost child. All eyes in the room turned to the form on the gurney.

Dazed and confused as he was, Chris was nevertheless acutely aware of the trouble he was in. He closed his eyes to feign unconsciousness. There was no need to pretend. The next thing he knew, he was in a four-bed hospital ward with Lisa sitting alongside. He'd come back far enough now to feel cold all over, and an awful ache in his right leg.

"Hi, Honey." Lisa had been leafing absentmindedly through a Swedish fashion magazine. She looked up, returning his weak smile with her own.

"How are you feeling, Mr. Macho Man?"

"Terrible. Silly. Terribly silly and sad. I seem to have made a real mess of things."

"I don't want to make you feel worse, but I have to agree. What were you thinking of, to take off skiing like that by yourself?"

"I guess I wasn't really thinking. I came home early, had time to kill and decided to ski down to find you shopping at the square. I don't know why, but instead I went into the park to ski for a while, and decided to try that little jump. Did Plotkin show up?"

"Of course. You left the Volvo parked outside, so he thought you were there."

"What did he say? What did you tell him?"

"I told him what I knew, which was nothing. I had no idea where you were. He looked very confused and took off. Said he'd have to wait until he got back from Moscow to see us."

"Shit!"

"I beg your pardon. You don't talk that way."

"Sorry. What a mess! How long am I going to be stuck here?"

"Not long. You should be released Sunday night or Monday morning. There's really not too much wrong with you outside of a broken leg and some frostbite on your cheeks. Mainly, they need to get your temperature up to normal and stabilized." He reached up to touch his right cheek, which was covered with thick creamy stuff.

Lisa lowered her voice so those in the other beds couldn't overhear. "Speaking of the mess, Mark Noble was here a few minutes ago. They were frantic down at the office when I told them you were missing. It was reported to the police. They're the ones who told us someone of your description was here in the hospital. Do you realize that the Station is now three officers short? Mike's away, Bill is still in the hospital at Karolinska recovering from the automobile accident, and now you."

"God!"

"It's a good idea to call on Him, all right." She pointed straight up. "You're going to need all the help you can get. How are you going to explain missing the meeting with Plotkin? Mark had some very colorful things to say about that when he was here."

"I'll be back at work on Monday. I'll worry about it then." That was clearly a lie. They both knew he would think about nothing else until getting back to work.

Lying in a hospital bed over the weekend was agony for Chris. The constant stream of visitors made it worse. For those who weren't connected with the Station, it was difficult to explain how he had done this to himself. "Oh, on a whim I decided to take off a day from work. The weather was so nice I went skiing." None of his friends understood. It was so unlike him.

Agency people were even less understanding. Mark Noble was third most senior in the Station and thus Acting COS until Chris was back on his feet. He came to visit on Saturday afternoon, carrying copies of the cabled reports to Headquarters and their replies. Headquarters was not charitable about Chris's injury. They wanted a full explanation as soon as he was able to prepare a cable, and his plans regarding Plotkin in light of these developments. Chris vomited much of Saturday night, worrying the doctors. He knew enough about his own body to realize that the nausea was from mental stress rather than his physical condition.

Lisa spent the last of Saturday visiting hours with Chris, worried sick herself because the doctors could give no reason for her husband's nausea. Chris himself was far more concerned about the impact of his screw-up on the future. Lisa couldn't shake the notion that with his physical symptoms and inappropriate behavior, Chris was having a nervous breakdown brought on by the pressure of his work.

CHAPTER ELEVEN

Lisa's eyes were moist as she left her husband's hospital room that Saturday evening. Tears began to flow when she found herself alone in the elevator car, and by the time she exited the hospital's main doors she was choking back sobs. Once in the car, she was seized with such wracking spasms that it was several minutes before she could trust herself to drive.

Missy was in good hands with a babysitter. There was no compelling reason to go home. She would have liked to visit Millie, the closest she had to a confidante, but what could she tell her? That she and Chris were caught in a web of intrigue involving a senior KGB officer?

When she finally started the car she was uncertain where to go. This aimlessness reminded Lisa of her dad, bringing on more tears as she thought of her cherished family life before both parents had left her. Every Sunday her little family had gone for a drive. The ritual began when Lisa asked her dad where he planned to take them. His answer was always the same: "We'll follow the hood ornament and see where it leads us."

And that's what she did now, wiping tears away with the back of her hand, gradually more dry-eyed as she watched with interest where the hood ornament would take her. With no apparent volition on her part, the car took her to a Bromma street-end that overlooked Lake Mälaren, not far from Missy's *lekskola*. It was a spot where she occasionally parked while waiting for her daughter. As the car cooled she hugged her winter coat around her, admiring the view made possible on this unusually clear night and allowing her mind to wander back to thoughts of her early life.

She put concerns about her present situation and what to do about it in a box that would have to be opened soon.

✳ ✳ ✳

Lisa was born in Arlington, Washington, a town north of Seattle. Her parents were second-generation Danes who came from Chicago to the northwest. Tomas was a pharmacist, running an old-fashioned drugstore in town. Her mother, Lisbet, was a homemaker. They were a quiet couple with some good friends and few activities outside the Lutheran church.

The thing Lisa missed in her early years was having a big family with relatives. She was an only child of two people who in turn were the only children in their families. Her parents were both in their mid-thirties when she was born, and by then their parents and most of their relatives had passed away. Her dad's uncle Thorwald lived in Chicago. He, too, died before she got a chance to meet him.

It was in September of her sophomore year at high school when Thorwald passed away. As his only living relatives, Tomas and Lisbet had to go back to Chicago to make funeral arrangements and take care of his effects. Lisa begged to go with them, but they insisted she must stay in school. Education came before everything else. It was a decision that saved her life.

The airliner carrying Tomas and Lisbet home from Chicago crashed on takeoff from O'Hare Airport, killing everybody aboard. To say that Lisa was devastated could not describe how the loss affected her. She was surrounded with friends but had no relatives. It was a distinction those around her didn't seem to understand.

Her best friend was Barbara Jensen, a classmate whose parents had also been best friends of her parents. Lisa and Barbara were often mistaken for sisters because they were so close and had the same surname. It was only natural that Barbara's parents would take her in as a foster child. She was a ward of the court, and would have been adopted by these other Jensens if she had wanted it. She did not.

The next year passed in agony. Not long past puberty, she changed from a sweet, compliant girl into a stubborn, withdrawn teenager. Once a straight 'A' student, she barely scraped through classes and was at outs with everybody, even Barbara. The Jensens tried to convince her that through adoption she'd become part of the family. They tried to treat her as 'family,' but it just didn't work. Nobody could understand. She was an orphan. She had no living relatives.

Reluctantly, the Jensens came to realize that they couldn't properly raise this girl. Something had to be done. That something came at Christmas of her junior year in high school.

The change was a move to Darrington, a logging town lying east of Arlington, nestled in the foothills of the Cascade Mountains. A childless couple, Maggie and Bert Brown, came from Darrington occasionally to visit Barbara's parents. They were touched when they learned from the Jensens about Lisa's difficulties, and offered just after Christmas to let her live with them. A new school and lifestyle might bring her around.

It seemed like a good decision, one that turned her life around at a difficult time. The Browns had an old frame house on the edge of the small town, well kept and with a wonderful big bedroom and bathroom upstairs for Lisa. Maggie and Bert had their room on the main floor.

Entering a new school in midterm, junior year, would be difficult for most. Strangely, it didn't prove difficult for Lisa. She gradually fell in love with both Maggie and Bert and began to emerge from her shell. Her usually bright personality and lively intelligence returned. Soon she had friends again. She took part in most of the social activities of school and town. Two things she didn't do. She no longer attended church—Maggie and Bert were not church-going folk—and she didn't date. Her blossoming somehow didn't include an interest in boys.

Maggie and Bert were more rough-cut than Lisa's parents, the other Jensens or friends she'd known in Arlington. Both had been raised in Darrington. Maggie finished high school but had not gone on to college. She worked as a checker in the local Safeway grocery store. Bert worked as a timber cruiser, measuring the timber resources in his company's forests. He was a logger at heart, a big man, rugged in looks and language. But for all the differences between her parents and the Browns, Bert and Maggie were able to reach Lisa and help her recover from that terrible loss of her parents.

Bert was laid off by the timber company in late March. He expected to be hired back in June. In the meantime they managed to get by on Maggie's income and Bert's unemployment checks.

In her senior year Lisa became accustomed to a leisurely morning before going to school. With so many credits earned already, she didn't have to be at school until third period. It was only a five-minute walk from the house, so she started sleeping in until after Maggie had gone to work at seven thirty. A couple of mornings she overslept, and Bert had to knock at her door to awaken her.

One morning in early April she awoke to find Bert standing by her bed. He'd never come in like that before. "You forget to knock, Bert?" she asked.

"Yeah, I guess so," he replied. "You're late again." She waited until he'd gone out and closed the door before getting out of bed.

The next morning he was there again, in robe and slippers. "Time to get up," he said.

She was awfully tired. "Maybe I don't want to. I could be late one day."

"Maybe if I got in on this side of the bed, you'd get out the other," he threatened, his tone making it clear that he was joking. This time she hopped out of bed in her pajamas and ran for the bathroom. By the time she went downstairs, he was gone, probably to the coffee shop where he often met a friend who was also out of work.

When the scene was repeated a few days later, Lisa decided to test him. "Go ahead," she said, "get in bed. I'm too tired to get up." He did, pulling the covers over himself and lying there on his back, hands folded on his chest, saying nothing.

"What do you want, Bert?"

"I want you to get up and go to school. School's important." Bert remained in bed, watching as she headed for the bathroom, carrying her outfit for the day. He was gone when she came out.

On Monday and for the next several school days he was there again. She stayed in bed until he got in with her. She tested him further: "I'm not going to get up today. I'll stay home from school."

"I said school's important. You have to get up." He put his foot against her hip and pushed. She turned her back to him and grabbed hold of the bedpost to hang on. "I'm not getting up."

"I know something that'll get you up." He turned on his side, put his arm around her and held her breast in his hand. His fingers searched and caressed gently. She shivered. Then she felt something starting to poke at her bottom. It wasn't his hand. "Actually," he said, "it's getting me up." He got out of bed and left the room.

When he next paid Lisa a morning visit he slipped into bed with no preliminaries, moving over to her and putting his arm around her again.

"Who are you saving yourself for?" he asked.

"Prince Charming."

"Maybe the Prince is here." Her breast was in his hand.

She was silent for a minute, trying to sort out her feelings. Some of it was a shivery delight. She loved Bert as a surrogate father, but she also admired him as a man. She was curious. Something had been skipped in the tragedies of her recent upbringing, leaving her confused but with a feeling that this wasn't right. She'd play it along and then cut him off.

"I'm getting up."

"You're right. It's time to stop and get you to school."

When he came again the next morning she was wide awake, had been for hours, waiting for him, trembling in anticipation, telling herself that before he came in the room, she was going to get up and stop this foolishness. But she was there for him when he slipped into bed. This time he'd shrugged out of his robe before getting in with her. He had nothing on.

"How can you do this to Maggie?" she asked.

"I'm not doing anything to Maggie. I'm doing something for you."

"I'm not ready for that."

"You're right," he said, "you're not ready." He left.

Twice that day at school—both times at her locker in the hallway—Lisa had trembling fits that brought her almost to fainting. Books under one arm, she put the other arm on top of her locker, laying her cheek against the cold steel. One of her girlfriends noticed the second time and tried to take her to the nurse. Lisa brushed it off as unimportant. But she was worried. Those scenes of the past week made it hard to concentrate on her studies.

That night Maggie and Bert took her to their square dance club as they had often done before. Everything was the same. Everything was different. Bert and Maggie said the same things to her and each other that they always did. The club was the same. The caller was the one the club always used, sing-songing his calls to the same crowd.

What was different was the way the men looked at her, brushed against her during the dances. What was different was the way she saw the men. And the women. She wondered about their sexuality, what they did with each other. And she wondered what the women were thinking about her, especially Maggie. Did they notice that the men were treating her differently, or was it all just her imagination?

Bert went to Seattle the next week, giving Lisa an opportunity to talk with Maggie about sex, maybe get a better picture of what was leading Bert to her room in the mornings. But somehow she could never get up the nerve to raise the subject. The closest was when she told Maggie that one of her classmates was pregnant and had decided to keep the child. That inspired a rare and brief lecture from Maggie: if Lisa ever decided to screw around, she'd better get some protection to avoid that happening to her. Did she want Maggie to arrange for birth control pills? Maggie's directness put her off. No, she wasn't screwing around and no, she didn't want birth control pills. Conversation closed.

The clock on her nightstand showed seven forty-five when she was awakened on the morning of Bert's return from Seattle. It was Bert slipping in beside her again, again with nothing on. He moved across at once, put his arm around her.

"Where were we?" he asked.

"You were talking about teaching me something."

"And you didn't want to learn."

"No."

"Want to now?"

She pulled the covers over her head.

"What's the point?" His fingers slipped down from her breast, caressing her body. She was getting aroused.

"Oh, for heaven's sake. Why don't you just do it and get it over with." She threw the covers off and lay on her back, legs and arms spread flat on the bed, looking like a rag doll tossed there by a careless child. She stared at the ceiling, refusing to look at Bert, wondering what he looked like. He laughed. It broke the spell. The good feeling left and was replaced by shame. She pulled the covers over both of them, first sneaking a peak. She was amazed at the sight of him.

"I guess you don't want to do it. Why did you laugh?"

"You really don't know much, do you?" He took her in his arms. She was stiff and resisting. He began by kissing her throat, her eyes, her ears, all the time with his hand stroking her, light finger touches. It wasn't until she began to relax that he finally kissed her full on the mouth. With that came the age-old ritual of making love. This was lovemaking by a very experienced older man who carefully led his pupil down the garden path, encouraging and enticing at every bend, preparing to the point where she was more than ready when they reached that final turn. It was a supreme moment of satisfaction, never to be repeated in her life so far.

Never by Matt, her only serious boyfriend before Chris. He was an experienced and competent lover but never took her to those heights.

Never by Chris, so inexperienced when they first went to bed together that she became his teacher. Her lessons ("women just know these things by their nature, Chris") served to bring them together into a thoroughly satisfying physical union, but never to those heights she found in a bed in a home on the outskirts of Darrington, Washington.

Never.

Lisa went to school that day in a daze, sure that everyone would see she'd lost her virginity. She felt ten feet tall, walking down the halls. But nobody treated her differently, and soon she was in the swing of all the activities leading to graduation from high school. It was three days away from her eighteenth birthday.

At dinner that night, Bert announced that he was going to Seattle again the next day. Lisa was stricken by the news and showed it.

"Don't look so sad, Lisa," Maggie said, "he'll be back in time for your birthday, and he's going to bring you a surprise." If she was puzzled by Lisa's reaction to the news she didn't show it.

Bert returned on the eve of Lisa's birthday, giving her hope of a very special birthday present the next morning. But it wasn't to be, because Maggie stayed home from work. She woke Lisa up early for a birthday breakfast and the surprise, a combination birthday and graduation gift: a portable typewriter to take to college. She was touched by their generosity. With Bert out of work, she knew they'd had to stretch their budget to afford it.

Her final three weeks of high school passed in a blur of normal school lessons and a continuation of Bert's lessons. He came to her again twice the following week, and several more times before graduation. He guided her down new paths with skill and patience. He set aside her worries about getting caught, about getting pregnant, with words and actions that prevented her stopping.

He was too patient. Twice she was late to school. The second time, Maggie heard about it.

At dinner that night, the beginning of the last week of school, Maggie said "Mrs. Carson was in the store this afternoon. She said you've been late for school twice recently, Lisa. You don't have to get there until nine thirty. How come you can't get up?"

Lisa knew she was blushing. Bert jumped into the conversation. "I'm surprised, Lisa. That's not like you. I've been leaving pretty early myself. Usually I knock at your door before I go. Maybe I'll have to come into your room to wake you."

Maggie's measuring glance took them both in. "I'm sure Bert would like to come into your room. Don't let him. Just get up when he knocks."

That at least gave Lisa an excuse for blushing. "I'm not letting any man into my room until I'm married."

"Nice to hear, Lisa," Maggie said, "but not many kids wait that long nowadays. Remember our little talk? The offer is still open."

On the morning of her last day at school he came to her the instant Maggie left for work. It was their last time together.

Bert and Maggie were proud parents at her graduation ceremonies. Many, many friends were there, including the Jensens from Arlington and lots of square dance club members. A reception at home for all the friends made the evening almost perfect. The only thing spoiling it for Lisa was the absence of any relatives in the crowd.

The following morning after commencement she went to school to help clean up, and then to a lunch for the school's editorial staff. When she returned home Bert's car was in the driveway, but there was no sign of him. Maggie was sitting at the kitchen table with a cup of coffee in front of her, untouched. She had been crying.

"Maggie! What's wrong? Where's Bert?"

"He's gone."

Lisa's heart fell. "Gone? How can he be gone?"

"He is, Lisa. Gone. I'm sorry we didn't let you know about it. It wasn't my choice, it was Bert's. He wouldn't let me tell you."

"Where's he gone? Has he left you? Left us?"

Maggie picked up her coffee cup with a trembling hand. "Damn, it's cold." She got up to throw the coffee in the sink, stood looking out the window with her back to Lisa. "He's gone to Brazil, if you can believe it."

"I don't believe it."

"Believe it." Maggie sat down again next to Lisa, who had sunk into a chair. She took both Lisa's hands in hers.

"But ... why?"

"The company isn't going to be able to take him back to work for a few months more. We make out okay with my paycheck, but he goes nuts hanging around the house and the coffee shop. He got an offer of a six-month job in Brazil, timber cruising in some of their forests. He thinks so much of you, he just couldn't tell you."

"But I love him. He's the only ... father, I guess ... I have."

"I know that, Honey, and he knows that. That's why he couldn't tell you."

Lisa took a clerking job for the summer in a local drugstore, reminding her of her dad's place in Arlington. She had a low-key social life. Though most of her activities were with Maggie, once in a while she went out with friends from school. She even went on a few dates, with encouragement from Maggie. But the girls and boys she'd known and liked in high school now seemed terribly immature. Lisa felt she'd moved far beyond them in life.

Late September and she was off to the University of Washington, the "U-Dub." Maggie drove her down to Seattle and helped her settle in a dorm on the beautiful campus. They parted with tears and Lisa's promises to write at least once a week, to go to Darrington for the holidays. Lisa went to the UW with lots of resources and every prospect of success. She lived off a trust fund left by her parents, still administered by the Jensens in Arlington. She had a high grade point, scored well in academic achievement tests. She declared a pharmacy major, with the romantic notion of following in her father's footsteps.

It was soon apparent that she wouldn't be a pharmacist; chemistry just didn't interest her that much. She switched to a communications major. That was better, if not totally satisfying. She was popular in the dorm, had many friends and dated quite a lot, especially enjoying the dances. But, like her friends in Arlington, the young people on campus seemed like kids to her.

A handful of visits with Maggie in Darrington reminded her that she was truly an orphan. With each visit their relationship cooled—not because Maggie had no feelings for this former foster child but because she was so invested in her relationship with Bert. His contract in Brazil had been extended, causing Maggie to travel there for the holiday season. Fortunately, the Jensens invited her to spend the holidays with them, and she found herself fitting in with their family better than in the days following the loss of her parents. As that relationship warmed, visits with Maggie became less and less frequent.

It was just a year after Bert left for Brazil that Lisa saw him again. Maggie had invited her for a weekend in Darrington following her first year at the University, a weekend that coincided with Bert's vacation from the job in Brazil. Maggie and Bert were so close after their long separation that Lisa felt left out. Everyone gave lip service to having a good time, but it seemed that the Browns were not comfortable with her presence.

It was at Sunday morning breakfast—a celebration of her departure—that the relationship between Bert and Lisa began its brief slide into non-existence.

She had been looking forward to seeing Bert again, wondering if he would show tenderness toward her or try to get her alone. He did not, leaving her even more confused about her feelings toward him. Those feelings were resolved when their breakfast conversation turned to her dating experiences at school. She told them about her current boyfriend, explaining that even though there was no firm commitment they were going steady.

Maggie was at the stove, so she could not see Bert when he turned to Lisa with arched eyebrows. "Sounds like you've found your Prince Charming. How's it going with that?" And then he grinned. The son-of-a-bitch.

In the year since their affair, Lisa had thought a lot about Bert's real motives in taking her down the garden path. Her thinking was confused by the tragedies that eventually led her to live with the Browns, but until this meeting she had remained charitable about his true reasons. How could a man who seemed so tender and loving want anything but the best for her? Now she had her answer, one that had lurked at the back of her mind.

She had been molested by a very experienced, clever man who had put his own desires far ahead of her welfare. Her life would always be affected by what he had done to her. Lisa did not believe that Maggie was aware of what had gone on between her and Bert, so she said nothing. Their relationship dwindled into a couple of postcards, Christmas cards with brief notes, and then nothing.

As for the times in bed with Bert, she decided that this was an unfair way for a girl to lose her virginity. She made a solemn pronouncement to herself that she was a virgin again, and decided that she would never, never reveal the episode with Bert to anyone; man, woman or future husband.

At the end of her sophomore year, Lisa decided to leave school to start over. It had to be a clean break, some job away from Seattle, Arlington, Darrington, the friends she'd known. That June she moved to Washington, DC, to take a secretarial position in the Navy Department. She was a good typist and had picked up enough shorthand in a night class in Seattle to pass a civil service examination.

It didn't take more than a month in DC for her to know that this was the right move. Her co-workers, the people she got to know in the rooming house where she lived, all seemed more mature than the people at the UW. The job, in a support unit for Navy armaments testing, was just okay. But it gave her a chance to meet many interesting people.

The most interesting was Matt Collins, a Marine captain who worked in a nearby office. Ten years her senior, he had seen combat in Korea. He was terribly good looking, respected by the men around him, and sought after by the women. They started dating.

As a single officer Matt lived well. He took her to all the right places in DC, loved to dance as much as she did. They hit it off right away, and right away he started putting pressure on her for sex. She told him she was a virgin, saving herself for marriage. After one date, sitting in his car outside her rooming house, he insisted on petting. The petting got heavier and heavier.

Finally she let him make love to her. It was a sultry, late summer evening. They had laid blankets out on the national mall near the Washington Monument. After hours of kissing and petting alongside many other couples, they fell asleep. Upon waking, Lisa saw that no one was nearby and let him do it. The act itself was quick and unsatisfying. She told him this was the last time unless he was willing to make a commitment. She relented, giving him a few more chances to redeem himself. In the end she graded him a "C-plus" and ended it. That was the last she saw of Matt, except at the office. At least he was a gentleman. As far as she knew he never told anybody about their brief affair.

In her own mind that encounter on the mall counted as losing her virginity, even if for the second time.

Early that fall she met Chris. A girlfriend at work was going with a young man who, she whispered, "worked for the CIA." The couple took her along one Sunday for a swim at a house in nearby Maryland, where the boyfriend lived. His three roommates also presumably worked for the Agency, though they claimed various employments with the State Department and Department of Defense.

The house and pool were filled with many young people. As the crowd moved from the pool area to a buffet in the house, she stayed behind. She walked by a young man sunning himself in a lawn chair at the end of the pool. Lisa filled out her bikini well enough to call attention to herself even among a lot of other good-looking girls.

The young man was tall and lanky, his pleasant face topped by crew-cut blond hair. *Relatively good looking*, she thought. A lopsided grin lit up his face, making her look again.

"Hi."

"Hi." She wasn't going to stop, but he jumped to his feet and stuck out his hand.

"I'm Chris Holbeck. I don't think we've met."

"I'm Lisa Jensen." She returned the handshake, feeling rather awkward. He was looking directly into her eyes, as though avoiding staring at her body.

"If you're not attached, why don't we eat together?" He was tentative, a little shy. *Why not?* They walked into the house together to get some food.

In no time they discovered their common roots in Washington State. It didn't take much longer to sense an attraction. They dated twice the following week, were soon talking daily on the phone. After a month they declared their love. By Thanksgiving they were engaged. They flew out to Seattle for that holiday, and Chris's family held an engagement party at their Edmonds home. They would be married in the same home at Christmas.

Lisa's near-instant falling in love with Chris was almost eclipsed by the way she fell in love with his family, especially Mor. Finally she had the prospect of a real family. At first Mor and Herman were doubtful about their son's whirlwind romance with this unknown girl and had tried to talk him out of the official engagement announcement. But they were won over almost as quickly as he had been. The party was next to the best Lisa ever experienced. The wedding, at Christmas, was the best. Except for the Browns, everyone she'd ever cared about was there from Arlington and Darrington. They mixed beautifully with Chris's relatives and friends. She was in heaven.

Her only disappointment was with the sex. During their dating and engagement she found Chris to be inexperienced. She told him about losing her virginity in the moonshadow of the Washington Monument, but held to her vow not to tell anyone about her experience with Bert.

The consummation of their marriage was a letdown for both. At that point she took matters into her own hands. She bought books on the joys of sex, insisted they study them together. Soon he got the hang of it, amazed at how much she was able to learn from those books. It took about six months for her to turn him into a considerate, skilled lover, who could bring her high, if not to the heights she seemed to remember from those long-ago days in Darrington.

* * *

After an hour the car had cooled so much that her coat no longer provided enough warmth. The reverie had extended beyond the warmth of her life before her parents' passing, to unsettling thoughts of her time in Darrington—the sexual pleasures contrasting with later hatred for Bert after she finally realized that his lessons had been motivated by his own selfish desires, and not by his caring for a vulnerable seventeen-year-old foster child.

Lisa checked her watch in the dim light of the street lamp. She'd been musing about her past life for more than an hour. It was time to get back home to relieve the babysitter.

CHAPTER TWELVE

Headquarters was strangely quiet about the Plotkin case. The reply to Chris's report on the missed meeting was remarkably low key. The quiet brought a vague sense of discomfort. Chris would rather have responded to out-and-out criticism.

Bisan impressed him by discovering that Plotkin was scheduled to travel on the night boat to Helsinki on February seventh. She went on that sailing herself and, through a guarded telephone conversation with Mark Noble, reported that she had not located Plotkin on the boat. She was quite certain he had not made the sailing from Stockholm.

Matters remained confusing on the home front. Lisa had changed again, once again becoming the dutiful wife she'd been before Plotkin came along. Dutiful, that is, in all matters except sex. She was no longer gone in the evenings. She took pains to recount her every move during the days, sharing everything as she had in the past. She was as attentive and loving as ever, with that one notable exception.

In early March even that changed.

It was an ordinary evening. Chris's hours weren't quite as long as earlier in the month. He arrived home at seven o'clock in the evening, tired and irritable. The cast on his leg was bothering him. The leg itched. He had taken to scratching inside the cast with a chopstick, even though his doctor strictly forbade it. He longed for a hot shower or bath with freedom from the cast. Tonight, at least, they didn't have to go out. His main plan for the evening was to take a bath, cast propped up on the edge of the tub, then to crawl into bed with a good book.

Lisa and Missy met him at the door. Missy threw herself into his arms, forcing him to drop his briefcase and hoist her up. Lisa joined in with a hug as far as she could reach around them both. His two ladies then took his coat and escorted him into the living room, where hors d'oeuvres and a drink were waiting for him.

Chris eased himself into his favorite chair. "Let me guess," he said, "I bet Mommy wrecked our car today."

Missy giggled. "No, Daddy. Mommy didn't wreck the car." She frowned and looked at Lisa. "You didn't wreck it, did you Mommy?"

"No, Sweetie, you know I didn't wreck the car."

"Then I bet it's something Missy did, to get me such great treatment. Did you get in trouble today, Missy?" She jumped into his lap, inadvertently kicking his cast. Chris tried not to wince. "Well, something's going on. You're always nice to me, but this is special."

"Shall I tell him, Mommy?"

"Sure, go ahead."

"Farmor is coming to stay with us at Easter." Farmor was the children's name for Mor—grandmother on the father's side.

Chris brightened. "Really! That's wonderful. But how did you find out?"

Lisa said, "Mor was so excited that she called about an hour ago. She and your dad were planning to visit this summer, but she's so anxious to see us in her country that she decided she had to come sooner."

The three of them chatted excitedly through dinner about this news, planning everything they'd do with Mor and the boys, who would be home for Easter vacation. After putting Missy to bed, Chris went upstairs to take his bath. He had just settled in the tub when there was a knock at the door.

"Want some help in there?" Lisa's voice was small, unsure.

"Oh, I don't think so, thanks. I'm settled in with a book."

"You sure?"

This was a real departure from her recent behavior. He was curious. "Come on in, Honey, I've got nothing to hide from you."

She came in and closed the door quietly. Looking pointedly at his naked body, she said "You really don't have much to hide, do you?"

He was startled. "What did you expect? I'm a celibate. I've been living the life of a monk."

Lisa sat down on the edge of the tub, carefully avoiding the cast propped up on the side. She picked up a washcloth, soaped it, and started washing his shoulders.

"You don't have to, not any longer." The washcloth went lower, over his chest, over his abdomen. He felt an arousal. He also felt resentment. What made her think she could turn him on or off at her will? He wasn't going to play her game. He took the washcloth and placed it out of her reach on the other side of the tub.

"What's going on here? I thought I was persona non grata with you as far as sex goes."

"A woman can change her mind."

"A woman needs to give a reason for changing her mind."

"This woman has a reason." She got up from the edge of the tub and sat on the toilet lid, staring at him seriously.

"Shoot."

"You know the reason I left your bed, Chris, whether you admit it to yourself or not. That's changed—not completely, but it's better. Ever since your accident you've been less withdrawn. Oh, you've been busy and gone a lot, but you're not off in space all the time like you were when you were so taken up with Plotkin."

"What else?"

"Mor's coming."

"So?" When she didn't answer, he went on, "So you think enough of Mor that you don't want her to catch us on the outs."

Lisa got up from the toilet, folded her arms over her chest and started pacing back and forth on the bathroom floor. "It's a lot more complicated than that, Chris. I can't explain what I've been feeling. Some of it would hurt you. A lot. Some of it is a lot of hurt I've gone through."

He looked up at her, thinking how hard it was to carry on a conversation from a position of power when you're lying naked, flat on your back, with a cast on your leg. "I'm a big boy. Tell me what it is that would hurt me."

Lisa smiled. "Nothing, my darling. Let's enjoy each other tonight." With that she pulled her dress over her head. She was wearing only panties underneath. Chris was overcome with urges too long suppressed. His resentment fled as Lisa slipped off the panties, kicked out of her loafers and got into the tub with him.

Their lovemaking that night was wild, considering the limits of a man in a cast. Lisa was insatiable, demanding. After the third time they joined completely, she fell instantly asleep. Usually it was she who complained about his falling asleep after lovemaking. He looked at the clock by the bed. Two o'clock in the morning. He lay there, unable to sleep, his leg aching again. As he thought about the evening, about the enjoyment of having sex again, he dwelled on how sweet Lisa had been. And how wild. She had always been an active partner in their relationship, but tonight had been different. She had demanded a lot, but had given a lot, too, anything he wanted.

Anything he wanted. The idea stuck in his mind. The more he thought about it, the more it seemed that her wildness was aimed at pleasing him rather than pleasing herself. Should he be pleased that she wanted to satisfy him, or suspicious of her motives? The more he wondered, the more confused he became. It was two thirty in the morning, time to sleep.

CHAPTER THIRTEEN

Saturday, March 22, 1969

There was a dance at the American Embassy. Chris later looked back at the fateful evening in terms of Shakespeare and the warning to Julius Caesar, "Beware the Ides of March," even though this event was a week later.

Chris and Lisa often avoided American Embassy functions, as they found it more interesting and rewarding to associate with people outside that community. In this case they decided to go because Norm Wykowski, the recently arrived Chief of Station, would be attending with his wife, Betty. They could help acquaint the Wykowskis with Embassy staff and spouses they hadn't yet met.

"What dress do you think I should wear?" Lisa asked. They were getting ready for the dance in the bedroom they once again shared.

"Why don't you wear the green one?" Chris hated being asked what his wife should wear. No matter what he answered, she never followed his suggestion. Why did she bother to ask?

"Chris! Pay attention. You know I wore that dress to the Joneses for dinner on Wednesday. They'll be there tonight with some other American business people. Be serious."

It was happening again. It always happened. "Then why don't you wear the purple one?"

"I don't have a purple dress."

Chris decided to try a different approach. He walked up to his wife, who was standing in front of the closet in her slip. "Love of my life, you are picking nits. You know the one I mean." He playfully spun Lisa around to face the closet, put his arms around her and pointed at the dress he had in mind.

She laughed. "Silly you, that's not purple, it's lavender."

"All right, so it's lavender." He took his arms away and patted her bottom. "So wear it anyway. It shows off your figure. Men will be falling all over each other trying to get a dance with you."

They bantered cheerfully for a few minutes more before she decided to wear an altogether different dress. It figured.

On this pleasant Saturday they had taken it easy all day. For a change, Chris had not gone into the Embassy in the morning to catch up on work. He'd had enough of that during the past six weeks. His cast had been taken off a few days before, and he was well enough to go for a walk with Missy, visiting the site of his disaster in Drottningholm Park. A few patches of dirty snow were all that remained of winter. Missy wondered aloud how anybody could break a leg on such a small hill. He worked on the cars in the afternoon while Lisa puttered around the house. It had been a good day.

He did wonder about Lisa. Though she seemed happy, there was a brittleness about her, a fragility that had developed over the past weeks.

They'd finished dressing and still had fifteen minutes before having to leave for the dance. As they walked down the stairs together, Lisa turned to him with eyes just a bit too bright. "Why don't we have a glass of sherry before we go?"

He was surprised at the suggestion. "I thought you were the one trying to keep me from drinking too much."

"It'll relax us for the party."

"I don't need to be relaxed. I feel great, except for this damned sore leg. Hope I don't have to dance much."

"Well, I'm going to have one anyway. Don't join me if you don't want to." She went to the bar, took out the sherry decanter and a couple of small glasses.

"Okay, okay. I guess it won't hurt." They drank glasses of sherry, poured nearly to the brim by Lisa.

The dance started out more enjoyably than Chris had expected. There was a good mix of Embassy people, couples from the American business community, and a sprinkling of Swedes. It had been organized by the American Women's Club, with Millie Jones as chair. Chris liked Millie. A little older than Lisa, Millie was not as good looking by half, but made up for it with an extremely warm personality. Her husband, Rex, was a glad-hander businessman whose warmth struck Chris as a lot less genuine. Part of that may have been a bias on Chris's side, as Rex had shown from the beginning of their friendship that he was fond of Lisa. Maybe a little too fond.

The Holbecks shared a table with the Jones couple, Norm and Betty Wykowski and the Brooms. It was a surprise to see Bill and Angela at this affair, a type of party they avoided most of the time. Chris learned during the evening that they were there on orders from the ambassador, who hadn't wanted to attend himself. To their credit, they made an effort to enjoy themselves and ended up having a good time along with everyone else.

After a fine buffet supper, a combo started playing. Chris danced first with Betty Wykowski—she was charming—and then with Angela Broom. By the time that dance was finished his leg was about to give out. He escorted Angela back to their table. She excused herself to go to the powder room, and he found himself sitting at the table with Millie Jones. They were the only ones there, all the others dancing or mixing with people at other tables.

"Where's Lisa?" he asked Millie.

She made a wry face. "Dancing with my husband. I love your wife dearly, but I wish she wasn't so damn good looking and sexy."

Chris looked at the crowd on the dance floor and spotted Rex and Lisa. They were dancing a slow dance, so close they looked as if they were one. "Should we worry?" he asked.

Millie laughed. "No, Chris. Rex may be thinking all kinds of lewd thoughts right now, but he wouldn't dare carry them out. He's got a thing about Lisa. He also knows that if he were to fool around with her or any other woman, I'd take a razor to his private parts. Besides, I trust Lisa."

"I'm glad to hear that. She's been acting kind of strange the past couple of months. I've been worried about her."

"You're right. We need to talk about it." Millie picked up her glass, rose to her feet and took Chris's hand. "Let's refresh our drinks and go someplace where we can talk. It's too noisy here." They went to the bar, then into the hall. A few knots of other people were there to escape the noise of the music.

"What is going on with Lisa?" Millie asked when they found a quiet spot. "Soon after New Year she was with us constantly. You must have felt abandoned. And then, since your accident, we've hardly seen her. She seems brittle."

"Just the word I chose to describe her earlier tonight," Chris replied. "But I don't know what it's about. She complains that I get too involved with my work. I've always been involved with my work. You're sure we don't have to worry about her and Rex?"

Millie was more serious now. "I'm sure. I meant what I said. Rex may come off to most people as a traveling salesman type, but way down deep he's a pussycat and darned good family man. He's always been faithful to me and a great father to our kids. You don't have to worry about him."

She interrupted herself and motioned to Chris to turn around. There, coming out of the ballroom, were Lisa and Rex walking hand in hand. Lisa whispered something to Rex then walked in the direction of the ladies room. Rex noticed Chris and his wife and came toward them. "There they are!" he said in his booming voice. "We were looking for you."

"I bet you were," Millie said. "Lisa may have been looking for Chris. I bet you were looking for a more private place."

"How you malign me, woman! And in front of her husband." He winked at Chris. "Let's dance." He grabbed Millie by the arm and dragged her back toward the music, leaving Chris to wonder what that was all about. He waited for Lisa to return from the ladies room, then took her back into the dance. She had been drinking more than usual.

"You and Rex were quite a sight out there." They were dancing in place, he moving his feet only slightly. He'd overdone it with that leg today. "You looked like you were making love right in front of everybody."

Lisa gave him that over-bright look. "We were. I could feel him enjoying it."

Chris was so shocked he dropped his hold. "I think you've gone nuts. How much have you had to drink?"

"Not enough by a damned sight. Let's get more."

"No way. We're going home." He took her by the hand. "Be a good girl now. Let's go back to the table and get your purse. I'll tell the rest of them that my leg has done me in."

To his relief she complied. The brightness in her eyes died suddenly, as if a light had gone out. Meekly she followed him to their table, holding hands all the while. Quietly and graciously she excused herself from the party. He began to understand that it wasn't drink that was making her act this way.

They walked in silence to the car. On the way home they exchanged barely a word. It was hard for Chris to hold an emotional conversation while driving. Lisa was quiet for her own reasons, whatever they might be.

At the house, with the babysitter paid and sent home, Lisa said she wanted a nightcap.

Wondering again at her unusual interest in drinking, Chris said he'd have one with her. It wasn't yet midnight. He lit a fire in the stone fireplace in the living room, then fixed a vodka tonic for Lisa and cognac in a snifter for himself. Might as well have their talk in the most relaxed circumstances possible. They settled in front of the fireplace, in easy chairs facing each other. "Now," Chris began, "can we talk about what's going on? Not just tonight but over the past months."

Lisa sipped at her drink. "It's late," she said, "and I'm very, very tired. I'm not sure I'm up to it."

"We have to. This can't go on. You'll destroy our family."

"*I'll* destroy the family? *I* will? How about *you'll* destroy the family? Or—let's be charitable—*we'll* destroy the family."

"I ..." Chris was about to argue, then changed his mind. "Okay, we're in this together. Let's say we're doing it together. Now, what's going on?"

"Well, for starters, I'm pregnant."

It took almost a full minute for that to sink in. Chris was sputtering when he started talking again. "Pregnant? You're kidding, of course."

"I've never been more serious in my life."

"You can't be pregnant. We just started sleeping together again a couple of weeks ago."

This time Lisa took a healthy gulp from her glass, set it down on the coffee table next to her chair, and folded her hands in her lap. She looked down at her hands, not meeting his eyes. "I didn't say that you were the father."

The pause was even longer this time. Chris stared at his wife, whose eyes remained fixed on her hands. "Jesus! Jesus Christ! Are you trying to tell me you've been unfaithful?"

She nodded, tears starting down her cheeks.

He slumped in his chair, stunned, glass still in hand. Suddenly, viciously, he threw the glass as hard as he could against the fireplace. Shards of glass bounced back, some hitting Lisa in the side of the face. She brushed them off absently with her hand. Now she looked at him directly.

"If you ever do anything like that again I'll leave. Permanently."

"Who was it?" he shouted.

"I'll also leave if you shout like that again." She was calm, intent.

"It was that goddamned Rex Jones wasn't it? I knew something was going on between you two. Millie and I even talked about it tonight."

Lisa was in no mood to be bullied. "No, it wasn't Rex. You should know better than that. I saw you talking to Millie, and I know her well enough that she'd have set you straight. The real problem we have, Mr. Intelligence Officer, is right here. You think you're so damned smart, such a good officer, an 'observer' as you like to call yourself. You can't even observe your own family, right in front of your eyes." Tears were coming, faster and faster. "You set it up yourself, watched it happen, looked and didn't see."

Chris felt drained, his strength ebbing, much as it had after he broke his leg. At the same time he felt some measure of calm overtaking the anger. "All right, tell me about it. Who was it?"

"A friend of yours. Sasha Plotkin."

He was caught between laughter and tears. Hit most of all by total disbelief. "What kind of sick joke is this? I don't believe you. You probably aren't even pregnant. What are you trying to do to me?"

"It's sick, all right, but no joke. You better start believing me." The tables were turning. Lisa was beginning to take control.

Chris got up, went to the bar and poured himself another cognac. Back at the fireplace, he scraped the broken glass into a little pile with his shoe, stood with his back to the fire. He was so charged with nervous energy now that he couldn't sit. He felt chilled.

"Tell me your fairy tale."

"No. I can't deal with that kind of sarcasm. Why don't we go to bed and talk about it tomorrow."

He sat down again so that he could better observe her face. "So what's it like to screw a Russian, if you did screw Sasha? Is he better than I am?"

"You would like to know that, wouldn't you? I won't give you that satisfaction. Ever. I will tell you how it happened, if you can listen for a change."

His features were set and hardened, but he nodded for her to go on.

In less than half an hour, Lisa told him her story. He tried to interrupt her several times with questions. She silenced him. "I'm sure you'll want to debrief me. But Chris, please just let me tell you what happened. What I felt. Then I want to go to bed and get some rest. We can talk tomorrow about where we go from here."

He nodded again. Slumped in his chair, beaten, he listened.

"I was," she said, "in a terrible state by the time of your accident. A lot of things had been building up ever since we left Madrid. It's been harder and harder for me to leave the places we've been, the friends we've made, watching the children deal with change, dealing with change myself. Dealing most of all with your marriage to the Agency. You're a good husband and father, Chris, better than many. But you're a husband and father second—second to your work.

"You're a pretty good lover. When you're interested. Something happened here, though, that's happened before. You lost interest in making love when Sasha came along. Only this time it was worse. I needed you more. A woman's interest in sex gets stronger at my time of life. You were even less attentive to my needs than before, at a time I needed you more, and at a time when everything about our lives was bothering me. I felt like you'd lost interest in being in love with me.

"Then you brought Sasha into our lives, here at home. I found him attractive, but had no thoughts that way. All I wanted was to help you get what you wanted out of this case so you'd come back to me in real life. You didn't get exactly what you wanted and you didn't come back to me. I tried, Chris, I really tried, because I loved you and wanted you, wanted us together the way we used to be. But I was mad, too, and in some ways I have to admit I wanted to get back at you. I was silly to act the way I did, running around town without telling you what I was doing, leaving Missy with a sitter too often. But I didn't do anything wrong during that time. I guess I was just trying to hurt you, the way I was hurting. You should know, too, that I was just as lonely in that bed in the guest room as you were in our bed. Maybe even lonelier.

"Then came your accident. It came at the peak of those feelings. I was so mad to be acting like a servant for you. I almost felt like a whore, with you as my pimp. Not in a sexual way, but doing everything you wanted me to do for another man.

"And then you didn't show up for the lunch with Sasha. I was frantic, mixed up with feelings of love and hate, worried to death that something dreadful had happened, and at the same time—I have to say it—thinking that you deserved whatever fate had brought you. I knew it had to be as serious even as death for you to miss that meeting.

"Sasha came right on time. He would. Just like you would. He seemed worried. He thinks like you. I'm sure his worry included concern for us but also a heavy dose of how whatever happened to you might affect him. He stayed about a half hour. During that time he paced here in the living room, thinking out loud. Finally, he said he had to know what happened to you, and asked me to meet him when I knew.

"I need a breather." Lisa was on her feet and headed out of the room.

"Wait! Wait! You can't leave me in the middle of the story." Breaking the story here was just too much on top of too much.

"Don't worry, Chris, I'm coming right back." She went upstairs to check on Missy, who was sleeping sweetly. Lisa used the bathroom and returned to the living room, where she found Chris in an easy chair with his head thrown back, eyes closed, but clearly not asleep. She refreshed her drink with ice only, which caught Chris's attention. He glared at her as she sat down across from him again and resumed her story.

"I agreed to meet him. I know, I know. It'll be hard for you to believe that I did it. It's even hard for me to understand now. But I agreed. He asked me to come to a little apartment down in Old Town. On the Wednesday after your accident.

"Oh, I argued at first. But he said if something bad had happened to you he'd need to see me. He insisted I not tell anybody about it, even you. He said there were some things he could tell me. That it would be to your benefit in the long run. I said I thought he was leaving for Moscow. He said he was, but there was still time to meet. Stupid? Of course it was stupid. I figured if you were okay I'd just tell you and play it from there.

"Then I found out what had happened to you. I was so damn relieved, and so damn mad at you. How could you have been so self-centered, to go out skiing— skiing for God's sake—while I was busy playing the whore for your friend, doing everything I could to help you with your case? There I was, down at the market getting ready for the lunch, thinking that maybe even the flavor of some dish might swing the case for you, and you were off skiing! I decided not to tell you until I'd met with Sasha.

"I went to the apartment at noon that Wednesday. It's a cruddy little place on the third floor of an old, old building in Old Town. Dark and smelly. No elevator. It was so dark in the hallway that I could hardly see which door to knock on. I was scared like I've never been scared in my life. Sasha opened the door before I knocked. He had been watching the hall through a peephole in the door.

"I stepped in. He closed the door. It smelled like fish, old cooking in the apartment. 'He's all right,' I said. 'I know,' Sasha said. 'Then, why am I here?' I asked. He didn't answer that.

"Instead, he put his arms around me. 'I'm so glad,' he said. 'So glad for you.' I stood there with my arms at my side, wondering what was going on.

"Then he drew me to him and whispered in my ear. Three little words, Chris, three little words. Not I love you. Not those three little words. Everybody says those three little words. Sometimes it's two little words. Luv yah. We say those two words to each other too many times from habit alone.

"What he said to me was, 'I want you.' He said, 'I want you.' Chris, Chris! If you could just understand what that did to me. Somebody wanted me. No conditions. No lies or half-lies. Just 'I want you.'

"I lost it at that point. I put my arms around him and we kissed. You'd probably like to know the details. I'm sure they'd even excite you. I told you I wouldn't tell you. But I'll tell you this much. We just fell into a dirty bed in that dirty little apartment and made love like it was the first and last time in our lives. No talking, no lies, not really making love but just good old-fashioned screwing. Yes, Chris, I did it for your friend, Sasha. What was I thinking about while we were doing it? I was thinking about you. And me. I was thinking about our children, and his wife. Crazy as it sounds, I was thinking that this was the ultimate way I could help you with your case.

"When it was over, we talked. I thought he would give me lunch, but we just lay there and talked. Lord, did he talk. After we'd talked for an hour—no, don't interrupt me, I'll tell you later—we did it again, and then he rushed me out of there. He said he had to leave quickly himself and needed to clean up the apartment before going. It sure needed a lot more cleaning than he could do in a short time.

"I agreed to meet him again that Friday, same time, same place. I intended to tell you about it afterwards, but couldn't. Every time I tried, I got all mixed up with that love and hate I felt, an old love and new hate, a love for everything you've been as a husband and father, and a hate for the CIA zombie you've become.

"That Friday it wasn't good at all. I was worried about getting pregnant. I'd stopped taking the pill when we stopped making love. I started to take it again right after the first time with Sasha, but I was worried I might be too late. The apartment seemed even smellier and dirtier than before. But most of all, Sasha had become more like you—preoccupied. He needed me less, and showed it. Like you, he went through the right motions and said some of the right words, with his mind a thousand miles off somewhere. Whatever he wanted that day had more to do with his business than with my body and soul. He didn't tell me much that would be of interest to you, and the sex was ... routine. During the act I started feeling ashamed. The feeling hasn't left me since, and now that I know I'm pregnant it's a lot worse.

"How did I know I'm pregnant? You know how regular I am. I'm almost six weeks overdue now. I wanted to make sure before I told you, so this Monday I went to my doctor and asked her to do a test without telling anyone. I gave her a urine sample and she called yesterday with the news.

"Sasha doesn't know, of course. I told him the last time we were together that I wouldn't see him again. He didn't argue. I think he knew and felt, too, that our little romance was over. He said he'd contact you as soon as he returns from whatever he's doing. He didn't mention an exact date, but I think he will be gone a fairly long time. I have little information about the reasons behind all the mystery. I know he plans to be in Moscow for a few days, because he talked about seeing his wife. Most of the things he told me had to do with his past.

"There isn't much more I can say, Chris. I'll tell you everything I can remember of what Sasha told me about himself, but you can get that better from him than from me. I can imagine what you're going through now, and I'm sorry and ashamed. If you want a divorce I won't contest it. But I think you need to feel sorry and ashamed yourself. Like I said, it was you who wanted us to get close to Sasha. You played such a big part in getting me into bed with him that you might as well have been there yourself.

"We've got a lot to talk about, but I'm very tired now. I just can't talk or even think anymore tonight."

Chris started sobbing as she finished. Huge, long sobs. Lisa came over to his chair, dropped to her knees in front of him and took his hands. "I'm so very, very sorry, Chris."

He pushed her away, so roughly that she sat down hard on the carpet. He looked at her angrily, then dropped down beside her and took her in his arms. They huddled together for minutes, both crying softly now. "Shall I sleep in the guest room?" she asked, finally.

"No, let's sleep in our room. We're in this together now."

In bed at last, Chris lay on his back with arms folded across his chest while Lisa lay quietly separate from him, silent tears flowing unchecked. He was bombarded by such an array of emotions that he could hardly think. Rage and the awful frustration of a cuckold competed with guilt over the part he'd played in Lisa's story. And fear. Fear settled over him like a wet, cold hand. He'd have to report all this to the Agency. What a disgrace! He'd be personally humiliated, maybe lose his job. Lisa would be disgraced. The children would suffer. Rage. Rage. Rage eventually was followed by a brief sleep marred by a troublesome dream.

He dreamed of Lisa's tears. Her tears had become so copious that they formed a small stream that flowed out the bedroom door, down the stairs to the main floor, then down the stairs to the garage. In the garage they became a river, flowing out the garage door. A little raft that Missy used in summertime fell into the river.

His last memory of the dream was of Missy on the raft, sailing out the door with the river, waving with a solemn expression and saying "Bye-bye, Daddy, bye-bye ..."

CHAPTER FOURTEEN

Sunday, Monday, March 23-24, 1969

They went to church the following morning. Chris, when he first awoke, would not have believed that they could get to church this Sunday after a night of such tension, such emotional and physical depletion. But somehow they managed.

The somehow was Missy. She came bouncing into their bed at eight o'clock. "Come on you lazybones! It's Sunday and we're going to church." How often she mirrored her parents' words to her. It was never difficult to get her to church. She loved attending Sunday school while her parents listened to the sermon. The Holbecks were members of the American Church of Stockholm, which they attended as often as their schedules allowed. Because of Missy's enthusiasm, they were regular churchgoers.

Chris awoke with an awful taste in his mouth, a headache, a dragged-out feeling and the need for a shower. He looked over at Lisa, trying to smile at Missy. *God!* The nightmare of the past evening hit him. He made an effort to push away the emotions that rushed back with that memory in order to deal with the problem at hand. Missy, and going to church. There was no way he could go to church today.

"Listen, Sweetheart, I'm going to take a shower and while I'm in there I'm going to think of ten good things we could do today besides going to church. Why don't we skip church today?"

Lisa joined in. "What a good idea!" At least they could agree on that much.

"No, no, no! I want to go to church. I've been cutting out pictures from my Sunday school book for our lesson today. Mrs. Smith will be mad if I don't come."

Chris went into the bathroom, leaving Lisa to deal with Missy. The shower revived him physically, so much so that he was surprised to discover how well he was functioning on so little sleep.

Lisa and Missy were tickling each other and giggling when he returned to the bedroom. "So, what are we going to do today?" Chris asked.

"Go to church, I guess." Lisa rolled her eyes. "Our young lady is not going to be moved from that plan." They were defeated. Chris ordered them both out of the bedroom so he could dress while they took a shower together. He wondered how he and Lisa would make it through this day.

As a lifetime Lutheran, Chris could go through the rituals of the service awake or asleep. Today he did it asleep. Or, rather, with his mind elsewhere. He didn't hear a word of the sermon, constantly thinking, ever more eager to hear the story Plotkin had told Lisa. They skipped coffee time after church in favor of going home to fix brunch and to plan for an exciting Easter time with Mor and the boys. It all seemed so hollow. At this point Chris wasn't sure they'd even be in Sweden at Easter.

After church he tried every trick possible to get Missy away for a while so he and Lisa could talk more about the events leading up to today, but nothing worked. They spent the afternoon with a calendar propped up on the kitchen table, travel brochures spread out, a big notebook filled with their plans. They went out to a simple restaurant for dinner, finally getting Missy in bed at eight.

Lisa came down to the living room after tucking her daughter into bed for the third and hopefully last time. "Shall we talk?" he asked her.

"I guess we'd better."

They talked until midnight. They talked about the possibilities of an abortion. On principle Chris was firmly opposed. He wasn't so sure in this case. Lisa was more liberal about abortion but wasn't sure she could go through with one herself; besides, she had been told that it was harder than most people realized to get an abortion in Sweden. They didn't reach a conclusion.

They talked about what this predicament would mean in terms of Chris's career. He started out with the firm conviction that he'd have to report the whole sordid mess in detail the next day.

Then Lisa related Plotkin's story. It was not the story of his KGB career but, rather, a life story. A fairy tale, Chris thought at first, made up as a way for Plotkin to get his wife into bed and keep her there long enough to have his way with her. But as he listened he became more and more interested, even going to his library shelves for books on Russian and Swedish history. Excitement began to grow. Maybe it was possible to salvage something out of this after all. Maybe he could get away with not reporting the relationship between Plotkin and Lisa to the Agency. Maybe. Maybe.

Exhaustion finally overtook them both. They fell into bed and held on to each other.

The workweek began so normally the next day that Chris almost believed the weekend had not happened. Passing Chris in an Embassy hallway, Bill Broom mentioned what a pleasant affair the Saturday party had been, and asked why he and Lisa had left early. Chris told Bill his leg was bothering him and he needed to rest it at home. A plausible excuse, and Bill didn't remark on Lisa's behavior. Perhaps nobody else other than Millie had noticed.

Monday went like most Mondays, with Chris catching up on weekend traffic from Headquarters. Much of the work in Langley piled up through the week and was sent off on Friday night. Chris spent an hour with Norm Wykowski, chatting about the various people at the party and Norm's plans for his new station. The more they talked, the more Chris liked him. He was already getting the hang of operations at Stockholm Station and seemed a pleasant man to deal with.

In the early afternoon Chris drove downtown to visit his doctor—a checkup to see how his leg was faring now that it was out of the cast. The doctor assured him that the leg would soon be back to full strength. Chris could speed the process through regular exercise.

He was just leaving the building—exercises for his leg on his mind—when he saw Plotkin walking toward him on the street.

"Chris! What a surprise!" The Russian seemed genuinely astonished to encounter Chris on the street like this.

"Sasha! What in hell are you doing here?" After all that had happened since they last saw each other, Chris was engulfed with emotions. Anger was at the top of the heap, but it was tempered by caution. He wasn't sure whether to accept the hand offered to him in greeting, but did so after a second's hesitation. There was a piece of paper concealed in Plotkin's hand, so it was obvious that this was no chance meeting. Chris was able to retrieve the note without a fumble. He slipped it into his coat pocket.

"I got back from Moscow yesterday," Plotkin said. "I just finished lunch and am on my way back to my Embassy. There's a bit of a hurry right now, but I hope we can see each other soon."

"I think—"

Sasha interrupted before he could say more. "Sorry, Chris, I've got to run. See you later." Plotkin turned, checked the traffic and darted across the street before Chris could even sort out his thoughts. *Jesus! What was that all about?* He didn't dare take the paper out of his pocket to read, in case they were under surveillance. It didn't matter who. Surveillance by the Swedes, the KGB or even his own people could put Chris in danger at this point, when he still had no plan of action. He walked quickly to his car and drove in a direction away from the Embassy.

With no destination in mind, he found himself driving to Gamlastan (Old Town), on the street where Lisa had met Plotkin. With a lot of difficulty he found a parking place on one of the narrow side streets. Despite his mental turmoil he had enough sense during the drive to check for surveillance, and was satisfied there was none.

In the parking spot, with the engine turned off, Chris leaned his head back and took a deep breath. He felt his heart pounding, hands sweating as he thought about the note. At last he allowed himself to retrieve the paper from his pocket and read it. It was typewritten in Swedish on a plain piece of paper: "Must see you on Friday. Follow these directions ..." Detailed instructions followed. The high-handedness of it infuriated Chris. Suddenly restless, he exited the car and slammed the door.

He walked back to the main street. There was a konditeri, a Swedish coffee house, at an angle across from Plotkin's safe house. He went in, ordered a cup of coffee and a roll, and took a window seat in the nearly deserted shop. He stared at the building housing the safe house, counted to the third floor and tried to identify the windows of the apartment Lisa had described. Anger boiled inside as he looked at the building, tried to picture the apartment. His mind drifted unbidden to the sexual encounter between his wife and his Sasha. How had Lisa put it? "We just fell into that dirty bed and screwed like it was the first and last time in our lives." *God!* What a perversion to dwell on those thoughts. He pushed back from the table and all but ran from the konditeri to his car, nothing more on his mind now than to get away from that place.

He didn't have to return to the office that afternoon, so he drove directly home from Gamlastan, his mind churning with the decisions he was forced to make after reading Plotkin's note. What to tell Headquarters at this point? How to react to this peremptory summons to a clandestine meeting on the target's timeline, on his terms, a meeting with a man who had not only cuckolded him but had made his wife pregnant? And the terms were certainly all Plotkin's. The date, the time, the place, the signals, even the means of getting to a meeting in Norrtälje had been spelled out clearly in the note Plotkin handed to him, a message on the stationery of Stockholm's Grand Hotel.

Chris and Lisa had no obligations that evening, which usually meant a pleasant break from a busy social life. Tonight, though, he anticipated a hellish scene with Lisa, talking into the early morning hours—balancing the pluses and minuses of an abortion, debating whether or not to inform Headquarters about Lisa's indiscretion with Plotkin or even if he should remain with the Agency ....

It went better than expected.

On this night they managed to speak quietly and respectfully about the affair and pregnancy, deciding to proceed for the time being as if the incident between Plotkin and Lisa had never taken place. Both were mentally exhausted, running on adrenaline, too overloaded to make more than this one decision, but surprised at how they'd been able to present a front of normalcy to their friends and associates.

This conversation cleared up at least one mystery for Chris—how Plotkin had found him on the street outside the doctor's office. He was too numb to be shocked that the information had come to Plotkin from Lisa. Sasha had phoned her mid-morning that day, not identifying himself but assuming she'd know him by his voice. She was surprised at how open he was on the phone in telling her it was imperative that he see Chris. Knowing about the doctor's appointment, she'd obliged with the information and tried to get the idea across—without saying it explicitly—that Chris was aware of their tryst and was most interested in meeting with his counterpart.

Chris's next task was to be convincing in his presentation of the situation to Headquarters while keeping the agreement with Lisa not to reveal her affair with Plotkin. Just as he had truthfully reported the facts of the missed meeting, he would fully report today's event outside the doctor's office.

And so he reported, and so did Headquarters regenerate the excitement and double-think of their earlier interest in the case. Chris was quite sure he would have to fend off a lot of unwelcome suggestions, such as wearing a concealed recorder for the meeting, condoning counter-surveillance by Station personnel or others brought in for the purpose. Being wired for sound was his greatest worry, because he had to be able to talk with Plotkin about the affair with Lisa (though not about the pregnancy, they had agreed). The counter-surveillance issue was less personal than professional. His gut instinct was that Plotkin was such a highly experienced clandestine operator that he would spot surveillance and scrap the meeting, something that simply must not happen at this juncture. Headquarters was not at all happy when he rejected these intrusive measures. He'd had to overcome Norm Wykowski's concerns, but once Norm was convinced he stood fully behind Chris. Acquiescence by the team back home was not gracious, coming with several caveats about any future meetings with the target beyond this one.

However reluctant their approval, it was given. Chris would have his clandestine meeting with Plotkin.

CHAPTER FIFTEEN

Friday, March 28, 1969

So it was, on this gray, late March Friday in Stockholm, a few inches of dirty snow signaling a reluctance to surrender winter, that Chris boarded a *T-bana* car en route to the meeting with Plotkin. The destination was Norrtälje, an historic town lying in the heart of Roslagen, a loose conglomeration of former coastal parishes lying north of Stockholm.

He left very early in the morning, parking his car near the end of the Green Line at Hässelby Strand, boarding a middle car and staying aboard to the station at Slussen, just south of the central part of Stockholm. There he sat for ten minutes in a nearby konditeri, eating (but not much enjoying) a roll with coffee. "Cleanse yourself first" Plotkin had written in the directions for the meeting. It griped him, being forced to follow an order like this, as if he needed instructions on how to avoid surveillance! So far so good on this stage of the journey.

A turn around the block, rubbing elbows with many working-class Swedes on their way to their jobs, nobody showing the slightest interest. Next he boarded a Red Line car bound for Mörby Centrum, the end of the line. He disembarked at the Tekniska Högskolan station for the next part of the trip, boarding a bus that would take him to Norrtälje. The bus was due to depart at 8:40 a.m. and would arrive at its destination close to 10:00 a.m.

"Arrive Norrtälje bus station on Bangårdsgatan." When he came to that station without incident, Chris was irritated all over again by the tone of the note, which he had consigned to bitter memory. If all was clear and the meeting on, he was instructed first to walk east for two blocks with a newspaper in his right hand. Chris thought the next instruction impractical: he was to shop for an hour and a half, have lunch at a designated restaurant, then walk to the site of the meeting. Norrtälje is a tourist town with scores of shops catering to foreigners who swarm to Roslagen during the summer. In this late winter season, few of the shops were open and few people were in them. He wandered through a large department store, looking around mostly in the men's clothing department. A small gift shop had the usual little red horses from Dalarna, the blue and yellow candlestick holders, the flags and other typical items attractive to tourists. Relieved when this stage was over, he walked to the restaurant specified in Plotkin's instructions. This choice was more practical. The restaurant catered to a commercial trade and was packed with businessmen. In his Stockholm-bought clothing, feigning great interest in a Swedish newspaper, he fit into the crowd.

Chris had been feeling confident up until the time he left the restaurant at thirty minutes past noon for the final stage of the journey. If it worked out according to Plotkin's plan, he was half an hour away from what should be the most momentous meeting of his life. His palms dampened and his heart thumped. How had he ended up in this kind of fix? He began to think he couldn't handle it. Maybe he should just turn around, go back to Stockholm, pick up Lisa and Melissa, retrieve the twins, quit the Agency and go back home to earn an honest dollar for an honest day's work.

Jesus! How did he ever get into this mess?

These were his thoughts as he entered the final lap. Norrtälje is close to the head of Norrtäljeviken, a long arm of the Baltic Sea, narrow as it passes through the town. The town surrounding this body of water has charming vistas, its many hotels and restaurants fashioned to take advantage of that fact. Plotkin's directions were now leading Chris on a path along the water bordered by houses and an occasional inn—wooden two-story buildings, well maintained and painted mostly a standard yellow or red. The buildings were so close to the water that the path was narrow. It was also quite straight, with a slight curve just beyond the inn where Plotkin wanted to meet. He confirmed the address on the door, kept walking past the entrance and around the curve.

There was nobody in sight. As though he'd missed his address, Chris looked around, turned on his heel, and went back around the curve—where again nobody could be seen on the path—pushed open the door and stepped inside.

The directions said: "Door on path open. Enter. Door on right."

With the outside door closed, Chris found himself standing in gloom. The place smelled like his family's summer home when first opened for the season— the dampness of the nearby water, a building long closed to outside air.

A yellowish light spilled from the only door in the passage, on the right. The door was ajar. He walked as silently as possible down the narrow passageway to peer into an old-fashioned Swedish sitting room, dark walls covered with dozens of framed paintings—landscapes, grim-looking men and women in nineteenth century clothing—a grandfather's clock, heavy overstuffed chairs and sofa, a ponderous round oak table covered with a lace cloth. Nobody in sight. He stepped cautiously into the room. The door closed. Plotkin had been standing behind it. Chris jumped, startled. Plotkin held out his hand. Chris refused to take it.

"I understand how angry you are, Chris." Plotkin dropped his hand.

"Probably not." Chris glared at him.

"We need to talk. Come in here. Take off your coat." He led Chris into an all-purpose room, much plainer than the sitting room. A door at the back of the room was open to a bedroom; a closed door at the side probably led to a bathroom. There was a single bed in one corner; a small stove, sink and old-fashioned refrigerator along the wall facing the water. An overstuffed chair was near another window with a standing lamp alongside, and in the middle of the room sat a square oak table with four straight-backed wooden chairs. Windows were curtained against the outside view.

The men were quiet as Chris shrugged out of his topcoat and was nodded into one of the chairs at the table by Plotkin, who went to the refrigerator. From the freezer he took a bottle of Russian vodka and a couple of frosted shot glasses, and from the cooler section two bottles of Carlsberg beer. Chris started to say something as Plotkin set these items and two large glasses for the beer on the table, but the man silenced him.

"Please, Chris. There will be time for us to talk about what is between us: you, Lisa and me. But before that I want you to listen to my story. You will always be unhappy with what happened between Lisa and me, but I think you'll be interested when I tell you the rest of the story. Will you hear me out before we discuss what must be discussed?"

As he was talking, Plotkin poured the shot glasses nearly full of vodka and poured beer in each of the other glasses. Finished, he raised his own glass of vodka, looked Chris in the eye and said "Skål!" Chris deliberately looked down at the table and refused to pick up the glass of vodka.

"I'm sorry you won't join me. I really do think I understand how you feel." Plotkin downed the vodka.

"You understand shit." Chris picked up his own glass and unceremoniously emptied it. "What is this place?"

"This place is safe for us both. It's the owners' room in this tourist inn. They're friends of mine who vacation in the Canary Islands at this time of year. They think I use it to be with lady friends. However you feel, it will do neither of us any good if we can't talk and work some of this out. Will you listen to my story?"

Chris reached across for the bottle of vodka, poured his own glass full again and refused to answer for a moment. Thoughts were spinning through his head as he tossed down all the vodka in the glass. Plotkin's tumble in bed with Lisa was an attack on his manhood, and the Russian's continuing control of the situation was compounding the insult. Was Plotkin actually carrying out a KGB mission to turn Chris by getting at him through Lisa? Maybe Chris was less of a man because he hadn't punched Plotkin in the face when he first saw him here.

"Well?" Plotkin looked at him quizzically.

"Well what?"

"Are you going to listen to my story?"

Chris felt pulled in different directions. His agency mission and his own natural curiosity made him want to hear what Plotkin had to say. His anger conjured thoughts of mayhem—he could grab the vodka battle, smash it over Plotkin's head, and run. *What the hell, why not?* He stared down at the table for a moment, realizing that as good as that might feel, it would only make the situation worse. Stretching his long legs under the table and slouching back in the uncomfortable wooden chair, he clutched the now empty shot glass and stared at the table.

"Go ahead."

Plotkin poured himself another vodka but left the liquor untouched as he began his story.

CHAPTER SIXTEEN

"The first thing you need to understand, Chris, is that I am not Russian. I'm every bit as Swedish as you, if not even more. Have you ever heard of Gammalsvenskby? No? Well, this is important to what you've seen in me. Not a state secret, just a little side box in history that few people know about. I have to give you a bit of a history lesson before you can understand me.

"The story goes way back in time, but I can shorten it by beginning with a Swedish-speaking people who were living centuries ago on the Baltic island of Dagö—free, landowning farmers and fishermen. They found themselves oppressed and eventually put into serfdom by a series of powers: German, Swedish and eventually Russian. They kept fighting against this oppression, but they lost the battle when even the land of the freeholders was taken away. In the late 1700s the oppressors were the Russians. An appeal to Empress Catherine II eventually led her to grant the Swedes land in 'New Russia,' a place on the Dnieper River in the southern part of the Ukraine.

"About twelve hundred people set out for New Russia, a brutal journey covering more than three thousand miles with no mechanized transport and the hardships of a Russian winter. Only some five hundred survived the awful trek to the Dnieper, and within the next ten years they suffered all kinds of suffering and epidemics. By the beginning of the 1800s only a few more than one hundred people were still alive.

"But these ancestors of mine were tough and determined people. They built their village, cultivated their land and some found a livelihood fishing on the Dnieper. They succeeded in building a true Swedish village in the heart of Russia, even kept their Swedish language through all that time. That's where the name 'Gammalsvenksby' (Old Swedish Town) comes from.

"Things had improved by the late 1800s. I've personally heard some of the older people tell of the good times they had then. Their lives centered in the Lutheran church built not long after the original group arrived, and they kept their language and customs. But things fell apart after the First World War and the Russian Revolution. There was no longer any law; chaos spread, criminal gangs stole and murdered."

Chris rudely interrupted the story. "What the hell does this fairytale have to do with anything?" He paced the small room for a moment then asked if he could have coffee rather than alcohol. After moving at a deliberate pace to put water and coffee in an old percolator pot, Plotkin sat down to wait for it to boil. He signaled to Chris to do the same. "If you want to hear me out, Chris, you need to sit down and listen without interrupting me. If you don't want to, that's fine; I'll deal with another service." Chris sat down.

"I was born into the middle of this post World War One mess in September 1925. My father had a small vegetable farm near the Dnieper River. My mother helped him on the farm and was a wonderful seamstress who earned extra money with that. Their names were Andreas and Anna Hinas. I was born Gustav. My father never knew me. Before I was born he was hanged from an apple tree near our house. He had tried to stop a gang from stealing vegetables from his little farm. My mother came home from a prayer meeting at the church to find him hanging there. She always seemed a little strange to me as I grew up. Her friends told me that she had never been the same after seeing my father dangling from that apple tree.

"With the loss of her husband and the lawlessness it must have been a terrible time for my mother, who somehow managed to keep the house and eke out a living with her sewing. It was an awful time, so bad that the Swedish Government and Red Cross worked hard to get all the townspeople out of Russia and back to Sweden. They succeeded in 1929 when I was going on five years old. There were about nine hundred people who finally arrived in Sweden on a ferry from Germany to Trelleborg. My first clear childhood memory is the excitement of getting off that ferry and being pushed into a huge crowd where I could see only knees. I was happy because everyone had told me that we were coming home.

"But if it was a homecoming, it was not a happy one. The group scattered, with many farmers settling on the island of Gotland, some even going to Canada. Others took low-paying jobs in the cities, my mother included. She got a tiny apartment in the Södermalm district of Stockholm and was lucky to be able to work as a seamstress because times were pretty hard then. What was unlucky was that she met Gustav Anderson and let him move in with us. I hated him and that he had my name.

"Gustav was a Swedish Communist who had been trained in Moscow as an agitator. There was an organized Swedish Communist resistance to bringing the people of Gammalsvenskby back to Sweden, and there was organized agitation among members of the group once they arrived. Gustav was part of that. For reasons I never understood—other than her mental state after seeing my father swinging from a tree branch—my mother was attracted to Gustav. Soon he was living with us in that tiny apartment.

"I hated this common-law stepfather. His weekday life revolved around working as a longshoreman on the docks at Stockholm Harbor during the day and going to Communist meetings at night. On Saturdays he often traveled around Stockholm to talk about Communism with the Gammalsvenskby refugees, trying to convince them to return to Russia. Saturday evenings he sat at the table in our tiny kitchen, drinking schnapps and singing Swedish folk songs. I must say he had a beautiful voice and seemed to know every folk song there ever was. But he also had too much thirst for schnapps, often got drunk and sometimes beat my mother. He never touched me. I'm sure he knew my mother would kill him in his sleep if he ever mistreated me.

"Except for Gustav I was enjoying my time in Sweden and doing well in school when I was yanked out of there and taken back to Gammalsvensby in 1937. Gustav and his friends had succeeded in persuading a couple hundred refugees to return to the Soviet Union a few years after their arrival in Sweden. Two of the Communist agitators went with them, but not Gustav and his new family. He preached about the Red Paradise that was supposed to be developing there in Gammalsvenskby, but wasn't enough of a believer to go with them on the return to paradise. I've never fully understood why he later changed his mind and took us there, or why my mother would be willing to go with him. Again it may have been her strangeness following my father's death. Gustav's decision had something to do with one of the two Swedish Communists who went with the group of returnees, a close friend who had begged his help.

"Whatever brought Gustav and my mother to that decision, I remember being seasick on a small private boat that took us from Stockholm to Tallinn, Estonia, and constant troubles with nasty authorities as we made our way to the Dnieper River by train and a few bus rides. It was my first lesson in the bureaucracy of Communism, which was well developed by that time. Estonia was still free and relatively easy for us travelers, but after crossing the border into Russia we encountered constant roadblocks, for purposes both real and imagined by commissars with their hands out.

"The chaos in the Ukraine at that time should have been known to my mother and Gustav. Contrary to promises of the Swedish Communists, the returnees had been unable to go back to their old lives and farms they had owned, and were even persecuted for their Christianity. There were mysterious deaths and disappearances.

"In the midst of all this Gustav seemed to take a leadership role in the small group of Swedish Communists. Physically he was as big and tough-looking as you might imagine a longshoreman to be. He had the kind of presence that made people avoid bothering him. Yet at the same time the nostalgia of his folk songs drew people to him. I have to give him credit; he was protective toward my mother and me, and toward his Swedish Communist friends, and I think he may have had some role in making the Swedish returnees lives a little bit better. But they were still miserable and regretting the awful decision to come back to the Ukraine.

"We found a little place to live, not much more than a shack just outside the old village on the right bank of the Dnieper, close to the road to Kherson and the Black Sea. The Swedish Church building still existed, but no services were held and there was no Swedish-speaking school. I didn't want to go to school anyway. I was mad at everyone, Swedish or Russian didn't matter. The greatest part of my anger was reserved for my poor mother, who I blamed for bringing Gustav into our lives with this result.

"She still ruled, though, and one of the rules was that I go to school. I was put into school a couple of miles down the road toward Kherson, a small one teaching in the Russian language. It existed under those circumstances mostly through the efforts of a dedicated Moscow Communist teacher whose interest in bringing Russian language and culture to the Ukraine reminded me of the Lutheran zeal in some of the Gammalsvenskby people. I didn't like him at first, but I was a bright and interested student and he eventually won me over. Inside of a year I gained native fluency in Russian and tried to reject speaking Swedish at home. My mother spoke Russian pretty well, and Gustav spoke it haltingly, but they insisted on speaking Swedish with me.

"The only good part of this mess was a developing friendship with a fellow student. He was a bright spirit, a smart and unusual character I later recognized in English-language studies at the University of Moscow. Your *Huckleberry Finn* was a standard in literature there, and I instantly saw that Mark Twain had written about Sasha. Sasha Plotkin. What a character that boy was! He was living with an aunt because his parents had disappeared. His aunt was very loose in playing the parent role, so Sasha could stay out for nights on end, skip school if he felt like it and wander around until he got hungry enough to go home for a meal. There were a lot of kids like that due to a kind of anarchy in the area and the loss of many parents eastward to Siberia or heavenward. Some of the boys gathered into small gangs, but Sasha was more of a loner until he and I met at school and came under the influence of Headmaster Oblonski. This man was a true teacher who saw some learning potential in Sasha and me. Before long Sasha was attending school most of the time. We often stayed after school for extra instruction from this remarkable man, and became fast friends outside of school.

"If my mother had known anything about our after-school activities she would have chained me to the house. Some of it was innocent fun like building little rafts and fishing on the river. But some of it was so dangerous I'm amazed now that we survived. There were camps along the river populated by those who had no place else to live or gangs who used their camps as bases for criminal activities. Sasha and I gave no thought to walking into those camps to beg food from people who were probably just as hungry but willing to share what little they had.

"The first time I ever got drunk was the summer of the year I turned fourteen years old. We'd walked into an all-male camp on the river—pretty rough looking men who claimed they were making a living fishing on the river. There wasn't much fishing gear around, but there was a still that was producing white liquor from corn they'd probably stolen from nearby farms. They thought it would be fun to get a couple of kids like Sasha and me drunk. We were ready. I was in such bad condition when I staggered home that night that I threw up just outside the door. My mother heard me, dragged me inside and slapped me across the face, once on each side, with Gustav watching happily. I'm sure he thought it was about time.

"This kind of fun was coming to an end. Headmaster Oblonski didn't talk much about the danger of war during regular class time, but he talked a lot with Sasha and me after school about Hitler's conquests. He was afraid Stalin was too trustful of Hitler.

"By the late spring of 1941 our little school was no more, Mr. Oblonski was nowhere to be found, and the general situation in our area was more chaotic than ever. Most of the young men had gone off to the military. I was a few months shy of sixteen years old and Sasha would be sixteen in June, both of us too young for regular military service. I was hoping my mother would give special permission for me to join when I reached that age in September, but terrible events overtook us. Hitler's Barbarossa operation was launched that June, a huge sweep of military power moving north and east from the Balkans through the Ukraine and eventually to the very gates of Moscow and Leningrad. We were in the way of an army group led by Field Marshal von Rundstedt, advancing toward the Dnieper River and Kiev. They were almost at the Dnieper after only three weeks of fighting.

"Although I'm sure Headmaster Oblonski's teaching and indoctrination was not intended to make soldiers of us, Sasha and I were prepared in every way to go to war. Sasha's aunt had disappeared earlier that spring, eastward bound to Siberia with others who had caused trouble one way or the other for the local commissars. He was staying mostly in her little home, living on handouts and occasionally eating at our home.

"The first strike of Barbarossa was the signal Sasha and I were waiting for. We'd made a pact that if war came to our area we would run away from home to join the military, regardless of our ages. And that's what we did. It was common knowledge in early July that a company of Soviet T-34 tanks had taken position a few miles upstream from us near the left bank of the Dnieper. We decided to raft across the river at night, sneak upstream following the river bank, then steal into the encampment and offer our services to the motherland. Foolish? Of course. That's why young men make such good cannon fodder. And perhaps not as foolish as you might think. Remember that we had long experience in stealing around on the banks of the Dnieper and entering encampments uninvited.

"The tanks were loosely dispersed under trees around a clearing a quarter-mile in from the river and not far from the beginnings of farm fields to the east, with guards posted at hundred-meter intervals in a circle farther out. We managed to creep between two of these guards without being seen or heard, crawl between two tanks, and present ourselves to a half-dozen men standing around a tiny campfire on the edge of the clearing.

"It's a wonder we weren't shot on the spot. As soon as they got over the shock and accepted that we'd managed to pass through their defenses, a runner was sent to get the captain in command of the unit. While they were waiting, there was a lot of kidding about which lucky men would be sharing blankets with these tender young lads.

"When the captain showed up we finally had enough sense to be scared. He was a banty rooster of a fellow, shorter than any other man there and spitting mad. He yelled at us first, then really got riled up as he chewed out the Sergeant of the Guard, who he demoted to Corporal on the spot. He took us to a little shelter he'd made for himself with a piece of canvas tied from his command tank to some trees, and heard our story in a calmer manner than he'd shown with his troops. Once he was convinced that we were who we said we were and really wanted to join the fighting, he located a couple of blankets and put us under one of the T-34s that was pointed east into the clearing. We'd talk further in the morning, he said.

"Sasha and I were far too excited to sleep much. We dozed for maybe a couple of hours, awakened before dawn and slid out from under the tank. As the sun was just clearing the horizon, Sasha hoisted himself up on the slanted bow of the tank. I sat on the ground looking up at him while we talked about our adventure, wondering where it would lead.

"In the distance toward the south we heard the growing roar of an engine unlike anything we'd heard before. Much louder than any boat we knew on the river, moving too fast for a boat but still seeming to be on the river. As the sound drifted away, we were speculating on what it might have been when Sasha's upper body imploded and a huge spew of blood and flesh splashed up on the turret behind him. Almost at the same time I heard a quick series of explosions followed by a roar—the same sound that had come from the river.

"I sat there stunned, unable to move as men poured out and from under the tanks, most of them just awakened by the noise. Captain Sibulsky was one of the first to come to this tank and see the results of the brief attack. There was nothing to do about Sasha, who was very dead with his chest blown out dead center. The captain ordered his platoon commanders to set up an immediate defense against further air attacks, had a blanket thrown over Sasha, then dragged me to my feet. I was in such a state of shock that I couldn't get up on my own.

" 'Listen here, Sasha,' he said, 'I know it's terrible for you to lose your friend. But it's hard for everyone else, too. This is the first combat these men have seen. We just came from a training site a hundred kilometers east of here. You've got to get yourself together here. We'll help you bury your friend ... what was his name?'

"Sasha? I thought to myself, why is he calling me Sasha? Doesn't he mean Gustav?

"You mean Gustav?"

"Yeah, that's it, Gustav. What was his last name?"

"Now I was coming out of shock and getting an idea. I was truly alone and about to help fight a Russian war. Wouldn't it be better to fight as a Russian than a Swede?

" 'Hinas. Gustav Hinas,' I told him.

" 'What the hell kind of a name is that?'

" 'Swedish. He was one of the leftovers from an old Swedish community that used to be down near Kherson.'

" 'Well, if you can handle it, why don't you get whatever your friend had in his pockets and take him down from the tank onto a blanket. I'll have some men help you bury him near the edge of the clearing. You have any religious feelings about it?'

"I could honestly answer no at that moment.

"And so Gustav Hinas died and was buried near the shores of the Dnieper River in the Ukraine, and Sasha Plotkin was reborn. The only proofs of identity that either of us carried were a letter Headmaster Oblansky had given us a few months earlier to show that we were students and not just idlers in the community, and well-worn identity cards issued by the Kherson Communist Party Headquarters. I found Sasha's letter—even dirtier and more creased than mine when I gingerly took it out of his pocket along with the identity card, a pocket knife and a few coins. I kept the knife and money and slipped my own identity card and letter from Oblansky into his pocket before we lowered him into a shallow grave and threw on enough dirt to make a small mound. I had cried earlier, but by now my tears had dried up and all emotion seemed to have left me. I wasn't much interested in putting a cross on the grave. But the troops who helped me seemed to think a cross would be called for because the deceased was a Swede. So we made one, tying a couple of sticks together with wire produced by one of the tank drivers. Once we planted that I said goodbye to Gustav and turned my back on a life that had only one really bright spot—a true friendship.

"Captain Sibulski let me sit with him and the platoon and tank commanders a bit later as they tried to figure out the attack. Finally they pieced it together from their own observations and radio messages from other units; it appeared a lone German fighter plane was making a reconnaissance up the Dnieper River at tree level when he spotted this platoon of tanks under the thin cover of the foliage. He pulled up to altitude farther up the river, headed east and then came at us out of the rising sun, firing his cannon in hopes of destroying one of the tanks. Ironically, 'Gustav' was the only human casualty, hit by a shell that didn't explode. As the Germans would learn in the next few weeks, the new T-34 tank was so well armored that this kind of attack could not destroy it.

"After that meeting Captain Sibulski put me to running errands for him, and soon I was too busy to worry about my situation. That afternoon a radio message came in with orders to pull out under cover of night in the direction of Kiev. We didn't know then that the Soviet defenses in the Ukraine were crumbling in the face of the huge German attack. It took us five days, traveling only at night, to get to Kiev with the rest of the Brigade and prepare for the coming siege. I acted during that time as the Captain's runner and errand boy. We built up a mutual respect that was very important to me in my situation.

"In Kiev Captain Sibulski took me to the railway station and bought a ticket to Moscow out of his own pocket. He gave me a handwritten letter of recommendation to any military service I might try to join, urging me to wait until I was at least as far east as Moscow. He was quite pessimistic about the Soviets' ability to hold the Ukraine very long, due to anti-Soviet feelings among the Ukrainians. He was right. Kiev was surrounded just weeks later and fell with a huge loss of life and surrendered troops. I learned later that the company I found on the banks of the Dnieper had gone west from Kiev to meet the advancing Germans. After fighting valiantly for a couple of weeks, they were destroyed to the last tank and man in a raid by German heavy bombers."

✳ ✳ ✳

RAP! RAP!

Chris and Plotkin jumped equally high in their chairs as someone or something hit the window on the path so hard it was a wonder it didn't break. Sitting with his back to the window, Plotkin swung around and pulled back the lace curtain far enough to see two schoolboys running down the path. "Not to worry," he told Chris, "it's happened before. They see the light in the window and like to play pranks on their way home from school."

Looking at his watch, Chris found it hard to believe that it was already past two o'clock. He'd been listening to Plotkin's story, entranced, for close to an hour, managing somehow to forget his anger, confusion and embarrassment over the fact that this man had cheated him out of a happy marriage. How could he have forgotten?

"I've got to use the bathroom," he said, "and then we really have to talk. How much time do we have here?"

"We could use the place all night if necessary, but I have to leave no later than four o'clock."

Chris found the bathroom where he guessed it would be. Plotkin had shoved the pot to the back of the stove when the coffee was done. Two cups, sugar and milk had replaced the glasses, beer and schnapps bottles. "Good idea," Chris said. "We'll need our wits to get through the next part of this."

"What do you think the next part is?"

"The first is what you have to say about your affair with my wife. Besides my personal feelings about your getting my wife to cheat on me, besides all that nonsense about friendship, I wonder if you can understand what kind of a position you've put me in with my agency. We'll talk about that afterwards, but I want to know about the first part."

Tears suddenly welled in Chris's eyes, and just as suddenly he felt a mixture of shame and anger. Shame at showing the weakness of tears in front of this man who was a professional and now a personal enemy. Shame that he hadn't been able to hold Lisa to the vows they both believed in so strongly when they married. Anger at Plotkin for being the one to seduce her. He turned his back on Plotkin to hide the tears, brushed at his cheek with the back of one hand. When he again turned toward him, Plotkin was seated at the table looking pale and drawn. Chris's brief emotional display had touched him.

"I am very, very sorry Chris. I know there are no words that will repair the damage I've done. But I want to finish my story. I truly hope you'll forgive Lisa someday for her part in this, and perhaps one day you'll even forgive me—though none of us will ever forget what happened. What I'm going to tell you in the time we have left here will help you forget those troubles for a while so you can deal with the challenges on your doorstep right now."

CHAPTER SEVENTEEN

Plotkin poured the coffee and they settled back at the table. He glanced quickly at his wristwatch and looked at Chris with raised eyebrows—should he go on with his story? Chris nodded, his expression glum. Plotkin took a sip of his coffee, set the mug back down on the table, and continued.

"Warfare suited me at that stage of my life. I was more than ready to fight for the Russian motherland after coming under the influence of Headmaster Oblonski and harboring such hostility toward my mother and Gustav. Captain Sibulski made a huge impression on me. The experience with his company of T-34s made me determined to become involved with tank warfare. I was Sasha Plotkin in my heart and thinking, better educated by far than most young Russians my age thanks to Mr. Oblonski's teaching, and ready to die in a tank for mother Russia. I was also very young, not even sixteen. Gustav was dead and buried.

"My dreams of fighting for the motherland were shattered when I arrived at Moscow Central Railway Station from Kiev. When I asked people at the station about joining the military they all but laughed at me. I was a skinny boy, not very mature physically and looking even younger than the sixteen years shown on Sasha's identity papers. Draft age was eighteen years at that time. Exceptions for enlistment could be made, but I had no parents to vouch for me. The need for wartime factory labor was great, though, and soon I found myself an apprentice at Military Factory No. 205 in Moscow, helping manufacture anti-aircraft aiming devices. I made it a practice to work harder than anybody else. Tests administered to set professional grades proved that I had the equivalent of a ten-year education. That put me in good with the factory leadership. With the German Army nearing Moscow the factory was moved to Saratov that October.

"In June 1942 when I (as Sasha) turned seventeen years, I got support from a senior military representative at the factory to join the military. He went with me to the military commissariat, where we learned that an accelerated course for infantry NCOs had been established. I was accepted and realizing my dream!

"After a month and a half—at graduation—we were made sergeants, lined up and sorted out by education. I was in the first rank because of my education and really pleased to be recruited to become a tanker. Before long I was at the Saratov Tank Academy, training in the same T-34 tanks that had been my introduction to warfare and this new life. I graduated in October 'with excellence,' was offered and accepted another three months of training and was then a lieutenant and platoon commander. I was off to war.

"I don't want to dwell on the war years. They passed quickly. You must know my record anyway from background checks through your agency. You probably know that I was much decorated for my part in the very successful tank warfare we waged against the Nazis. I was promoted on a fast track. In July 1943 I was a captain and company commander when more than a thousand of our tanks defeated the German Army at Kursk. I was badly injured when my command tank was hit and burned there, but I managed to get out and continue leading my troops in part of an attack on the left flank of the line, first from the ground and later from another tank I commandeered. I was cited for personal heroism and leadership in that battle and nominated for the Hero of the Soviet Union award. It was not granted. In its place I received another highly respected award, Order of the Red Banner. I was disappointed, but other military awards and a lot of respect came my way. Gustav was still dead and buried.

"My final war days were in the battle for Berlin, as our Soviet forces raced to beat your troops there. By then I was a Major and brigade commander, with a distinguished military career and enough medals to keep me comfortably in the Soviet Army for the rest of my life. I was offered a permanent commission but turned it down. I couldn't tell you why. At times I've wished that I'd stayed on in the military.

"During my wartime experience I hadn't thought much about my changed identity. I was thrust into the role of Sasha Plotkin suddenly, and then found myself caught up so entirely in the war that the potential fallout from that switch of names hadn't occurred to me. As I entered civilian life in a tightly controlled bureaucratic state, with all the forms and background checks required for everything from ration cards to top-level jobs, I began to think long and hard about what I'd done on that day the real Sasha Plotkin died. Not daring to go back to the Ukraine with a different name, I read everything possible about the fate of the residents in the Kherson Oblast. It was grim reading. Many had been hauled off to Germany to work in factories there, where they were given such short food rations that a lot of them died. I have every reason to believe today that my mother,

Gustav and most of the other Swedes who had returned to Gammalsvenskby did not survive the war.

"There were times right after the war when I considered going to the authorities and making a clean breast of my identity. But that foolish idea faded as I found myself able to build a civilian life despite my lack of proven background. As one who'd had his background documentation wiped out, I was in the company of hundreds of thousands—maybe even millions. Some seven million people were killed in the Ukraine during the war, and with Stalin's scorched earth policy as the Army retreated from the attacks of Barbarossa, little evidence of life was left in many of the villages and towns. As time went on I found myself more and more comfortable as Sasha Plotkin the civilian, and I spent a lot of time and thought in building this identity. The Kherson Oblast official records were in reasonably good shape after the war, so by mail I was able to get copies of Sasha's birth certificate and identity card. I was sure of his mother's name, took a good guess at his father's, and of course knew the aunt who had cared for him before being sent to a Siberian camp. I was afraid the aunt's anti-Soviet behavior that led to her going east might reflect badly on this identity, but my being a war hero removed a lot of doubts.

"During the Battle of Berlin, I became friendly with a doctor in the field hospital serving our unit. Yuri was a wonderful fellow, totally committed to mending all those bodies broken in war. When called on he would work the clock around more than once, but in our idle times he was full of fun. We played cards together, smoked endless cigarettes, and talked and talked. Yuri talked so much about medicine that he got me interested and even encouraged me to become a doctor myself if I survived the war. I survived. Yuri didn't. He was killed in a truck accident just as we were entering the outskirts of Berlin.

"So it was because of Yuri that I enrolled in the Second Moscow State Medical Institute in the fall of 1946 to start my medical career. It didn't last very long. Many would-be doctors find they aren't cut out for that profession because they can't stand the sights and smells of sickness and surgery. During the war I'd seen more of that than most doctors see in a lifetime. No, blood and guts didn't bother me. I am simply not a scientist. The preparatory studies in chemistry, biology and physics were not interesting to me, while something else was.

"There hadn't been much chance for hobbies during the war, but I did pick up an interest that I followed almost like a hobby: the German language. I had taken a simple German phrase book with me from the Saratov Tank Academy. Being so dedicated to fighting the Nazis, I felt that everything I could learn about Germany and Germans would make me a better soldier. In addition to the phrase book I was able to get more advanced texts and studied them whenever possible. I also took every opportunity to exchange words with prisoners, so by the end of the war I had a good knowledge of the language.

"Germany was advanced in medicine compared to the Soviet Union at that time, and German-language texts were a basic part of medical studies. Instruction in German was part of the preparatory curriculum at medical school. Medical students were required to have a good reading knowledge of the language. The instructors in German were amazed at my knowledge. Concluding that it would be a waste of time for me to study German at the level taught there, they allowed me to enroll in advanced German language classes at the Academy of Foreign Languages that is part of Moscow State University. It soon became clear that I had a real talent for foreign languages, and within six months I withdrew from the medical school and started studying full time at the language academy. In addition to German I studied English and French. I found English more to my liking than French. I had to be careful not to reveal that I was also a Swedish-speaker, which was not easy. As you know so well, Chris, modern Swedish takes many words from both German and English.

"The resolve not to reveal my Swedish roots was sorely tried in the fall of 1947, when by chance I met a young Swedish girl in the cafeteria at the language school. She was a student at Moscow State University, daughter of a rather prominent Swedish Communist, not very pretty but with an attractive personality. Ulla was taking a year's course at the university. She had been brought over to the language school by a Swedish instructor who wanted to give her students practice with a real Swedish-speaker. Ulla and I went out a couple of times, but I lost interest because of her rabid ideology. All she could talk about was communism and how it would save the world. My loyalty at the time was to mother Russia more than to communism and the Soviet state. Though I certainly supported the Soviet Union and all it stood for, I found other things such as literature, art and culture more interesting to talk about.

"The KGB changed how I dealt with Ulla. It won't surprise you to hear that the KGB was active for many reasons at Moscow State University, including officers assigned under cover as instructors and in administrative positions. This activity grew along with the increase in the number of foreign students coming to the university after the war. It gave them an opportunity for counter-intelligence against possible agents among the foreign students, and a means of spotting potential recruits for the ranks of the KGB. I was first approached by the KGB in connection with my relationship with Ulla. The agent who contacted me was from outside the school apparatus. He said that from time to time the KGB used students like myself for help in maintaining a watch on certain foreign elements who might not be what they seemed. Ulla was one of these, he said. I was asked to keep up the relationship with her, to report on her contacts, activities and political statements.

"I did so happily enough. After the excitement of warfare it was pretty humdrum stuff with a pretty humdrum girl, but I enjoyed a good fortnightly lunch with an interesting fellow from the KGB until Ulla returned to Sweden. Again you won't be surprised that this was the initial approach for my recruitment into the KGB. There were problems in vetting me because of thin bona fides for the background check, so it took longer than usual for me to be fully cleared and entered into training. Years later I met a fellow KGB officer who began his career as a young recruit in one of the State Security offices in Kherson Oblast. He recalled doing inquiries involved with my background check. The investigation included interviews with people who knew my aunt and me, and they remembered that I was a loner who had finally come under the wing of a Russian schoolmaster, only to disappear from that area during the Nazi attack in the summer of 1941.

"The rest, as they say, is history. It's a sad history in a way. Sad for me to think that my fine young friend, Sasha Plotkin, is dead these many years in a grave that must now be unmarked and untended. I told you earlier today that this story might not remove the hurt I've given you, but that it might help you forget for a time, might keep you occupied. It all comes down to the fact that Gustav Hinas is no longer dead and buried in the Ukraine, but alive and well and sitting in front of you. How did he rise from that grave to come here today? That's the rest of the story and I have to tell it very quickly.

"I want to defect. I want to defect a week from today. I want you and your service to get me out of Sweden next Friday without the KGB and the Swedes having any hint beforehand. I will not work in place for you. I will not go back to Moscow first and get more information or help you in any way as an agent. Once I'm safely out of Sweden and in the United States I'll tell your service whatever they want to know about my life in the KGB and whatever I know about KGB operations anywhere. But I won't give you much current information before then, other than what I've given you so far and what I'm about to tell you—my reasons for my doing this."

CHAPTER EIGHTEEN

M arch 28th is just a week after the vernal equinox, when night and day are about equal all over the earth. In Roslagen that means the long nights of winter are half over. Spring is in the air and the sun doesn't set until after six o'clock in the evening—on those days when it's not covered by clouds. Spirits rise.

On this day in 1969 the clouds parted just as Plotkin made his startling declaration, bringing light into the otherwise gloomy room. Torn by the conflicting allegiances to his wife and job, thinking he'd come to this meeting primarily to salvage a few remnants of honor from the situation that had developed between Lisa and Plotkin, Chris now found all his faculties and energies suddenly brought into focus on Plotkin and the work laid out for him. His spirits rose.

"I need more coffee." Chris got up to fetch the pot from the stove, pouring himself another cup and offering some to Plotkin. He looked at his watch. "It's about three o'clock now. Do you really need to be out of here by four?"

Plotkin nodded. "I'll be leaving exactly at that time by way of the street entrance on the other side of the inn. I want you to wait for about a half hour and then leave the same way you came in."

"Your sudden decision to defect makes me think you're in trouble. I'm glad to have a week to make the arrangements to get you out of the country, but isn't it dangerous for you to wait so long?"

Plotkin smiled. "No, Chris, I'm not in trouble. At least I don't think I am. This is something I've thought about for the last couple of years, so it's not as sudden as you seem to believe. Part of the suddenness you see is that I want a clean break and no pressure to stay in place. I'm not driven by ideology. My feelings on that haven't changed since we discussed them at your home. If your government doesn't want me under my terms I'll go to the British. You're cut from about the same cloth."

"So what are your terms? My people are going to want to know something about your motivation and bona fides as a defector; what you're willing to do for us in return for bringing you in."

It was Plotkin's turn to look at his watch. "Let me tell you quickly the rest of my story and then we'll talk about details."

✳ ✳ ✳

"As I said, my relationship with Ulla was the beginning of my recruitment into the KGB. Ulla is not her real name. I'm holding that back because her position in life now is one of the more important pieces of information I'll share with you once I'm out of Sweden. I spent about six months in a relationship with her in Moscow, then turned her over to an experienced KGB officer who recruited and trained her as a sleeper agent.

"That turnover took place about the time I was vetted and began a year of training. The training was what you'd call after-hours, because I needed a cover of some kind and therefore stayed at language school. I was directed to add Swedish to my list of language studies. With difficulty I managed to do just fairly well in those classes, which were most useful to me because I was able to work on improving a pretty basic vocabulary and to develop a standard Stockholm dialect. My success with Ulla and the Swedish language led to my first assignment abroad—actually a part of my continuing KGB education. I spent a year as a foreign student at Stockholm University, mixing with many other nationalities and meeting clandestinely with a KGB officer who was part of the residency there. I spent a lot of time learning how to assess people and how to prepare useful reports.

"Sweden at that time was still quite poor as a result of its neutrality in World War II. If only they had attacked the Allies they could have shared in some of the wonderful help your government gave to its enemies like Germany, Italy and Japan. I heard a lot of grumbling about that. For my own part I played a pretty moderate communist line in talks with other students. I downplayed my role in the military during the war, telling people it was a terrible experience that I just didn't want to talk about. Frankly, I didn't see that much difference between the Soviet and Swedish experiences at that time, so I wasn't attracted away from my beliefs. That was important, because complete loyalty to the Soviet Union and being a non-Jew were two basic requirements for admission to the KGB.

"My training was not the usual for a KGB recruit. I never entered a known KGB building. I was never allowed to hint at my KGB connections, even with friends who worked in government. There was a reason for that. Because of my language abilities and, I believe, my proven coolness under fire, I was destined to work abroad as an illegal agent under the KGB First Chief Directorate's Department S. You should have a record of my wartime service. You might have a record of my language studies in Moscow, and perhaps know of my academic year at Stockholm University, 1948-49. But I have reason to believe that for all your agency's background checks you have found no reference to me for the period from 1951 to 1959. I won't give you all the details yet, but I will give you a brief outline. Until I'm out of Sweden I beg you not to make any more inquiries within your own agency except the most discreet possible. My life could be seriously endangered otherwise.

"After the training was completed in 1951, I changed my appearance by adding thirty pounds to my weight, growing a mustache and wearing horn-rimmed glasses. Looking like that and using a forged passport, I entered Canada at Montreal, rented a car and drove to Vancouver, British Columbia. The cover was that of a naturalized Canadian citizen of Swedish origins, now moving to Vancouver to open a small photographic studio. Which I did, in one of the Vancouver suburbs. I had to smile to myself when you and Lisa talked about your home in Washington State. I visited Seattle many times for equipment and supplies to build up my little business, and have to agree that it's a beautiful place. I had good success with the studio, concentrating mostly on family portraits, pets and the like. I have to say that I'm an excellent photographer, so I got as much business as I wanted.

"That was actually just a way-station, a two-year period to build cover for a mission in England. In 1955 I was able to get a British entry visa and work permit to open a similar photographic studio in a small town outside Portland, a bedroom community for the Portland Navy Base and installations like the Underwater Weapons Establishment. The Politburo and Soviet military had realized the huge importance of nuclear weapons on ballistic missile submarines, so they put information on U.S. and British submarines and their nuclear weapons among the top intelligence priorities. When you think of the time, training and other efforts that went into my assignment in England, you will have an idea of how important that was.

"I was in place there until 1959, and so successful that I received several medals. My reassignment to Moscow KGB Headquarters that year came at my own request. I had lived as an Illegal for eight years, and I was getting on in age without having had a chance to marry and have children. I spent a couple of months of decompression and debriefings in a dacha outside Moscow, during which I was able to lose the extra weight. In 1960, with my mustache shaved off and horned rim glasses gone, I went to work in Department 'S.' My few old friends not with the KGB accepted the legend of my working for the Ministry of

Foreign Affairs without prying. By now they knew better than to ask.

"This story of my mission in England should ring bells with you. No? Think about that area of England for a minute. Still nothing? Think about Gordon Lonsdale. Yes, you would know that name. I should think that would be a textbook case for your agency's training courses.

"Konan Trofimovich Molody is one of the most celebrated KGB Illegals of all time. You know him as Gordon Lonsdale, because that was the identity he adopted in Canada before moving to England about the same time I went there. Our operations were run in parallel and compartmented from each other, though his was broader in scope and he was more visible socially and in the businesses he ran so successfully. He truly is a gifted man and so good in business that he made money for the KGB with his companies. But the reason you recognize Gordon Lonsdale is that in 1961 he got caught with his fingers in the pie at the Underwater Weapons Establishment, with two of his agents convicted and himself sent to prison on a twenty-five-year sentence. I worked with him at KGB Headquarters after he was released in a spy exchange in 1964. Because our operations were compartmented from each other, I had not known about his existence until I returned to Moscow in 1959. I've talked with him many times since he returned to Moscow and went back to work in Department 'S.' He claims to have known about my operation while he was running his own in England. That's a problem for me, and you can tell your masters that it's one of the reasons I want to leave the Soviet Union.

"Corruption and cronyism are a part of any monolithic state. I was able to rationalize that fact as the price citizens pay for stability in such a huge, diverse country as the Soviet Union. The problems are much worse in the Politburo and KGB than in the Soviet military, which is one of the reasons I began to feel sorry that I hadn't stayed on in the military. And Molody's case is a good example. For all his cleverness he's a profligate, given to heavy drinking and sexual athletics with an odd assortment of women. Other reasons were given for his being caught by the British, but I wouldn't be surprised if his drinking and womanizing didn't play a part. His low morals were overlooked by the KGB because his reporting put them in good standing with the Politburo and top levels of Soviet leadership. When he returned from England he was treated like a hero, given medals more important than mine and treated like a celebrity.

"In my view he was a failure. I had a chance to compare our operations after my return to Moscow. The scope of reporting from his agents was broader than mine, which was mostly confined to intelligence on undersea navy and nuclear weapons matters. My reports in that field were at least as good as his. You probably know that the British have always felt there were more Soviet agents in that area who weren't caught. They're right. They weren't caught because they weren't Molody's agents, they were mine. I had three primary agents providing good intelligence on underwater warfare. Two of them are still producing. The third has retired with a nice annuity given in thanks for his work. I had to fight hard with upper levels of the KGB to make that happen. Your masters will be pleased to learn their names.

"It was absolutely right that our operations were compartmented from each other. But I resent Molody knowing about mine, while I was not told about his. It's a great example of the favoritism running through Soviet society. I ran the same dangers, worked just as hard and cleverly, produced intelligence at least an equal to his reporting. But he was favored and still is favored. Molody continues his loose ways in Moscow. Last time I saw him he looked awful. I doubt he'll survive much longer if he keeps on drinking the way he does.

"Another reason I want to leave has to do with my name—or, rather, Sasha's name. Not all Jews in the Soviet Union are named Plotkin. Not all people named Plotkin are Jews. But there are a number of famous Russian Jews named Plotkin, and the name has a Jewish flavor. The thin background information on Sasha makes it impossible to say that he wasn't of Jewish origins, or that he was. My acquaintance who did some of the background check in Kherson thought it likely that the family was White Russian and believed that Sasha's grandparents belonged to the Eastern Church. Sasha never mentioned that to me, but I took comfort in the thought that it could be proof that I was not Jewish in my identity as Sasha Plotkin.

"What's in a name? While going through life you develop enemies along with friends, especially if you make a name for yourself as I did during the war. I never thought seriously about all this until all known Jewish elements were removed from the KGB First Directorate during the purge of 1952-53. I heard about it from a KGB Illegals agent handler in Canada who knew my Plotkin identity. This fellow was weird to start with, and thought it funny to kid about whether or not I'd survive the purge with a name like that. I did, of course, but have worried about it through the years. When I'm at a lower ebb I sometimes wonder if I didn't receive the Hero of the Soviet Union award because someone in the Politburo was afraid to take a chance in giving that top award to a person who might be a Jew.

"And then there was the Prague Spring last year. What a tragedy! I believe the invasion and all it cost in lives and prestige for the Soviet Union centered on intelligence. Not so much that the intelligence was poor, but like so many cases throughout history, it was misread. Our leadership was blinded by a conspiracy theory blaming the United States for prompting the actions leading to the invasion. Another example of a monolithic state striking for the wrong reason.

"Now, Chris, let me finish this before we run out of time to plan my disappearance. You and your masters need to accept the fact that ideologically

I'm not changed from what I described during the visits at your home. I'm disaffected from the Soviet Union, yes. But I don't have much admiration for a United States that commits atrocities against the population of Vietnam in the name of democracy, or a Britain that has forgotten it's no longer a colonial power while conducting itself as if it still were. Practically, though, I believe I'd be safer and happier in your country than anywhere else. In return for your government giving me safehaven, I'll pledge to tell your agency everything I know about past and current KGB operations. But only after I'm safely in the United States and under your protection. My dream is to settle somewhere pleasant in the United States under a different identity. Even though I'm getting on in years, I would still like to marry there and raise some children. Maybe I could teach or do language tutoring. Or even be a photographer again.

"My wife? I met Marina when she and I were contemporaries starting out at medical school. We had dinner together a couple of times, but nothing sparked. She got her medical degree, married and divorced while I was out of the country. Things did spark when I returned. We married in 1961 and have had a good relationship as far as it goes—which is to say without children. There's a lot of respect but not a lot of love between us. My defecting will be tough for her, but she has so much attention and admiration for her medical work that I think she'll be okay.

"My life is in your hands, Chris. We won't be able to communicate between now and next Friday when you pick me up. I have to assume that your government will agree to my terms, and that you will do everything possible to protect me before then. Please do whatever you can do to restrict the information at your Headquarters. You also should know that our local counter-intelligence people have a good line on your office and your people. Be careful that you don't change your patterns or bring in other Agency people who might be identified to the KGB. And most of all, don't try to follow me during the next week. That could be fatal.

"My life is in your hands."

CHAPTER NINETEEN

Saturday, March 29, 1969

It was ten o'clock the next morning, Saturday, when Chris came home after meeting with Plotkin. His hair was tousled and his clothes wrinkled. He needed a shave and after such a long time in the same clothes he smelled bad even to himself. For most of thirty hours he'd been awake and away from home.

"I'm home!" His usual homecoming greeting brought Missy tearing out of the kitchen. The big wooden spoon in one hand almost put out his eye when she leaped into his arms. "Hi, Daddy." Once in his arms, she leaned back to stare at his haggard face. "You smell bad, Daddy!"

"You don't smell so good yourself, Kiddo. You smell like vinegar. What have you and Mommy been doing to make you smell like that?"

"It's going to be Easter!"

"What's vinegar have to do with Easter?"

"Daddy, Daddy." She mimicked her mother in pretend disgust at how dense he could be. "You need vinegar to dye Easter eggs. Mommy said."

"But why would you be dyeing Easter eggs now? Easter's not for another couple of weeks."

"Wrong, Daddy. Wrong. Mommy says Easter is a week from tomorrow, and tomorrow's called Palm Sunday. Farmor is coming this afternoon to spend the Easter holiday with us, and the twins are coming tomorrow. Mommy says." She slipped from his arms to run to her mother in the kitchen. When Chris followed he found Lisa in a colorful apron and with a colorful face. She'd smeared dye on her forehead while working with the Easter eggs.

"You look awful, Chris. Are you okay?"

"He smells bad, Mommy." Missy was holding the edge of her mother's apron and looking at her dad suspiciously.

"Hail the conquering hero! I've been away from home for more than a day, and after a couple of minutes here all I've heard is that I look awful and smell bad."

"I'm sorry, Honey. You must have had a couple of rough days. Why don't you take a shower and change into some other clothes while I clean up our Easter egg mess and make you something to eat. Then, when Missy's gone, we can sit down and chat about what's going on."

"What's going on, Mommy?" When Missy was worried, a furrow formed between her wide-set eyes. She had caught on to the tension between her parents.

"Nothing to bother your beautiful little head, Sweetheart. Remember all the plans we made for Farmor's visit? Daddy and I have to go over those and make sure everything will work out. And remember, your brothers are coming next week!" With a glow of motherly love, Lisa leaned down to gather Missy into her arms. It was a struggle, now that her little girl was four years old.

Chris was fading fast. "I hope I don't fall asleep in the shower. If I'm not back down here in fifteen or twenty minutes you better come check on me."

* * *

Half an hour later, Lisa had stored the colored eggs in the refrigerator and taken Missy to Millie Jones' home for a children's lunch party. Still no sign of her husband. She decided to check on him. Her heart ached when she found him on the bed in their room, on top of the covers and still wearing the same clothes, so deep in sleep that she had to make sure he was breathing. He was. Deeply, quietly, in another world that had never been fully accessible to her. The world he was in now was certainly inhabited by the Plotkin case, with all the twists and turns of tradecraft, worries about Headquarters reactions, about the Swedish authorities, and now about the stability of his job itself. In many of the other dream worlds conceived during their marriage Lisa was certain she played no part. Like it or not, she was a major player this time. Missy was a sensitive, sweet girl who was right to worry, "What's going on?" Lisa would let Chris sleep for now. She might even leave him home to get Missy and go out to the airport to meet Mor. But before this Saturday was over, before midnight of this day, she was going to corner Chris in a quiet spot where they could talk. And she was going to ask the question.

"What's going on?"

Chris was still deep in his dream world when the time came for Lisa to pick up their daughter and head out to the airport. Anxious as she was to learn what had happened in the meeting with Plotkin, Lisa thought it best to postpone their talk and planning until the day was over. She left her husband at home, fetched Missy from Millie's house, and headed for the airport.

✲ ✲ ✲

Mor strode through airport customs in her regal manner. She enveloped Missy in a big hug before greeting Lisa and asking about Chris, paying scant attention to the answer. Instead she turned to Missy to converse in the Swedish language. Lisa knew that Mor's joy at returning *home* was spiced by the fact that now she could speak Swedish with one of her grandchildren. Her happiness in observing Mor's pleasure was tempered by the fact that the usually bubbly Missy had been replaced with a quiet, shy little girl.

"What's happening, Missy?" she asked her daughter, when Mor excused herself to powder her nose. "Aren't you glad to have Mor here? Isn't it fun to talk Swedish with her?"

"Is that Swedish? She talks funny."

"Can't you understand her?"

"Yes, I understand her. But she talks like some of the people do on the kids' radio program I listen to in the mornings. She sounds like Papa Bear in the story about the three bears."

Lisa had trouble holding back her laughter. This was a pretty serious matter for Missy, but it was funny to her. No expert in Swedish herself, she understood from Chris that his mother's Swedish was completely fluent but tinged with the flavor of Dalarna Province, an accent used in the theater for playing parts of woodsmen and other rural people—a natural for the Three Bears. It was what Mor had heard while growing up.

She tried to explain this to Missy, but in their short time alone she could only convey to the four-year-old the need to be nice to her grandmother. A naturally cheery and resilient child, Missy was soon telling Mor all about *lekskola*, her friends, her toys, her brothers, and everything else important to her world. Lisa could understand about half of this Swedish conversation-turned-monologue as they collected Mor's luggage and drove back to Stockholm. What a good feeling to have grandmother and small child enjoying each other in this way!

It was suppertime when they finally arrived home in Bromma. As they went into the house, Mor started inquiring more sharply about Chris's whereabouts and why he couldn't come to the airport.

"He pulled an all-nighter," Lisa told her mother-in-law, "and has been sleeping all day. I'll get him up for supper."

"For Heaven's sake, what is an all-nighter?"

"Every once in a while, when they have important messages coming in and going out at the Embassy, he has to stay there until the wee hours of the morning. He doesn't tell me much about it, and I've learned not to ask."

"That work of his!" Mor made a sour face of disapproval.

Missy and Lisa helped Mor carry her luggage to the guestroom, where Lisa left the two of them to start supper and wake up Chris. Supper preparations wouldn't take long. She lit the gas stove to warm a hearty lentil soup made that morning, took the open face sandwiches out of the refrigerator so they wouldn't be too cold for serving, then went upstairs to check on Chris.

He was in his waking-up mode, still on top of the covers in yesterday's clothes, on his back with hands behind his head, eyes closed. "What time is it?" he asked.

"Six o'clock."

"Jesus. So early. I don't have to get up this early."

"Six o'clock at night, silly. Mor is here and we'll have supper in half an hour or so. You better shower and shave before she sees you in this condition."

"How'd she get here already? I thought we were going to go out and pick her up at Arlanda on Saturday afternoon."

"Chris! Chris!" She spoke sharply. "Wake up. Get with the program. You're so exhausted you're talking nonsense. It's Saturday, late Saturday afternoon. You've been out of it ever since your meeting with Plotkin and whatever else you were doing after that. Mor's going to start worrying if you don't get in that shower."

With a groan he rolled over to put his feet on the floor, sitting with elbows on his knees, hands supporting his chin. "You're right. I'm beginning to remember." He rose to his feet a bit unsteadily as Lisa left, quietly closing the door behind her.

⁕ ⁕ ⁕

They spent a pleasant evening together, these three generations of the Holbeck family. A long hot shower followed by a blast of cold water had revived Chris to a point where he almost enjoyed the evening, spoiled for him only by insistent thoughts of the professional and personal complications of the Plotkin case. Missy and Mor continued to enjoy each other, chattering away in Swedish and playing card games. Mor finally announced herself in a state of collapse about nine o'clock, already past Missy's bedtime. By ten o'clock her snores were rattling the door of the guestroom. This didn't seem to bother Missy, even though she slept with her door partly open. A peek into her room showed the little girl sleeping sweetly and quietly, surrounded by her menagerie of stuffed animals. It was time to talk.

Chris went to the basement to select one of the better red wines in his modest collection. Lisa worked briefly in the kitchen, preparing a plate of cheese and crackers, placing them on a teak tray with two crystal wine glasses. They took the treasures upstairs to their bedroom, which doubled as a sitting room. Two overstuffed chairs faced each other, a table between them. Lisa placed the tray on the table. She had changed into her nightgown and a light green, floor-length robe that complemented her variable eye color. For his part, after the shower Chris had exchanged his grubby suit for a pair of Levis and a fresh white dress shirt with the cuffs rolled back a turn, a combination that Lisa found attractive. As she fussed with the food on the tray, he opened the wine and filled their glasses. Finally they were seated across from each other. Chris lifted his glass to his wife, and she responded by lifting hers. They made eye contact in the Swedish fashion before tipping the glasses to drink.

"Skål," he said. With his eyes still locked on Lisa's, he added, "Just another Saturday night in the Holbeck home."

Lisa had already started a sip of the wine. This remark struck her as so ludicrous that she choked, spilling wine onto her chin and nightgown. Her giggle threatened to turn into a roar of laughter.

"Shhh," Chris warned. "Shush. You'll wake Missy and Mor." Now Lisa had a napkin over her mouth and was standing, but bent over with laughter that was turning into hysteria. Chris started to laugh along with her. He stood also, reaching across the small table with his free hand to straighten her up and get her to look him in the eyes again, trying to move on to the serious business before them. As she removed the napkin from her mouth, Chris felt a wave of love for this woman, a flood of emotion like a burst dam. He reached out to place his wineglass on the windowsill, alongside the bottle of wine. She did likewise. They kissed deeply across the table, overcome by these tensions so suddenly released, so moved by the moment that they rushed to the bed.

They talked before midnight, just before Lisa's deadline. Both had showered; Lisa was in a fresh nightgown and Chris had changed into pajamas and a robe. This time, as they sat across from each other, Lisa didn't wait for a skål. "So, Chris," she said, "What's going on?"

He told her what she needed to know.

He told her that he and Sasha had met at an inn in Norrtälje, and that Plotkin had expanded on the story he'd told Lisa about Gammalsvenskby.

He told her that Plotkin had decided to defect at the end of the coming week, which he now realized would be Good Friday.

He told her that this so-called friend seemed genuinely remorseful for the damage caused to their marriage.

These things Chris told his wife because she had a need to know. Not, perhaps, in the official sense, but certainly in light of some of the decisions they would soon have to make.

He did not tell her that he would meet Plotkin at one of the entrances to the park at Drottningholm at 2:55 p.m. on Friday, in a car borrowed from a long-time agent in Malmö, in the south of Sweden.

Because she had no need to know, he didn't tell her that the car would be picked up in Malmö and driven to Stockholm by a married Agency couple who were specialists in disguise and documentation. After the pickup by Chris, Sasha would be taken for a two-night stay at a Stockholm safe house, where he would be given a disguise and documentation as a Swedish businessman.

Chris did not share with Lisa one of the challenges that had kept him at the Embassy all night, part of the negotiations with Headquarters over the methods to pull this off. They had wanted to send a three-person surveillance team to track Plotkin's movements up to the time of the pickup. Chris was firmly against this, both because of Plotkin's plea in this regard and because a team unfamiliar with Stockholm would have little chance of success. In an exchange of several cables, a compromise was reached: The team would come to Stockholm as quickly as possible, spend the week familiarizing themselves with the territory, but not act until after the pickup. They would start tailing Chris at an agreed upon point about five minutes drive from Drottningholm, follow along to the safe house and make occasional sweeps by the safe house during the couple of days Plotkin would be there. Unbeknownst to Sasha they would be following when he left Stockholm on Easter morning in the car with Malmö plates, along with the man/woman team who had brought it to Stockholm. After arriving in Malmö and leaving the car on the street, they would be there as Sasha and his escorts walked to the hydrofoil dock to cross to Copenhagen, making their way to Kastrup Airport and a flight to New York.

Chris did not tell Lisa all these things. There was one important matter to discuss: her pregnancy and what to do about it. The wine bottle was empty and it was almost two o'clock in the morning when that matter had been settled. They dropped into bed, as satisfied with their decision as possible under the circumstances, too exhausted to make love again but feeling the need to hold each other.

The following afternoon the twins would arrive from school in Switzerland to spend the Easter Holiday. They would share their news at a Palm Sunday family dinner, later on with friends and colleagues.

Lisa was pregnant. In the fall they would be blessed with the addition of a sixth member of the family.

They didn't care if it was a boy or a girl. Just that it be a healthy, happy child.

CHAPTER TWENTY

EASTER WEEK
Sunday, March 31, to Sunday April 6, 1969

SUNDAY OF THE PASSION (PALM SUNDAY)
Luke 19:28-40
Psalm 188:1-2, 19-29

Blessed is he who comes in the name of the Lord
(Ps. 118:26)

The Reverend Bill Stewart was serving as Pastor of the American Church of Stockholm. He had been ordained in the Lutheran Ministry shortly before Christmas 1941, two weeks after Pearl Harbor. Everything seemed to happen at once. The week after Christmas he received a direct commission in the U.S. Navy with the rank of Ensign. The first week of January 1942 he entered a month's course at the Navy's Officer Integration School at Newport Rhode Island. At the finish of the course, this "thirty-day wonder" was sent to Norfolk, Virginia, to join the carrier *USS Hornet* as an assistant chaplain, sailing into war on an historic mission to launch the famous Doolittle raid on Tokyo. In the nearly four years of naval warfare experience that followed, Bill Stewart survived the sinking of the *Hornet* and nearly constant duty aboard other carriers involved in the intense naval warfare experienced by the United State Pacific fleet.

Now a reserve Navy Captain long retired from active duty, Pastor Stewart surveyed his flock from a chair alongside the pulpit as they entered the American Church of Stockholm. This being Palm Sunday, the church would be overfilled with worshippers, mostly local American businessmen and officials, with a sprinkling of Swedes with some connection to the United States. As he watched the Holbeck family enter the sanctuary he was delighted to see Chris's mother—Mor, as they called her. She had visited before and enlivened the services with her regal presence and a soprano voice that soared above others during the hymns and responses. Pastor Stewart was a particular friend of the Holbecks and especially close to Chris, with whom he shared a love of boats and the sea.

At the end of the service, as the recessional hymn was sung, Pastor Stewart's determined strides took him outside to the portico at the church entrance for farewells, a bright, sunny day God had given the parishioners to celebrate the beginning of Easter week. The Holbecks were the last to emerge from the entrance hall.

"Easter's next Sunday!" said little Missy, who looked sweet in a sunny yellow dress and bonnet.

"Thank you for reminding me, Sweetheart." Pastor Bill squatted down to meet her at eye level. "Mrs. Smith tells me you're one of her best students in Sunday school."

"Let Pastor Stewart say hello to your grandmother, Missy." Lisa was anxious to get home. The twins would be arriving in mid-afternoon, and there was much to do to get ready for a big family week.

Greetings were finished and his family had already headed for the car when Chris came out of the church. He had hung back to help straighten out the chapel. As they shook hands warmly, Pastor Bill leaned close to speak quietly into Chris's ear, "You look tired!"

"And a Happy Easter to you, Pastor Bill."

"What's going on with you and Lisa? You both look sad and worn out at a time when you should be joyful, with most of your family around at Easter. Anything I can do to help?"

"Not now, but maybe we could get together for a talk sometime this week. How about Wednesday?" Chris was not at all sure he'd be free that day, but it might work. Uncertain of what he could share with Bill, the one thing he knew was that he needed comfort from an outside source.

Pastor Bill gave Chris a hug. "You've got it," he said. "Give me a call."

* * *

Lisa had pulled their car up in front of the church, waiting for Chris with Mor and Melissa in the back seat.

"Dear Lord!" Mor exclaimed, "Look at that! It gives new meaning to the expression 'bear hug.'" At six feet, four inches, and 250 solid pounds, the pastor was big enough to fit the 'bear' description. The impression was enhanced by a full ginger-colored beard and hair the same color with no gray, cut about an inch long. The bright sun, still low in the sky at that time of year, shone like a spotlight on the pastor, turning his hair to copper. "Look at that!" she repeated, nudging Melissa, "doesn't he look like a grizzly bear?"

"Maybe," Missy replied with a puzzled look, "but he doesn't talk like a bear."

Lisa whirled around in the driver's seat to aim a meaningful glare at Missy. "Bears don't talk, Missy. You know that."

"But pretend bears can talk, Mommy, just like on—" Chris's fortuitous arrival prevented her from continuing.

In the late afternoon Chris and Missy headed for Arlanda airport to meet the twins, flying in from their school in Switzerland. Mor had taken over the kitchen to prepare her own version of Swedish meatballs. Lisa's sous-chef duties included listening to Mor's thoughts on raising children, the main thesis being that American children should be raised in America, not abroad.

The happy atmosphere of the day continued through picking up the boys. After dinner that evening they gathered in the living room, where the family sat in a circle, and the conversation became more serious. They talked about family, about the boys' school in Switzerland, about Missy's *lekskola*. A perfect time for the announcement.

"Your dad and I have something we want to share with you tonight," Lisa began, "and of course it's especially nice that Mor is here to get the news. We hope you'll all be as excited about it as we are."

Mor clapped her hands together. "You're coming back home!"

Lisa had no chance to disillusion her before Missy clapped her hands together in imitation of her grandmother. "I'm going to have a baby sister!" Lisa and Chris looked at each other in amazement.

"Not exactly," Lisa said.

Mor's expression turned grim. She'd gotten at least part of the message. "What's that supposed to mean? You're not exactly having a baby? Or it's not going to be exactly a girl? It doesn't seem you'll be coming home."

Missy jumped down from her chair, running over to leap into her mother's lap and give her a hug. Lisa's eyes were wide with awe. "How did you figure that out, Sweetheart? I don't know if it will be a girl or a boy, but we are going to have a baby and your father and I are really excited."

"How *did* you figure that out, Missy?" Chris was concerned that Missy had overheard some of the heated conversations between her parents.

"It was easy. There are too many boys in our family. The biggest surprise I've always wanted was to have a baby sister, and I could tell that Mommy had a really big surprise for us."

The twins were sitting quietly, forgotten in the exchanges with Mor and Missy.

Chris turned to them. "So what do you think, guys?"

Mark's face had no expression. "That's nice, I guess."

Matthew's eyes were wet. "I thought you guys would have had all that making babies stuff figured out by now." He jumped to his feet—a tall, skinny, vulnerable fourteen-year-old boy with tears coursing down his face—and hurried out of the room. The others sat in silence, listening to the echo of his feet stomping on each step of stairs leading to the upper part of the house.

"What was that all about?" Chris turned to Mark as the best possible authority on his twin brother. His expression blank, Mark simply shrugged and pushed back in his chair—arms folded, legs extended.

"What the hell was that about?" Chris was getting angry now, turning to Lisa for help. "You need to go talk to him. This is nonsense."

"*I* don't need to talk to him. *You* need to talk *with* him." Lisa still had Missy in her lap, sitting alongside Mor, who was nodding slowly in agreement. It was Chris's turn to stomp out of the room.

Matthew was lying on one of the twin beds in the room he shared with his brother when they were home. The tears had dried but his eyes were red.

"So what's up, Buddy?" Chris pushed his son's feet to one side and sat at the foot of the bed.

"I don't want to talk about it."

"You know we have to talk about it, Matt."

"And don't call me Matt. If you let us be together more, you'd know I want to be called Matthew."

"I can respect that, but I still don't understand what all this anger is about. Our having another child should be the beginning of something good, something wonderful. You saw how excited Melissa is about it, and you know how your mom and I feel."

"Missy's excited, sure, it's just what she wanted. But I don't know about you guys. Farmor looked upset, Mom wasn't really looking all that happy when she told us, and you've just been mad at everybody. Are you really glad about it, Dad?"

"You bet I am. I think it's neat to have a big family. How come you can't be happy with the rest of us?"

Tears started in Matthew's eyes again. Not outwardly sobbing, he was taking deep, shuddering breaths. "I'm sorry to say this to you, Dad, but I don't think you're a very good parent. You can't take care of the kids you have already. Why should you have more?"

The hurt stabbed right through Chris's chest. His voice was almost a whisper. "How can you say that to me, Matthew? I've worked very hard to keep this family together and happy."

Matthew rolled over with his face to the wall. "You've worked hard, that's for sure. That's why we see you so little. But how can you say you've kept us together when Mark and I have been in Switzerland all this school year and probably will be there the next couple of years?" He reached around into his back pocket to drag out a grimy handkerchief, blowing his nose loudly as the crying subsided.

"I thought you two were happy there. That's the best school we could find for you in Europe."

"It's a good school. It's a great school, Dad, but I just don't want to be there. I want to be with you and Mom and Missy. I'd really like to be in Edmonds with all of you, and Farmor and Farfar, and doing all the things we do on home leave like fishing and hiking. That's home. This is a nice house, but it's not home. Can't you understand that, Dad?" It looked as if he might cry again, but with an effort he choked it back.

Chris felt terrible. "Does Mark feel the same way? He's never said anything like this."

"You know Mark. He sucks up to you and Mom because he's a real Goody two-shoes." He reached out and circled Chris's wrist with his right hand, squeezing hard and looking directly at his father. "You know me, Dad. I'm the honest one. I always tell you how it is. I'm your number one son."

Chris recognized the twinkle that had come back to his oldest (by thirty-five minutes) son's eyes. He removed the hand from his wrist and dragged Matthew to him for a bear hug rivaling the one he'd received from Pastor Stewart that morning.

As he left the boys' room he said, "Come on downstairs when you feel up to it. We'll try to get some games going."

Monday of Holy Week
Isaiah 42:1-0
Psalm 36:5-11

Your people take refuge under the shadow of your wings.
(Ps. 36:7)

Operational plans for the Plotkin defection included using Bisan as the local contact for Headquarters' surveillance team to familiarize them with Stockholm.

At the office Monday morning, Chris learned that she had balked at playing the role. Mark Noble met Bisan at a suburban café on Sunday night to brief her on plans for the week. She'd cut him short with a demand to see Chris before she continued active in any operations. Further, the meeting would have to be at eight o'clock Monday evening in her apartment. For operational reasons they had never met there or used her apartment as a safe house, keeping her as clean as possible from overt contact with the Embassy and Station.

"That little bitch! What it comes down to, Chris, is just what I told you before. I don't think I'm that bad a guy, and I don't think she really dislikes me. She either has the hots for you or she feels more secure when she's under your wing. We're going to lose her if you don't meet her there tonight."

Bisan, Bisan. Here was a support agent who could pass as a Swede or an American, who could move comfortably through many parts of Swedish society, who had proven she had the guts to tackle any kind of task assigned her in the past year. It looked like he had no choice but to meet on her terms.

Bisan was the daughter of Robert West, a U.S. Navy warrant officer, and Ingrid, a former Swedish employee at the American Embassy in Stockholm. Robert had been assigned to the Naval Attaché Office in Stockholm soon after the end of World War II. It didn't take him long to fall in love with Ingrid and move into her small apartment. A year later she was pregnant with what would be their only child, Bisan. The couple married and began the life of a Navy family, eventually enjoying an assignment at the Naval Academy in Annapolis, Maryland. Bisan had just turned six years old when they arrived at the Academy. Six happy years there ended tragically when Robert was hit with a cancer that took only a few months from diagnosis to death. Mother and daughter returned to Sweden within weeks of the funeral, unable to visualize a happy life in the States without Robert.

Chris met Bisan during a visit to Gothenburg made at the request of his parents, who wanted him to meet relatives on his dad's side. He'd not been looking forward to the visit, but found it a blessing in disguise after meeting Bisan. A friend of one of his distant cousin's daughters, she was invited to a party the family gave in honor of Chris's visit. They were no sooner introduced than she caught his eyes and his ears.

Taken individually, Bisan's features were not remarkable. Her jaw was rather strong, her cheek bones high. Her nose was short, her eyes blue or green depending on the setting. Her hair was blond but closer to light brown than the nearly white hair seen on some Scandinavians. She was not very tall, quite slim and small-boned with an attractive figure. The packaging was not special; what was inside the package was. She radiated such good humor and natural lust for life that he felt immediately drawn to her, so much so that after a few minutes he realized that he'd paid no attention whatsoever to the distant cousin. He did his social duty with the cousin, circulated around the crowd for a time, then returned to Bisan to sit down and chat with her.

It was then that he learned of the girl's fluency in both English and Swedish. He was especially interested to find that she lived in Stockholm, working there for a tourist company that provided a range of services from guided tours to entertainment ticket sales, from hotel reservations to transportation arrangements of all kinds. She was also connected with various foreign embassy people and those involved with travel, such as the Soviet Intourist representative.

If Bisan had a weak point as a prospective support agent, it was her foreign language fluency outside of the native ability in Swedish and English. She admitted that the German and French tourist groups she led were entertained by the way she butchered their languages.

Within two weeks of that party the Station received clearance for the recruitment of Bisan as a support asset. She happily agreed to Chris's pitch. After a couple months of practice in surveillance, elicitation exercises and other bits of tradecraft, she began assisting the Station in a variety of ways. As they trained, worked and traveled together, Chris was more and more tempted by this attractive young woman. In order to resist that temptation, he shifted her control to Mark Noble.

Now he had no choice but to accept her demand. He could think of no other way than through Bisan to secure support needed by the surveillance team. Meeting her meant ducking out on a dinner party for Mor hosted that evening by Millie and Rex Jones. Lisa would be terribly unhappy about that. So be it.

Chris took extraordinary precautions in approaching Bisan's apartment building, located on Grevgatan in the Östermalm district of Stockholm, an old building that had been renovated twenty-five years earlier. Most of the apartments here remained under rent control, which meant that a new tenant had to pay key money to take over a reasonably priced rental or, as in Bisan's case, inherit the right to the apartment. An elderly great aunt had loaned it to Bisan a couple of years earlier—a terrific break for a young woman starting out on her career with a salary that otherwise wouldn't cover such a nice living arrangement. The aunt, a straight-laced Free Baptist, made it available with some strict caveats to protect her ownership under rent contol. No wild parties, no roommates, nothing to prevent the aunt from returning when released from the nursing home. Which clearly was not going to happen.

It was also a terrific break for the Station in case they ever needed such an apartment for a safe house.

"You're late," she said as he entered the apartment. Dressed in green pedal pushers and a matching short-sleeved blouse, spectacles pushed up into her hair, without even so much as lipstick for makeup, she looked like an American college girl interrupted in the midst of studying for an exam.

"I didn't know you wore glasses."

"Only for serious reading. I said 'you're late.' I seem to remember my training officer telling me how important it is to be on time for a clandestine meeting."

"And I seem to remember that same officer telling you that meetings would not be held at your apartment until he made an exception."

"Well, Herr Training Officer Almighty, you're the one who forced the exception. You're the one who forced me to work with Mark, and he told me you're the one who would be giving the orders I'm supposed to follow this week. Number One: I don't like working with Mark. It feels like he's undressing me with his eyes every time we meet. When I get up in the morning of a day to meet him, I put on a long skirt and a blouse that buttons up to the chin. So I'm not going to meet with him anymore. Number Two: You're late." She motioned him into a comfortable chair in the small living room. "Would you like something to drink? I've got a couple of cold Heinekens in the fridge."

"Thanks. I'll take one but don't offer me more. I'm driving. Sorry about being late. I took a lot of precautions against surveillance. When I arrived there were a couple of old yentas in the reception area downstairs, yakking away. Like I told you during training, here in Sweden it's the old ladies you have to watch out for—the nosiest bunch of people I've seen anywhere. I wasn't about to come into the building while they were there, so I took turns around the block until they were gone."

As he talked, she opened the beer and poured it into mugs. Accepting the Heineken, he raised the glass in a brief toast. "Thanks, and by the way Mark is a first-rate nice guy and married. You don't have to worry about him trying anything funny with you."

"I'm not sure I agree with you about his trying, and I know what he has in mind wouldn't be funny. If you want me to keep working, it's going to have to be with you or nobody."

"I don't remember that being part of the agreement you signed."

"It wasn't, but you can't make me continue. You or nobody."

"How about I introduce you to somebody else, not Mark?"

"You or nobody." She raised her glass to him in a toast. "It's really nice having you here. Thanks for coming!" She put down her glass. Sitting catty-corner from Chris—he at the end of a sofa and she in an armchair—she reached out and took one of his hands in both of hers. Her blouse parted, revealing some cleavage. Her eyes softened. Chris felt his cheeks go warm, a sheen of sweat break out on his forehead.

"You've got to understand, Bisan. This is strictly business. I'd never cheat on my wife."

Her eyes changed from soft to mischievous. "No? I seem to remember a time in Copenhagen when it was only a phone call that kept you from cheating on your wife. I think the real reason for you turning me over to Mark was that you're afraid of me. Afraid of what might happen when we're together."

Chris blushed. He stared at her without speaking.

She dropped his hand. "Don't worry, Chris. If you think I'm proposing something you're wrong. You think I could have some kind of romantic interest in a man old enough to be my father? That time in Copenhagen was nothing, just the drinks we had. I was only teasing you. Don't flatter yourself that I would have gone through with it."

What an insult! "Old enough to be your father? I don't think so."

Bisan didn't let him continue. "It was exciting when you first asked me to work with you and your people. I enjoyed our training time together, and some of the assignments like going with you to Copenhagen and taking the night boat to Helsinki to look for that man. Being half American I feel some loyalty, but I have to tell you, Chris, that it's getting harder and harder with all the bad feelings here in Sweden against the United States. My Swedish half tells me those people demonstrating against your involvement in Vietnam are right."

"I'm not in love with our being in Vietnam myself. But what does that have to do with your being safe?"

"I don't go around telling people that I'm half American, but quite a few people know it, and I feel like they're looking at me suspiciously. It may sound silly to you, but I'm nervous. You're the one who talked me into doing this work, you're the one who trained me, and you're the one I trust. Nobody else. Take it or leave it."

"You've got me in a hell of a bind here, Bisan. My week is chock-a-block full for a lot of reasons. It's Easter week, my mother's visiting from the States, I've got boys back here on Easter vacation from school, and this operation going on. Can we agree that I'll brief you tonight on the operation, and meet you during the week as necessary, but that you'll consider working with somebody else after that?"

Bisan sank lower in the chair and pouted. "You or nobody." That did it. He couldn't waste more time on arguing with her.

"Okay, okay. Let's leave it at that and get to work." He pulled a notebook from the breast pocket of his suit jacket, opened it to a page where he'd made some cryptic entries on meeting places and schedules for the surveillance team, and got ready to brief her.

"Wait a minute, Chris! Does that mean you agree? That I won't have to work with somebody else?"

Chris sighed. "You're leaving me no choice. Frankly, I don't have anyone else available to do the job, and I know you'll do it well."

"Thank you." Her eyes softened again.

"You're welcome. We'll talk next week about our future relationship, but for now let's concentrate on this week." They spent another hour together planning Bisan's involvement with the surveillance team during the following days. She seemed satisfied with his promise to work with her, and there was no return of her earlier coquetry. Chris was able to keep his mind on the business. In the back of his mind, though, he kept wondering about the show of cleavage, hand-holding and soft-eyed looks. He'd never understand women.

The family was abed when he got home—Mor and Missy asleep, a Beatles tune drifting from the twins' room. Lisa was propped up in bed, reading a novel.

"Hi, Honey, how did it go? Were you at the Embassy or a meeting?" She reached for his hand and kissed it, gently. He had told her only that he wouldn't be able to go with the family to the Jones's party for Mor.

"It was a meeting." He took off his suit jacket and sat down on his side of the bed, starting to undress. "I can't give you the details, but I'm beginning to think that we're going to be okay with this situation we've got on our hands. Nothing special from the meeting tonight, but just a growing feeling that it's all going to work out."

"What a relief. I sure hope you're right." Lisa put her book on the nightstand. "Mind if I turn out the light?" He didn't and she did, leaving him to dress in the semi-darkness of the bedroom.

"And I realized something tonight."

"What's that?"

He slipped into bed. "Remember how I've told you that the kind of work I do for the Agency amounts to being a manipulator of people, and that I'm not always comfortable with that?"

She reached out and drew him to her in a "not tonight let's just be comfortable with each other" embrace. "Yes, Honey, I do remember that."

"I feel sometimes like we're trying to play God. We're manipulating people, talking them into doing things they really don't want to do, claiming we'll protect them even though we're not absolutely sure we can. There's a lot of responsibility in these relationships. You know what?"

Lisa was dropping quickly off to sleep. "What?" she barely managed to murmur.

"I'm beginning to think that I'm not all that good at playing God."

Lisa answered with a gentle snore.

Tuesday of Holy Week
Isaiah 49:1-7
Psalm 71:1-14

From my mother's womb you have been my strength.
(Ps. 71:6)

Chris arose on Tuesday morning with the feeling he should do something special for Mor to make up for missing last night's dinner in her honor. Lunch, he thought, a very special lunch with just the two of them, mother and son, giving them a chance to visit about the family in ways they couldn't do with everyone else around. He'd take her to the Operakälleren Restaurant—the finest eating establishment in Stockholm. Shortly before he left for work, she came downstairs in her robe. He put his arm around her and gave her a kiss on the cheek before extending the invitation.

Mor's eyes danced with excitement at the prospect. "Your father would never take me there when we visited Stockholm in the past. He's made of money but too cheap to spend it on that kind of place."

Tuesday morning at work seemed the beginning of a return to some kind of normalcy in the Station offices. Most everyone was there. The Plotkin case activity had simmered down; there was still heat underneath and a bit of steam, but not the crazy rolling boil of last week's preparations. Chris took care of some paper work, then left on foot at 11:30 a.m. for the long walk to the restaurant. He'd be waiting there when Lisa dropped Mor off in the car, and later would escort his mother to a nearby subway station for her return home.

Mor was brimming with excitement when she arrived and took her son's arm to parade into the restaurant.

"Would you like something to drink?" Chris asked.

"Yes, I believe I'll have schnapps with a beer chaser."

Chris was astounded. "Schnapps? A beer chaser? I've never in my life seen you drink like that."

"Isn't that what you have with your business lunches? Is it only the men who can drink schnapps? Just because we don't do it at home doesn't mean that I might not like to try it. I thought maybe this would be like a business lunch for you, eating downtown on a weekday."

All the women in his life were going crazy. "First of all, Mor, I really don't drink much during the day. I might have a beer and one shot of schnapps at a diplomatic or business lunch as you call it, but usually not even that. I find it too hard to work in the afternoon if I drink much during the lunch hour."

"Why don't we have a beer and schnapps anyway? I promise to have just one of each." Mor was determined to do this lunch the Swedish way, or at least her perception of it.

This was not quite as Chris had envisioned lunch with his oh-so-Swedish mother. So be it. He ordered schnapps and a beer for both of them.

"Never mind. Let's talk about something more important to us both, like my children and your grandchildren. Don't you think they're pretty great?"

"They're better than that. You and Lisa are lucky to have such wonderful children. I wish I was lucky enough to share in your joy."

"Why in the world should you not be sharing in the joy?"

"Silly Boy. How in the world can you not understand, when you've kept them away from me all these years?"

"Mor, Mor. We have this discussion every time we meet. I guess you'll never understand my need to do the work I do, and that it meets my needs best when we live abroad. We started sending the boys home to you during summer vacation as soon as they were old enough, and when Missy is older we'll send her, too. I'm sorry to say that I think you're asking too much when you suggest I give up my career."

"I bet Pastor Stewart wouldn't think it was too much to ask."

Chris was still trying to digest that one when the drinks arrived. "And are my guests ready to order their meals?" The waiter graciously gave them a few more minutes to look over the menu, a high cuisine featuring many entrees unfamiliar to both. Finally they ordered a beef steak and a green salad. It was time to try the schnapps. Though Chris had advised Mor to take about half the shot glass of schnapps at one time, she sipped it. "Kära Gud!" She couldn't believe how strong it was. Her eyes watered as she took a large gulp of beer.

"That's why I suggested you take about half at a time. Schnapps is not like a southern sipping whiskey in the States."

Mor was recovering from the shock of her first sip, even beginning to look as if she might have enjoyed it. She raised the shot glass in a toast to her son. "Skål!" She emptied the glass and followed it immediately with another slug of beer. His mother was truly full of surprises today.

"What's this about Pastor Stewart, Mor? Why in the world would he agree that I should quit my work and move back to the States?" Before Mor could reply, the waiter arrived and presented their entrees with a flourish.

"We talked about it after church on Sunday," she replied once they had started on the meal. "I told him how much I miss you and Lisa and the grandchildren, and wish we could all be together. He said that it would certainly be ideal to have a family like yours living close by the grandparents."

"I'm sure he would say that. What he probably didn't tell you is that he has two daughters living in California, one with three kids and one with two. It would be ideal if they could all live in one community in California, but the fact is that one daughter lives in Sacramento, another in San Francisco, and Bill and his wife Marta live here. He and I have talked about that, about the pain of separation, but he has a calling and it's to the church. To the Lutheran church here."

"You don't have a calling."

"Of course I do. My calling isn't to the Lutheran church, but it's a calling nevertheless."

They were interrupted by the waiter, checking to see that everything was all right with their meals and drinks. More schnapps? More beer? His mother was looking so glum that Chris suggested they break the rule and split another bottle of beer.

The rest of their lunch conversation was filled up with small talk about the food and the restaurant. They had passed on dessert and were enjoying a remarkably good cup of coffee before Chris felt he had to return to that sensitive subject of work taking his family away from the grandparents. It seemed only fair to toss some kind of bone to Mor to help her feel good about this lunch she had begun with such anticipation.

"I want you to know, Mor, that I love and appreciate you very much. So do Lisa and the kids. I'm especially glad that you raised Björn and me in the church. It's given me solid ground for the marriage with Lisa and for being a parent. I think I have an idea of how you feel when we're not around you all the time. With a career like mine I can never be sure where the next assignment will be or how long it might last. One thing I can tell you for sure: Lisa and I are agreed that if we're ever separated for a long time by this crazy business I'm in, she and the kids will stay in Edmonds until we can get together again. And the same is true for when I retire. That's not really so many years away when you think about it. Then you'd have us near you all the time." He tried to push out of his mind the fact that staying on with the Agency was still a fragile proposition.

Mor smiled, almost shyly, a smile tinged with sadness. "I'll be very old by then. I'm actually feeling pretty old and tired right now. It was a wonderful lunch, but maybe you were right about the dangers of drinking during lunch. I'm ready to go home and take a nap."

Chris paid the bill. He put his mother in a taxi instead of taking her to the subway, paying the driver in advance. As he kissed Mor on the cheek and gave her a goodbye hug, he felt a special love for this mother who was criticized for her Swedish pretenses, for being too-too Swedish, but whose real being was oh-so-caring, oh-so-loving toward him, his children, Lisa, and all her family and friends. He was a lucky man in many ways.

WEDNESDAY OF HOLY WEEK
Isaiah 50:4-9a
Psalm 70

Be pleased, O God, to deliver me. (Ps. 70:1)

Chris attended a morning service at the American Church on Wednesday. Maybe he and Pastor Bill would have a moment for coffee after the service.

His mind was as far away from the service as it had ever been. This morning his thoughts dwelled on Bill Stewart, and what he could tell the pastor about his troubles. Bill couldn't help Chris ease his mind if he didn't know what was on his mind. How much should he reveal about the events that had led to the weaving of this web that ensnared him?

This was a special case. From the intelligence point of view it was a special case because Bill Stewart was a Captain in the U.S. Navy Reserve, and had done his two weeks' mandatory active duty in the office of the U.S. Military Attaché at the American Embassy in Stockholm. Through that service he was fully aware of Chris's position and knew the identities of most of the Station personnel.

But this was also a special case in a personal way, which was even more important to Chris. Nils Schmidt, the maritime shipping man Chris had met early in his time in Stockholm, owned a beautiful old sailing boat moored on Sweden's west coast. Bill Stewart had become acquainted with Nils separately from Chris. And so the two Americans, acquainted only as pastor and parishioner until then, found themselves invited to crew on Schmidt's boat during a ten-day cruise the previous summer, sailing from its west coast port into the Baltic. As the only Americans in a six-man crew, they bunked together and shared personal information they'd never have an opportunity to discuss in social settings on land.

There were only a couple dozen celebrants at the service, mostly elderly Swedes who emigrated to the United States as young people then retired in Sweden, living on their U.S. Social Security checks. When the others drifted off after the service, Pastor Stewart took Chris by the arm and led him the short distance behind the altar to his little office. An automatic coffee maker was a permanent fixture on the credenza behind his desk. The first order of business was to pour them each a cup.

"You look a little better today, Chris."

"Thanks. I feel a bit more rested."

"So you're here looking for me to give you salvation? You're questioning your faith?"

"I have questions, Bill. Of course I have questions. The older I get the more questions come, and the more difficult they are."

"So what is it that's brought you to this point?"

Here it was, Chris thought. He had to tell his pastor something, if only as a way of escaping from this situation he'd put himself into. "You'll be the first outside the family to know: Lisa is pregnant."

"That's it? Lisa is pregnant? My Dear Lord Above! Why in the world would that bring you to the point of coming and—if you'll pardon the expression— crying on my shoulder? Is Lisa sick, in danger from the pregnancy? Something wrong with the fetus? This should be a time for rejoicing, but here you are down in the dumps. I'm beginning to be seriously worried about you, my boy."

"None of the above." Chris straightened his back and sat more erect in his chair, stung by the remark about crying on Bill's shoulder. "I'm discouraged. Whenever we get together Mor reminds me of how I've hurt her by keeping the kids away, and when she heard there'd be another it gave her just one more reason to complain. It tears at me, makes me feel like I'm selfish to follow a career that keeps me overseas. She also reminds me that there's a fine job in the family towboat business in Seattle that I could have any time I want it."

"That's it? Sounds to me like you've got the world by the tail. A beautiful family, plenty of money, interesting work here and another job waiting at home that should be a fantasy for anyone loving the sea as you do. There's something you're not telling me here, my friend."

"You can't appreciate how hard it was last night when Lisa and I told the family about the pregnancy. Matthew was so mad he ran upstairs. When I went up to talk with him he accused Lisa and me of being bad parents because he and Mark have to go to school in Switzerland rather than living with us or at home in Edmonds, where they really want to be. The general message was that bad parents should figure out where babies come from and take steps not to have any more.

The only happy one of the bunch was Missy. She wants a baby sister and she'll probably be mad at us if the baby turns out to be a boy."

"Something still doesn't fit." Pastor Bill leaned back in his comfortable office chair and hoisted his feet up on a corner of the desk, already scuffed from this kind of treatment.

The moment of silence was broken by ringing of the modern, banana-shaped Ericsson telephone sitting on the pastor's desk. He answered it. "Lisa? Amazing! How did you know to catch him here? Yes, he's right across from me." He handed the phone to Chris.

"Yes, Honey. No, that's fine. Everything okay at home? Good. I'll catch a taxi up to the Embassy right now." He put the phone back down on Bill's desk.

"You can guess what that was about. Somebody didn't get my message that I was attending the service this morning. I'm expected for a meeting at the Embassy." Chris stood and moved toward the office door.

"Not so fast." The pastor jumped to his feet and blocked the way to the door. His eyes bored into Chris's.

"I suppose you'll justify running out like this as your part in keeping us all safe from Communism or whatever. Just know that I'm not fooled. There's something going on in your family that's seriously wrong. You need to share it with me, or some other trusted friend. And soon, Chris. Don't let this fester much longer."

Chris reddened, and his eyes dropped away from Bill's gaze. "I truly respect you, Bill, and I hope we can continue this conversation another time. But it's absolutely necessary that I leave right now. I'm sorry. Thanks for putting up with me."

Bill gave Chris's shoulder a squeeze with his big paw of a hand and stepped aside.

THURSDAY OF HOLY WEEK
Exodus 12:1-4 [5-10] 11-14
Psalm 116:1, 10-17

I will take the cup of salvation and call on the name of the Lord (Ps 116:11)

He had lied to Pastor Stewart about being late for a meeting at the Embassy. This lie was in addition to the several sins of omission he'd committed in talking with Bill about his problems. *Oh what a tangled web we weave, when first we practice to deceive.* Those words were on his mind as he ran the daily gauntlet of Marine Guard, Embassy receptionist, elevator, and electronic lock on the Station's office door. Peggy, the staffer who did most of his support work, greeted him normally. The call Lisa had relayed was not urgent. Peggy needed Chris's signature on some documents going to Headquarters, and simply wondered if he would be at work in time to sign and place them into the outgoing pouch.

As he sat down at his desk, Chris tried to put aside his personal problems and the routine responsibilities of the office in an effort to focus on the Plotkin pickup the next day, Good Friday. Other Station personnel were excited about the upcoming resolution of the case, discussing it at every opportunity. The surveillance team was in town. Bisan had already spent several hours with them, orienting the crew to the city and routes that would be important to this mission. Mark Noble was handling the couple who would be taking care of Plotkin's disguise and documentation and driving him out of Sweden.

Chris's last remaining task before the pickup at Drottningholm next day was a meeting with Bisan, who had signaled through coded phone messages that her briefings of the surveillance team had been successful. Now she needed his assurance that everything was in order. They would meet late this afternoon in an obscure coffee shop in Gröndal, a southern district of Stockholm not frequented by people likely to know either of them.

The meeting with Bisan proved to be surprisingly business-like, satisfactory in every way. She had carried out her assignment without a glitch and written a crisp and complete report. She did not play games or flirt as she had the last time. The chief emotion he felt in parting from her was pride. Pride in the fact that he had personally spotted, recruited and trained this young woman who was turning into a first-class support agent.

After dinner at home, Chris was pleased to learn that Mor and Lisa would be out at a bridge game that evening. With Missy in bed and the twins playing foosball in the basement game room, this was a perfect opportunity to mull over his options. The current course of events could lead to outcomes ranging from career advancement to family disaster.

He went to the kitchen to heat up some coffee left over from breakfast. While it was warming he looked in the cupboard above the stove. There he found a bottle of Remy Martin cognac, about a third full. He poured a shot, or maybe two shots of the cognac in his mug before filling it with the leftover coffee. Good thing he did. The coffee would have been undrinkable otherwise.

In the living room Chris eased into his chair, feet up on an ottoman, and rested the warm mug on his belly, thinking. The more he drank from the cup, the more his spirits sank. Half an hour later he repeated the visit to the kitchen. Little coffee remained, so he had to put more cognac into the cup to make a decent drink.

✳ ✳ ✳

Marta Stewart was awake, sitting up in bed reading another of her historical romance novels, which her husband Pastor Bill referred to as bodice-rippers or even trash literature. For all his criticism, she'd caught him more than once staring at the revealing covers on her books, and even one time found him reading a few passages. Men!

Her man was sound asleep, snoring not so gently when the bedside telephone rang, a fairly unusual event in this parish. Emergency calls after ten o'clock at night were quite common in some of the urban churches they'd served in the States, but this congregation was for the most part older, more conservative, less prone to getting themselves in trouble. She picked up the receiver quickly in hopes that the ringing hadn't disturbed Bill. "Yes? This is Marta Stewart."

"Is Pastor Stewart available?"

"He's here, but he's asleep. It's quite late. Ten thirty, in fact. May I ask who's calling?"

"Sorry, Marta, it's Chris Holbeck. Something of an emergency. I hate to wake him, but I really should talk to him tonight."

Pastor Bill was alert and already reaching for the phone. In the Navy he had experienced many late night watches and shipboard emergencies, and in his current position he had often responded to anguished calls from parishioners calling for succor at all hours. Marta mouthed Chris's name.

"What's happening, Chris? Are you okay? Is the family okay?"

There was a moment of silence before the reply came. "Yeah, I'm okay, Padre. So's the family."

"And …?" When there was no immediate reply he went on: "I'm sure you called this late for a good reason, Chris."

"To say I'm sorry." The reply was close to inaudible.

"For what?"

"For not being completely truthful with you this morning. I do have personal problems, but there are many things that make it difficult to tell you the details. I need to do that."

"You know this is one of the busiest weekends of the church season, Chris. I hope you're not talking about getting together tonight or even before the service on Sunday."

"No, no, not before Sunday. Maybe after the services on Sunday morning?"

The pastor looked at his wife, whose eyebrows were raised in question. She mouthed a message: "What's going on?" He smiled at her.

"That might be tough, Chris. We've got a bunch of people coming for dinner in the late afternoon. I'll have to check with Headquarters and let you know. Give me a call on Saturday. I'll have a better idea then."

"I'll do that. Thanks for being such a good friend, Bill. Thank you for being my pastor. Thank you, thank you." Chris hung up the phone.

Marta was curious. "What was that all about? Is he going to be okay? Do I get the idea that I'm now Headquarters?"

With a bemused expression, Bill stretched over to give her a peck on the cheek before turning his back away from her reading lamp. "I'll tell you more about it tomorrow. You know, Love of My Life, that God protects drunks and fools. I believe Chris was a little of both those things tonight. He'll be okay. Oh, yes, and you are my one and only earthly Headquarters."

GOOD FRIDAY
Isaiah 52:13-53:12
Psalm 22

My God, my God, why have you forsaken me? (Ps.22:1)

Chris and Lisa's bedroom on the top floor of their home extended across the back of the house, facing east. About five o'clock on this Good Friday morning, Chris left the bed he shared with Lisa, taking a comforter to one of the pair of overstuffed chairs next to the window. Sleep had eluded him most of the night. Now he was watching for the dawn. A little after six o'clock, a cloudless sky lit up with the promise of a beautiful day. He hoped it was the precursor of a good outcome to the case that had engulfed him too long. By sundown this night, Plotkin should be in the safe house, preparing for the journey out of Sweden.

Still unable to sleep, he arose an hour later. Showered and dressed in another half hour, he walked softly downstairs to make coffee. Breakfast would be a roll and slice of cheese eaten at his desk in the office. To his surprise, someone was in the kitchen before him. Missy was sitting quietly at the kitchen table with a bowl of cereal in front of her, a favorite picture book spread out to one side.

"What are you doing up so early, little girl? I thought you didn't have to go to lekskola today."

"I'm not a little girl anymore!" She was miffed. "I got out my own cereal and milk. I got up because I don't want to miss my radio program. Did you know there's a bear on that program who talks like Farmor?"

"Mommy told me about that. You have to be careful not to tease Farmor about that, Sweetie."

"I don't tease her. I can't even say anything about it because Mommy won't let me. I don't see why not. It's just ... it's just ..."

"Just what?"

"It's just the way it is!"

That was hard to argue with. With his coffee perked and poured, Chris tidied up after Missy and tucked her in under an afghan in the living room, waiting for her eight o'clock program. Before leaving for work he went back upstairs to waken Lisa and let her know that their daughter was now grown enough to fix her own breakfast.

Morning at the office seemed endless. Chris found it hard to focus on deskwork and business brought to him by other Station personnel. He took a mid-morning coffee break in the Embassy cafeteria, swapping sea stories with the Naval Attaché. Back in his office the clock finally ticked all the way up to noon. Time to leave for the pickup.

The first order of business was to drive into town and park on a side street in order to spend some time shopping along Götgatan, choosing the southern part of the city to check for surveillance. For lunch he bought a couple of varmkorv—Sweden's version of the American hot dog—then window-shopped for nearly an hour before going back to his car for the final leg of preparation. From there he drove into the central business district of Stockholm, then many miles west to the town of Blackeberg, where he parked briefly to buy a newspaper and take the opportunity to check further for surveillance from the viewpoint of a pedestrian. Back in the car, he headed southwest through the residential streets of Södra Ängby, then joined the last road to his destination, Drottningholmsvägen. At exactly 2:55 p.m. he arrived at a parking lot near the northwestern entrances. Plotkin was nowhere in sight.

There were two other cars in the parking lot, both empty. About five minutes after his arrival a woman came out of the woods carrying an infant in a backpack, walking toward one of the cars. Chris picked up a sandwich he'd bought while shopping and began eating it, hoping any observer would take him for a nature lover enjoying a late lunch in the park. The woman's path took her directly in front of his car. He held the sandwich to his mouth as she passed with a faint smile and nod.

Ten minutes went by with no sign of Plotkin. Twenty minutes .... When this meeting had been planned it was agreed that Chris would wait no longer than twenty minutes at the park. Sasha was certain that he'd be there at the appointed time. So certain that he wouldn't consider an alternative. "If I'm not there, you probably will never see me again," he'd told Chris.

Such a bleak prospect! Despite the agreement, Chris waited another five minutes before giving up. The other car in the lot was still empty, and he'd seen nobody after the woman left with her baby. He drove by the planned rendezvous with the surveillance team, the empty passenger seat in his car signaling a meeting at 7:30 p.m. in a small restaurant at Islandstorget with the head of the surveillance team and Bisan. Chris would drive there and park a few blocks from the restaurant, while Bisan and the surveillance team member she knew as Tom arrived separately by Tunnelbana, the Stockholm urban rail and subway line.

Chris drove directly back to the Embassy to send a report of the failed meeting to Headquarters. There was no difficulty in writing this report because there wasn't much to say. Plotkin was a "no show." The Station would do everything possible to learn what had prevented his defection.

The meeting with Bisan and Tom was predictably glum. There were no limits to the depth of Chris's disappointment, to which was added a feeling of guilt that he'd let everyone down—these two, his comrades at the Station, and all those at Headquarters whose expectations had been dashed.

Without specific directions from Headquarters, Chris ordered the team to take up a light surveillance of the Soviet Embassy and Plotkin's residence building to see if they could pick up any sign of him. Bisan was working the next morning as a guide on one of the Stockholm sightseeing boats. Given her work schedule that day, there seemed little chance of her being able to elicit any information about Sasha's travel. Despite the odds, Chris arranged to meet her at four o'clock the next afternoon, Saturday, hoping that she might have learned something. They would rendezvous in one of the Stockholm konditeris they had used before. He was tired of the super sleuthing they'd been practicing and ready to go back to a reasonable level of security precautions.

There were no other assets to help him in this case.

SATURDAY OF HOLY WEEK
Genesis 1:1-2:4a
Psalm 136:1-9, 23-36

God's mercy endures forever. (Ps. 136:1b)

Bisan was already seated with coffee when he arrived at the konditeri, wearing an expression that puzzled him. With his own coffee in hand, he joined her at the table. She had a half smile on her lips, but she looked more amazed than happy.

"Well?" he asked.

She leaned across the table to speak in a low voice. "I have good news and bad news. Which do you want first?"

Chris was annoyed. This was no time to be playing games. "Give me the bad news first."

"Just as we expected, I could get no information about your friend from my contacts today."

"So what could the good news be?"

Now Bisan smiled broadly. "Two minutes ago I found out what happened to him. To your friend."

"How could that be?"

"I'll guarantee it. Two minutes ago I learned that he left here yesterday on an evening SAS flight to Paris."

Chris was shocked. "That can't be. It just can't be. How could you sit here and learn that?"

Bisan was so excited that she was wriggling around in her seat as she pushed a copy of the Stockholm newspaper *Aftonbladet* across the table to Chris. "Someone left this newspaper on the table. I read it while I was waiting for you. Take a look at page three."

He did. There on page three was a photograph taken at Arlanda Airport the previous evening, showing the Soviet Ambassador and another Embassy officer as they were about to board an SAS flight to Paris. The accompanying article reported that the Ambassador would not comment on the purpose of the trip, but it seemed that it was in connection with multi-national discussions about Vietnam then underway.

Though not named in the caption, the man standing alongside the Ambassador was Aleksandr Elyovitch Plotkin.

EASTER DAY
Acts 10:34-43
Psalm 118:1-2, 14-24

On this day the Lord has acted; we will rejoice and be glad in it (Ps. 118:24)

On Easter morning Chris awoke with thoughts of his family and the pleasant day ahead. It had been a long time since his first thoughts of the day turned to anything but work—worries about the many bits and pieces of cases and programs that needed to come together neatly if his particular intelligence efforts were to be deemed successful. More recently those thoughts had been dominated by the Plotkin case and the horrendous personal problems that had ensued.

But today was today. Ever since filing last night's report to Headquarters about Plotkin's departure with the Soviet Ambassador, since releasing the support teams to return to their home territory, he felt a burden had been lifted. Logic told him that the burden would be heavier rather than lighter in the future. There would be a lot explaining to do and a lot of Monday morning quarterbacking by Headquarters.

Logic be damned! Today was today and he was going to enjoy every minute of it.

* * *

Lisa had sensed a change in Chris when he returned home on Saturday from the meeting with Bisan. Mor and Missy were already in bed when he came in to find his wife playing a wild game of Monopoly with the boys. With Chris sitting alongside as the game wound down and joining in the laughter and fun, Lisa began to think that Plotkin must have shown up someplace and defected after all.

It was puzzling to learn from Chris—once they were all in bed and the two of them were talking in low voices—that Plotkin was gone. Gone to Paris. It didn't make sense that her husband would appear relaxed and happy after what had happened to his plans. Everything was left up in the air, unsettled. How could he be more relaxed? He didn't know.

She asked him again this Easter Sunday morning as they lay comfortably in bed, thinking about getting up.

"Odd, isn't it?" he said. "You're right, I do feel much better today than I have in weeks. Somehow the Plotkin thing feels done, over. That must seem silly to you, considering all we've been through and what I'm going to have to deal with after this fiasco with Plotkin. But what can Headquarters say? I reported all the specifics of the case honestly. I provided all the information he gave us. We'll do everything we can to figure out what prevented Sasha from defecting. Beyond that there isn't much to do, except to see if he turns up someplace or we get news of him through other sources."

Chris reached his arm out for Lisa. She scooted over to his side of the bed as he turned to embrace her. "The most important thing now is that you and I stick together completely. You never saw Plotkin except during his visits here and at Palmstjerna's. We're going to have another wonderful child who will be a blessing to the family, a little girl."

Lisa pulled back, the better to see Chris's face. "What do you mean a little girl? We don't know that!"

"It's got to be a little girl."

"What makes you say that? It doesn't 'got to be' anything but another healthy, bright, delightful child in the Holbeck family."

"Nope. We have to have another girl this time."

Lisa was beginning to catch on that Chris's sense of humor was returning. "Okay, Mr. Know-It-All, what's your story this time?"

"I know Missy well enough to have figured out that her life will be ruined if she doesn't get the baby sister she's counting on. She'll grow up to be a miserable teenager, probably drop out of school and never get a job, and she'll be living with us for the rest of our lives. You've got to have a girl!"

Lisa picked up her pillow and started hitting him with it. "You (bash) are (bash) something (bash) else (bash)."

Soon Chris was using his own pillow in defense. They were having such a good time with their pillow fight that they didn't hear the knocking on their bedroom door. Mark opened the door with Matthew right behind him. They both looked worried.

"What's going on here?" they asked in chorus.

"Are you guys seriously trying to kill each other?" Mark continued. "You woke us up with all that noise." The boys' expressions showed they wanted to believe this was all in fun, but weren't at all sure.

"Sorry, boys, we were just settling who's going to fix breakfast." Lisa tried to get her nightgown back into a place more suitable for viewing by her children. "I won. Your dad's going to make pancakes while the rest of us get all dolled up for Easter Sunday. Stick your heads in Missy's and Farmor's rooms, will you, and tell them it's time to rise and shine."

When the boys were gone, Chris took her in his arms for a real embrace. "I don't remember that you won."

"Doesn't matter much because you're going to fix breakfast anyway. You don't take long to dress. I've got to get myself and Missy ready, and you know Mor takes forever." With that she pulled her nightgown up and off, deliberately wagging her hips as she walked to the bathroom to shower.

✻ ✻ ✻

Somehow they made it to church on time. Somehow, as he often did, Pastor Bill seemed to have prepared the sermon especially for Chris. All the parishioners connected in a similar way to the sermons of this truly talented and deeply spiritual church leader. As in all the Easter services back through his many years, Chris once again heard the story—the truth, he believed—of the rebirth of Christ and the promise of rebirth for those who believe. But this year was different. This Easter he felt truly reborn, and in truth, he was.

When Pastor Bill said goodbye to the Holbeck family in the church entry, he and Chris exchanged meaningful eye contact and a handshake that was even heartier than usual. "You are looking very good today, Chris, very good indeed. I'm pleased to see you all looking so happy and well." Nothing was said about their telephone conversation on Thursday.

"I'm feeling that way, Pastor, and your good sermon helped seal it. Thanks!"

Dinner, preceded by an Easter egg hunt in the Holbeck yard, was a shared affair that included the Rex and Millie Jones family along with their children, another couple and some unattached staff people from the Embassy. A card table placed at the end of their dining room table allowed room for fifteen people to gather around a sumptuous feast put together by Lisa, Mor and Millie Jones—ham, meatloaf and au gratin potatoes respectively. Then the games began, rounding out a truly fine day.

Later that night in bed, Lisa said, "The day was everything I hoped. Do you think—"

"Yes," Chris said, giving her shoulder a squeeze. "I believe we can move on, now."

As usual Lisa slipped off into dreamland before Chris. As he lay there enjoying his memories of the day, a thought occurred to him that he felt might be sacrilegious. Then again, maybe not.

It was great to be reborn.

CHAPTER TWENTY-ONE

On May 15, 1969, U.S. Marine Major Björn Holbeck was killed in action during an operation known as Oklahoma Hills, southwest of Da Nang in Quang Nam Province. In a letter from the regimental commander, his parents learned that his death came as he was trying to rescue a sergeant wounded in an earlier round of fire. Chris flew to the States for his brother's heartrending funeral service, spending a few days in Edmonds consoling his family.

* * *

On November 2, 1969, a baby girl was born to Lisa and Chris Holbeck. At a weight of five pounds, four ounces, she might have been premature but was not. In fact, she was born almost exactly nine months from conception in a shabby apartment in Gamlastan. Chris and Lisa christened her Lisbet Maria Holbeck, and took pains to make sure that their friends knew how much they fussed over their little "premature" baby.

* * *

On June 1, 1970, Chris Holbeck received notice that he was being transferred to service in Vietnam. The family was not permitted to accompany him. During what would be a two-year tour, they could remain in Sweden, live at their home leave point in the States, or move to Bangkok, where more frequent visits would be possible. They decided to move the family to Edmonds, where Chris enjoyed a brief vacation before flying to Vietnam in mid-July.

PART THREE

CHAPTER TWENTY-TWO

Four Years Later
Thursday, November 9,1972

As the SAS flight from Washington approached Copenhagen, Chris looked out from his window seat at the cloud cover expected during this time of year. Sleep had eluded him during most of the flight. In less than an hour, about seven o'clock in the morning, he would be taking the long walk at Kastrup Airport, the long walk leading up to the first of the lies he would be telling in the next few days. The long walk up to entry procedures—passport control and customs.

"And what brings you to Copenhagen, Mr. Holbeck?" the officer at the control booth would ask as he leafed through Chris's passport. He had marked "pleasure" on the immigration card as his reason for entering Denmark.

Another question on the immigration card asked for the name and address of the hotel where the visitor planned to stay. Chris marked that as "unknown." He planned to tell the passport control officer that he'd be looking for a hotel after going through the entry procedures and would first of all try to get into the SAS Hotel in Copenhagen. With few tourists coming to Denmark in November, it shouldn't be hard to find a room there.

Whatever happened, once off the plane he needed to be at top form. He swiveled his head back and forth, trying to ease the tension in his neck muscles. After using the toilet facilities to brush his teeth and accepting a last cup of coffee from the stewardess, he felt more ready to deal with the assignment.

Passport control was a breeze. The control officer was a smiling, friendly fellow who was much interested in the visa stamps in Chris's passport. He flipped back and forth through the pages, enough to piece together an assignment to

Vietnam of about two years, with occasional leaves in the U.S.

"You must be military, then? In Vietnam?" The question was far from hostile. Quite a few Danes favored the U.S. position on Vietnam.

"No, I was a civilian." Chris was hoping he wouldn't have to elaborate on that.

"I see." As he said that, the officer pulled out a watch list book, opened it to a page that apparently held the "H's," and ran his finger down the page.

"Ah yes, I see!" The officer's smile was broader still. "Have a wonderful time in Denmark, Mr. Holbeck." He stamped an entry into the passport and handed it back to Chris, who had no trouble interpreting this. His Agency affiliation was well known to the European security services, most of which were friendly to the U.S. The passport officer saw nothing sinister in a CIA officer entering Denmark, but the entry would be reported to the Danish security people. Chris didn't think they would relay that information to the Swedes. He certainly hoped not.

After picking up his single piece of luggage, he found the customs control point to be easier still. Customs cards had been filled out by all passengers on the plane, stating whether or not they had anything to declare such as money, liquor or cigarettes beyond the limits allowed, or agricultural products banned for import. Along with most other passengers, Chris stated he had nothing to declare and walked through the green entry sign designated for these people. At the ground transportation area on a sidewalk outside the airport, he was met by a vicious wind, blowing dust around passengers waiting for taxis and hotel shuttles.

Chris was headed for a bus that carried passengers directly to the Copenhagen docks for boarding a hydrofoil boat to Sweden's southernmost city of Malmö. Travelers using this means to reach Sweden would be crossing the Öresund, the body of water between the North and Baltic Seas. Chris had experienced the smooth ride of hydrofoils in good weather. He wondered what kind of ride the passengers would have today in the growing wind and rough water not uncommon to the Öresund.

Before buying a ticket and boarding the bus, Chris tore the SAS tags and his own identification tag off the luggage. From here on he would speak nothing but Swedish. He knew there was a rather desultory customs control on arrival in Sweden, with immigration officers on hand to check passengers who declared themselves as not being Scandinavian. He expected no problems passing himself off on that end as a Swede.

By eleven thirty on this Thursday morning, Chris found himself on the most uncomfortable boat ride of his life. There had been some question whether or not the hydrofoil would depart on time in the nasty little storm that had blown up in such short order, but at the last minute the skipper hurried people aboard. It was a rough trip and a long hour before a bedraggled bunch of passengers got off the hydrofoil in Malmö. The only look most of them got from Swedish customs and immigration officials was one of sympathy.

A very short taxi ride took Chris to the main railway station in Malmö, where he bought a first class ticket for Stockholm. A one o'clock departure would get him into Stockholm in the early evening. Now he was full into it. The operation was underway.

CHAPTER TWENTY-THREE

Chris stayed in his seat on the train rather than using the dining car, ordering a ham and cheese sandwich and a beer. Toward the end of the journey from Malmö, the food and drink, together with a comfortable train ride, combined to help him sleep—a deep and dreamless sleep. He was awakened by a slowing of the train, accompanied by the clanking of couplings between cars. They were passing through Stockholm suburbs just a few minutes from the destination. He started gathering his gear. Slowly. He intended to be last off the train in order to observe the other passengers. The chances of his being followed at this point were close to nil, but good habits make for good operational security.

Yesterday afternoon, DC time, there had been an exchange of "eyes only" cables between Headquarters and Stockholm COS Norm Wykowski, setting up a first meeting between Wykowski and Chris. As of the last cable before Chris flew out of DC, Wykowski was still searching but not making a commitment for a safe house where Chris might stay in Stockholm. He wrote that he was considering a couple of possibilities that he would review with Chris when they met in Stockholm. Their meeting was scheduled as a car pickup outside Åhléns City Department Store on Klarabergsgatan. Wykowski would make the first pass at 8:30 p.m. and pass twice more at ten-minute intervals. If Chris hadn't shown up by then, he would give up and go home to await a phone call.

It was only four blocks from the central train station to Åhléns, an easy walk with the light luggage Chris was able to carry with a strap over his shoulder. Though the train arrived exactly on time, Chris missed Wykowski's first pass. He had dawdled too long getting off the train and double-checking for surveillance. The second pass was successful. He saw Norm driving a black Volvo similar to the one he had used in Stockholm.

After a brief exchange of family news, Chris got down to the nuts and bolts of their meeting. "So, Norm, what wondrous luxury apartment have you arranged for me tonight?"

"You might be surprised" was the answer.

"Surprise me."

Wykowski gave him an address on Grevgatan. It sounded familiar.

"That sounds like the address of our support agent Bisan. I checked at Headquarters and was told that she made good on her threat to refuse further contact after I left for Vietnam."

"Almost true." Norm was driving aimlessly in the northern residential suburbs of Stockholm now, using their time together in the car to make whatever arrangements would take them through tomorrow, Friday, just a couple of days before the scheduled meeting with Plotkin.

"What does 'almost' mean?"

"After you went to Vietnam I realized what a gap that left us, losing Bisan. I figured an older guy like me might be able to get around her objections, so I called and set up a lunch meeting. She's delightful, isn't she? I presume you kept your hands off her during the time she was your agent. It must have been hard. So to speak."

"Yes. And yes. But ..."

"She turned me down on helping us out again. But she was willing to see me every three or four months for lunch, just to keep in touch. What that really meant was that she wanted to hear what was happening with you. I told her that you continued on in Vietnam, going home to see your family every few months. Outside of my charming personality and good looks, I'm sure getting news of you was what kept her seeing me.

If it hadn't been so dark, Wykowski would have seen Chris reddening. "You know, I thought we'd settled that just before the Plotkin case went south. Remember that she insisted on being run by me and not Mark Noble? The first meeting when I picked her up again was in her apartment. I thought she was coming on to me and made the mistake of saying something about it. She made it clear in no uncertain terms: what interest would a young woman like her have in an older married man, one who has children and is obviously settled down?"

Norm was reversing his course, turning around and heading the car back toward town. "I didn't think you were that naïve."

"What's naïve?" Chris was insulted. "What's naïve about that? Either a woman is interested in you or she isn't. Bisan made it very clear that she respected me as a professional in my field and as a ... man. I almost said 'father figure,' and I think it's likely that's what it was. Did you know she lost her father when she was just a little girl?"

"Well, Chris, women remain a mystery to me as they do to most men. You may be right, but I'm not so sure. From what you told me of the tensions between you and Lisa over this mission, and this situation where you're going to be alone with a young, attractive woman who thinks the world of you for whatever reason, you're going to be facing some real temptations. Let me give you five short words of advice. Keep it in your pants."

"Not to worry, Norm, I can handle it. Let's hope her needs are being met by someone else, which brings me to questions about the apartment. Is her aunt still alive? Does she still keep the apartment pretty much to herself to satisfy the aunt? Does she have a boyfriend?"

"It's yes, to all the above. The aunt is totally bedridden now. Bisan does have a boyfriend who sounds like a good match for her. He's first officer on one of the Danish Maersk Line ships. We're in luck that he sailed just a couple of weeks ago on a trip to Thailand. He does stay overnight sometimes in the apartment, but according to Bisan she still doesn't use it for big parties and only once in a while for casual visits by girlfriends. A lot of us are better off because of Bisan. Her aunt gets to keep the apartment and Bisan gets a great place to live. Her mariner boyfriend has a fine girl to come home to. I imagine that both their needs are met, as you suggested. And we get to use the apartment for a few days."

"How did Headquarters react when you asked that Bisan be cleared again?"

"I didn't ask."

"Seriously? You didn't ask?"

"There wasn't time. As far as I understand, we have carte blanche to run this operation in whatever way it's going to work. Headquarters has put a lot of responsibility on us, and I think this is a good time to tell you the ground rules." Wykowski was circling the northern suburbs, buying more time before he delivered Chris to the safe house.

"I understood I had mostly a free rein here."

"I understood that, too, but don't forget that you're in my territory. You're a good operator and I trust you more than most, but think about the fact that you'd have been up a tree if I hadn't arranged a safe house for you. You need me, and I need you not to screw up our position here. I don't want you doing anything outside that safe house without clearing it with me first. That begins with my telling you that you won't be stepping a foot out of that apartment before Saturday."

"You can't be serious."

"I'm dead serious. Have you thought about how you're going to get Plotkin out of Sweden if he wants to defect? What kind of documentation and other support you can get to carry the operation forward, however it turns out?"

"I know that whatever it might be will have to come through you."

"So let's understand each other, Chris. You can take all the credit you want if this operation is successful, but while you're here in Sweden, I'm still your Chief of Station and I'll be calling the shots." In the dim light of the streetlamps, Wykowski noted Chris's glum expression.

"Cheer up, Chris, you've got to know there's no way you could carry it off all by yourself. My first worry when this came up on the screen was how we'd ever get Plotkin out of Sweden without alerting the Swedes and doing further damage to our relations with the country. I started working on that right away, and I have a solution I think you'll like."

With that, Wykowski turned the car once more toward Grevgatan and briefed Chris on the plan he'd developed. At first hearing, it seemed wildly impossible to carry off, but as they talked Chris became more and more intrigued. The plan could be successful and personally exciting at the same time. The main problem for Chris was that it would keep him cooped up in Bisan's apartment until noon on Saturday, with nothing to do but read and watch TV—if Bisan had a TV set. Chris couldn't remember from his one earlier visit if there was a TV in the apartment. If so, he hoped the government-controlled programs had improved a lot during the couple of years he'd been gone.

CHAPTER TWENTY-FOUR

Where is he? Where in *Hell* is he?

Bisan was prowling around her apartment like a jungle cat in heat. She smiled to herself at the thought. She'd been told that Chris would be coming not long after nine o'clock, and now it was almost ten.

Ever since having coffee with Mr. Wykowski yesterday afternoon she'd felt an awakening. Not that she was in love with Chris Holbeck. Never that. He'd misunderstood her mood that one time. She made it clear to him that there was nothing like *that*. He was much too old and already married with children. Much too old. Not bad looking, though. It was hard to understand some of the feelings she had when she was with Chris, feelings that welled up right behind her breastbone and made her all funny inside. Bisan put a lot of thought to that during the time Chris was gone from Sweden. She decided it was because of their clandestine arrangements, their meetings in places like Malmö, Uppsala, Gothenberg, even Copenhagen. Funny it had never been the same with Mark Noble. She sneaked around with him, too, but she never got to the point of feeling as comfortable as she did with Chris. Mr. Wykowski was definitely old. She was comfortable with him, but then their arrangement wasn't really clandestine, just a quiet lunch together once in a while.

Where is he?

With lights dimmed in the apartment she adjusted Venetian blinds on windows looking out on Grevgatan to where she could look down through the mostly-closed slats to see the street. Traffic was scarce this time of night.

Then she saw him walking fast, a bag hung over one shoulder. She'd recognize that walk anywhere. She ran to the intercom on the inside of the hall door, ready to press the release button the instant he buzzed her apartment. When the signal came she released the lock immediately, not giving him a chance to speak into the monitor in the front hall of the building. Standing by the door, she could hear the elevator called down to the ground floor, then ascend. Her heart was pounding.

Bisan, Bisan, she told herself, *you're acting like a fourteen-year-old school girl.*

With one eye glued to the peephole, she waited and listened as the elevator passed her floor on its way up. Now what? Still she watched and listened. A few moments later she could hear the stairway door open. There was Chris in front of her door. She opened it before he could press the bell. She should have known the delay was due to Chris's obsession with operational security. He had taken the elevator to a higher floor and walked down, "just in case." In her time working with him he was often unable to answer her question: "In case of what?" She teased him: "You see spooks everywhere." He'd smile with that crooked grin she liked so much: "That way the boogey man doesn't catch us."

Not wanting any more accusations of messing with his hormones, she was dressed modestly for the occasion in a yellow wool bathrobe—demure and belted high—moccasins on her feet hiding the painted toenails. Her makeup was simply a pinkish lipstick put on an hour earlier then refreshed thirty minutes later when she noticed that biting her lip had worn most of it off.

In one motion Chris slipped the bag off his shoulder, closed the door with a back kick, and gave Bisan a big hug that he obviously meant not to overdo in strength or duration. Bisan knew he was truly glad to see her again, that he really cared about her. She thought of the times—every six weeks or so—when her Danish mariner friend Peter Nielsen showed up at the door. The hug would be longer. She'd stand on his feet and he'd walk her into the bedroom, where they would frantically tear at each others' clothes until they reached nirvana.

Still, her fourteen-year-old heart was pounding. Somehow she had to separate these two different kinds of feelings—the intense physical and romantic sensations aroused by Peter and the heart-pounding excitement of change, of the unknown, of the challenges and dangers that came along with Chris. And, she thought ruefully, she had to quench some physical and romantic reactions that arrived with him, too. It must be the romance of spying that kept these forbidden ideas surfacing.

His arm was draped around her shoulder as they walked into the living room, quite generous in size by Stockholm standards, small for a U.S. apartment. There was just enough room for a sofa, two armchairs, a coffee table and an occasional table against one wall, all close together. Besides the living area there was a bathroom, a small bedroom, and a tiny kitchen.

As if suddenly realized the intimacy of having his arm around her, Chris dropped it and asked to use the bathroom. Afterwards he peeked into her bedroom, walked into the kitchen, then stood in the living room carefully looking around.

"Looks like you're—what do you call it?—casing the joint," Bisan said, as she arranged a couple of beers and some snacks on the coffee table.

"You're right. That's just what I'm doing. I want you to know, Bisan, how much we—how much I, personally—appreciate your taking us in this way. I don't know what Norm told you about why I'm here. Sasha Plotkin, the guy you were looking for on the night boat to Helsinki when I was here before, is back in town or will be soon. I'm meeting him on Sunday. This is a very sensitive operation. There are few people at our headquarters who know about it, and here it's only Norm, you and I. So we can't let any information at all slip out."

He sat at the end of the sofa. Bisan was in the armchair. She slid the tray with beer and snacks over toward him and raised her glass. "Skål! Welcome. Norm Wykowski gave me some idea of that, although he didn't tell me it would be Sasha Plotkin we'd be looking for again. What he didn't make clear was how long you'd be here."

"That's because we just don't know. The first thing is that I'm going to be staying here all day and night tomorrow. Norm doesn't want me sticking my head out of this apartment except when it's absolutely necessary. I need to avoid being seen by somebody who knew me when I was living here. I'll be going out for a few hours on Saturday during the day and then again on Sunday afternoon. That's when we'll know if Sasha will be coming back here with me."

"Back here? Mr. Wykowski didn't tell me anything about that!"

"We don't know what Plotkin wants. But if he wishes to defect, he'll need someplace to hide until we can get him out of the country. He'll have to be here a few hours at least, maybe even a couple of days."

With that, Bisan took a deep pull on her beer. "Where would we put him? I don't have room for two men in this little apartment!"

"Where were you planning on my sleeping?"

"I thought you could sleep in my bed and I'd sleep on the sofa. But if there are going to be two of you it's going to be awkward. The one bed in the house is big enough for two, but I can't think of any good combination for the three of us. Can you?"

"I can't think of anything acceptable to everybody," he replied with a smile. "Whatever happens I'm not going to let you sleep on the sofa. I'll sleep in this room until Sunday. If Sasha comes we'll figure out something, even if it means my sleeping on the floor. I've done enough camping out that I can handle that."

They came to agreement that Bisan would stay in her bedroom and Chris would sleep on the sofa. They'd cross the Plotkin bridge when and if they came to it. Another half hour of chitchat went by quickly as Bisan told him about her Danish boyfriend Peter, and Chris told her about his family.

Bedtime. Bisan brought a pillow and comforter for the sofa. She excused herself to use the bathroom first, then told Chris she'd be up at 7:30 a.m. to go to work. After work she was going out with girlfriends. "Pub crawling, or whatever you call it. I won't be home until late. Sorry to leave you home alone all day and evening. You'll find plenty of food in the icebox and cupboards. Just help yourself."

It was difficult for Chris to sleep. The sofa was six inches too short to allow lying full length, leaving three options—curling up in an awkward fetal position, lying with his feet propped on the low armrest, or resting his head at a painful angle on the other armrest. A frustrating hour of experimentation left him sleepless and in the head-on-armrest position. The bedroom door opened. He closed his eyes almost shut to make Bisan think he was asleep, but could still see as she swung the bathroom door open and turned on the light. In the flash before the door closed he could see she was wearing only panties and a short, sheer top. After the toilet flushed, she stood in the doorway looking in his direction. Her figure was silhouetted against the light for the moment before she returned to her bedroom.

The rest of the night was still more difficult. Chris was tormented by thoughts of the difficulties with Lisa and plans for the case ahead. Perhaps even more by that last glance of Bisan's figure, provocatively lit from behind. Sleep wouldn't come. The last time he checked his watch it was 4:10 a.m. Finally exhaustion overtook him.

Chris barely stirred as Bisan dressed and left for work. Rising at nine o'clock, he faced one of the worst days of his career. Inactivity was always hard. People seemed to think that the CIA offered nonstop excitement, but in truth most of his days were taken up with paperwork; the heart-stopping activities were a small part of it. To wake up knowing you would be cooped up by yourself for twenty-four hours in an unfamiliar apartment with nothing to do but wait—now that was boredom!

He found coffee already brewed in the kitchen and fixed himself a simple breakfast. The only reading material he'd brought with him from the States was a paperback mystery finished and left on the plane in Copenhagen. His salvation lay in the many reading materials in the apartment, from Swedish periodicals and novels to a nice collection of American literature. Watching Swedish TV on an old black-and-white set was far from satisfying, especially at a volume low enough to be undetectable in the adjoining apartments.

After many hours of reading, Chris heated up a simple dinner of meat and vegetables Bisan had left for him in the refrigerator. He went to bed (if the sofa could be called that) at nine o'clock, this time facing away from the bathroom door. He didn't need more temptation. Convinced that going to sleep would be nearly impossible, he was nevertheless in dreamland when Bisan came in quietly about midnight. The sound of a key in the door awoke him. Once again he feigned sleep while she very quietly got ready for bed and used the bathroom. Eventually he drifted off to sleep again.

CHAPTER TWENTY-FIVE

Saturday, November 11, 1972

Saturday morning began early. At six thirty Chris swung into a sitting position on the couch, the comforter draped over his shoulders. He was on his way to relieve his bladder when Bisan breezed past with a cheery "good morning," beating him to the bathroom. Fortunately it was a matter of moments before she reemerged in her yellow robe, face shiny from a quick morning wash, hair casually brushed back. She looked about seventeen years old. Chris grabbed the clothes he'd laid out for the day and headed for the bathroom, keeping the comforter wound around him to hide the fact that he was wearing only jockey shorts.

"You want some breakfast?" Bisan looked as cheery as her "good morning" had sounded.

"Sure, thanks. You seem awful happy for someone who got so little sleep. Why are you up so early?"

"What? Are you checking up on me? I thought you were asleep when I came in last night. People my age don't need as much sleep as certain older people."

"Touché."

"What are your plans for the day?" Bisan said as she moved about the kitchen, opening and closing cupboard doors, searching the refrigerator shelves.

Chris felt silly standing by the bathroom door, the comforter still draped around him, clothes over one arm. "I'll tell you when I finish in there."

Twenty minutes later he'd brushed his teeth, shaved, and was dressed in his travel clothes. Nothing fancy was required for the afternoon with Norm Wykowski. He followed the aroma of bacon to the kitchen, where Bisan was fixing a typical American breakfast. Better than that, she was making plättar, the dollar-sized thin pancakes, one of his mother's most successful Swedish recipes.

"My favorite! Thank you. I only get those when my mother is around."

"I hope these are up to her standards. They should be. My own mother is a very good traditional Swedish cook, and I think she got me started making plättar when I was about five years old. So what is it you're going to do today?" She gestured for him to sit at the kitchen table as she laid out trays of plättar and bacon, a pitcher of orange juice and a thermos jug of coffee. The day was definitely starting out better than yesterday.

"What a treat! The first thing I'm going to do is enjoy this wonderful breakfast. I have to wait until close to noon before I leave to meet Norm Wykowski."

"What are you and Mr. Wykowski going to be doing?"

"We'll be setting up things for a meeting with Plotkin. If he shows up—and I think he will—the most likely scenario is that he'll want to defect. It will probably take us a couple of days to arrange the best way to get him out of the country."

Bisan said, "I'm going out myself in about a half hour. One of my favorite jobs. A posh British group rented a limousine for a few hours and wants a good English-speaking guide besides the driver. I really enjoy showing off the city that way—lots more fun than guiding on a bus—and the tips are usually good. To tell you the truth, I've missed the small salary you were giving me when we worked together. What time will you be back?"

"Quite late, I think."

"What's quite late?"

"I really don't know, but probably sometime between eight o'clock and midnight."

Bisan went over to a chest of drawers, pulled out the top one, and reached into the back to fetch a ring of keys. "I'm not going out this evening, but you'd better have keys to let yourself in on the chance that I'm asleep when you get back. This one opens the door downstairs, and this one gets you in the apartment door."

A delicious breakfast. Chatting away with a good-looking young woman in cozy surroundings. Looking forward to a day of adventure. This was more like it. Thoughts of Lisa and the children hovered at the edge of his consciousness, but he let them drift away. Time enough for that when this case was resolved.

After breakfast he helped Bisan clean up the kitchen and went to the door with her when she was leaving. She surprised him with a brief hug and quick peck on the cheek. "Good luck!" And she was gone.

This morning's wait was much easier than the boredom of yesterday because of the action to come. At eleven forty-five Chris hit the street, walking briskly up Grevgatan as if it were his morning stroll. He crossed Karlavägen and kept heading north on a quiet, weekend street. Five minutes later a brief blast of the horn on Norm's Volvo alerted him to the pickup. The car had barely stopped before Chris jumped in, on the way to this new adventure.

"You ever been in the Stockholm Archipelago before?" Norm, dressed as casually as Chris, was aiming the Volvo north, along the Baltic coast.

"A couple of times. When Bill Stewart and I crewed on Nils Schmidt's boat that summer, he dropped us off at Sandhamn at the end of the cruise. Bill and I came back to Stockholm on a passenger boat. I wasn't real impressed with the Archipelago. It's pretty, but not much compared to our San Juan Islands in Puget Sound. Ever been there? I bet you didn't know that there are more than one hundred seventy islands in the San Juans."

"I've been there, and it's pretty spectacular. But I bet you didn't know there are twenty-five thousand islands in the Stockholm Archipelago."

"You're kidding!"

"Not at all. And I hope you don't try to make comparisons like that while we're with Nils today. This is a huge favor he's willing to do for us. A huge favor."

"You know I wouldn't do that, Norm. Have you ever seen or been aboard the *Valhalla*?"

"Never, but I've seen pictures. She's an old boat, isn't she?"

"Very old. What they call a 'Colin Archer.' Colin Archer was a famous Norwegian shipbuilder who built the Fram, the ship that sailed to both the north and south poles. But he's also known for building very safe pilot and life boats that saved a lot of lives in the late 1800s, and he built many fine yachts. Some of them are still sailing and even winning prizes in long-distance races. I think the *Valhalla* was built around the turn of the century. Besides superb maintenance that's kept her in Bristol condition, the main changes have been to put in a Volvo diesel auxiliary that drives her about seven knots, and a whole bunch of electronics."

The two men rode in a comfortable silence for most of the forty-five minutes it took them to get to the town of Östanå, to board a ferry for the short trip to Ljusterö, one of the larger islands in the Archipelago and a jumping off place for many Swedes who own summer homes in the islands. The plan was for Schmidt to pick them up at a small port on the east coast of Ljusterö, taking them in his private boat to the island where his was the only home. He'd been planning to winterize the house this weekend until Norm Wykowski met with him to make the proposal they'd refine today. Schmidt thought their best chance for a lengthy and secure meeting with Chris would be on what amounted to a deserted island amid a chain of other islands that were nearly deserted at this time of year.

Their host was waiting on the dock when they arrived, feet dangling over the side, a Greek-style fisherman's cap pushed far back on his full shock of white hair. Chris knew that the Swede had to be in his early sixties, but an athletic build and agility made him seem at least ten years younger. Once on his feet he put his heels together, bowed slightly from the waist and extended his hand for a formal greeting. This shipping tycoon had not lost his old world manners.

"How the hell have you been, Chris? Thank God you're back safely from Vietnam!" He went from the handshake to putting an arm around Chris's shoulder, then patting him on the back and aiming him at their island transport. "Come along, Norm. I saw you already on Thursday, but I haven't seen this chap for years."

"I know, I know, Nils. It's good to have him back."

The boat taking them to Nils' summer home was a 1930s vintage Chris Craft runabout, a twenty-footer nearly identical to a boat kept at his family's summer home on Lake Sammamish, east of Seattle. "I can't believe it, Nils. What are you doing with my boat here? I'm surprised to see you running it in the Baltic." He told Schmidt about the Holbeck family boat and that he'd always considered these runabouts to be lake boats.

"In the summer this part of the Baltic is more like a lake than like a sea. I took her out of the boathouse today to give the old girl some exercise before real winter sets in. We'll see how the weather goes. If it's rough later in the day we'll leave this beauty at the island and come back in a utility boat. Would you like to drive us out there?"

Chris was delighted to accept the offer. With Schmidt giving directions, he steered in a southeasterly direction over glass-smooth waters, reveling in the way the boat ran at some thirty-five miles an hour, the way it hunkered down in the turns. The lowering sky threatened worse weather later in the day. Approaching the end of the twenty-minute trip, Chris looked astern at the beautiful arc of the boat's wake as they cut through a narrow slot between two low-lying islands and aimed toward Schmidt's home. The scene would remain with him forever: dark gray water fading into light gray sky, framed by almost identical green islands bisected by the curve of the boat's travel.

As they approached Schmidt's island Chris saw a major feature that made it attractive for boating life—a snug harbor on the east side with a hook of land from the south that allowed a narrow entrance and protected the cove. Schmidt aimed him at a three-bay boathouse with an open door on one of the bays. They drifted into the slot for the Chris Craft, which had powered slings to raise it out of the water for storage.

"We'll leave her in the water until it's time to go back. That's the boat we'll use if it's too rough for this one." Schmidt pointed to a gray boat with a small cabin forward and long afterdeck, utilitarian but well kept. The third bay was empty, waiting, Schmidt told them, for a power cruiser being built for him in Florida.

Leaving the boathouse, they walked on a switchback path leading to family living quarters, perched atop the island in a position fully exposed to the weather, allowing views in all directions. The house was large, more modestly furnished than Chris had expected given Schmidt's wealth. It had an open beamed, plain wood construction on the interior, with many windows to take advantage of the views, most of them shuttered at this time of year. Upstairs, their host told them, were a couple of bathrooms and sleeping quarters, including two dormitory rooms with several bunks in each. "One is marked 'Boys' and the other 'Girls,' " Schmidt said, "but in the face of today's society, my wife and I have given up trying to police who sleeps where when we have visitors."

The downstairs was mostly taken up by a single great room, furnished with a couple of sofas and several occasional chairs and tables, well-used almost to the point of shabbiness. Other than a small toilet room, the only apparent concession to luxury was a modern kitchen furnished with every device a devoted chef might want. Chris remembered that cooking on the trip aboard the *Valhalla* had been rotated among the crew members, and that the crew looked forward to the days the skipper took charge of the galley. True to that memory, Schmidt headed directly to the kitchen, where a table had been set for three. In minutes he had produced a variety of open-faced sandwiches—smörgås—taken from the refrigerator and placed on the table along with bottles of beer and a frosted bottle of schnapps from the freezer.

The Station Chief had only a rudimentary knowledge of Swedish, and Schmidt's command of English was excellent, so they spoke only in that language for most of the day. Lunch talk began with the guests' insistence that in light of the important business they had to conduct, they could only afford to drink one shot of schnapps. Schmidt playfully told them he would not consider the proposal they were making unless they agreed to two shots. How else could they consider such a serious matter in a properly relaxed atmosphere? Besides, they would be there several hours and he had plenty of coffee to serve after lunch. The two Americans pretended reluctance before they happily agreed, and lunch conversation stayed in a light vein with the host talking mostly about Swedish history and life in the Archipelago.

When lunch was finished they settled with coffee on the south side of the great room in front of the tall windows, unshuttered and offering sweeping views of other islands in the Archipelago. Chris deferred to the Station Chief to begin planning the operation that would extract Plotkin from Sweden. If, indeed, Plotkin wanted to leave. If, indeed, Plotkin showed up at the meeting tomorrow. It was all very iffy, but at the heart of any successful operation was a plan that covered all contingencies.

"First," Wykowski began, "we want to thank you for even considering becoming involved in this operation. There's no way I can minimize the risk to you if we go through with it. Nils, you know far better than I the possible consequences of being caught smuggling a foreign national out of the country."

"Yes, yes." Schmidt waved one hand impatiently. "I've thought my way through all that. I've survived a few scrapes in my business life, and those taught me that the way to avoid more scrapes is to plan carefully. Let's plan!"

"Okay, here we go. You should know that the only people in Sweden who are currently aware of this operation are the three of us and the keeper of the safe house where Plotkin will be stashed until we can move him. We assign code names for ourselves and people like you, and I've been employing very secure communication channels due to the sensitivity of this case. Anytime a Soviet intelligence officer defects to us in a third country we have to be very careful that the Soviets don't get wind of it early and try to snatch him back, or that the third country security services don't save them the trouble."

"What's this third country? Are you talking about Sweden? You know how I feel about the current Swedish government. That son of a bitch Olof Palme has just about driven me out of the country. A lot of my friends have left through the years because of taxes. I've held on because I love this country. Even the extremes of Social Democracy couldn't drive me out. But Palme's taking sides with the Soviets on the Vietnam situation and allowing your military deserters to stay here—and to demonstrate against your Embassy, for God's sake—is driving me crazy. I'm one of those who think it's shameful that Sweden stayed out of World War II and that some of our most important people cozied up to the Nazis. Now we have our leaders cozying up to the Communists, the other side in that war. It's a disgrace!"

Chris and Wykowski exchanged a glance. They had never seen such vehemence about politics in Schmidt, or in any other high-powered Swede for that matter.

The Swede noticed their surprise. "Sorry, I get a little carried away on the subject. I don't resent the taxes as much as my friends do because we Swedes truly take care of our people, much better certainly than you do in the United States. That costs a lot. What I do resent is that we can't seem to take the right stand on important issues in the world. Neutrality may be useful, but it's useful like eunuchs are useful. Once you cut off their balls they grow big and strong but you can never be sure if they will serve the harem or the master.

"There I go again. Do you really think Palme would use the security services to find Plotkin if he defects?"

Wykowski took the question. "I'm not sure who would have responsibility for a decision like that. I'll guarantee you that the Soviets would immediately inform your foreign ministry that one of theirs was missing and request an immediate search. The ministry would certainly inform Palme, and I imagine the decisions regarding a search would be made in consultation with the appropriate ministries."

Schmidt got out of his chair and started pacing in front of the view windows.

"You know now how I feel and that I'm willing to take the chance. What are we going to do about a crew? I've single-handed the *Valhalla* before, but that was around here in the Baltic during the summer. I wouldn't consider doing that in the kind of weather we have at this time of year."

Chris spoke up. "Nils, do you think you could handle her outbound with two good sailors, and with one good sailor on the return to harbor?"

"Probably so." Schmidt showed his surprise. "But where are we going to get those sailors? I've been worrying about which of my various crew members would be both free to go along and able to keep their mouths shut. I can think of many who would like the adventure, but only a couple I can trust to keep quiet about the reason for the trip." He paused. "Would one of those sailors by any chance be you, Chris?"

"That's right. I'll be the one who doesn't go back to port with you. That was kind of immodest of me, but I am a good sailor. I hope you'd trust me to give you a hand outbound."

"Of course, of course. You're a fine sailor, Chris. I'm beginning to see the rest of the plan here. Would the other sailor, the one who'd stay with the *Valhalla*, by any chance be a mutual friend who once sailed into the Baltic with us?"

Again it was Norm Wykowski's turn to answer. "That's right, Nils. I think you know that Pastor Stewart is a reserve U.S. Navy officer, a captain in fact, with top secret clearance. He comes into the Embassy pretty regularly to touch base with the Naval Attaché. On Thursday—the same day you and I met—I got him up to a secure room in our office and propositioned him to give you a hand with the *Valhalla*. I understand he's a pretty good sailor. Oh, and by the way, he agreed."

"Bill Stewart will be a great crew member." Schmidt looked relieved. "We got along fine when he and Chris crewed with me. It's not like we're going to be using lots of sails. I'm planning to motor all the way out the cut and into open water; maybe even all the way to the transfer point depending on the weather. There won't be much deck work until the pickup. That could get interesting at this time of year in the Skagerrak. You haven't told me much about the transfer, other than we'll be meeting an American submarine."

"I won't have detailed information on that until tonight," Norm replied. "From what I hear, you and your boat can take just about anything that's thrown at you. The things concerning me now have to do with meeting Plotkin, getting him moved into a safe house, and then moving him from there to your boat on the west coast. My problem at the moment is that I don't have a car that isn't identified with one of us."

"What kind of car?"

Chris broke in, "The most important thing, Nils, is that it not be identified with one of our Station people or be an attention-getter—you know—too flashy looking or too old and beat up. Something in between. There'll be four of us if this works out: you, me, Bill Stewart and Plotkin. Something big enough so we can be comfortable on the long drive would be nice, but the rest of it is more important."

Schmidt, who had been pacing by the windows, broke off and went to the kitchen to get more coffee for his guests. He was evidently taking time to think something out, as he dawdled there longer than necessary. When he returned with the coffee, he sat in one of the easy chairs facing the two Americans and said, "How about a not-very-shiny dark-blue 1967 Volvo station wagon?"

"It sounds ideal. Do you know of one we could borrow?"

"Yes indeed. It's parked near the dock where I picked you up on Ljusterö. My wife and I both drive BMW's, but we have this station wagon to haul things back and forth from home to the island. During the summer we leave it on Ljusterö quite often so we don't have to put a car on the ferry from Östanå. Yesterday, when I came out here from Stockholm, I brought the station wagon because I had some gear I wanted to bring for winterizing this place."

Both Chris and Norm Wykowski jumped at this chance. But now they had to work out the logistics. In the next hour and a half they went through another pot of coffee and the sandwiches left over from lunch, finding satisfaction in the food and drink and the development of what seemed a workable plan with minimum security exposure. Rain continued to splatter against the windows on the south side of the great room, a rat-a-tat that beat faster and faster as the afternoon progressed. By the time they wrapped up the planning and took dishes into the kitchen area, it was a steady downpour driven by a wind that in Chris's experience would bring small craft warnings on Puget Sound.

"I don't suppose we'll be taking the Chris Craft back to Ljusterö in this weather," he said. The three of them were tidying up the kitchen, stacking dishes in the state-of-the-art German dishwasher and getting ready to leave on the next step of this venture.

"No, no," Schmidt answered, "no way would I take that beauty out in this weather. We'll take the utility boat."

"What'll you do with the utility when you leave?"

"An old fisherman on Ljusterö has been our winter caretaker for years. I'll have him tow the utility back to the island with his own boat. He'll put it in the boat house and check that everything's secure. Weather permitting he visits about once a week to check things out."

It was not long before they were huddled in the short forward cabin of the utility boat, headed back to Ljusterö through dimming twilight, small seas and a heavy rain that gave minimum visibility.

They parted at the dock at Ljusterö, not to see each other again until—or if—the operation came off. Nils Schmidt went to find a phone to call his caretaker with instructions about the utility boat while the CIA pair drove directly to the ferry. They were second in a line of a dozen cars, guessing that the others were mostly people going into Stockholm to celebrate a Saturday evening. One of the cars joining the line was a non-descript blue Volvo station wagon. They paid no attention to it then, or on the ferry, or on the road to Stockholm.

The final pre-operation meeting with Pastor Stewart took place soon after their return to Stockholm. Norm Wykowski called him from a public phone on the mainland side of the ferry from Ljusterö, with a pre-arranged signal setting up a meeting an hour later in a Gamlastan konditeri. During the meeting they chose a pickup-spot a few blocks from Pastor Bill's home in the event Plotkin defected and Bill would be needed to help sail the Valhala. Telephone and visual safety signals were agreed on, and twenty minutes after they'd ordered their coffee Bill Stewart was on his way back home to finish preparations for Sunday's sermon.

"You've given me some good ideas for my sermon tomorrow," he told his friends as they parted.

"As long as you don't feel you have to tell them what you'll be doing next week," Wykowski commented.

"Don't worry, my friend," Pastor Bill replied, "I don't have to justify myself to my congregation, only to God. And He and I understand each other on these matters."

"Time flies when you're having fun." Wykowski was driving Chris back to drop him off a couple of streets away from Bisan's apartment. "Or if you'd prefer another cliché—tomorrow's the big day." He pulled into a street-side parking space.

"Thanks for everything today, Norm. You came up with a great plan."

"Let's chat for a minute before you go back to Bisan's place. I want to make sure you're okay with all the arrangements for tomorrow." They went over their plans for a few moments before Chris left the car for a circuitous route to Bisan's building. He let himself in with the keys she'd given him that morning. Bisan was not at home. She must have gone out with her friends again. Needing a good night's sleep before the big day, he straightaway got ready for another night on the couch.

When he came to his customary meditation after prayers on this important eve, he started thinking about the family he'd been shoving to the back of his thoughts much too long. An onrush of guilt brought him to his feet, throwing the covers back and pacing Bisan's living room. Dear Jesus, how had he rationalized abandoning them the way he had, never getting in touch during these many days he'd been gone? A few laps around the small room helped him rationalize once more. Certainly Bob Brewer would contact Lisa to let her know that her husband was alive and well. Back on the couch and under the covers, he felt better and was soon asleep.

"Chris! CHRIS!" Someone was trying to wake him, a voice he didn't recognize. Not a voice, actually. More like a whisper, hissed more loudly with each repetition. What now?

"Jesus, Chris, wake up!" Now he was swinging into a sitting position and could see it was Bisan who had finally brought him around with a hard shake.

"What's wrong? Do we have a problem?" He was still groggy but conscious enough to worry that something had happened to make Bisan act that way.

"You're lucky that I came home just as you started. There would have been hell to pay if you'd wakened the neighbors. Just think what my aunt would have to say if she heard about that from her friends on this floor."

"What's 'that'?"

"Just as I came in the door you started calling out, loud, over and over, a woman's name."

Chris was jolted fully awake. The dream was coming back to him. He thought it safe to ask the next question.

"Dare I ask who I was calling out to?"

Bisan sat down on the arm of the couch, staring at him. In the dimness, he could see she was looking at him sternly, but then she grinned, giggled a bit, gave him a shove to the shoulder and headed to her room. She spoke softly from the doorway of her bedroom before closing the door.

"From the way you were calling out, it seems you were making love to a woman in your dreams. I'm pretty sure, too, that what I heard was 'Lisa, Lisa, Lisa.' Good night, my friend."

CHAPTER TWENTY-SIX

Sunday, November 12, 1972
Edmonds, Washington

The skirt was wool, a dark-green plaid fitted nicely to the trim figure of the woman wearing it, except for the handful clutched by a small, teary-eyed girl.

"Mommy, Mommy, I need you!"

"I Am Talking On The Phone." Each word was enunciated as clearly as Lisa was able in the middle of frustration with her youngest daughter, who was tugging at the skirt and probably making it unfit to wear, and with a telephone call that was raising more questions than it answered.

The clear enunciation brought a howl from Lisbet, followed by gasping sobs: "but ... she won't ... let me!" Lisa felt like clobbering her, but they were both saved by Mor coming to the rescue of her youngest granddaughter. She scooped Lisbet off the floor, where the three-year-old had collapsed in anger and tears, and carried her off to do battle with Missy. The two girls usually got along beautifully, but of late the tension in their family was reflected in the girls' moods.

Missy, now almost eight years old, had even repeated a phrase overheard at a cocktail party her grandparents hosted for the Tows senior staff: "Is it true, Mommy, that we have to be careful what we wish for?" Missy and her mother were having a cozy bedtime chat together in the room the girls shared, while Mor gave Lisbet a bath.

"Sometimes, Sweetheart. I think what it means is that we have to trust God's plan. If we pray for something that we really want but it's not part of the plan, we might be sorry if we get it. Did you get something you prayed for that you don't like now?"

"Kind of."

"What do you mean, 'kind of'?"

Missy moved closer to Lisa on the bed, kissing her cheek and laying her head on her mother's shoulder. "I don't want to talk about it."

"I can't make you talk about it, but maybe you'd feel better if you shared it with me."

"I don't want to talk about it because it makes me feel bad." Lisa saw that her daughter had tears in her eyes. She shifted positions to take Missy in her arms, patting her on the back as the girl began to weep.

"It's up to you, Sweetheart, but I still think you'll feel better if you tell me."

Missy extracted herself from her mother's embrace, took a Kleenex from the nightstand to blow her nose, then sat down on Lisbet's bed facing Lisa, with her arms folded, grownup style.

"Okay. It's about Lisbet. I prayed and prayed for a baby sister, and when she came I loved her more than anybody." She paused. "Except you and maybe Daddy. Now I don't like her so much. She bugs me all the time."

"You shouldn't feel bad about that, Missy. You remember how cute puppies and kittens are when they're real young. But then they grow up. The kittens start biting and scratching everything, and the puppies make messes in the house and chew up all your good things. You just have to be patient and help Lisbet grow up to be as nice a girl as you are."

Lisa wished that was all there was to it.

All she heard after she hung up the phone was a blessed silence. It seemed Mor had mediated the squabble between the girls. The quiet was soon interrupted by some rattling and running water sounds from the kitchen. She guessed Mor was preparing for one of their coffee and spritz cookie chats.

She guessed right. After peeking into the girls' room to see them coloring cheerfully on papers laid out on the floor, Lisa went to the kitchen in time to watch Mor take a batch of cookies from the oven. Mor's mood was dark. Lisa expected to be chewed out by her mother-in-law, who had come to favor her youngest granddaughter.

Whatever Mor's intentions about their chat, they were soon deflected when she learned that the telephone call had something to do with Chris. "It was Chris! Why didn't you tell me?"

"Not Chris, Mor. It was a message from Chris, a call from a friend in Washington. It was very confusing because his friend Bob was trying to cover up all the secret stuff, and that just made a muddle. All I could understand was that Chris had someone call Bob to say he loves us all and would be home before long. Whatever that means."

"But that's good news, isn't it? Why are you still looking unhappy?"

"Think about it, Mor. All the time Chris was in Vietnam, two whole years, we'd been planning this move. Chris and I, Missy and Lisbet would be going to Virginia for an assignment at Headquarters, the boys staying back here with you and Herman to finish high school. All tied up in a neat little package. The renters have already left our house in Vienna and we've got crews fixing it up for the four of us to start living there, with Matthew and Mark joining us in the summer before they're off to college. Now what?" Her angry voice started to tremble. "Now what, Mor? Your son is off to God-knows-where doing God-knows-what, and we're stranded here with you and Herman, not knowing whether to stay, go to DC, rent a house in Edmonds again, or ..." She broke off the tirade, too angry even to cry.

"Drink your coffee, Dear, and have a spritz. They're good for you."

Mor's attempt to calm Lisa worked, not for the reason Mor thought, but because Lisa found the idea of spritz cookies being good for one's health so ludicrous, loaded with butter and sugar as they were. She took one anyway and smiled inwardly at Mor's fractured logic.

"Thanks, Mor. I've heard our men talk about steadying boats with ballast, and I think you're my ballast. You help steady me when I need it, and I appreciate your doing it right now, when I need it more than ever."

"When are you going to make a decision about what to do with this wonderful family of yours?" Mor's mood was still somber.

"I don't know how I can make any decisions until Chris lets us know his plans, whenever that might be. I can't tell you how disappointed I am or how angry I am at Chris. I hate to say that about your son, but I can't lie to you, Mor. You're very special to me, the only mother I have now."

"What are you going to do? Just wait for some word from Chris or that agency he works for?"

"I don't know what else I can do. His friend Bob—the one who called just now—said he would call again in a couple of days. He expected to hear from Chris again about that time."

They had moved into the living room during the conversation. Now Mor stood with coffee cup in hand, gazing out the picture window at a steely Puget Sound bordered on the west by gray-blue Olympic Mountains. "We can only hope."

Just then a high-pitched scream sounded from the girls' room. Lisbet. "Mommy, Mommy!" Tear-streaked again, she came running into the living room, clutching a colored page in both hands. "Mommy!"

Lisa arched her eyebrows at Mor. "You really think there's hope?"

Chapter Twenty-Seven

Sunday, November 12, 1972

On Sunday a spatter of rain and a rattling of the apartment windows conspired to awaken Chris before dawn. He came into the real world from a feverish night on Bisan's couch, sweaty and disoriented. It was hard to sort out dreams from reality, but he remembered Bisan waking him during the night, bringing back that very real dream of being with Lisa. After that he thought he'd never get back to sleep, but he must have slept. He felt reasonably well-rested and curious about the time. It was still dark, but then the sun would not rise until after eight thirty this morning. Reaching over his head to retrieve his wristwatch from an end table, he angled it in the scant light from the bathroom until he could just make out the time. Seven o'clock. Not bad.

As Chris showered, shaved and dressed, he heard not a peep out of Bisan. He pulled on a fresh casual shirt to go with the same gray slacks worn on the trip to Nils Schmidt's island home. He would add a warm, dark-blue windbreaker when he left the apartment. He was quiet as possible while cooking oatmeal, which he enjoyed along with breakfast rolls and coffee. Before the Plotkin pickup Chris planned to check thoroughly that he was not under surveillance, but there was no set time he had to leave the apartment. Three or four hours should do it, meaning he wouldn't have to leave before ten o'clock at the earliest.

An hour of reading went quickly, even if it was hard to concentrate on the late nineteenth century Swedish novel he found on the library shelves. Now it was half-past nine, and he'd still heard nothing from Bisan. Maybe she had gone out before he awoke? Chris was in a worrying mood, and here was one more thing to worry about. Was she okay? Listening outside her bedroom door he still heard nothing. He hesitated before turning the doorknob as quietly as possible, then pushing the door open just far enough so that he could see the bed.

There she was, staring at him with a wry smile on her pretty face, lying on top of the bedcovers and clad modestly in old-fashioned pajamas that revealed nothing more than head, hands and feet. "Is there something you want, Chris?" He knew she was teasing him, but couldn't resist a jolt of excitement at what seemed an invitation.

"I'm going to be leaving soon. I just wanted to check that you were here and okay."

"Come in here and tell me again about the plans." Bisan moved to one side of the bed and propped herself up on the pillows, patting the bed to show him that he should sit on the other side.

"I've made coffee. Why don't you put on a robe and we'll sit in the kitchen for a few minutes before I have to leave."

"Don't be stuffy, Chris. Nobody's going to know the shocking truth—that you were on a bed with me. Sometimes I think you are such a-a-a *prig*. Is that the right word?"

"I hope not. I don't like to think people would believe that about me. I'm just careful."

"Okay, but you're too careful sometimes. Get me a cup of coffee and bring it in here." She patted the bed again. "Remember, you need me to keep this place safe for you. I need to know everything about the plans."

With that Chris gave in. He fetched a cup of coffee for this so-called agent, thinking about the fact that she wasn't even cleared for the operation. A lot was riding on Bisan's good sense in keeping up the appearance of a normal life around her apartment and keeping her mouth shut.

"That wasn't so bad, was it?" She teased him after he handed her the coffee and sat down beside her on the bed. "Tell me everything."

"You know I can't tell you everything."

"You take things so seriously, Chris. Can't you tell I'm teasing you?" She hit him playfully on the arm, nearly spilling coffee on both of them. "Can't we just go over things again, like when you're going to be back here today, who you'll have with you, and when you're going to want me here to act as your courier?"

And that's what he did. Sitting alongside Bisan on her bed, Chris reviewed what would be happening. He might or might not bring Plotkin back with him to the apartment. Plotkin might or might not spend the night. Or two nights. Depending. In other words she should be prepared to have one or two guests for up to a few days while showing the outer world that she continued to lead her normal life, alone, waiting for her Danish lover to return from his latest sea journey. Chris (and Plotkin, if he showed) would do everything possible to help her keep up the pretense by staying as quiet as possible and getting into and out of the building with the least possible fuss. If Plotkin did not return with Chris this evening, Chris himself would be gone within twenty-four hours.

Bisan's most important duty for today would be carrying a message to Norm Wykowski and bringing one back in return. Norm and Chris had gone over several possibilities for communication, but they always came back to using Bisan as a courier.

"When will you return this afternoon?" Bisan was no longer in her light-hearted teasing mode.

"That's hard to predict. If I return with Plotkin it will probably be sometime between three thirty and four o'clock. If he doesn't show, I may go into other meetings and get back later, maybe early evening. So I'd like you here this afternoon by four o'clock at the latest. Remember, you have that meeting with Norm a few minutes after five."

"I remember, I remember. But how in the world are you going to get in and out of this place without calling attention to yourselves? One man, like you, isn't so unusual, but two big guys coming in together could really raise some curiosity—especially if a couple of older lady residents are hanging out in the lobby, just visiting. They do that sometimes. I can see them watching the indicator above the elevator door and seeing it stop on my floor. 'Aha,' they'd think, 'Now she's taking them on two at a time. A real ménage à trois.' "

"I can't imagine the old ladies around here would have such dirty minds."

"Jesus, Chris, you really are a prig. Young or old, man or woman, they're human, and humans think like that, even though people such as you won't admit it. Anyway, my morals are beside the point. People know I've had lovers here occasionally, and some might even know that my Danish mariner stays over whenever he's in town. But two men at once is just too much. Can't you enter one at a time?

"No way. I don't want to be separated from Sasha, even for a minute."

"Then we need some way to make sure the old ladies aren't hanging around in the lobby."

She and Chris worked for almost half an hour trying to solve this problem. Chris was less concerned than she because he had twice been able to get in and out without calling attention to himself. They were almost at an impasse before Bisan agreed that Chris and Plotkin would enter together, take the elevator one floor higher than her own and go down the stairway to her floor.

* * *

Chris was driving Nils Schmidt's Volvo. Following the first part of the plan worked out at the island home a day earlier, Schmidt had parked the car on

Artillerigatan, about three blocks from Bisan's place. Chris was given a spare key. With the license number memorized and key in hand, he had no trouble finding and driving off with the vehicle that hopefully would transport Plotkin on the first leg of his journey into self-imposed exile. And on the second leg, too, if the plan worked out.

Eleven fifteen in the morning. After an hour of driving around in Norrmalm, the city center, he was crossing Strömbron, the bridge to Gamla Stan—where so much emotion had been invested during that previous life in Stockholm—the site of the tryst between Lisa and Plotkin. Probably, he thought, this was a case of punishing himself for the stirrings of guilt he felt over whatever part he had played in the coming together of those two. No sign of any interest in him so far. Realizing that he was following a crazy bend in his psyche, he parked briefly and strolled by the Soviet safe house where the affair had taken place. He noted nothing more than the expected lull of the season between crowds of tourists during the high time of summer and early fall. This more modest crowd of locals could enjoy the beginnings of the Holiday season without having to rub elbows with German, French, Italian, American and Japanese tourists.

At half-past noon, he crossed Kungsbron toward Bromma. Chris's senses were on the alert, his hands moist on the steering wheel. An older BMW sedan—not unlike the car Chris was driving in age and condition—had been tailing him for five minutes, cutting into traffic about three cars behind and keeping that position as other cars entered and left the stream. It could be innocent, but Chris was taking no chances. He had already scrapped original plans for getting to the first checkpoint on the way to meet Plotkin. Rather than staying on the main drag to Brommaplan, he turned south on one of the neighborhood streets, keeping an eye on the BMW. As he slowed, the sedan blew by, and he could see a single driver—an older woman wearing a large hat—a most unlikely setup for a surveillance vehicle.

At one-o'clock precisely, Chris's Volvo slowly entered Höglandstorget, driving past five cars waiting to pick up passengers from the spårvagn, a quaint trolley that ran from the main subway station at Alvik, near Kungsbron, to his former home at Nockeby. Having ridden the trolley many times on the journey back and forth to the Embassy in Stockholm, he knew that this stop was one of several on small squares at the centers of their surrounding neighborhoods. He cruised past the cars waiting at the station to pick up folks getting off the trolley. One of them was a black Volvo, the driver a middle-aged man wearing a fedora. Chris made a turn around the block and again drove by the waiting cars, noting that the middle-aged man in the Volvo was still wearing his fedora. As Chris entered the square, circled the block and drove past again, Norm Wykowski was signaling with the hat still on his head that he had seen no vehicle surveillance or other interest. That was a thumbs-up for the first checkpoint. Forty-five minutes to go before the next checkpoint.

He arrived at the final checkpoint at 1:45 p.m., this at a similar station named Olovslund, the last stop before Nockeby. The procedures and signals were the same, with the same results. The pickup was a "go." It appeared safe to meet Plotkin. With hands still damp, and suffering the full, heavy weight of responsibility—to his family, to the Agency—Chris turned the Volvo toward Drottningholm.

The storm had abated during the morning hours, wind becoming a breeze, rain turning into drizzle. But now, in the vicinity of Drottningholm park, breeze and drizzle had reverted to the earlier wind gusts and bursts of rain. A strange place to meet at this time of year. If Plotkin were waiting on foot he would be soaked. Chris couldn't imagine that he would be in a car, though anything was possible when going on such little information.

No more than a minute from the time Chris pulled into the park and turned off the engine, he saw Plotkin coming toward him out of the woods bordering the parking lot. In a business suit—no hat or topcoat—he was soaking wet. He jerked the passenger door open, fell into the seat alongside Chris and slammed the door. "Let's go, let's go!" Chris responded by putting the car in gear the second the engine turned over, driving as quickly as he dared out of the parking lot in the direction of Nockeby, the last stop on the trolley line, the last checkpoint for surveillance before heading toward the Grevgatan safe house. He was driving across Nockebybron before he felt it was safe to take a look at Plotkin.

The KGB officer wore a serious expression on a face that seemed to have aged more than the two and one-half years since Chris had seen him. Seeing Chris look at him, Plotkin repeated in a more normal voice: "Just get me the hell out of here Chris. Let's go! Let's go."

The thrill of the chase had pushed Plotkin's liaison with Lisa to the back burner. But now the thoughts, the feelings, the anger, all were hanging like a shroud between Chris and his passenger. Focusing his eyes back on the road, he was struck by the realization of how much time he'd spent on the operational plans, the mechanics of arranging a pickup of a KGB officer. He couldn't shake thoughts of the dichotomy of this meeting, of a personal relationship splintered by Plotkin yet forced to continue because of both men's professional needs.

It was easier not thinking about it. He interrupted his own mental gyrations to come back to the present. "I won't drive faster than the limit, Sasha. We don't want to do anything that would call attention to us in any way."

"Agreed. You can imagine that I'm nervous about this whole thing. Where are we going now? It looks like we're heading toward your old home in Nockeby."

"Same area but not the house. I'm going to swing by the Nockeby tram station before we head toward the safe house where we'll spend the night. While we're driving there, why don't you start by telling me what led you to this, what's going on? I need to have an idea of what we're up against before we get you out of the country."

"I'm not telling you a goddamn thing until we are out of the country. Not even then. Not until we're on American soil."

"You're playing with a weak hand, Sasha. You're not going to get out of the country without my help, and before I expose any of our people or assets to you, you're going to have to give me some reason to trust you. You've given me a good personal reason not to trust you, so unless you want to start cooperating now you can get out of the car at Nockebytorg and take that little tram to wherever in hell you want to go."

As Chris spoke they were arriving at Nockebytorg, the small market square where he and Lisa had often shopped together on Saturdays. Trying hard to push such thoughts out of his mind, he concentrated on the task at hand. Plotkin sat quietly beside him, a grim expression on his face.

"I know I'm too valuable for you to do that, Chris, but I also understand that you have to answer to your masters just as I've had to do these many years. What can I tell you to make you understand that I'm serious?" They were passing Norm Wykowski's Volvo now, parked in the square with a scattering of other cars. Norm was still wearing his hat.

"How about the names of those agents you claimed to be still working around the Portland Navy Base in England?"

Plotkin gave a short bark of laughter, more scoffing than humorous. "Not likely. That teaser I gave you is the kind of thing that will keep your agency eager to get me to the States."

"You need to satisfy *me*, Sasha, not my agency. Give me something I can believe and use before we go much farther." Wykowski was still wearing the felt hat as Chris swung the Volvo back in the other direction. "We've cleared the main checkpoints and we're on our way now to the staging area to get you out of here. I'm serious about putting you out of the car if you don't satisfy me with something important."

"You wouldn't," Plotkin said, but Chris caught a glance of body language that indicated doubt.

"You better believe I would. Something's triggered your contacting us again. You need to realize that my investment in this isn't so great that I can't afford to let the operation be blown. I'm seriously considering leaving the Agency anyway. I could go back to the Seattle area any day and get a position with my family company that would pay two or three times as much as I make now. Besides satisfying Lisa and the kids, it would get me back on the boats I enjoyed so much before I went into this kind of work." Chris was now steering the car toward

Stockholm, hoping the threat would work. He didn't, in fact, think he had the guts to blow the operation, but his thoughts were leading him more and more toward leaving the Agency and permanently joining Lisa and the family in the Northwest.

"Okay, okay! I still believe that you wouldn't dare give up this operation for something like that, but I'll give you a case to titillate your people. It will also explain why I'm here and some of my past movements as well."

Chris still had his doubts. "Before you try to titillate me, I notice you aren't carrying a briefcase. Do you have any documents with you? What kind of papers did you use to get into the country?"

"Sorry to tell you, I haven't brought any written secrets of the palace with me. And as far as getting into Sweden, I took a train to Helsinki, and flew from there to Stockholm, using the same diplomatic passport from my days here at the Embassy. Nobody checked the passport after I entered Finland. Can I get back to my story now?"

Disappointed, Chris nodded agreement.

"This gets back to my girlfriend Ulla at Moscow State University. I believe I told you when we met in Norrtälje that while in Moscow she was recruited by the KGB as a sleeper agent, but I don't remember giving you any details. She was encouraged to get a Swedish Government job, preferably in the Foreign Office, and to tone down her communist rhetoric in order to be more acceptable to Swedish technocrats who were beginning then to play a major role in running the Government, and who were mostly Social Democrats. Ulla played her game very successfully, switching her allegiance to the Social Democratic Party, playing a role in that party and rising in government circles. She was—and still is—an eternal student, managing to get a Ph.D. from the University of Stockholm in political science. And that, of course, helped put her ever more deeply into SDP circles."

He was interrupted by Chris slapping the steering wheel of the Volvo. "Stop right there! Stop! You know damn well that's not the kind of information that's going to get my headquarters excited. Give me something that directly affects the security of the United States."

"I will, I will. But hear me out on this one, Chris." Plotkin sat up taller in his seat, turning toward Chris, leaning against the passenger door. "I still don't want to toss you any bombshells—and believe me, I have some—but I think you'll like this one. What if I told you that Ulla was activated as a Soviet agent in 1967 and is now one of the principal advisors to Prime Minister Olof Palme?"

Chris tried to appear unimpressed. This wasn't the kind of thing he was hoping for, but it would surely be of interest to Washington. Palme was a thorn in the side of U.S. policymakers dealing with Vietnam, often appearing pro-Soviet in his foreign affairs statements. The Vietnam War led all others on his list of issues in opposition to U.S. policy. Anything showing a weakness in Palme or his government could awake a lot of interest.

"How was it that she was activated?"

"The KGB had followed her rise in the SDP and Swedish Government with much interest. There were several thoughts of activating her earlier, but the decisions not to do so were wise. Pressure to bring her on board was strengthened in 1967, when Palme became Minister of Education and brought Ulla to that office as one of his protégés. Although I was still in the Illegals Directorate—Ulla was no Illegal—I was consulted about the case a number of times because of my original involvement, my Swedish language ability, and a continuing interest in matters Swedish. In the fall of 1967, when it began to appear that Palme had a chance of becoming Prime Minister, the decision was made for activation and I was chosen as the officer to do the job. I came to Stockholm in September 1967 to meet her for the activation, traveling under diplomatic cover. That was a fateful meeting in many ways.

"I first met her on the street in Stockholm for the activation. She recognized me instantly after all these years, practically jumping into my arms. I slipped her a note asking for a meeting in one of our Stockholm safe houses. She came right on time, accepted her assignment without question, and gave us only one problem: she wouldn't meet with anyone but me because she trusted me so much. On my return to Moscow I made it clear to my masters that her insistence on that point was more because of her attraction to me than for security reasons. I thought we could find another officer she would trust. But events overcame that.

"The Politburo was inordinately interested in having an agent at the heart of the Swedish Government, not so much for intelligence but for influence. The KGB Chairman keeps top levels of the Politburo briefed on operations that can affect political matters, and in this case the interest skyrocketed. Here was an opportunity to influence Palme to stay on a track beneficial to the Soviets—at that time mostly regarding policy toward Vietnam—through directions given to one of his trusted advisors—"

"Hold it, Sasha. I've got to concentrate on something here." Chris was swinging around another square for the final safety check before proceeding to the safe house. Norm Wykowski was again signaling no problem with surveillance. "Okay, Sasha, go ahead."

"I think," Plotkin went on, "that the Chairman gave out too much about the operation in a couple of ways. First, he was too optimistic about the agent's ability to carry out this kind of operation; and second, he told the Politburo types that this was a female agent in love with the recruiter, meaning that the recruiter would have to handle her."

Chris could empathize. "I think the first part is common to all intelligence services and their governments, but pegging you as the handler sounds kind of strange."

"Indeed! It gave me and the leadership all kinds of problems. I'd never had a diplomatic posting, and I was an Illegals body, still working for the most part as a handler of our own department's agents in a number of countries. I'm sure you agree that you just can't switch these things on and off. But the leadership thought that the safest way to deal with her would be by having somebody on the ground. In the end they brought the Ambassador to Stockholm back to Moscow for briefing sessions with the KGB. Now aware of the Ulla operation, he agreed to my assignment in Stockholm and to giving me a cover job with light duties. So I was slipped into my Embassy assignment, arriving soon after New Year's, 1967. Internally in the KGB, I was still an Illegals type. I would spend some time on activities in support of Illegals in Sweden; Ulla's reporting would go through that channel.

"I sometimes met Ulla when she was traveling abroad with the Prime Minister. It was easy for her to explain our meeting times as her opportunity to shop, and since the Swedes had no minders on her it was easy to slip away to a safe house in one of those cities visited by the Prime Minister. It all worked very well. I never thought the results were worth the trouble, but the Politburo was truly impressed with the way Palme appeared to be influenced by Ulla against the U.S. and the Vietnam war. It seemed to me that Palme had the right opinion about the war and that he naturally refused to play the American line. His thinking wasn't much different from some other western leaders. He was less tied to the Americans than many and could afford to be honest about it. That was fine with me as it raised my stock with the KGB. Up to a point.

"That point came at an unfortunate time for me. And for you. Just before Easter, 1969—a couple of days before I was to meet you to turn myself over to your people—Ulla sent an emergency message that she would be traveling with Palme to Paris for an unannounced meeting. It was surmised to have something to do with the Paris Peace Talks that had begun, still in secret, with General Le Duc Tho. Naturally I was instructed to travel for a meet with her there. The Ambassador was going for an unrelated reason, which gave me cover to travel with him. That meant canceling my Friday meeting with a local Illegal, the one who would have given time to have you pick me up with none of my colleagues around. There was no way to let you know, and with so much attention placed on me right then I couldn't take a chance of just walking away."

They were nearing the Grevgatan safe house by the time Plotkin had reached this part of the story. Chris interrupted him. "I really want to hear the rest of the story, Sasha, but we're almost there. I'm going to park in that space up ahead, and we'll walk for about three blocks to the safe house. You can finish while we're walking. I want you to know that there will be a young woman in the safe house some of the time while we're there. She's extremely reliable, and she knows who you are, but I don't want us to discuss any operational matters in her presence."

Chris parked the Volvo in about the same place it had been, and the two men walked together, buffeted by rain and wind. Plotkin managed to relate briefly that he had been called unexpectedly back to Moscow from Paris, where he found himself in trouble. As will happen in such bureaucracies, his successes had raised jealousies, and this in turn led to a reawaking of suspicions regarding a Jewish background. He spent nearly a week in a KGB dacha outside Moscow, where he underwent interviews with a number of KGB officers reviewing his background from childhood to that time. During that week he came to believe that someone had spotted him at Chris's home, but there were no accusations of wrongdoing, only ominous periods of silence while the interviewers stared at him with apparent hostility. He was finally sent back to his former job, managing operations out of the Illegals Directorate. There were no apparent restrictions on his activities within the Soviet Union, but the various passports he'd used through the years were not available to him. He continued to be the agent handler for Ulla, despite the rules having been changed. During their first months of meetings she had been trained in secret writing communications, rarely used. Now the exchange of letters with secret writing became her only means of communication, as she continued to refuse meetings with KGB officers other than himself.

They arrived at Bisan's building. Both men had been using their trained abilities at checking for surveillance, with nothing spotted. Chris was happy to see that nobody was in the lobby. Still, he and Plotkin rode the elevator one floor above the safe house, and they walked quietly down the staircase before letting themselves into the apartment. Bisan was nowhere in sight.

"What is this place? Is it safe?" Plotkin was looking around the apartment with an air of great suspicion.

"You've just proved it safe," Chris said.

"How's that?"

"If you don't know about it, I should think it would be safe as far as your KGB comrades are concerned. I have no reason to believe it isn't safe from the Swedes or anybody else."

Reluctant to put wet garments in the small coat closet, Chris took spare hangers from the closet and hung his jacket and Plotkin's suit coat over the tub in the bathroom to drip dry. Plotkin's pants were almost as wet as his coat, but he refused an offer to hang them with the coats. Instead, he took towels in the bathroom to soak out as much water as possible and folded an additional dry towel to sit on, so as not to damage the furniture.

"You need to know, Sasha, that this apartment is owned by an elderly lady who now lives in a nursing home. Her niece lives here now. I'm not going to play any games with you about this, since you could look around and learn about her anyway. Her name is Bisan. She knows about the operation up to this point, but no details about you and nothing about how we're going to get out of Sweden. You will find she is young, but I want you to treat her with great respect. She's very nice, and she deserves it."

"Of course. Of course!" Plotkin waved a hand dismissively. "I always treat people with respect. But where is she?"

"I honestly don't know and don't care; that's her business and I trust her. I can tell you that she will be back here by four o'clock at the latest. After meeting us she will be carrying a message to my outside contact, reporting that we're together here and ready to follow the exfiltration plans."

"Which are—?"

"You don't need to know the details yet. The Volvo we were in just now has already been moved by a gentleman who will pick us up tomorrow at a different location around five thirty in the afternoon. There'll be one other person, and I'll let you know then the plans from that point."

"Okay, okay. But we will be going to the States? You're going with me?"

"Of course."

"Where will I live after I've served my purpose for your agency?"

Chris had taken a couple of beers from the refrigerator and they were now drinking them in the living room. "I haven't the slightest idea. It could be anywhere in the United States where you'd best fit in under a new identity. I doubt that you or the Agency would want to publicize your defection."

"Sometimes it's done."

"Sure, but it's not appropriate for me to talk with you about those possibilities, because I'll have nothing to do with them. I'll escort you back to the States and help get you settled with the debriefings, and then I'm gone."

"Gone?"

"Gone as far as you're concerned. Out of loyalty to the Agency I'll see you through this exfiltration. But then I want nothing more to do with you. You must certainly understand that."

Plotkin was sitting on the sofa with both feet planted on the floor, leaning forward and staring at the hands folded on his knees. "I understand."

"And that's something we need to work out before leaving this apartment." Nervous now, Chris was on his feet, pacing back and forth in the small living room. "Unless you've blabbed to somebody, the only people who know about you and Lisa are the two of you and me. I've never reported it to the Agency and never will. This could give us problems when you're interrogated at Headquarters. I think you'll find it a friendly interrogation—much friendlier than you'd get by your own people—but they will give you a polygraph exam. Do you think you can manage not to talk about that painful episode in our lives?"

"Of course."

"They may ask about our relationship, especially because of some of the odd things that happened just before you failed to show up for your first try at defecting. And since you met a couple of times with Lisa and me at our home, they could ask some questions about that relationship and your feelings about her. Can you get through a polygraph exam touching on those subjects without revealing your ... your other contact with Lisa?"

"Of course."

Chris stopped pacing and loomed over Plotkin, who still sat in the same position on the sofa.

"Goddamn it, Sasha, what do you mean 'of course?' Do you have any idea how hard it is to fool a truly good polygraph examiner?"

"Of course."

Chris fell heavily into an easy chair facing Plotkin on the sofa. "Remind me that we have to speak softly in here. Sorry I raised my voice, but you're driving me crazy with answers like that. Why do you think you can beat a lie detector so easily?"

"Because I've done it. Many times. And with an American acting as the interrogator."

"Really. How did that come about? Were you actually being interrogated by a United States agency?"

Seeing that he'd deflected some of Chris's anger, Plotkin relaxed a bit and smiled. "Not really. The officers assigned to the Illegals Directorate receive a lot of training to avoid being caught in the act, and what to do if caught. That includes training to beat the polygraph with practice using an interrogator with native ability in the language of the interrogation. I was considered good at it."

Chris returned his smile with a wry one of his own. "I bet you were."

Before either could go further they heard the sound of a key in the door lock. Plotkin was halfway to getting on his feet when Bisan breezed in, all smiles and graciousness. Her KGB guest bowed slightly as they were introduced by Chris with first names. Bisan's first action was to scold Chris.

"Why are you serving beer to my guest at this early time on a Sunday? You may drink beer later, but this is closer to teatime. I'll put on coffee and bring out the lovely Danish pastries I bought yesterday. You may continue while I prepare." With that, she headed for the kitchen, leaving Chris with a genuine smile as he thought how alike her actions were to Lisa's in the same situation.

Plotkin's expression was quizzical. "Is she real?" he asked Chris quietly, hoping that Bisan could not hear.

"Very real," Chris almost whispered, "and quite a young lady. She's half Swedish and half American, totally loyal to the United States. After a bit she'll be leaving to carry a message, but she won't be gone long and we'll be spending the evening with her. You may see her early tomorrow morning if you don't sleep late, but then you won't see her again. If luck is with us, we'll leave here before she returns from work tomorrow."

"I feel awkward." Plotkin indeed looked uncomfortable. "What can we talk about when she's here?"

"Anything that doesn't have to do with this operation or any other operations. There's plenty to talk about. I don't think she's ever traveled in the Soviet Union. You could tell her a lot about your country—Russia, I mean. You can talk to her about Sweden, or even her experience as a very young girl in the United States. Literature, poetry. Look at this book collection here."

Plotkin got to his feet and started looking over the collection of books, while Chris went into the kitchen. Bisan had the pastries warming and coffee percolating on the stove. Chris whispered in her ear, "Tell Norm it's a go from this side."

Bisan whispered back, "Is that all I'm going through this meeting arrangement for ... to tell him that?"

"Yep."

"That's a lot of trouble for a few little words."

"He may have something more complicated to send back with you, or not. This is the most secure way we can decide whether or not we're going ahead. Sorry to put you to all the trouble."

Bisan offered one of her most fetching smiles. "It's no trouble. You better get back to our guest." She playfully grabbed his shoulders and turned him to face the doorway to the living room, giving him a little shove.

As he entered the room, Plotkin asked, "Everything all right? You have a funny look on your face."

"Everything is just wonderful, Sasha."

That seemed to be proven during the time before Bisan had to leave to meet Norm Wykowski. Most of the time was taken up with Bisan's questioning him about Russia, and it went so fast that all were surprised to notice it was time for Bisan to leave for the meeting. After she was gone Plotkin went back to nervous fidgeting.

"What's this meeting all about?"

"It's really very simple, Sasha. Bisan is taking a short message to the person coordinating our exfiltration, saying that you and I are safely in this apartment and ready to proceed. She'll return with another short message. Hopefully that will be an answer that we'll be able to leave Stockholm tomorrow afternoon, or the following afternoon at the latest. If it's anything else, I'm sure we'll be able to work it out."

If anything, this information seemed to make Plotkin even more nervous. He prowled the living room, looked briefly at one of the old Swedish books. He checked out their sleeping arrangements, offering to sleep on the floor of the living room to allow Chris's sleeping on the sofa. After a brief argument, it was settled that Chris would sleep on the floor this night, while they'd switch positions if it was necessary to spend another night here.

They had settled down to read when again there was the sound of a key at the door to the hall. Bisan returning from her meet.

Before taking off her coat she came into the living room, looking back and forth between the two of them. "I have a message for you. It's a go for tomorrow, whatever that means."

CHAPTER TWENTY-EIGHT

Sunday, November 12, 1972

The rest of Sunday evening went pleasantly, thanks to Bisan. She prepared a good supper, but more than the food it was her bright personality and insatiable curiosity about everything in the world around her that eased the great tension both men felt about the exfiltration operation beginning the next day.

After dinner Bisan played records of Swedish folksongs, which she thought of as background music. She was wrong. Plotkin asked her to turn up the volume so they could really listen, and he began singing softly along with the music. He didn't have much of a singing voice, often just mouthing the words silently with his eyes closed. Bisan looked at Chris during those times with eyebrows raised in an implied question: "How in the world does he know all the Swedish folk songs?" Chris made a palms-down dismissive gesture. This wasn't the appropriate time to discuss it.

Bisan being Bisan, there was no waiting for an answer. At the end of the second LP record she asked Plotkin directly, "How in the world do you know the words to all those songs? I don't have a single Swedish friend who would know so many."

Plotkin took the question in stride. "My Swedish-language instructor at Moscow University loved the folk songs and thought that music was a good way to teach the language. It's funny but true that I learned all those Swedish songs in the Soviet Union." Chris was impressed by the facile evasion of his answer, wondering how successful Agency interrogators would be in getting information from Plotkin.

For the most part Chris stayed out of conversations between the other two, sitting back and enjoying Bisan's skill at making a guest feel welcome. He also made several mental notes about Plotkin's reactions to her questions, mostly truthful as far as he could tell.

The evening wound down about half past nine o'clock. Bisan said "I have to get up bright and early, so I'll say both goodnight and goodbye. If you happen to be up in the morning, I'll say goodbye again." Plotkin responded by standing to shake her hand, giving his little bow to formality as he thanked her profusely. Chris also stood, taking her by the arm and steering her into the kitchen.

He whispered in her ear, "Thank you, Bisan, not just for this but for all you've done. I'll remember you all my life."

He started to hug her in a fatherly way, which she preempted by reaching up to take his face in her hands. Her kiss, somewhere between warm and passionate, lingered. It was a kiss that Chris Holbeck would truly remember for the rest of his life.

CHAPTER TWENTY-NINE

Monday, November 13, 1972

Both men feigned sleep the next morning when Bisan quietly let herself out of the apartment at seven thirty, not wanting to go through another goodbye. Greeting the day, they found a typical Scandinavian breakfast on the kitchen table: hard-boiled eggs, breads, cheese and deli meats, with coffee kept warm on the stove. Before eating they took turns in the bathroom. With the light travel case he'd brought on the trip, Chris had all the tools and the advantage of clean underwear. Having brought nothing, Plotkin had to make do. He found an unused toothbrush still in its wrapping in one of the bathroom drawers, which he confiscated from Bisan, hoping she wouldn't mind. He used a disposable razor found in the bathtub enclosure to shave, and an underarm deodorant he hoped would not smell too feminine. He laid it on thick, sure that his clothing would have to survive at least one more day before he could get a change.

Nine thirty in the morning. Almost seven hours left to spend in silence. No conversation beyond very low voices or whispers. No radio. No records. They washed the dishes quietly, debated leaving a thank-you note for Bisan, quickly discarded that idea. They didn't even dare flush the toilet for the rest of the day. Each man scanned several Swedish-language books before settling down to read during this long waiting period. With all the appearance of being absorbed in their books, neither man afterwards would be able to recount anything about the book he was reading, even the title. Not long after noon Chris mimed eating to see if the Russian was interested in lunch. Plotkin shook his head "No." Chris nodded agreement.

Five o'clock in the afternoon. With a thumb pointed at the door and a glance at his watch, Chris signaled that it was time to leave. Standing by the hall door and ready to go, they listened for noises in the hallway. Hearing nothing, Chris used the peephole to double check. They exited quietly and chose the stairs to go down to the main floor lobby. Chris was pleased to find only one elderly lady in the lobby, engrossed in some mail she had just taken from her box in the row of mail slots on the back wall. They left via the main door into sparse foot traffic, heading for a rendezvous with the Volvo, its driver and passenger.

They were picked up almost immediately. In planning the exfiltration, Chris and Norm Wykowski decided that the shortest street exposure would be best at this point, some twenty hours after the Soviets would have discovered Plotkin's disappearance. Accordingly the two men walked a half-block south on Grevgatan, turned right and then right again at the next street. There they found the Volvo station wagon parked on Skeppargatan, with two men seated in front. Chris indicated that Plotkin should be seated in the right-hand rear passenger seat. He got in behind the driver.

Following the plan worked out on Saturday, Nils Schmidt had picked up the Volvo on Sunday evening, soon after Chris brought Plotkin to the Grevgatan safe house. At three o'clock in the afternoon he met briefly with Norm Wykowski, not much more than a brush pass in the Men's Clothing Department of Åhléns Department Store. The only words spoken came from Wykowski as he slipped an envelope into Schmidt's hand: "There's something for you, and please give the note to Chris as soon as you see him."

Before starting the car and pulling out of the parking place, Schmidt dutifully handed that envelope to Chris. "You need to read this right away."

In the envelope was a handwritten letter from Norm Wykowski:

> *Good Luck, Chris! You'll need it.*
>
> *I've been awake since two thirty this morning, when the Ambassador phoned me at home. He had been called by the Swedish Foreign Minister, who in turn had been called by the Soviet Ambassador to Sweden. These calls concerned the kidnapping of a named Soviet diplomat by a western intelligence service, with the intention of spiriting the official out of Sweden. Our Ambassador was also informed that the Foreign Ministry has been in touch with the Swedish Police, who've responded by putting out an APB, not only here but with notification to Interpol.*
>
> *Keep the faith!*
>
> *Your Friend*

Chris felt like he'd been punched in the solar plexus. He'd expected a lot of interest and action on the Soviet side, but not the makings of an international incident. Sasha Plotkin must be privy to a very special kind of information for the Soviets to have raised the case to this level. How much of this note should be shared with his fellow travelers?

Before that, introductions and explanations were necessary. Chris tapped Nils Schmidt on the shoulder. "Many, many thanks, Nils." Then he reached forward to shake Bill Stewart's hand. "And to you, Sir! Sorry to take you away from home on your days off. Have you met Sasha?"

"I don't believe so." Pastor Stewart reached back to shake Plotkin's hand.

"I don't think we've met," Plotkin said, "but of course I know who you are, Captain. You're with the Naval Attaché office at your Embassy." The other three men laughed, much louder than would have been appropriate on another occasion, a result of the tension all had been feeling.

Plotkin had a hurt expression. His pride had taken a blow. "But you are a Navy captain. The military is hardly my specialty, but I know I've seen pictures of you going into the American Embassy in uniform."

"True enough. I'm there fairly often, though usually not in uniform. I'm a Naval Reserve officer. My real work is shepherding a flock."

Chris jumped into the conversation. "He's Pastor of the American Church of Stockholm. Which, incidentally, is a mission of the American Lutheran Church. You're meeting a fellow Lutheran.

"You know Nils Schmidt, of course. I want to assure you that these gentlemen are not agents of the United States in any way other than being generous and courageous in helping to get you safely out of Sweden because they believe that's the right thing to do. Their careers are on the line here, so we need to be grateful.

"I'm not going to talk yet about the details of our plan to move you to the United States. You'll see it unfold as we go along. You all need to know that the letter I just received from our coordinator informed us that the Soviets have filed a serious complaint with the Swedish Government, to the effect that a western intelligence service has kidnapped Sasha. The Swedish Police have distributed an All Points Bulletin to be on the lookout for him."

Schmidt was now driving on Valhallavägen, headed for the E4 and Sweden's west coast. "Jesus Christ! That really is serious. I wasn't counting on anything like that." He turned to look at Pastor Stewart briefly. "Sorry for the language, Bill, but this could turn into a terrible situation for all of us."

"Don't worry, Nils," said Bill. "What I want to know is how Chris and Sasha interpret this. They're in a better position than you or I to review the situation and recommend damage control."

No one spoke for a minute, as each of the four thought about his own personal situation, should he be stopped by the Swedish Police. The silence was broken by Chris. "You need to know, Sasha, that we'll be driving to the west coast and on the road for about seven hours. My own opinion is that the Swedes will give lip service to the Soviet Ambassador's complaint. They'll have notices posted at the airports and train stations, and probably in the police stations that provide highway patrols. I doubt that they would go so far as to establish road blocks, but they might give a special look at passengers boarding planes or trains. Any roadblocks would be on the main roads going out of Stockholm, but I think the chances for that are so small that we'd be wasting our time by taking side roads or any other kind of evasive action."

Nils spoke up. "I agree with Chris that it's unlikely we'll meet roadblocks. Practically unthinkable. But this sure as hell scares me. Problem is, with this government we have in Sweden I can't imagine what they would do to me if I were picked up."

Plotkin spoke up. "I think Chris has understood the situation quite well. The lip service part, especially. In nearly every department of my Embassy, the officers complain that their Swedish counterparts talk cooperation but don't follow up. I believe you have an expression for it: 'They talk the talk but don't walk the walk.' We have some sympathizers among the police, but in general the Swedish authorities do only what they absolutely have to do legally in helping us. That doesn't mean I'm not frightened. Like Nils, I don't have much idea of what the police would do if they found us all together. If they physically tried to get me into the hands of Soviet authorities, I would do everything possible to escape that fate, including killing myself.

"Also, Chris, I feel like you're leading me into a dark tunnel, with no way of knowing where it comes out. You're taking me to the west coast for what? Is there a plane that's going to pick me up? Are you going to put me into a box and ship me somewhere? How am I going to get out of here? I hope you have a very safe plan."

"I'm sorry to keep you in the dark, Sasha. The less you know, the better off you are in this business. So all you have to do now is settle back for a few hours and pray if you feel like it. We'll see what happens. We won't be stopping at a gas station to fuel up. Nils has extra gas in the trunk of the car. He'll pull onto a quiet side road when it's necessary to gas up again, which should only be once. You can take a leak then. Try to hold it to that once. If you really can't, tell Nils and he'll find a place to pull off the road. Did you bring the sandwiches and drinks for the trip, Nils?"

"They're in that box on the floor between you and Sasha."

Plotkin, still nervous, was not so easily put off. "If we're stopped, what's the cover story?"

"We're friends on a trip to Oslo. Nils has an office and apartment there, where he does sometimes take guests for a few days of business or relaxation."

An uncomfortable silence followed. Finally, Plotkin made a suggestion. "If I have to identify myself, I think it would probably be best for me to be a Swede. I could pass as a Swedish photographer. But the only documentation I have with me is as a Soviet diplomat. I can't show that!"

"Even if we're stopped by the police, as passengers we may not have to show identity documents. It's a sure thing that Nils would have to. If worse came to worst, and the authorities wanted you to ID yourself, you could claim the wallet with all your documents was stolen just before you came on this trip."

"But what if I were searched?"

"Good point. What all do you have in your pockets? You sure as hell have to get rid of any identifying stuff like your passport. Better to be picked up with nothing in your pockets than with what you have now." Plotkin emptied his pockets of everything but a few Swedish coins and folded everything into a piece of notepaper, which he hid under the floor mat in the rear seat.

In the back of the car there was no more talk. Chris and Sasha were deep into their own thoughts as the car passed Västberga on the way to joining the E3. If Plotkin paid attention, he would wonder why they were taking such a southerly route when the cover story was a trip to Oslo.

CHAPTER THIRTY

Monday evening, November 13, 1972
En route to the west coast

The exfiltration party had covered about two-thirds of the distance to their destination. Though tired and tense, the travelers were growing more optimistic about completing this phase of the operation. The sandwiches provided by Nils were eaten, one thermos of coffee was emptied and a second held in reserve for the driver. Both Chris and Bill Stewart offered to relieve Schmidt at the wheel, which seemed a sensible safety measure considering that the man otherwise would be driving in stormy weather for many hours with only one short break. He refused the offer. "If we're stopped for any reason, we'll get through the situation best if a real Swede—and the real owner of the car—is at the wheel." Wise words, as it turned out.

The break was taken at ten thirty in the evening, when they were about fifteen minutes away from reaching Mariestad on the E3 highway. With his fuel gauge showing close to empty, Nils did not want to take a chance of running out of fuel while passing through a city. He'd hoped to make it to the turnoff for Lidköping on the smaller Highway 44, where there would be less traffic. But with four good-sized passengers and a can of gas in the back, his trusty old station wagon had used more fuel than usual. Given that fact and everybody's need to pee, he took the first turnoff onto a county road. Two pieces of good fortune made the stop possible and relatively pleasant. First, there was no traffic on the side road during the five minutes they parked in a gated turnout to a farm field. Second, the weather had eased to a light sprinkle of rain and gentle breeze, which meant that fueling with a gas can was much easier than in the middle of a storm and their time out of the car was more agreeable. The road was narrow and the distance to the gate was short, forcing Schmidt to back and fill when it was time to return to the highway. At one point he lightly touched a gate post with what he presumed was the bumper.

By eleven thirty they were on Highway 44, halfway to Lidköping from the E3. Chris and Plotkin were sound asleep in the back seat, Bill Stewart dozing alongside Nils when the rearview mirror alerted Nils to another car coming up fast from behind, blue lights flashing. He slowed and pulled off onto the shoulder of the road.

Chris was awakened by a pulsing blue light and Nils Schmidt muttering, "Shit!" As he raised his head he saw a scene that was well lighted by the headlamps of a vehicle behind them. He had just started to realize what was happening when the dark-blue uniform of a Swedish Police traffic officer passed the window. Nils was already rolling down his side window when the officer arrived to stand alongside the car. He was a tall fellow, so tall that he had to stoop a long way down to look at the driver. He gave only a cursory glance in the car as he asked the driver for his license and identity card. Nils produced both without saying a word.

"Good Lord," the officer said when he'd seen the documents. Now he got down on his haunches alongside the driver so that Schmidt could see him. "Don't you know who I am, Nils?"

Nils replied in Swedish. "Lars! I'll be goddamned! Lars Lindblad! I never see you except in good weather when you're racing those little dinghies. What are you doing this far from Uddevalla? That is where you live, isn't it?"

"I might ask the same question. What are you doing out on a miserable night like this?" Officer Lindblad dropped his initial cordiality and his face grew serious.

"Well, Lars, I can tell you it's not for fun. My friends and I are on our way to Oslo for a business meeting tomorrow. We couldn't get away from my offices until after the close of business this evening." Schmidt seemed relaxed and casual, though he had to be going through hell.

"But why are you taking such a southerly route to get to Oslo?"

Schmidt didn't seem fazed by the question. "I haven't seen my boat—the *Valhalla*—since she was laid up in harbor at Hamburgsund in late September. Same slip as when you sailed with me on that trip a couple of years ago. This is going to take us longer, but it gives me a chance to make a quick check on a new watchman. Ulrich died last summer and I'm not entirely comfortable with the fellow who replaced him. They tell me that Bengt Larson is a bit of a drunk.

"Let me ask you a question. Why did you stop me? I know I wasn't going over the speed limit. I haven't gone through any stop signs. There haven't been any for a long time. My old Volvo may look a little worn, but she's in Bristol condition. It's good to see you, Lars, but you didn't stop me to say 'hello.'"

"If I had known it was you I might have. No, I stopped you because your right rear tail light is out."

"Can't be. I checked all the lights when we stopped for gas an hour ago." Schmidt felt this might be some kind of trumped-up charge just for the excuse of checking on his passengers.

"Sorry, but it's true. Come out here and take a look for yourself." Officer Lindblad stepped back in order to let Nils open the driver's door.

Schmidt's passengers were more worried than Schmidt seemed to be. In the light shining through the back window Chris could see that Plotkin was quickly losing his cool, even putting his hand on the door handle as if ready to bolt. He nudged the KGB officer with his elbow in order to make eye contact and shake his head slightly, warning him not to panic.

Plotkin spoke very softly in Swedish, "I hate boats. I get deathly sick on boats." *Fine time to learn that.*

"Tell me about it later, not now," Chris whispered in return.

* * *

Meantime, Nils Schmidt found that his friend Lars was correct. The tail light on the right side was not lit and the glass was cracked. The reason was obvious. While he had backed into the gate post at the rest stop, he had hit the tail light, not the bumper. Cursing himself for a fool, he borrowed Lindblad's toolbox. The fixture wasn't badly damaged and the bulb had just been loosened. A little wiggling got it lit right away, so the only remaining problem was the cracked red glass cover. He was sure the police would not stop him again just for that.

While doing the repair, Schmidt kept up a lively conversation with the police officer. All about sailing, which was the only thing they had in common. The advantage he had over Lars Lindblad lay in the fact that bigger really is better, at least when it comes to sailboats. The *Valhalla* was the envy of the sailing community in Scandinavia, a boat very few could afford to buy, and still fewer could afford the upkeep of a wooden boat that size. The experience of sailing on her was to be treasured. Schmidt treated it as a boat to be sailed hard, not for family vacations. Consequently he took only experienced sailors on summer cruises. Lindblad had enjoyed that experience just once, and his questions made it obvious that this was an adventure he'd like to repeat. Schmidt played shamelessly into that desire, talking while he worked on the car about plans to sail to Iceland on a three-week cruise in July. Would Lars like to go along as a crewman for a week of that voyage?

Would Lars like to go? Schmidt smiled to himself. Did it snow in the Alps? Lindblad was holding the toolbox for Schmidt as he worked, asking questions about dates and who else might be aboard. His caution at the beginning of the stop had been thrown to the winds. When the repair was done, Schmidt gave the man one of his business cards, first writing the dates on the back. In parting, the officer said he would not be writing up the stop in view of the fact that nothing was really wrong. It didn't hurt, Schmidt thought, that Lars had received the invitation of a lifetime.

Falling into the driver's seat, Schmidt started the car and took off, rising slightly in his seat to settle into a more comfortable position. "Jesus Christ!" he said. "And I'm not going to apologize this time, Bill. You can take that as a prayer of thanks!"

"No need, Nils. I was praying pretty hard myself for a miracle. Some might think it self-serving, but not me, not under these circumstances. I guess our prayers were answered, but I can't understand how God helped you get out of that one."

"I just about had to sell my soul. I've spent years planning for a three-week trip on the *Valhalla* to Iceland this coming summer. A lot of my sailing friends would kill for a chance to go along on that trip, so choosing a crew has been a bitch. I've had my crew lined up for a year now, and just about all the plans have been completed. So I did something I thought I could never do.

"Lars Lindblad is a really fine young guy and a wonderful competitive sailor in some of the smaller boats. He loves the *Valhalla* and really enjoyed the one trip he took with me into the Baltic. I offered him a berth on that trip to Iceland. I can't tell you the problems that will create with my sailing friends. You saw what it did, though. He was eating out of my hand by the time we finished back there. About the only thing I can do now is pray that one of my older crew members dies before July."

Staring straight ahead, Stewart said, "God sometimes works in mysterious ways."

Schmidt continued driving into the blustery weather, silent now, mulling over how he was going to manage crew positions for next summer's cruise. He turned on the car radio, tuning it to a classical radio station. The program was devoted to choral music, putting their small team in a nostalgic and somewhat sad mood as it headed into the unknown.

After his pronouncement about God's mysterious ways, Bill Stewart started to nod off. Those in the back seat were all too alert. Chris did his best to ignore Plotkin, who had been glaring at him ever since realizing they would be leaving Sweden by boat. He'd managed to keep the man quiet as long as Officer Lindblad had been outside the car. Plotkin remained quiet for the first five minutes of their resumed journey, his expression thunderous. Finally he said, "Why did you not tell me we would leave by boat? I hate boats. Especially small boats!"

They were speaking quietly, but Chris was uncomfortable with the others hearing the conversation so he switched to Russian. "Do you mean you get seasick?"

"I get boat sick."

"So you suffer from motion sickness? How could you ever ride around in tanks with that condition?"

"No, No! I do not suffer from what you call motion sickness. I suffer only from boat sickness."

Chris was teetering between exasperation and alarm. "Then how could you bounce around the countryside in war tanks? I don't understand why riding on a boat should be that much different."

Plotkin was becoming increasingly aggravated. "Tanks don't rock, they just beat the hell out of you. It's that rolling motion that gets me on a boat. This is really serious. I didn't tell you much about that private boat from Stockholm to Tallin when I was just eleven years old. It was a little boat and the Baltic was stormy. I got so sick that I was afraid I was going to die. Then I really got sick, so sick that I was afraid I might live. My mother seriously feared for my life. I was sick for weeks after that, probably five kilos lighter in weight when we reached Gammalsvenskby. That was a terrible beginning to a terrible time. I've avoided boats ever since."

"You told me once that you were going to take the night boat to Helsinki."

"I lied. It was a diversion. I had a reservation but didn't use it. I've never been on that trip. It's hard to live in Scandinavia without being on a ferry boat or two. I've done short trips on some, when it was calm, but most of the time I fly. Nothing else bothers me, just boats. I can't leave here by boat!"

"Be realistic, Sasha. There's no other way. We've gone to huge trouble to get you safely out of Sweden. You're damned lucky that this could be arranged and that we have friends like Nils and Bill who are willing to put themselves in danger for you."

Hearing his name, Schmidt spoke up from the driver's seat. "What's going on back there? I thought we were going to keep to English so all of the team knows what's happening. If there's an argument, let's keep it to a language we all understand." Bill Stewart, shaken out of his half-slumber by the angry voices, added his agreement.

"Sorry, Gentlemen." Chris leaned forward between the front seats to speak to the others in English. "It turns out that our friend here is deathly afraid of boats. Says he gets seriously ill on anything smaller than a ferry boat sailing in smooth waters. He wants some other way to get out of Sweden."

"Yes, yes! Some other way." Plotkin was so upset he was nearly shouting.

Nils Schmidt's voice rose to match the Russian's. "I'll be goddamned. Some other way? Do you have any idea of what Chris has gone through to get you this far? Do you realize that Bill and I are going so far out of our way to help you that our lives could be changed forever?" His anger spilled over. "What kind of an idiot are you?"

Chris interrupted as Plotkin spluttered a retort. "Please, gentlemen, please. This kind of thing does nobody any good." Then, turning to Plotkin, he continued in English: "Sasha, the fact is that you will be leaving Sweden by boat or not at all. We have no backup plan. This is it. If you want to run once we've reached our destination, you'll just have to run. We won't try to overpower you. There's no way we want to bolster your government's case by physically kidnapping you. So face it. Either you go with us by boat, or you stay. And you need to know that if you stay we'll disown you. We'll claim that nothing like this ever happened, that it's just another example of Soviet disinformation."

A couple of minutes of silence followed. Plotkin sat glumly, hands folded, rubbing his thumbs together. Occasionally he unclasped them, using his right hand to rub his forehead, a nervous gesture Chris had noted before. "How big is the boat? How long will we be on it? Where are you taking me?"

Schmidt jumped in to answer the first question. "My boat is famous for being seaworthy. She's a very big sixty-five-foot sailboat, an old one built especially for the North Sea. You'll have as comfortable a ride as you can get on those waters. Chris can tell you the rest, if he's of a mind to do it now."

"Thanks, Nils. I think it's time for you to know the rest, Sasha, but remember that if you jump we'll claim that all this is the fevered imagination of some Soviet citizen. You won't be on the *Valhalla*—Nils' boat—very long. Probably about four hours, give or take an hour. We just have to get outside Swedish waters and then transfer to an American ship. Before you start asking questions about that, let me say that I simply can't give you the details on that ship right now."

"What kind of ship?"

"You already know I can't tell you. You'll find out when it happens."

"Why can't you tell me? I need to know."

"Get serious, Sasha. You're threatening to leave us, and you think I'm going to give you more operational information to share with your service?"

"I won't share it."

"You're right. You won't share it because you won't have it. I said, get serious. Are you going with us or do you want to give up the game right now? Like I said, there's no point in our trying to restrain you. You already crapped out on me once. If you do it again you can say goodbye to any future chance of defecting to the States. Or the Brits, for that matter. Make up your damned mind. We could drop you in the next town that has a rail line and go on to Oslo for a good time with Nils. What's it going to be?"

Plotkin continued looking glum. "I will go with you. But I want to know more details before I step on the boat."

"Give it up, Sasha. You'll know when it happens. As we Americans say, 'Shit or get off the pot.' What's it going to be?"

"I need more time to think about it."

"You get no more time." Chris was tired of sparring with this supposed friend turned personal enemy turned pain in the ass. "Nils, how far is it to a town where we could drop our friend Sasha?"

"Uddevalla. We're half an hour away. It's another half hour from there to the boat."

"There you have it, Sasha. Half an hour to decide if you want to give this up. Another hour in the car if you decide you want to go through with it this time. What's it going to be? I can't believe that boat sickness would keep you from acting on a decision that's taken so long to make."

"You don't understand how afraid I am of getting on a small boat. It would be like purposely putting myself into a situation of torture. I'll take the half hour."

"What will you do if we leave you in Uddevalla?"

"I've come through a lot of tight spots. I'm pretty sure I can manage to get out of Sweden without the Swedes or my service knowing it. Just leave me alone for a while. I need to think about it."

Chris said nothing in reply. He was flying by the seat of his pants, wondering how other operatives would handle such a unique situation. It was a serious gamble to threaten Plotkin with leaving him in Uddevalla. The man was a highly experienced, clever operator, who could just possibly manage an escape from Sweden on his own. The fate of this operation would be decided in part during the next minutes. If Plotkin decided to go with them, there was some chance now that they could pull it off. If he insisted on leaving the party in Uddevalla, Chris would have to figure out what to do from there. Actually, he didn't want to think about it, preferring to wait until the moment came. It was not worth straining his tired brain cells until the actual moment came.

Plotkin stared out the window for about ten minutes, folding and unfolding his hands, rubbing his thumbs together, stroking his forehead from time to time. Finally, he said, "Okay, let's go to the boat, wherever that is. But Nils, you better have a bucket ready and keep me away from the deck. I know I'll suffer, and I want to suffer quietly, someplace inside with my bucket. Alone. Nobody putting his hand on my shoulder to ask if he can help."

A collective sigh went up from other members of the party.

CHAPTER THIRTY-ONE

Tuesday, November 14, 1972

With the exception of Plotkin, all members of the exfiltration party had been to Hamburgsund on Sweden's west coast, a couple of hour's travel north of Gothenburg. Nils Schmidt spent time there with his boat, while Chris and Bill Stewart had visited only once, when they helped Schmidt sail the *Valhalla* into the Baltic.

Coming down from the low hills of the Swedish west coast—now on the level runout to their destination—three men in the party viewed the scene before them with memories of its high season. Plotkin, already depressed by the thought of going out on a small boat, was visibly disheartened by the scene. In fact there wasn't much to see, what with the darkness, rain and wind.

Hamburgsund is one of the larger small towns situated on the Swedish west coast in the province of Bohuslän. The province is a magical playground in summer, swarming with Swedes and foreigners. The geography is unique, with low hills bordering the rocky coastline. The town is protected on the west by Hamburgö, a fairly large island reached only by private boat or a small car ferry painted a bright orange color. As the party approached, the ferry was tied up for the night on the mainland side, brightly lit by overhead lights on the dock. For Plotkin, this first real view of Hamburgsund was a spooky sight in the foul weather.

"Sweet Jesus, what's that?"

Schmidt laughed. "Don't worry your head, Sasha. That's not my boat. It's a car ferry."

"It doesn't look much like a car ferry to me. I hope your boat is bigger than that!"

"Not really." Schmidt swung his Volvo to the left, around a number of darkened buildings, coming to a rest in the parking lot of a small marina. He left the headlights burning. "There she is!"

"Where?" Plotkin was pressed forward between the front seats, looking for the boat he would be traveling on.

"Right ahead of us. The sailboat."

"But it's not even as big as that ferry boat!"

"Believe me, in this weather you'll be better off on the *Valhalla* than you would be on that ferry. We're wasting time. According to the schedule, Chris, we have to be out of here before two o'clock. Sooner if possible. Sunrise this morning is about seven thirty. For real darkness we'll want to transfer before five thirty.

"Shake a leg, everyone. Bill, take off the spring lines and stow them below. We don't want them on deck in this weather. We'd lose them for sure. Chris!" Schmidt reached in his pocket for a key ring, taking off one of the keys and handing it to Chris. "Do you remember those lockers over there? Mine is Number twenty-seven. You'll find some survival suits in there. We'll need just the two. Nothing else from the locker, so close it up and bring the suits. I'm going aboard right now to open up and get the engine warmed." The wind was rising as he spoke.

The group had been standing in front of the Volvo. With those words Plotkin sagged back against the hood of the car, then jumped up to go to the locker with Chris. "Why only two survival suits?"

"Because you and I are the only ones who will need them." Chris took a mean pleasure in frightening Plotkin still more, knowing that it wasn't very smart or operationally sound to do so. To Hell with it. He didn't care anymore.

Yes he did. "Don't worry, Sasha, they're just a precaution to keep us safe and warm when we transfer at sea." Yes, he did care. Yes, he cared about his own integrity, about how his actions affected his family. He cared about being a fine model of a man to his children. Plotkin had to be kept aware that their so-called friendship had ended, but that did not mean that Chris could treat him any way other than in a professional, humane manner.

He had to keep this guy focused on the task at hand. "While I'm doing this, you better go back to the car and retrieve the stuff we put under the floormat. You don't need to hide your identity documents now."

As Plotkin started toward the car and Chris was unlocking the storage unit, a new figure appeared on the scene. A short fireplug of a man, a burly fellow dressed against the storm in hooded oilskins, walked toward Chris with the wide stance of a seaman, rolling rather unsteadily and shouting hoarsely. "What are you doing in my locker?" He turned to look at the *Valhalla*, light now shining from the cabin portholes. "And who the hell is on my boat?"

This was not a good development. Chris guessed correctly that the man sputtering before him was Schmidt's watchman for the boat. "I thought the *Valhalla* belonged to Nils Schmidt."

"'Course it does. But when he's not here it's my responsibility, just like I'm responsible for that locker you're breaking into." Chris edged toward the sailboat, hoping that Larson would follow him and not see Plotkin, who wisely had ducked into Nils's station wagon and hunkered down. Pastor Bill, having stowed the spring lines, squatted down on the far side of the boat where he was hard to spot in the dark and burgeoning storm.

Nils Schmidt was coming back on deck as the two men approached the boat. He responded to the unwelcome presence of his watchman with the same apparent ease as when they were stopped on the road by Lars Lindblad.

"Good to see you're on the job, Bengt. We were passing by and wanted to make sure the old girl was snugged up for the storm. Come aboard and have a drink." He asked Chris to finish checking the locker and wait for him there.

When Schmidt had gone below with his watchman, Bill Stewart jumped onto the dock and joined Chris at the locker. The six-by-eight-foot space was a cozy shelter from the storm. Hoping Plotkin would be smart enough to stay in the car, they closed the door, turned on the overhead light and held a two-man war council.

Stewart said, "I think somebody up there is lying down on the job. I presume this guy who showed up is the watchman. What do we do now?"

"The easiest thing would be to throw him in the drink," Chris answered, "but obviously we can't do that. How about we lock him in here? The latch on the outside is padlocked, so he couldn't get out before you and Nils return from the run out to sea."

Stewart was sitting on a large coil of rope. "Good plan, but how do we pull it off?"

The two men took their time discussing just how such a plan might work, from inventing an excuse to lure Larson into the locker to physically snatching him off the boat. They finally decided to wing it. Chris would go back to the *Valhalla* to see if he could steal a moment with Nils Schmidt to discuss the plan, while Pastor Bill would hide out in the car with Plotkin.

Chris opened the door, poised to dash through the storm. The scene before them changed the plan. Schmidt was making his way across the dock toward town with an arm clasped around Bengt Larson, who was lurching even more than when he first appeared. Given the extra time, Chris went back to the original plan and chose two of the bright orange survival suits. After closing and securing the locker, he and Bill Stewart headed for the boat. They rousted Sasha from the car along the way. At the boat they found that Nils had left the engine idling. Judging from the size of the scattered raindrops, heavy rain would soon accompany the storm. They climbed aboard and found the rain gear required for deck work. Stewart remained on deck to keep an eye out for Schmidt's return, while Chris and Plotkin went below. It was only moments before the skipper came trotting back to his boat.

"I turned Bengt over to his wife. They live just a few hundred meters up from the docks." He struggled into his own rain gear—hooded oilies essential in this weather.

Shouting down the companionway, he told Chris to put Plotkin in the forward cabin. "There are covers on the portholes there. Be sure to slide them into place before you turn on any light in the cabin. Here—you can use this flashlight until you get that done." Chris caught the flashlight and was moving forward when Nils called to him again. "Chris! You better check in the galley on the way and rustle up a bucket. I don't want to come back to port with a cabin full of puke!"

The *Valhalla* had cleared the dock and was nosing into the waterway when Chris came back on deck. "I notice you're not showing any lights, Nils. Do you plan to run this way?"

"Absolutely. We should be able to slip out of here without raising too much curiosity. I don't figure on using running lights until we're well out to sea."

"How about meeting other traffic coming into the harbor?"

"Unlikely at this time of year. There's obviously no pleasure boat traffic in this weather. With a storm coming, the commercial fishermen will have already returned to port. I know the channel like the back of my hand, so we shouldn't have any trouble. You fellows can help keep a lookout."

Chris didn't like the proposition. Not because of the danger of running without lights, but because of the appearance of stealth. "This part of it is your show, Nils, but the idea worries me. What if someone has been watching and sees us depart that way?"

"I'm sure nobody has seen us. At this time of year the town closes up tight by nine o'clock in the evening. There's a watchman at the ferry dock, sleeping in a shack. He's there just in case of fire or an explosion; something drastic. Nobody's seen us."

"Yes, but what if? Seems likely to me that anybody seeing us running without lights, anybody who was alert, would call the authorities. I know I would. I bet you would, too. The first thing that would enter my mind was that someone was stealing your boat."

The idea of his boat being stolen hit a chord in Schmidt's mind. "I think you're right. Let's keep the noise down while we get ready." He turned on the running lights. They motored quietly through the maritime center of activity for

Hamburgsund, passing the brightly lit ferry.

"How long before we hit the Skagerrak?" Chris asked the skipper.

"It's about one of your land miles, so we'll make it in a little under ten minutes. It'll take another ten minutes or so to clear Hamburgö and get into the open waters of the Skagerrak. That's where we'll feel this storm, coming right up the slot between Norway and Denmark. We'll be on a northwest heading, so the weather will hit us on the port bow. It looks to be a gale, or just short of it. That's no problem for this boat. It'll be more of a problem for the passenger, and it seems to me it's going to be a real bitch to transfer you and your friend. Norm gave me the latitude and longitude, and approximate time to rendezvous with the submarine. I also got some blinker light recognition signals. Do you know any more details?"

"You know more than I do."

"When Norm gave me that note for you, he also gave me one with the directions. What I know is that we're meeting an American sub as close as possible to five thirty in the morning. The latitude and longitude put us about mid-point on a line between Fredrikstad in Norway and Skagen, at the northern tip of Jutland. I guess that's as neutral a spot as you could find politically without running all the way out into the North Sea, but it's about as bad as you could find as far as weather is concerned. It's often a nasty piece of water at this time of year. You'll see that as soon as we break loose from the shelter of Hamburgö."

They were nearing the entrance to the channel now and beginning to feel long swells gently raising and lowering the *Valhalla*. Chris wondered how his so-called friend was faring down below. "How far is it from the channel entrance to the rendezvous point?"

"I charted it out to eighteen nautical miles. I figure we'll make about six knots over the bottom in this storm, so you can plan on a good three hours. Throw in more storm and we'll probably hit it a bit after five thirty. I'm not very concerned about getting there. What does concern me is first of all how we're going to get you and Sasha transferred to a great big rounded tub of a submarine. I'm wondering, too, how Sasha is going to survive. That was quite a show of panic he put on back there about getting seasick. Do you think it was genuine?"

"I'm sure it was. It looks like a real phobia, coming from a time when he was a young kid and got very sick out on the Baltic. When I left him below he was acting embarrassed about it." Now Schmidt spun the large wheel at the stern of the boat, bringing the *Valhalla* onto a southwesterly course, getting ready to round Gåson Island for a final turn northwest to their destined rendezvous. The surge had turned into higher, shorter waves. With the wind and waves coming from dead ahead, the *Valhalla* was getting spray over the bow. Chris was impressed by the steadiness of the boat, which cut determinedly through the waves with a minimum of pitching.

Soon after making the turn they were joined by Pastor Stewart, carefully making his way aft after serving as the bow lookout in the channel. "How are we doing? It looks pretty nasty out there."

The skipper replied: "You can already see that this old girl handles weather well. Chris, take the wheel for now and keep her on the same heading. I need to go below to the navigation table to get the Loran C set up and work out our exact bearing to the rendezvous point."

Chris was beginning to get a feel for steering the boat when Schmidt's head popped up out of the companionway. "Turn the wheel over to Bill, and get down here right away!"

When Chris dropped down the ladder into the salon area, he was met by a worried skipper. "I don't have time to go looking for Sasha, but you can see from here that he's not up in that forward cabin."

"Don't worry, Nils, I'll take care of it. He must be in the head."

The marine toilet enclosure was a small compartment on the port side of the boat, big enough to sit on the toilet but cramped for kneeling in front of it. When Chris moved forward he could hear the sound of retching over the noise of wind, waves, and the creaking sounds of a wooden boat. He rapped on the door. "Sasha! Are you okay?"

There was no reply for a moment. Then, "Do I sound like I'm okay?"

"It must be awfully cramped in there. Wouldn't you rather sit out here someplace with a bucket?"

"Go away, Chris, just go away! I told you I don't want any kind of sympathy. Go away!"

"Okay. I'll be back down in a while to check on how you're doing."

Chris didn't bother Schmidt as he passed through the compartment where the skipper was working out the navigation. It was not long after he rejoined Pastor Stewart on deck that Schmidt came up hurriedly and took over the wheel. He checked his watch in the dim light of the binnacle, counted down four minutes from the last position he had taken with Loran C, then came to starboard on the final course to the rendezvous. The change brought an uncomfortable ride that took the motion from pitching to a combination of pitching and rolling that could best be described as wallowing. Despite the hatred Chris felt for Plotkin at one level, he could not help but feel sympathy for him in these conditions, a motion of the boat that could not have been better designed to guarantee seasickness in anyone the least prone to that condition.

And so they continued through the early morning hours. Schmidt went below every half hour for a Loran C check on their position, discovering with each check that the weather was having less effect on their course than he expected. Their speed over the bottom was holding close to his prediction at a bit over six knots, and corrections to the course bearings were keeping him hopeful of arriving at the proper time and place to meet the sub. At four thirty in the morning the waves had tapered off to three or four feet, and the anemometer was showing winds down to a steady eighteen miles an hour, with gusts not much higher than twenty-five. On his last visit below, Chris had found Plotkin stretched out on a lower bunk in the forward cabin, pale but alert. He wouldn't say much, but seemed to perk up at the news that their transfer to a bigger vessel should come within the hour. There was nothing in the bucket on the deck alongside him. Through the awful sickness he had managed to put everything that came up into the marine toilet.

"In about half an hour," Chris told him, "I'm going to come get you so we can start putting on the survival gear. We'll do that in the compartment where we left the suits, then go up on deck to await the ship we're planning to meet. Do you think you're going to be able to handle that?"

"I could handle the Devil himself if he could get me off this boat!"

Back on deck, Chris talked with the crew about plans for meeting the sub and transferring the two men. Once they were underway and on course for the rendezvous point, Schmidt had shown Chris and Pastor Bill the instructions from Norm Wykowski. They were brief, beginning with the time for meeting, and then the latitude and longitude of the rendezvous point. Upon first seeing each other, the two craft would exchange light signals. If the sub crew was not satisfied that the *Valhalla* had identified itself properly with these signals, they would dive and not return. When they found each other the *Valhalla* was to be positioned in the lee of the sub, standing off about one hundred yards. "Do not take any action to effect or assist the transfer." After that order, the instructions briefly indicated that the two subjects to be transferred must stay on deck and wait for action by the sub's crew.

Plotkin, though pale and weak, managed to get out of the bunk on his own when the time came, and to climb into the survival suit with only a little help. Chris observed Sasha carefully while he was trying to zip up the front of the suit. From the light spilling out of the forward cabin he could see that the man was still sick, his Adam's apple bobbing frequently as he swallowed, but he was no longer retching. He'd make it.

The men were ready to go up on deck just as the skipper headed down the ladder to check on their progress. Schmidt stayed below to make a last check on the boat's position while the two to be transferred sat down on deck in their orange suits, one on the port side of the boat and the other to starboard, with their backs against the cabin. From that low position facing aft they saw Pastor Bill behind the great wheel at the helm, his height and bulk exaggerated by the angle of view. The sky cleared as the storm seemed to ease. Stewart threw his rain hood back, away from the head of prickly ginger-colored hair that defied the dampness. With his height and bulk, hair and beard, and half-smile of expectation, Pastor Bill Stewart looked for all the world like a Viking ready to explore new lands.

The skipper called up from the companionway. "We've arrived! Put her up into the wind, Bill, and slow to idle. It's only five twenty in the morning. Let's see if we can hold this position while we're waiting for our friends to pop up."

CHAPTER THIRTY-TWO

A Sturgeon Class fast attack nuclear submarine, the USS *Rockfish*, was assigned to rendezvous with the *Valhalla*. With pressure brought down at most-secret levels from the Director, CIA, through Chief, Naval Operations and the appropriate Naval Special Warfare Groups, a submarine would have been found in good time, but not as quickly as in the case of the *Rockfish*. She proved to be in a fortuitous position to handle the task.

While on a three-month assignment in North Sea waters off the coast of Norway, the *Rockfish* developed problems with the steam turbine, fired by a nuclear reactor. She was still able to run submerged at reduced speed but needed a repair before completing the mission. The closest secure port was Holy Loch in Scotland—where the U.S. Navy maintained a refit facility for nuclear submarines at the former World War II Royal Navy Submarine Base—with three submarine tenders and a large dry dock.

The diagnosis and proposed fix for the problem required replacement of two valves, each a different type, and neither available at the Holy Loch facility. Queries to the home port facility, the General Dynamics Electric Boat Division in Connecticut (builder of the *Rockfish*), and the manufacturer of the steam turbine, brought an estimate of time required for shipping of the parts and completion of the repair as fifteen days. Commander Ronald Smith, skipper of the *Rockfish*, requested and received permission to grant leave to a limited number of his 115-man crew; a remaining complement of officers and sailors would be sufficient to run the submarine efficiently and safely, if not at full battle-readiness. Included among those lucky enough to get leave were two Navy Seals, members of a famed Special Forces group trained in unconventional warfare, counter-guerilla warfare and clandestine operations. Together with the two Seals still on the boat, they formed a team that would conduct an exercise as part of a large NATO maneuver—penetrating a beachhead on the northern Norwegian coast to clandestinely retrieve a dummy object two miles inland and return it to the sub. The task was scheduled late in the *Rockfish's* mission, so their scenario would not be affected by the stand-down.

The repair schedule went awry—in a way that favored the Plotkin mission. Replacement parts arrived in five days, with repairs completed so quickly that the *Rockfish* was ready for a sea trial by the sixth day after her arrival in Holy Loch, making it possible for the boat to be fully operational. But she was shy almost ten percent of her men, which meant she was not battle-ready. Initially it was decided that boat and crew could rest and wait for those on leave to return before conducting the sea trial. But that would not be the case.

Norm Wykowski dreamed up the idea of a submarine escape on the night of Wednesday, November 10th, about the same time Chris Holbeck was back-grounding on the Plotkin case at Headquarters. As a veteran officer communicating with other veterans who hand-coded cable messages in the old days, he knew how to communicate accurately with the fewest words possible. It was important not to show a hand to the Soviets through an upsurge in cable traffic sent from the Station. Gary Llonis took immediate action on the plea for a submarine pickup, exploring opportunities through the CIA Director and top Navy brass. The speed of response was nearly miraculous. Within a half-day it was learned that the *Rockfish* was in a stand-down situation at Holy Loch, awaiting crew on leave to return before a full complement permitted resuming the current mission. She could reach the Skagerrak in less than thirty-six hours and would not need the full crew to be operational for this kind of assignment.

By Saturday morning, November 13th, the details had been worked out, signatures placed on the Top Secret orders, and a message relayed to Commander Smith via a secure broadcast to the sub. The *Rockfish* skipper was happy to comply. Lying at dock with a restless crew was not his idea of submarine glamour. Local cover for the mission was set up via normal channels through a cable ordering him to do a shake-down cruise while waiting for the rest of the men to return from shore leave.

At her cruising speed underwater, the *Rockfish* had more than enough time to reach her destination in the Skagerrak on schedule. Though there was no indication of hostile interest in the voyage, the skipper chose to employ evasive maneuvers to use up the extra time, planning his navigation to reach the pickup site about an hour ahead of the appointed time. On site the submarine idled in circles at a hundred-foot depth, watching sonar for arrival of the exfiltration boat. Two large cargo ships passed to the southwest of their position during that time, headed for Copenhagen or other Baltic ports. Their route took them far enough away from the position that they probably would not have a visual sighting of the sailboat the *Rockfish* was expecting.

At five o'clock that Tuesday morning, the sonar operators reported sighting a slow-moving vessel approaching from the southeast, traveling at an estimated six to seven knots. That speed, and size estimates from the sonar, indicated that this was the vessel they were expecting. At five twenty the vessel hove to, only five hundred yards from the sub's position at the time. This must be it. Even so, as a matter of precaution Commander Smith decided to wait until five thirty exactly before surfacing at a reasonable distance from the boat.

* * *

If the crew aboard *Valhalla* was looking for a great surge as a submarine burst out of the water, they would have been disappointed. *Rockfish* was brought up in a gentle rise to the surface near the *Valhalla*, a gray ghost.

If not dramatic, the appearance was awe-inspiring. At 292 feet in length, *Rockfish* dwarfed the sixty-five-foot sailboat. The very bulk of the submarine, lying low in the water, topped by a sail structure rising high into the air, was truly a magnificent sight.

Commander Smith drifted his sub on the surface to a spot some one hundred yards upwind of the *Valhalla,* sheltering the smaller vessel with the bulk of his submarine. As the sailboat crew watched, they could make out in the dim light a half-dozen figures climbing on deck through a hatch aft of the sail, bringing an object with them that couldn't be made out in the low light condition. Though there was little doubt on either boat as to the other's identity, for the sake of security they exchanged light signal strings provided through their respective controllers—Nils Schmidt rather awkwardly using a powerful flashlight while the signalman on *Rockfish* used a proper blinker signal light.

An inflatable life raft was being readied for the transfer. In silhouette it was possible to see that two of the crewmembers were dressed differently from the others. The reason was clear when the raft was inflated and ready to go. As it was thrown into the water the two wet-suited swimmers dove in after it. Before long they headed for the *Valhalla,* one on each side of the raft, towing it over for the pickup. From a distance all of this seemed to be done with calm efficiency, making it appear that transfer to the *Rockfish* would be an anticlimax to the adventure of leaving Sweden. But when the raft with its swimmer power had traveled a dozen yards it dipped out of sight from the sailboat, obscured by the waves.

Valhalla was still headed into the weather. Chris and Plotkin were now on their feet and standing in the same positions as before, aft of the cabin. Chris could see that Plotkin, who was riveted by the scene, was more apprehensive than sick as the raft alternately came into view and disappeared. Drawing closer to the sailboat, raft and swimmers stayed in view and the crew could see there was a line attached to the raft, rigged so the deck crew on the submarine could haul it in on the return trip from the *Valhalla*.

Shortly before the swimmers brought the raft alongside, Nils Schmidt removed a section of rail on the starboard side, leaving a gap where the two departing the vessel could slip through and drop into the raft. The transfer was looking more precarious all the time. The *Valhalla* pitched softly in the waves, the lightweight raft riding their surface. It would be rising and falling several feet while alongside the sailboat. Not an easy boarding for men dressed in clumsy survival suits.

Schmidt readied two light lines as the swimmers approached. He threw one to the closest swimmer as the raft arrived, giving the other end to Chris. The second line went to the other swimmer. The skipper handed his end of that line to Pastor Bill, who now had the most difficult task of any aboard the boat. He was performing a balancing act at the helm—steering with his left hand and holding the second line to the raft with his right as he strove to let out line and bring it in. Meanwhile he had to deal with the changing levels of boat and raft while at the same time keeping *Valhalla* headed into the weather.

One of the swimmers yelled "Let's go, let's go! We need to get out of here. You guys will have to jump in when we're closest."

Chris in turn yelled at Plotkin, still standing behind the cabin on the port side, "Get over here Sasha. You go first." The KGB man moved cautiously across the boat, hanging on to rails atop the cabin whenever possible. Chris was holding on next to the gap in the starboard rail. He grasped a fold of Plotkin's survival suit to steady him. With no other purchase now, Plotkin was at his mercy.

"I'll tell you when to jump."

"I'm not sure ..." But he jumped when Chris and a swimmer yelled at the same time, landing awkwardly. A swimmer quickly moved around to the side of the raft to help him. "Move as far forward as you can!" he yelled. A moment later Chris jumped in at the maximum height of the raft's rise, landing partly in the raft, partly on top of Plotkin. It was not much of a drop, so neither man was hurt. They adjusted their positions and readied themselves for the ride across to the submarine. The swimmers released the lines to the *Valhalla*.

"Godspeed!" cried the skipper.

"God Bless!" cried Pastor Bill.

They maintained *Valhalla* in the same position, watching as the raft was hauled to the *Rockfish* at an unexpected speed. With Commander Smith urging them on from the conning tower, his deck crew was racing to bring the raft home as quickly as possible. A faint light of coming dawn streaked the eastern horizon, making the submarine skipper nervous. He wanted to get his crew and their passengers aboard as soon as possible in order to dive out of sight.

This made for an uncomfortable trip for the passengers. Riding buoyantly on top of the waves during the crossing to the sailboat, the raft with two big men aboard was now slamming into the waves, sending water cascading over and in. It was half full of water by the time they arrived at the submarine. Strong arms reached in to pull them aboard the sub.

There followed an amazing burst of coordinated activity, a blur that would be hard for them to describe in the future. While the deck crew deflated the raft, Chris and Plotkin were hustled below through the open hatch. Leaving his second-in-command at the helm, Commander Smith stood at the foot of the ladder. He instructed his passengers to remove their survival suits before going forward to the officers' quarters. A farewell wave from the two remaining crew on *Valhalla* at first went unseen in their haste to prepare *Rockfish* to dive out of sight. Finally, the last sailor on deck spotted them just as he was dropping into the open hatch and gave a vigorous two-arm wave before buttoning up for the journey back to Scotland.

If the sailor had stayed on deck another five minutes, he would have seen the *Valhalla's* sails raised in the moderating weather, preparing to beat a southeasterly course back to home port. A couple of old salts like Nils Schmidt and Pastor Bill Stewart were not going to miss the chance for a good sail on a boat that once again had shown its worth in saving lives.

CHAPTER THIRTY-THREE

Monday, November 13, 1972
Edmonds, Washington

As her husband saw the first hint of dawn on Tuesday, November 14th, experiencing the surge of adrenaline that comes with a first-rate adventure, Lisa sat in her parked car in Seattle's University District, trying to sort out her feelings. The sense of confusion and indecisiveness that had been dragging at her had been overtaken by euphoria at the prospect of finding closure.

It was late evening on Monday. She was reluctant to start the car and embark on the road for home before taking the time to think it all out, to make the crucial decisions arising from the $150 session. The best money she'd ever spent.

* * *

Since the Plotkin fiasco in Stockholm and her husband's transfer to Vietnam, Lisa had tried to be completely open with Chris, sharing with him every last snippet of her life at home in Edmonds with their four children and his parents. She felt good about that. The more she shared with Chris by letter and occasional telephone calls while he was in Vietnam, and when snuggled up to him in bed during the brief times he'd been home, the less she had to think, the less she was bothered by feelings she'd never been able to share. Feelings about being orphaned. Feelings about being seduced at the age of seventeen by Bert Brown. Feelings about ... about ... well, her true feelings about her youngest daughter, Lisbet. These she had never shared, even with her husband.

The only time Lisa had truly opened up to Chris was the terrible night she had revealed her affair with Plotkin. That confession had resulted in endless talk,

talk that was concerned with practicalities—whether or not to have an abortion, what to tell family and friends, what might be the effect on Chris's career. Not about feelings. There was a choking point in conversations where she couldn't go further. Not with Chris. Not with Mor. Not with anybody. That is, not with anybody except Elle, an acquaintance from her university days who had become a therapist working with troubled women.

Eleanor Bates—Elle as she preferred to be called—lived in the same dormitory with Lisa during her two years at the University of Washington. A class ahead of Lisa at the UW, she was called The Brain by girls in the dorm, who regularly asked for her academic help. Elle had later earned a PhD in psychology. She took the doctoral sheepskin to a low-rent office over a bank in the University District, scotch-taped it to the wall behind her desk in the office, and opened for business as a clinical psychologist for women only. Before long Elle's appointments calendar was so crowded that she rarely took on new patients. Women who had known her as a tutor for classes at the UW now also found Elle to be the best tutor for matters of the mind.

When a very confused, very hurt Lisa returned to the Seattle area with her children, one of her first moves was to renew friendships from earlier days. These attempts at building a new life outside the family structure were mostly disappointing. There were squeals of delight when she met her old friend Barbara Jensen for lunch at the Yacht Club in Everett. By the time the pleasant meal ended, both women realized they had grown in different directions. They continued to see each other every six months or so, but the joys of a childhood friendship never returned. The same was true with former classmates from the UW. There was no feeling of intimacy in these relationships, nothing that would make her comfortable enough to discuss deeply personal matters. She needed somebody to talk to, a sounding board, a confidante. When Lisa learned about Elle's success as a clinical psychologist, she decided that she must have her as a counselor.

When reached by phone in the office, Elle greeted Lisa warmly, but only laughed at the idea of taking her on as a client. "My dear Lisa, I could not take you on because my appointments calendar is full. I haven't accepted a new client for almost a year. But I would love to see you and hear directly about some of your adventures abroad. Could you have lunch with me here in the University District?"

That suggestion prompted lunch a couple of weeks later, and after a second lunch Elle was persuaded to take Lisa on as a client. Since the therapist/client relationship began it had been something of a standoff; their developing relationship seemed more friendship than professional. Seventy-five dollars for an hour in the evening every couple of weeks seemed a reasonable price to pay for friendship and some welcome time off from the family.

But a standoff it was. The client was not sharing her true feelings. Lisa realized this but could not open up.

Her fifth session was something of a breakthrough. Up to this point Lisa had related most of the facts of her life before and after the UW experience. Of course she left out the abuse by Bert Brown, and nothing, nothing could ever persuade her to admit to the brief fling with Sasha Plotkin.

On this night Elle didn't want to let Lisa get away with answering questions with questions, clamming up when the therapist probed more deeply into situations and the emotions they wrought up. She was too experienced as a therapist not to read between the lines.

In talking about the loss of her virginity, Lisa reminded Elle that she had been raised in a strong Lutheran Church culture until the age of fifteen, living with kind, nurturing parents who took it as a given that any decent woman would not be sexually active before her marriage. The loss of her parents, followed by experiences with foster parents and in college, had given her a more liberal view. She went on to relate that she nevertheless remained a good girl until losing her virginity in the moon shadow of the Washington Monument. Something in the way she told the story led Elle to doubt that this was the woman's first time.

Lisa's talking about her four kids raised another red flag for Elle. It was understandable that this mother would be proud of her teenage twin boys, bound for college in the fall, and that she would be devoted to an eight-year-old daughter who was incredibly smart, talented, loving, etc. But she talked most about the baby of the family, the little girl named Lisbet, providing unusually detailed explanations about her birth and development, how she had this one of Lisa's traits and that one of her husband's. The therapist had listened to enough of the so-called facts. Now it was time to start boring into the psyche.

Once they were settled, she asked if Lisa had any time constraints this evening. Elle had two hours available for this session. Would that work with children at home? Not a problem. She and the kids had moved in with the in-laws in preparation for the planned transfer to DC. Chris's mother enjoyed babysitting her grandchildren.

"Good. Let's figure, then, on going the full two hours. I don't have another session after yours, so it works out well for our treatment strategy. You've given me a good picture of your life up to now. We need to delve further into your emotional life.

"You've told me several times about how Chris was often gone during your marriage, sometimes for weeks at a time. How did this make you feel?"

"How would it make you feel?"

"I'm the one who's supposed to be asking questions here. How did it make you feel?"

Lisa brushed at some lint on her sweater. "I'm really interested in hearing how it would make you feel. Maybe then I could understand how I should feel."

Elle tried not to show her annoyance. "I'll be frank, Lisa. I've been talking with you to get an outline of what you wanted out of these sessions, what you thought I might do for you. A treatment strategy if you will. It's a beginning to the kind of trust, confidence and confidentiality needed for my clients to feel they can be open with me so I can help them. Somehow you and I haven't been able to establish that kind of relationship, even with the advantage of having known each other in the past. Why do you think that is?"

"Why won't you just answer my questions?"

Elle stood, then sat behind her desk. This was the first time she'd taken that position during sessions with Lisa, usually sitting in an armchair alongside the desk. "I'm tempted to end this therapy series."

"You wouldn't."

"I wouldn't leave you hanging. I would recommend a psychiatrist who might probe more deeply than I'm able to do as a clinical psychologist. But I don't think you need that. I think you need to get serious about this therapy by starting to be honest with yourself. Frankly, what you're doing with turning my questions back on me, by denying that you have feelings, is just a lot of crap. You're being emotionally dishonest. There's something in your background that you're hiding from me. Whatever it is, you surely remember it. I suspect that you skirt that memory, putting it back in storage when it rises to consciousness. Instead of dealing with the surrounding emotions, you've shut down or denied some of the feelings that control our lives. All this seems to have confused you so much that—if you truly believe what you've been telling me in these sessions—you've lost some understanding about the emotions that guide our lives. Does any of this make sense to you, Lisa?"

"I guess so."

"Am I right about an incident you're covering up?"

"Yes. I have to go to the bathroom." Lisa walked out of the office, into the dim hall, and found the public lavatory that serviced the five assorted offices on this floor. Not very well kept. She didn't really need to pee, so she just washed her hands and face, wrestled the dispenser into giving up a couple of sheets of paper towels, and returned to Elle's office.

"Where were we?"

"The incident you're not talking about."

"Oh, that."

"We can end this now, Lisa. I won't charge you for the time we've been together this evening, and we'll just call it quits. Or, you can decide that you truly want to work with me. Many of my patients start out our sessions with the thought that as a therapist I'll be doing all the work while they just sit back and get healed. Not so. The client—that's you, Lisa—must do the work. I am only the guide." Elle slipped out of her desk chair and moved back to the one alongside the desk.

"I want you to be honest with yourself in sharing with me what seems to be a troubling spot in your life. One that's never been resolved. Think you can do that?"

"I can try."

During the final hour of that session Lisa unburdened herself of the story of Bert's seduction. Once started, she was amazed by the details remembered, the emotions evoked, the real tears shed, as she described the first sexual act. Lisa was racked with sobs as she described her final acceptance of the fact that she'd been conned, cynically seduced by an older man.

Elle listened calmly, taking a note here and there but not commenting in any way other than to cluck in sympathy and hand tissues to Lisa. At the end she asked, "How do you think you'll be able to find forgiveness for this?"

"I don't think I can ever forgive Bert."

"I'm not just talking about Bert. I didn't hear you say you were raped."

"I was telling you about a confused young girl who was taken advantage of by an older man."

"Right. But I didn't hear you say that he entered you against your will, forced the continuation of the relationship, or that you reported it to his wife. Maggie, was that her name?"

"C'mon."

"Oh, I know there are a lot of justifications for not doing that, first and foremost being the insecurity of losing your parents and not wanting to lose the home you found with Bert and Maggie. But what you let Bert do was not something that the Lisa raised by your parents would have permitted. It seems clear that the basic virtues they taught would conflict with the freer spirit Bert developed in you. It was easier to bury those virtues in your subconscious than to resist a tempting man. The resulting conflict is pretty obvious.

"The first thing you need to do, Lisa, is to reflect on all the details you can remember about that time. Think about how Bert felt, about his motivation looked at from the experience of all these years, your expectations of him as a foster father. Then add up what it's costing you to hang on to the bitterness of this memory, and how you can grant him some forgiveness, or at least some understanding."

Lisa tried to suspend the disbelief, the disappointment in Elle's lecture. Her therapist ignored the touch of sarcasm in Lisa's tone when she asked for suggestions as to how to do this.

"I'm hesitant to suggest, but perhaps through an act of atonement."

Lisa struggled with the concept, thinking she would somehow have to make amends.

"Atonement has other meanings than to make amends. It can also mean something like 'bringing into harmony.' Wouldn't it be nice if your present weren't bedeviled by your past?

"Just as I suggested that you didn't have to let Bert do that to you, I also suggested some of the reasons you need to forgive yourself. The loneliness and confusion arising from the loss of your parents would be one reason. I'm sure you can find many other reasons if you're willing to devote time to meditate over these issues. If you then bring these conclusions back to our sessions, we can find a door that opens to your understanding, your forgiveness of yourself for whatever part you played. And I'd bet that continuing this kind of approach will not only lead to a better understanding of Bert's role, but to a lot more happiness for yourself."

If it was true that Lisa's spirits lifted somewhat during the ensuing months, wrestling with feelings about time spent with Bert, it was also true that they sank steadily in the fall of 1972 as Chris's return approached. On the surface they had resolved many of the issues arising from the Plotkin affair. The practical ones, headed by the agreement that there would be no abortion. But now that she was more in touch with her feelings, working hard to be honest and forgiving about the past, now that she was putting memories of Bert to rest, she had shifted her meditation more and more in Plotkin's direction. More and more she realized that she was carrying out a charade in these sessions with Elle, not sharing what certainly was a principal driving force in her present life.

Tonight, Monday, November 13th, changed that. After the terrible argument with Chris over the call for him to meet again with Plotkin, after threatening to leave him, she had set about reversing much of what had been done in preparation for a move to the CIA Headquarters area. She called the real estate agent to advise that their Virginia home could be put on the rental market again. She re-enrolled Missy in her local elementary school for the winter session. Getting Lisbet back into the private pre-school was not so easy. It was an excellent facility with a long waiting list. They'd already tapped the next child on the list to take Lisbet's seat. Tears, a friendship with the owners, and a sob story about the vagaries of government assignments resulted in their making one more seat available. She was engaged in a whirlwind of activity until Friday, when she arose with the realization that there wasn't much more she could do before speaking with her husband again. What now?

After the kids were off to school, after her ritual morning cup of coffee with Mor—a conversation skirting as much as possible any discussion of the family crisis—Lisa took a long, leisurely bath before changing from her robe to clothing for the day. During that relaxed time she remembered the upcoming session with Elle next Monday. Perhaps this was the time to bring the last skeleton out of the closet. Chris would be furious if he knew she was even thinking about it. Beyond furious if she acted on the idea and he learned about it. One of the nice things about dealing with somebody like Elle was the confidentiality. Therapists like Elle were sworn to secrecy about anything they learned from clients, weren't they? The longer she soaked in the bath, the better she liked the idea.

After getting dressed, Lisa used the extension phone in her bedroom to call Elle, only to be connected with an answering service. She'd forgotten that Elle did pro bono work at the battered women's shelter on Fridays. Frustrated that immediate action wasn't possible, she left a message for Elle: "Tell her that Lisa Holbeck called and would like a two-hour session next Monday evening. She needs the extra time because there is more to share now." Monday morning brought word that Elle was able to give her two hours that evening.

And so Lisa had met with her therapist, and so she had spilled the beans—*all* the beans—about the affair that led up to the pregnancy and birth of her youngest child, more about some of the stresses of family life with a "diplomat," and finally the fact that the affair was with a Soviet KGB officer who was targeted for defection by Chris, who was actually a CIA officer.

She felt not at all guilty about revealing all this to a therapist who could never repeat the information to anyone. She did not divulge any details about her husband's role with the CIA or his current mission. That damned current mission. There wasn't much she could have said anyway, since the only thing she knew was that it involved Plotkin.

* * *

Sitting in the car, musing about that long, cathartic session, Lisa had to make some kind of personal decision that would justify her action in relating all of this to Elle. What had she learned? What advice had she received from Elle that would change her life? Her children's lives? Chris's life? Something that would make their family whole again.

Soon into the half hour she'd been contemplating these questions, a Seattle police cruiser had drifted by her parked car. Now it passed her again, the policeman on the passenger side giving her and the car a long stare. Time to move. She drove west to the I-5 freeway and headed northbound.

During the twenty-minute drive to Edmonds she arrived at a solution she believed would satisfy the needs of most of the family.

At home not long after nine o'clock, Lisa found her two daughters already tucked into bed and asleep. Mor said it had been a quiet evening with no arguments. The boys were studying in their room.

Lisa arose at five o'clock the next morning to a muted alarm. After washing her face with cold water, she fetched the address book from her purse, sat down beside an extension phone in her room, took a deep breath and dialed a number in Virginia. Two rings and a friendly woman's voice answered.

"This is Lisa Holbeck. Is this Kathy Brewer? Do you remember me?" Although housebound by chronic disease, Bob Brewer's wife had been a gracious hostess on the only two occasions the women had met, parties for some of Bob's associates in their home.

"Of course, Lisa, I remember you well and hear news of your family through Bob. I understand your husband is back from his tour in Vietnam."

"*Was* back. He's off again someplace and I really need to talk with him. A family thing. Not an awful emergency, but important enough that I'd like him to call me. I know he and Bob are close. Bob's probably at work by now, but could you please ask him to get a hold of Chris and have him call me? I can't tell you how much I'd appreciate that."

"If I could, I would. I'm in the same fix you are. Bob left early this morning on a trip. He didn't tell me where he was going, but promised to call me in a couple of days. I'll give him the message then, but I hope you'll have contacted Chris on your own by that time."

"Not much chance of that, I'm afraid. Please do give Bob the message. How are you doing, Kathy? Is everything pretty much the same for you?"

Kathy's voice was cheerful. "Yes, about the same. I have a loving husband and a nice home, so I'm better off than many women my age. Can't really complain."

Lisa teared up at the thought of a woman so constricted in her life yet so cheerful. "You're a wonderful person, Kathy. I'll appreciate your getting that message to Bob, and I'll keep you in my thoughts. Bye-bye."

She hung up after Kathy signed off, got back into bed and pulled the covers over her head.

CHAPTER THIRTY-FOUR

Tuesday, November 14, 1972
Aboard the *Rockfish*

"Welcome aboard, gentlemen. I'm the skipper, Ronald Smith. Please follow me as soon as you have those survival suits off. We've got the retrieval crew coming down that ladder."

As Smith led them forward through a central passageway, Chris said, "Thanks, Commander. Your deckhands were great, especially the swimmers. I'm Chris, and this is Alex. I don't know how much you've been told about us."

"Enough to know that you're part of a highly classified operation and don't want too many questions. By the way, to give credit where credit is due, the swimmers aren't part of my regular crew. They're SEALS, who are aboard just for one mission. It was a lucky break we had them with us. We would have picked you up one way or another, but it was a lot more efficient having them in the water."

They came to a space on the port side that served as both wardroom and officers' mess. Nobody was there when they arrived. Smith invited them to sit at the table and poured three cups of coffee from a carafe kept warm on a sideboard.

"First thing I have to do is check on your health. Any wounds, diseases or other health concerns? Would either of you like to talk with a medic before we settle in?" Both visitors said "no," looking baffled by the question.

"Sorry, that's standard procedure. I was watching from the conning tower when you came across from the sailboat. That was a wild and wet ride. It's a good thing you had those survival suits, or you'd be damn cold now. I'm sure you noticed that everybody aboard wears blue coveralls. I'll ask one of the officers to find a couple of pair for you to use while you're with us, and we can make arrangements to wash and dry your skivvies when you get into the coveralls. You can dress in your own clothes when we land."

"When will that be? Where will we be landing?" Information provided to the exfiltration group had not included such details as the port of origin or destination of the submarine.

The skipper looked first at one man and then the other. He knew that Chris was an intelligence officer and that the other passenger was a foreign national, but not much beyond that. "Sorry to say that information is classified, though I can say we'll be welcome at the port where we land. I can also tell you that you'll be aboard for a couple of days, so you can judge your activities from that.

"We need to agree on some rules while you're aboard. I'm assigning you to an officers' stateroom just forward of the wardroom here. I'll take you there when we finish this chat. The stateroom is for three officers. It's a bit cramped, but besides three bunks it has chairs and three fold-down desks. We're not at full crew complement so you'll have it to yourselves.

"I expect you'll want to spend most of your time in the stateroom. You probably have many things to talk over and reports to write, so I'll get you pens and paper. Just as your operation is classified and largely unknown to me, most of what goes on in this boat is classified as well. For that reason I'm asking you not to go anywhere else but your stateroom, this wardroom and the bath facilities while you're aboard, unless you're accompanied by me or my executive officer. By the same token I know you won't want my men to learn too much about you and your operation, even though all of them carry high security clearances. I'll leave it up to you, Chris, as to how much contact you want with the crew. The main issue will be at mealtimes, and the fact that officers not on duty hang out here. Do you want to eat with the officers, eat here before or after our regular meals, or eat in the stateroom?"

Chris hadn't considered such details. "I suspect your staterooms are not exactly like those on a luxury liner. We'll get a little stir crazy if we're confined to a small stateroom for two or three days. Why don't we begin with eating here after the officers' meals, with the option of coming out occasionally to stretch our legs and move about? How do we handle contact with the officers who might be in the wardroom at the same time?"

"That's up to you, Chris. You'll have to judge what you can say. The guys on this boat are a disciplined bunch. They know what they can and can't share with you. I should think the problem would be more of what you and Alex can talk about. How can you carry on a conversation if you can't say anything about yourselves? Does Alex speak English? I haven't heard him say a word."

"Alex speaks English as well as you or I. But he doesn't much like boats."

Sasha finally spoke up, "On the contrary, Chris, I like this boat very much.

It's quiet, it has a smooth ride, and it doesn't roll or jerk around. The only thing I noticed was when we tipped forward to go under the sea. Now it's as smooth as being on an airplane in good weather."

He turned to Commander Smith. "I was a tank commander in World War II. It was my life at the time, so I accepted the realities of that kind of warfare. Consider that outside of the extreme dangers, you're locked up tight in a cramped, hot, metal box that stinks of diesel smoke and jolts your whole body about every other second. I'm beginning to think I should have enlisted in the submarine service."

Chris laughed. "He's changing his tune, Commander. Alex hated every minute, probably every second of the time he was on the sailboat that brought us out to meet you."

"That's true," Alex said, "but I can't understand how you can call both this submarine and that thing we came out on 'boats.' They're completely different animals."

The skipper smiled. "I'm glad you like our boat, Alex, and you certainly speak English well. We really should call a halt to this conversation, as there will be some hungry officers ready for breakfast just a few minutes from now. I'll pass the word for them to use their own judgment in talking with you, and ask that they not be too nosy. Let me show you the stateroom you'll be using. You can settle there for a couple of hours, then come back here for something to eat."

Neither of the visitors returned to the wardroom for breakfast, or even for lunch. By the time they changed into coveralls, gave their laundry to a sailor and washed up, they had been awake and under stress for almost forty-eight hours. A catnap or two during the drive from Stockholm to the Swedish west coast had not been enough to stave off the exhaustion hitting them now, magnified by an easing of tension after reaching *Rockfish*. The two men climbed into their narrow bunks. Although the atmosphere was foreign to both of them and the future uncertain for them both, they fell asleep immediately and stirred not at all for the next ten hours.

* * *

Plotkin was first to awake. Hearing Chris's light snoring, he tried to go back to sleep but could not. He left his bunk, much in need of the bath facility they called a "head." There he relieved himself and found that some thoughtful soul had left a couple of new toothbrushes and a tube of toothpaste next to one of the wash basins. He brushed his teeth, washed his face and dampened his hair, combing it with his fingers. Returning to the stateroom he noticed that the laundry had been returned, neatly folded and left on one of the chairs. He sat in another chair, wishing Chris were awake. Hunger pangs were coming in waves, not surprising since he'd emptied his stomach many times over on the *Valhalla* trip. He was tempted to go to the wardroom by himself but quickly rejected the idea. The crew might not like to see a foreign national wandering about by himself.

"Chris. Chris! Wake up. It's time we got something to eat."

* * *

Chris struggled awake, at first disoriented by the unfamiliar surroundings. Oh, yes, that was Plotkin calling. They were still on the submarine. "What time is it?"

"It's five o'clock in the afternoon by my watch, Stockholm time, meaning we've slept ten hours. It's dinnertime and I'm hungry!"

"I guess I am, too, but I won't know much until I take a leak." Chris jumped down from his bunk and all but ran for the head. After washing up, he was especially grateful to the kind stranger who had left the toothpaste and brushes, not only for his own sake but because it was another gesture of care for the well-being of the visitors. Unhappy as he was with Plotkin, anything that would help the man feel welcome would be a step toward establishing the atmosphere of safety and security that would help smooth the way for the debriefing that would begin within the next hour. He returned to the stateroom and the two men went into the wardroom.

Three officers were just finishing their meals, and a sailor was clearing the table. They introduced themselves by first name, with handshakes all around. One was the Executive Officer, also named "Chris," who asked if the visitors were hungry.

"We sure are," Chris replied, "but it's hard to know which meal you're serving. We arrived just before breakfast and slept a long time, so this should be supper. Is that right?"

"Right on," said the other Chris, who asked the mess man to bring two more meals. "That was an awfully wet and bumpy sailboat ride. I was in the conning tower watching as you came across, and took over from the skipper when he went below to welcome you. Congratulations for getting to us safely."

"Thanks, Chris, it's sure good to be warm, dry and rested up."

Chris was impressed with the dishes put before them. Pork chops, green beans, applesauce and a coleslaw salad were followed by a dessert of brownies, all of it devoured hungrily by the two men. Both guests and the officers, who were enjoying coffee and relaxing after coming off watch, watched their words carefully; no one wished to violate security protocols. Chris and Plotkin related the adventure of sailing out to meet *Rockfish*, avoiding any details about the trip to the Swedish west coast. Chris recounted a couple of stories concerning his towboat experiences in Pacific Northwest and Alaskan waters. Plotkin repeated what he had told Commander Smith, about how content he was to be on this submarine after the harrowing sail boat trip to the rendezvous, and how submariners' lives were so much better than the lives of those who fought in tanks during World War II.

Plotkin endured some friendly ribbing about that. An older officer had served as an enlisted man on diesel submarines operating in the Pacific late in that war. "You might not have been as comfortable," he said, "if, like me, you'd been in one of those old subs sitting on the bottom of the sea while Japanese destroyers dropped depth charges all around."

"Ah," Plotkin countered, "perhaps not. But one time, after escaping into an artillery barrage from a burning tank, I had to decide whether to take cover under a tank that might explode at any minute or take my chances on open ground."

The officer laughed. "We'll call it a draw, shall we?"

It was tempting to continue this relaxed conversation, but Chris was eager to hear Plotkin's reasons for defecting at this juncture and, of course, to begin learning what valuable information he had to offer. At the same time he dreaded beginning a conversation that would open old wounds.

Chris waited for a lull in the conversation. "Gentlemen," he interjected, "Alex and I need to retire again. Thanks so much for your hospitality. I hope we'll see you again in the next couple of days."

Plotkin followed his lead back to the stateroom where, with unspoken consent, they prepared to begin the debriefing. Chris folded down the outside two of the three desks in the stateroom, leaving a comfortable space between himself and Plotkin. He gave Plotkin a pen and one of the pads of lined paper provided, fully intending to confiscate later any notes the KGB officer might make during the debriefing.

"So, Sasha, how are feeling? I mean how are you really feeling, not what you told the skipper and those officers out there."

"I told them the truth. I feel good, and I'm truly glad to be off that little boat and on something big, solid and smooth like this submarine."

"I'm surprised, Chris said, "that you feel so good. Here you are, leaving your motherland, leaving a wife, leaving your friends and comrades in the service, leaving all of them forever. I know you're a brave man, but doesn't it frighten you even a little bit, wondering about your future?"

"I certainly wonder where I'll be and what I'll be doing a year from now. But I accept that in the meantime we have a lot of work to do to justify all this." He swept his hand in a circle, indicating the submarine.

"It sounds as if you feel better about the United States now, compared to when we talked in my home. That seems a long time ago now, doesn't it? A very long time ago."

"Two or three years. Not really so long." Plotkin shifted further from the desk, hooked both elbows over the back of the chair and stretched his legs nearly straight out.

"Well," Chris said, "it's understandable that you feel nervous about your future. Barring an unlikely accident on our way to the United States, you're safe and in good hands. You'll be surprised at how well our people will treat you."

Plotkin unhooked his arms from the chair back and leaned forward toward Chris, his expression direct and serious. "Please understand me here, Chris. My feelings about the United States, the Soviet Union and any of the so-called superpowers have not changed since our conversation on the subject. I'm still as disaffected from all of them as I was then, for the same reasons."

"Then why did you come out?"

"For the same reasons I planned to come out before, when I was short-circuited by the Ambassador's trip to Paris. Like I told you, I was hauled back to the Soviet Union and put on ice, still working but not allowed to travel and restricted in access to intelligence."

"So why did they let you out this time?" Chris was looking about the cramped cabin, as though avoiding Plotkin's eyes.

"I would have thought you could put two and two together, Chris." Plotkin said, willing Chris to meet his gaze. "I assumed you would understand that I was permitted to travel to Sweden because once again the Kremlin in its infinite wisdom insisted on a meeting with Ulla. She had continued her KGB ties through the secret writing channel I told you about, providing a lot of information that was more highly rated than it deserved. Because of its ratings, it held Politburo's interest. That exerted some pressure on the KGB to get back into direct contact, which became still more urgent as the Paris Peace Talks on Vietnam were thought to be moving toward a settlement. They wished to learn how a settlement would influence Palme's attitude toward the United States and its European friends, and which measures could be taken to maintain his supposed friendship toward the Soviet Union.

"This posed a problem for my masters. They were hoist with their own petard. Having overstated Ulla's importance as a source and particularly her influence with Olof Palme, they had to build up the pace and depth of our relationship to satisfy the Kremlin. The secret writing exchanges urging her to arrange travel for a face-to-face meeting in the Soviet Union or in Europe brought responses that delayed a decision. She refused to come to the Soviet Union or to meet anyone but me. They tolerated her behavior for some time, but with the international political climate in flux as the Vietnam War now seemed to be coming to a close, they renewed their pressure.

"My personal situation with the KGB remained about the same. I continued to work the Ulla case as a sideline to my duties in the Illegals Section. That included everything I'd done before the Stockholm assignment, with the exception of traveling abroad. I was in limbo. Nobody treated me badly or said anything about my being in a position of less authority. But there was an aura of watchfulness. Some documents I knew existed no longer existed when I asked for them. It was never suggested that I travel abroad in support of my operations as I had occasionally in the past. I no longer had access to my various passports and identification documents. I was in bad odor, either due to jealousy over some of my successes or continuing questions about my 'jewishness.'

"Whoever it was in the KGB hierarchy that was holding me in this limbo, he or they must have relented. The Politburo may have put such pressure on them regarding acceleration of the Ulla case that they finally had to give up. About three weeks ago I was called into the office of the Chief, Department 3 of the First Chief Directorate. I was instructed to prepare for a trip to Stockholm, beginning with a secret writing exchange to make arrangements for a face-to-face meeting there with Ulla. I was to report the results of the exchange immediately without revealing the information to anybody else. I did as instructed, the outcome being that Ulla agreed to a meeting on Monday, November 13th, when she would take a personal day of leave.

"Again I did as instructed, reporting back to Georgi Ivanovich Androsov, then serving as Chief of the Third Department, which I'm sure you know covers the U.K., Scandinavia, Australia and New Zealand. Georgi and I had been acquainted for years but were not friends. Our relationship in connection with the Ulla case had grown quite difficult after my return from Stockholm. I attributed his dislike to his carrying some of the baggage for whatever KGB elements were hostile toward me.

"I was excited about the possibility of a trip to Stockholm and had been planning in my own mind how to arrange a meeting with you. But when I reported to Georgi the date and time for the Ulla meeting, I sensed that getting away to meet you would not be easy. Georgi was unusually friendly. He said it was about time for him to get reacquainted with Sweden, so he'd be joining me on this trip as an excuse to visit Stockholm. He and I would travel there together on the Thursday prior to the Monday meeting with Ulla. We would visit with the KGB officers and the Ambassador at the Embassy on Friday; then, before I was to meet Ulla, we'd enjoy ourselves over the weekend with some serious sightseeing and shopping around Stockholm. I posted the letter to your mail drop in Germany, the one you gave me at the end of our meeting in Norrtälje, hoping it was still active.

"My concern was justified. Georgi and I shared a room together at the Grand Hotel. He stuck to me like glue, day and night. I began to think that we'd be disappointed once again. I'm sure you know that Georgi by himself couldn't prevent my escape. I could easily get away from him while he was sleeping or in the bathroom. My worry was that Georgi's role was as a red herring, trying to make me think he was the only minder while others were tailing us everywhere we went. I dared not be obvious in checking for surveillance, since Georgi—an experienced operator himself—would observe my behavior and guess what was on my mind. I bided my time.

"My plans were of course based on the hope you had received my message sent to that mail drop and would be there to meet me on Sunday. I figured that my best chance for getting away from Georgi and his friends would be during lunch on the last day before meeting you. By then they would have noted my contentment with the situation and concluded that I showed no signs of bolting. The best circumstance would be lunch in a restaurant near the Stockholm Central Railway Station. I'm sure you are as aware as I that the station not only receives and sends out trains to all part of Sweden and beyond, but also houses subway lines that extend out in all directions to Stockholm suburbs, five different lines going through the central station—T-Centralen.

"Sunday morning Georgi and I arose early—the genuine habit for both of us—complained mutually about our hangovers from eating and drinking too much the night before, and went for a half-hour walk before having a continental breakfast in the hotel dining room. Besides complaining about how he was feeling, Georgi went on and on about the cost of our visit and how expensive everything was in Stockholm.

"We were planning to rest for a couple of hours before having a big lunch followed by an afternoon of sightseeing. Lavish meals and high living were eating into expense money that Georgi hoped to spend on souvenirs. It was a real break when he asked if I knew a restaurant in Stockholm that had good food without costing so much. Just the opening I'd hoped for. When I was at the Embassy in Stockholm my comrades and I collected a list of such restaurants, many of them serving food as good as the expensive ones.

"After our rest, I took the lead as we walked in a light rainfall up Vasagatan to Klarabergsgatan, where there was a small, excellent restaurant a block and a half from T-Centralen. There are many entrances to the subway and train central station, including escalators from Vasagatan going down to the subway level. *If* the restaurant was still in business, *if* it was open Sundays, *if* it looked good and cheap enough to Georgi, *if* I could somehow get out of there and into the maze of the subway tunnels without being followed, I might get myself to the rendezvous point in time to meet you. *If*, of course, you had received my message, *if* you understood the rendezvous place, and *if* your masters had approved the operation in light of the earlier failure.

"That will give you some idea of my feelings during that walk up Vasagatan,

Chris. Besides all those 'ifs,' I thought about the consequences of the change I'd decided to make, leaving a decent if not very loving wife and her family, a government position that was well-paying and rewarding—even if my current situation was a bit tenuous—and embracing an uncertain future in a nation whose international policies were objectionable to me even if they were different from those of the Soviet Union. I had only an hour to change my mind.

"Georgi liked what he saw on the restaurant menu posted in the window. He grumbled about the cost not being all that cheap, but went in anyway. There was a good crowd there for lunch. Georgi was in an expansive mood after eating the first course of a large meal he'd ordered, spouting off about the rise of communism now that the United States would have to admit defeat in Vietnam. While I agreed with much of what he said about Vietnam, I found the rest of it the same stale stuff of the Soviet Communist Party line that helped make up my mind. It was time to go. Permanently.

"I would have to leave the restaurant no later than one o'clock in order to get to the rendezvous by two in the afternoon. Georgi was still waiting for his dessert course when a clock on the wall of the restaurant made the last tick of the noon hour. One o'clock. I could wait no longer. 'I have to pee,' I told Georgi, 'I'll be back in a minute.'

'I've got to go, too,' says Georgi, 'they're taking forever with that torte.'

"We made our way between the tables to a doorway leading to the restrooms, very close to the service door used by wait staff. There was just one stall and one urinal in the men's room, and the stall was occupied. I pushed my way to the urinal. 'I think I need to go more than you do, Georgi, and you take too long.' It had been a joke all weekend that Georgi, at his age, took a long time before he could get his stream going. He stepped up to the urinal as I left it.

"I washed my hands and dried them on a couple of paper towels before I heard Georgi start to pee. Just about that time the chap in the stall came out. An unsanitary fellow, he headed straight for the door without coming to the basin to wash his hands. 'I'll see you back at the table,' I called to Georgi, leaving him to stop his stream (if he could), zip up and run after me if he was worried.

"The rain had started coming down hard while we were eating. I planned to leave through the kitchen and its service entrance. With that heavy, cold rain I knew how good it would be to have my topcoat and fur hat, hung on a coat rack near the entrance to the restaurant. It took a millisecond to decide how dangerous it would be to pick them up and leave that way. Instead, I pushed the swinging door into the kitchen and walked deliberately through. One of the cooks shouted at me, but I just kept walking, opening the service door into the alley. Up to that point I had moved at what I considered a normal pace. When I shut that kitchen service door behind me, I started running through the rain, arriving so quickly at the escalator on Vasagatan that I wasn't very wet as I entered the tunnel leading to T-Centralen.

"You see many people running for trains without attracting attention, so I ran all the way up to the kiosk where one pays for travel. The first subway train leaving was on the Blue Line. I got my ticket, ran to the train, sat at the end of a nearly empty car away from the windows, and nearly vomited. If I was more frightened than that during wartime I simply don't remember it. I thought of getting off at Rådhuset—the Stockholm City Hall—but changed my mind and stayed on to the interchange at Fridhemsplan. There I waited ten minutes for a Green Line train bound for Hässelby Strand. I had taken no time to check for surveillance as I made that mad dash from the restaurant to T-Centralen, and dared not look out the window once I was on the Blue Line car. While standing on the platform at Fridhemsplan, I felt exposed. Only a few passengers were using the transportation on that Sunday, but I had those ten minutes to observe carefully in all directions. I feel certain that nobody was following me at that point.

"I would like to know—and I'm sure you and your people would like to know—if I was followed while with Georgi in Stockholm. I can give you my best guess. I do believe that Georgi was sent along to make me feel more comfortable than I should if I were going to defect. That makes sense only if they also had some other surveillance on me, probably a pair of watchers either brought in from home for the job, or KGB staffers at the Embassy who were assigned after I was there. They would be informed of the day's plans in advance. With Georgi as what you might call the 'inside man,' they wouldn't have to follow so close that I might detect them.

"It's likely that my theoretical surveillance team was in the restaurant, perhaps even before we arrived. Georgi made a routine call to the KGB man on watch before we left the Grand Hotel for the walk to the restaurant, reporting our plans for the day. I didn't pay much attention at the time, but I'd already told him the name of the restaurant before his call. That's the ideal way to run a surveillance: have somebody tell you in advance where the target is going.

"If you put yourself in the shoes of those watchers, you can imagine what confusion would come from the kind of escape I described. They would certainly have seen Georgi and me go to the men's room. They may not have seen me come out behind the other fellow who had been there, as it was the blink of an eye from the time I popped from behind him and went through the service door. Even if they had seen me, it would take some time for them to spring into action, run through the kitchen and follow me through the rain. If they existed, I'm sure I shook them off."

Chris was taking detailed notes as Plotkin spoke. Now he was tiring of the self-congratulatory narration. "That sounds reasonable, Sasha, but how did you get from Fridhemsplan to our rendezvous? And with all due respect, I have to say that you seemed scared as hell when I picked you up there in the park. How does that jibe with being sure you weren't followed?"

Plotkin took the implication in stride. "I've arrived at much of this after thinking it over during the last few days. Remember, Chris, that when we met there at Drottningholm I'd been hiding in the woods in the downpour, cold and soaking wet, no hat, no coat, and only an hour away from making that break. I can't change what you believe, but I know in my heart that I'm telling you the truth.

"As for how I got there ... After boarding the Green Line train, I stayed on through several stops and got off at Brommaplan, which you certainly know because it's not far from where you lived. You know what a busy center of activity it is during the week, with cars and taxis meeting people on their way to shopping or coming home from work. On that Sunday only a few people got off the train. I was last off, and nobody seemed interested in me. But getting from there to the park at Drottningholm turned out to be the most dangerous part of the experience.

"Think, Chris. Here I was, dressed nicely in a business suit, but without a coat or hat. Dashing out into a rainstorm, looking for a taxi. A casual observer might think that it was just some idiot who'd forgotten his coat and hat and was trying to get to his home nearby.

"But not the taxi driver. Where should I tell him I wanted to go? To a home address like your old place in Nockeby? In that awful rain he would want to wait to make sure I got in the door safely. Where, then? The park? I had only twenty minutes left before our scheduled meeting. Now he, too, would think me an idiot. But I told him to go there anyway. I didn't feel I had a choice.

"Luckily, the driver was a friendly fellow who thought I was a Swede. When he expressed doubt about leaving me in a place like that and wondered why I would do something so crazy, I told him it was an affair of the heart that couldn't be known to certain people. My lady friend would be picking me up within minutes. When we reached the park there were no other cars in the parking lot. The driver wanted to wait until I was picked up. To get rid of him I doubled the fare on the meter and asked him to come back in a half-hour. I would not be there, I told him, but if I was he could deliver me to the nearby mental hospital at Blackeberg. He appreciated the tip and the humor, shaking his head as he drove away.

"I stood under the shelter of a tree next to the parking lot until he was gone, then moved back farther into the woods where there was less chance of being seen. As you know, I was soaked, cold and shaking. The fear you saw in me came from my concern that the taxi driver would return with the police. My behavior must have seemed very odd."

Chris called a halt to the debriefing. "Let's take a break here, Sasha. Give me a few minutes to review what I've got before we start again. Do you want a cup of coffee or to take a break in the wardroom?"

"No. I'm fine. What do you think, so far?"

"It doesn't matter what I think. I'm just a scribe, taking down your story as you tell it."

"It's not a story. It's the truth!" Plotkin shouted, his face flushed.

Chris reined in some bitter thoughts and replied in as normal a tone as he could muster, "You're either being supersensitive or misinterpreting my use of the word 'story.' I didn't mean to imply that you were telling me a fable—something interesting but not factual—only that I'm doing my best to transcribe your narrative. It's not my place to judge the truthfulness of what you've said so far or will say in the future. That's up to the experts you'll be working with over the next few months. And, of course, your own conscience."

Plotkin appeared contrite. "Sorry, Chris, I guess I was being supersensitive. I think I'll climb into my bunk for a rest while you do your review."

Chris dutifully went through his notes, jotting in the margin here and there but really doing it for show, trying to impress Plotkin with his detachment from the narrative, merely greasing a machine that wouldn't start running until arrival in the States. Now he was at a point that demanded use of the brief, scribbled interrogation guide written by Gary Llonis and handed to him by Bob Brewer just before departure for Stockholm. It read:

> *What pushed the button that made him leave at this time?*
> *Full story of his exit up to meeting you. Does it ring true?*
> *What does he have to say that would bear on the situation we discussed?*
> *Good luck!*

Now that he had the envisioned source in the stateroom with him, he could act on those requests. Through reviewing the notes, Chris folded his arms on the desk and rested his head on them. He wanted to think through the discussion, how it fit into the picture Llonis wanted to develop from information available to Plotkin.

Plotkin had satisfied the first two points listed in the interrogation note, coming up with the information on his own. So far Chris found Sasha's escape story to be genuine. It was logical in the context of the operational climate in Stockholm, and even had the satisfying element of an overbearing superior getting his comeuppance.

During that first conversation at Chris's home in Stockholm, Plotkin had appeared to be honest in describing his disaffection—not only with the Soviet Union but with all superpowers—and he had gone much further than that in their meeting in Norrtälje. As disgusted as Chris was with the affair with Lisa, as angry as he was with Sasha, as easy as it would be to burn him with attacks on his honesty, he felt in his heart that this KGB officer was telling the truth about his motivation to defect. The timing seemed logical. Still, something remained unsaid. And unasked, for that matter. He would stop playing the self-proclaimed scribe and start acting like an interrogator.

"Sasha! Are you awake? Ready to start again?"

"Aye aye, Sir!" Plotkin jumped down from the bunk and stood at stiff attention. "At your service, Sir!" It seemed to be done in good humor rather than mocking Chris.

"Can it, Sasha. At ease." They went back to their positions at the desks.

Plotkin began: "I think I have to say now that I appreciate the way you and the crew on this boat have treated me. And Nils and Pastor Stewart. It seems like everyone worked hard and took chances to get me away, and I'm grateful. When you first picked me up I told you I wouldn't give details of operations until I was in the United States."

Chris interrupted: "You're on a United States naval vessel. That qualifies as being in the States."

"I don't know much about submarines, Chris, but I'm certain this boat cannot reach the United States in two or three days. We have to be going to another country before we get to the States."

"That's splitting hairs, Sasha. Actually it's bullshit. With all this talk about being grateful, I'd think you would want to help out the people who've helped you. So far you've given us a couple of adventure stories and a description of a case you yourself think is over-rated."

"I told you I would give you Ulla's name, only later."

"I don't give a crap about Ulla's name."

Plotkin appeared shocked. "But think how important that case was to the Politburo. If they were so eager, I'd think you'd want the details."

Chris was silent.

"I've got the details on my agents in England all memorized. I can give you addresses, telephone numbers, biographical information—all that when we get to the States."

More silence from Chris, who was doodling on his note pad.

"What the hell do you want? That's valuable information."

"You're right. If you ever make good on those promises, our interrogation team will be happy to get all the details. But that's all you're giving me—promises. And the information you're referring to is not what I'm looking for."

"Goddammit, I don't know what you're talking about. Here I try to be honest and open, and you're questioning my integrity." Plotkin picked up the pen on his desk and threw it back angrily.

"Is that 'honest and open' as when you took Lisa to that fucking safe house in Gamlastan? If you think this is difficult, wait until you meet our interrogators. They'll be very nice as long as you're cooperative, but things won't be as nice if you act then like you're acting now with me."

That stopped Plotkin. He was silent for a full minute before saying, "I know we have to talk about Lisa, but please, please, let's do that as the last thing before we get off this boat. I understand the point about information I might have, but you're too experienced to be naïve about this, Chris. If you were on your way to the Soviet Union to share information with the KGB, would you not give just a few teasers before being safe and comfortable in your new life? I'll admit that what I've mentioned so far is only the surface. Information on the Illegals Section and its operatives both in Moscow and abroad will probably be most important. I'll certainly give your people all that when I get to the States."

"Not good enough, Sasha. If we have time while we're on this boat I want to get it, but that's not my priority. Have you ever heard the term mole?"

"Yes. A penetration agent."

"Does the KGB ever look for one in their ranks?"

"All the time. It causes a lot of personnel problems. The paranoia about Jews in the service is partly that, partly anti-Semitism."

"Did you ever run an operation to recruit a mole within the CIA?"

Plotkin picked up the pen again, this time turning it slowly while he gazed at his hands. "I don't want to talk about these things until I get to the States."

"I'm afraid you're going to have to, whether you want to or not. Look, Sasha, when we started out I thought we were developing a friendship that might lead to where we are now. At the same time I thought it might be a genuine friendship —a real bonding between two men of like minds, even if not on the same side politically. But you blew that when you got Lisa to go to your safe house. So far we've been dealing with you as a friend. You have an option here. You can be a friend, telling us honestly and openly what you know in response to our questions, or ..."

Chris hesitated. He was flying blind here, unsure of what controls could be used in this case. A moment of thought, and then he went on, "Or you can make yourself a hostile player in our game. Believe me, the treatment will be a lot different from what you've had so far. Not cruel, but definitely not as pleasant.

"I hate to threaten you. My dream was that you would defect to the United States and be resettled in a place where we could see each other now and then after I retired, remain friends. That was probably an impossible dream to start with, and certainly that dream was dashed after I learned of your involvement with Lisa. But angry as I am about that, I feel that you're essentially a decent person, one who should be treated decently. You need to accept the facts of life here, Sasha. You can play our game or accept the consequences."

Without saying a word, Plotkin climbed back into his bunk and stared at the ceiling. Finally he said: "Give me a half hour to think about this, Chris. I understand your anger. I don't think you understand my position, and probably will never understand how affected I was by the sight of you and Lisa as a family, your life together with your children. What I did was indefensible. If you learn nothing else from me, I hope you will accept the fact that I wouldn't be here today, wouldn't have begun the actions that have brought us together, if it hadn't been for the goodness of your family life in Stockholm.

"Please give me that half hour to reconstruct my involvement in the one operational experience that might have resulted in what you're talking about. A half hour."

CHAPTER THIRTY-FIVE

Tuesday, November 14, 1972
Edmonds, Washington

L isa's ritual morning coffee time with Mor was less satisfying than usual. They sat in the living room in their customary chairs, overlooking another gloomy, late fall day in Edmonds, Mor still in her robe and slippers, Lisa fully dressed. Mor out of sorts for some reason. Lisa full of herself, excited, wanting to share with her mother-in-law the news of her transformation but not yet ready, not yet sure she would reveal to Mor or anyone else the full array of changes she found in herself. They sat in silence for the most part, sipping the strong, black coffee of this Swedish-American household, lost in their own thoughts.

"Yah, Lisa, doesn't that look like one of our boats out there?" Mor had spotted a small vessel, the only one to be seen other than the two ferries plying back and forth between Edmonds and Kingston, across the Sound. "My eyes aren't so good now. Can you tell?"

Lisa's younger eyes were able to see the TOWS painted in large letters on the stack of the tug. "Yes, Mor, it's running fast without a tow. Are you feeling okay? You're awfully quiet this morning. Anything I can do to help?"

"I'm so sad about what's going on between you and Chris. I worried all night and now I'm sitting here still worrying and wondering what's going to happen to the children if—God forbid—you and Chris don't make up." Mor pulled a wad of Kleenex from a pocket of her robe and held it to her tearing eyes.

"Don't worry so much, Mor. I think I've found a way that Chris and I can once again have a happy family life with the children."

Mor brightened. "Does that mean you'll be living in Edmonds, all of you?"

Lisa felt sorry for giving Mor false hopes. "No, Mor, it doesn't mean that. I'm sorry if I gave you that idea. And it doesn't mean we won't be living here, either. I only meant that I'm going to try something to bring Chris and me back where we were, where we should be—not a physical place, but a place of understanding."

"What can you do? I've never seen my boy so angry as when we talked to him after he went fishing. Sometimes I think he loves that agency more than he loves you and the children, loves me and Herman." Mor dabbed at her eyes again with the Kleenex.

Lisa reached out to pat Mor's knee. Now she was feeling teary herself. "I've thought that sometimes too, Mor. That's usually because he's out of town, gone to some other country, or gone far into his own mind—considering a complication having to do with his work, off in space somewhere, not paying attention to me and the kids."

"You still haven't said what you can do."

"I'm not completely sure yet, but part of it depends on you, Mor. I'd like to fly to DC and spend time with Chris when he gets back from wherever he is now. Problem is, I don't know when that will be. By his usual standards it should be in the next two or three days."

"So you will talk some sense into that son of mine? Make my Chris come home to stay?"

Lisa smiled. "No, Mor. He may need a little sense talked into him, but I'm going to tell him that I've come to my senses. He and I need to talk about the thing that's most important—our marriage. I know how you feel about the grandchildren. You may feel they come first, but I see our marriage as the first priority if we are going to care about the children and tend to them as we should."

Mor regarded Lisa with suspicion. "What gave you that idea?"

"I've heard that idea many times. It's the same one you hear on the airplane when you fly to Scandinavia: 'In case we lose cabin pressure, put on your own oxygen mask before you put a mask on your child.' It means that you have to be capable yourself before you can help somebody else."

Now Mor was downright dour. "That doesn't tell me why you would run off by yourself with only a hope of seeing Chris."

Lisa was disappointed with this turn of the conversation. She'd imagined that Mor would leap at the opportunity to have full charge of her beloved grandchildren while both their parents were away. She had underestimated the strength of Mor's desire to have Chris's family living in Edmonds, all of them, forever and ever.

"You know, Mor, that I had a long meeting with my therapist last night. She led me into a new view of my marriage and family and helped me to realize that my anger at Chris goes beyond his being away from home too much or being obsessed with his work. This is very personal. I need to have a frank discussion with him—away from home, away from the children, and away from his work. If he's willing to do that I'm sure we can fix our problems. That might mean he would continue his work—only with a new understanding about my obsession with his being gone so much and his preoccupation with work that interferes with our family life. It might also mean his giving up the Agency and returning to live here. No promises, Mor. First I have to get a hold of him and see if he'll agree to meet and talk over these things. I can't do any of it without your help."

Mor seemed to warm to the idea. "You mean my help as in taking care of all the children."

"Yes, Mor. It could be for a few days, or even a week or ten days. I don't know how long I might be gone, but one thing's certain: this is the best chance for our marriage, and the best chance all the children have for a normal life and happy future. Will you do it?"

"Of course, Lisa. You hardly have to ask me that."

"I love you, Mor." Lisa took a step to Mor's chair and bent down to give her mother-in-law a hug. "You're the best mother-in-law and grandma there ever was."

CHAPTER THIRTY-SIX

Tuesday, November 14, 1972
Aboard the *Rockfish*

A t half past ten o'clock in the evening, Plotkin jumped down from his bunk to find Chris with his head down on the desk, asleep again.

"Chris. Chris! Wake up, damn it, this is supposed to be a debriefing. I'm beginning to wonder who's running this show."

Chris stretched and yawned. "I don't think I'll get caught up on my sleep in this lifetime. Who's running this show? You're welcome to the job. As long as you sit here and tell me what I want to know, you can run the whole thing. I think by now you know how the information should be prioritized. Especially the item you've just been thinking about."

Plotkin was back at his desk, chair pulled out so he could face Chris. That was the last item they had discussed, the one that sent him to his bunk for half an hour. "I know. I know. I can't understand why you're so interested in this information right now, since the skipper told us you can't send anything out from the submarine. I'm trusting you about what happens from here, that we will go directly to the States without delay when we land wherever we're going to land. I don't feel good about this. Not good at all."

"What can I say that'll make you feel better?" Chris felt he was right on the edge of a coup, yet not quite there. "I wasn't involved with planning our travel, so I can't tell you what will happen when we land. I can only guess that we'll be met by some of my fellow officers and flown directly to the States, probably in a chartered private jet or military transport."

Plotkin wasn't satisfied. "That doesn't tell me much. If I give you information that could be acted on right away, and you pass it to your people when we land—wherever that is—the KGB could be alerted immediately and possibly get to me before we go to the States."

"That's a big stretch. How could that happen?"

"How about an intercept of your signals?"

Chris was doubtful. "You mean to tell me your service has that kind of resources? That they could instantly intercept and decode a message we might send from 'wherever?' I'm no expert in that area, but I don't think so."

"Signals intelligence is only one possibility. Remember that I ran a KGB operation in one of the British ports for several years, alongside a parallel operation. I have no idea where we're going on this boat, but if it's Portland I'll really be worried. The KGB is still running sources there, successors to my operation and Lonsdale's. They probably have agents at other ports as well, especially if they have to do with underwater warfare. If they've been alerted to look for me or any unusual activity pointing to my escape, well ... the shit could hit the fan."

"Still unlikely."

"But still possible, no? And if you don't like that one, how about a mole in your service? You asked me to identify one. If there were a mole in your service, and if I identified him right now, what would you do with the information? You can't send it from this boat. When we land at 'wherever,' I imagine we'll be met by some of your people. If you give them the name of a mole right then and there, what are they going to do with the information? Send it to CIA Headquarters? Great! The mole reads the message, passes it on to the KGB and disappears. I'm feeling less and less good about having come over to you."

"I can't give you any guarantees, Sasha. You and I both know that what you say is possible. But you know as well that those are the kinds of things we protect ourselves against. I'm going to share some thoughts that might help you feel better.

"This has been a very restricted operation. To my knowledge there are only four of my people plus a couple of communicators who are fully aware of what's going on. You can add the limited knowledge of the three people you met on the way out of Sweden—Bisan, Pastor Stewart and our sailboat skipper, Nils. You must know, must have done it yourself, that sometimes in this strange business you just have to take chances, act on your own gut instinct. I'd trust my life to any of those three. Bisan is young, but she grew up in a hurry when her father died and she and her mother had to face the world together. She's proven her reliability. Pastor Bill lived through World War II as a Navy chaplain and spent many hours floating in a lifejacket after his carrier was sunk, holding hands and praying in a circle of sailors. He's a true patriot. And Nils Schmidt? He's as solid as they come. You know that Pastor Stewart and I have sailed with Nils and a small crew. You get to know people in that kind of situation, and I trust Nils. That leaves me."

Plotkin sat up straight in his chair, startled. "What do you mean, that leaves you?"

"I don't want to be maudlin about this, Sasha, but you need to remember what I told you about our beginning this as a friendship, a friendship you destroyed by luring my wife to your bed. Friendships are built on trust, and you certainly destroyed that trust. I hope we can keep some of the trust in this part of the relationship. I'm going to trust you to be open and accurate when you tell me all you know about your service. You need to trust me to use good sense in what I do with the information. If we're able to leave for the States immediately after landing with the submarine, I may not send anything. Better to wait until we get to Headquarters and decide at the highest levels what to do with it. Trust me."

Plotkin was slouched down in his chair now, arms folded, a glum look on his face. He said nothing.

Chris was beginning to feel glum himself. "What about it? Are we agreed? Can we go forward with the understanding that we trust each other in this part of the relationship?"

"I guess so." Plotkin stood up. "I've got to use the head, and then let's get a cup of coffee before we start again." He looked at his watch. "Did you realize it's going on midnight, our time?"

"I don't think the clock time has much meaning to us while we're on this boat."

After using the head, the pair found some cookies alongside the coffee pot on the sideboard in the empty wardroom.

✵ ✵ ✵

"I have no certain knowledge of a mole in the CIA or any other western intelligence service," Plotkin began when they were back in the stateroom, "but I did participate in an operation that might have produced such an agent. This was after I'd twice visited your home in Stockholm. My involvement began when I was ordered to travel to Moscow, in early March of 1969.

"As you gain time and experience in a Soviet organization, the secrets you discover become all the more dangerous. Certainly the KGB is a perfect example of that. You may have many acquaintances, but must be very selective in choosing friends within the organization, especially close friends, and most especially confidants with whom you might exchange this kind of information.

"Except for the very top, politically-controlled positions in the KGB, I believe relatively few officers have friendships that extend to the level of confidant. Friends outside the KGB? Of course. Mine are a mixture of in-law relatives and people with whom I shared various school experiences. A few ex-military. Most of my good friends from those days were killed, and I don't enjoy sitting around rehashing battles, won or lost. Inside the KGB I've had many friends. I've gone to their weddings and baby christenings, gotten drunk with them when they divorced, gone to their parents' funerals and even a few of their own funerals. We've talked over old operations—these friends and I—but we've been careful in talking with each other about current operations. Never, never have I shared with these friends the kind of feelings I shared with you in Norrtälje.

"I do, though, have one friend who I considered a confidant. For the purposes of this story I'll call him Sergei. I absolutely will not give any details about Sergei until we reach the States. Sergei and I never shared conversations leading to the kinds of feelings I expressed to you about the world beyond the Soviet, simply because we are careful people and wise. We did, however, share some operational details of a kind I would not trust with other officers. I believe he felt the same.

"Sergei was the young KGB officer in the State Security office in Kherson Oblast I told you about earlier, the one who had done some of the inquiries involved with my KGB vetting. He surprised me by sharing that information, which many would not. We met when he was in Department 1 (U.S. and Canada). I was there to be briefed in preparation for my assignment to Canada. We developed a friendship that—for me, at least—became closer than any other in the KGB. It blossomed after my return from the assignment in England. We spent much time together outside the KGB offices and eventually brought our families together. I truly value Sergei as a friend. For that reason, and because of the family connections, I want to be careful not to harm him when the information comes out about my defection.

"All this background is important in what I'm about to tell you.

"When I was called back to Moscow I was afraid my visits to your home had been discovered. Instead, I was put in touch with my old friend Sergei, who had been put in charge of a special operations group targeted at American intelligence people abroad. CIA employees were at the top of the priority list, but all the other United States intelligence agencies were included—Army Intelligence, Navy Intelligence, etc., plus your National Security Agency signals intelligence people. Sergei's group monitored worldwide contacts with these people as reported by KGB residencies and took operational control of any that looked especially promising. An example would be if I had reported my contacts with you in Stockholm. His group was staffed with a mixture of KGB officers who had served in the residency in Washington—some who had experienced contacts with American Intelligence people in other assignments abroad—and a few counterintelligence people transferred from Directorate K. Of course I was delighted to work with Sergei and found the case for which he wanted my help quite interesting.

"I was happy to be assigned to the operation because of where it would take place: Istanbul. If you haven't learned much about the former Constantinople, you should. I've always been fascinated by the idea of one city lying in two continents, Europe and Asia, and being such a crossroads of many nations and cultures. Yet I never got a chance to visit there until this operation.

"I was also fascinated with the case itself. This was an attempt to recruit a CIA employee, a member of your Istanbul Station. She had come to the attention of a Russian employee of Intourist who was co-opted by the KGB Residency and reported routinely on all his western contacts who had any kind of governmental position. He met Roberta during a dinner party hosted by a common acquaintance, an employee of the Turkish Foreign Office whose one claim to fame was an administrative posting to the Turkish Embassy in Paris. This Turk and his wife had become friendly with Roberta during their Paris tour, meeting first at some large diplomatic parties and eventually beginning a more private relationship with family dinners and picnics that included Roberta. Our Intourist contact, Mikhail, thought that there was a sexual interest between the Turk official and Roberta, but he didn't know the Turk well enough to probe. Mikhail was a bachelor and had his own designs on Roberta.

"He had reason to believe that she might be a willing partner. Encouraged by his KGB contact, he had a couple of dates with Roberta and saw her at another dinner party at the Turk's home. Mikhail has proven to be a good people-reader. Although Roberta had the appearance of a carefree party girl, she was deeply troubled. She seemed to be in her mid-thirties, moderately attractive with a good figure and a nice face that was beginning to show the wear of too much partying, too much smoking, too much drinking. She claimed to work in the Consular Section of the American Embassy in Istanbul, but he had never seen her at work there during occasional visits in connection with his Intourist responsibilities.

"After those contacts with Roberta, Mikhail and his KGB handler came to the conclusion that she worked for the CIA Station. The residency mounted a week-long surveillance of her activities, confirming that conclusion through the weakness of CIA people congregating with each other socially, especially in popular restaurants they liked to visit. Roberta mingled more often with identified CIA employees than with those in the Consulate.

"Finally, on their last date before the reporting that resulted in mounting an operation, Mikhail drove her home from an hours' long restaurant dinner where Roberta drank far too much. Parked outside her apartment, they got as intimate as a couple can comfortably manage in a parked car. Mikhail had taken advantage of Roberta's heavy drinking throughout their time together. In the afterglow of their back-seat experience he questioned her rather directly, using the reason that he would like to begin a serious relationship. Roberta never named the CIA, but expressed some bitterness over how she was treated by her employers. She considered herself well-educated and good enough to compete with the officer corps, as she put it, but had been turned down for training to become an officer. She had hoped to get that kind of training between her assignment in Paris and this assignment in Istanbul. Instead, they'd given her some lower level training for a couple of weeks and sent her here as an officer's assistant, which involved going out on the street sometimes but not often.

"With these developments the case was turned over to Sergei's Special Operations Group. He seconded one of his officers to the Istanbul residency on temporary assignment, with a first priority to rent a safe house where Mikhail could take Roberta for their trysts. A suitable place was located in quick order and outfitted with hidden cameras and recorders.

"Soon there were many reels of tape showing her athletic sexual abilities. When I was given an opportunity to review all the material collected there, I was much less interested in the visual tapes than in the recorded conversations. Through the several months of the operation before I came into the picture, Roberta slowly revealed more and more displeasure with her employers and dropped some tantalizing remarks about people who were of interest to her superiors. Most were Soviet citizens, some members of our residency there. Putting it all together, we had to assume that she was a CIA intelligence assistant in a section of the Station devoted to penetration of the Soviet Embassy.

"Discussions with Sergei and other members of his group centered around blackmailing Roberta with the sex tapes. I personally feel that blackmail is both distasteful and of questionable value for this kind of operation. They wanted me to travel to Istanbul and recruit Roberta, using blackmail as a tool. Sergei's reason for choosing me was that I am one of the best near-native English speakers with an American accent (okay, maybe a little bit Canadian). He thought I would be the most likely to succeed with this recruitment. I know there was some grumbling in the unit about Sergei bringing a friend into the operation for this purpose, which not everybody saw as necessary. I agreed to make the attempt to recruit Roberta with the understanding that I wouldn't use the sex tapes as blackmail if I could recruit her with other motivation, such as ideology or financial reward. In truth, the notion of an ideological recruitment seemed laughable to me, but I thought financial motivation might work both because she seemed in her conversations to want better things than she could afford, and because it would give her a chance to screw her bosses. More than once I heard her complain on the tapes about not getting the advancement she deserved.

I was in the midst of gathering my passport and documents under a different name, preparing for the trip to Istanbul, when a cable arrived informing us that Roberta was being re-assigned to Washington. When she told Mikhail about the transfer, she seemed happier with her situation. In the terms of their relationship he wasn't able to probe deeply, but answers to a few questions led him to believe that the transfer would have her doing similar work with more responsibility. She would be leaving about three weeks after that cable arrived in Moscow.

"This was good news and bad news. The prospect of recruiting a penetration into the very heart of your agency was terribly exciting to those of us working the case in Moscow. For me, though, the prospect of trying to recruit a happier Roberta, a person who seemed on the brink of gaining more satisfaction with her work, was less exciting. If she was happier with her work, she would have less motivation to accept the offer I planned to use. I was still resisting the use of blackmail to bring her around to our side.

"I'm sure you and your comrades experience the same kind of highs and lows as I experienced in my KGB career. This case had both. Two days after the arrival of the cable announcing Roberta's departure, I flew to Istanbul via Frankfurt. The cover for this mission was tourism. I was met by 'my friend, the Intourist expert on Istanbul' (Mikhail), who installed me in the safe house he used for meetings with Roberta. Anyone who pried would learn that we were good friends from student days at Moscow University, and Mikhail would be introducing me to the wonders of Istanbul. We did, in fact, tour many interesting sights while I was there.

"Mikhail brought some food to the apartment that first evening. We spent hours reviewing the case. Remember that he was a co-opted agent, not a staff officer, which meant that he had only a little training in clandestine activities. He was a charming fellow who got by on good looks, a natural ability to understand the motives that drive people's actions, and a large measure of chutzpah. At the end of that evening I was not happy with the local control officer who had been handling the case. One of the important things missing in my review of the files while still in Moscow was the fact that nobody appeared to have been looking into Roberta's opinion of Mikhail other than how he performed in bed. Did she consider him a worthy person of interest for her own office? Had she been reporting the contact with him all this stime? I suspected the oversight came from a concern that the answers might not be what the local handlers wanted to hear.

"The next day Mikhail and I began by satisfying my personal reason for wanting to be part of this operation—tourism. We started at Hagia Sophia and almost ended the day there. I was so struck by the beauty of that huge building, the mixture of cultures and religions it has represented for almost fifteen hundred years, that it was hard to tear myself away. We went briefly to the Topkapi Palace— fascinating in itself—but ran out of time. We wanted to be back at the safe house before five o'clock in the afternoon. Mikhail had a brief meeting scheduled with his KGB control officer (I would not be meeting directly with anyone from the residency), to check on any new developments or messages prior to that evening's activity—my first meeting with Roberta. I thought for a time that it would be my last meeting with her.

"The plan was for Roberta to come to the safe house. Mikhail would tell her there'd be another person with them that evening, an American friend who was visiting Istanbul for the first time. His friend would be staying at the apartment for a week while Mikhail showed him the historical and cultural sites in the city. Mikhail was sorry, but their dates would be limited to restaurant meals or driving around the city during this time.

"Just as Mikhail warned me, she arrived about fifteen minutes late, surprised to find that Mikhail was not there. I acted embarrassed and offered apologies for Mikhail, who had called to say he wouldn't be able to see her this evening because of an Intourist group arriving unexpectedly. I turned on as much charm as I could. 'Come in, anyway. I know you were looking forward to dinner with Mikhail. I can't offer you dinner, but I was just about to have a drink and some snacks if you're interested.' She was.

"My first impression of Roberta was an exaggeration of Mikhail's description. She was taller than I expected, probably one hundred seventy-five centimeters or so, with more natural beauty. Very dark hair tied into a knot at the back of her head and a pale complexion set off by bright red lipstick. As Mikhail said, her classic features were marred by a look of general debilitation—dark circles under amber eyes, wrinkles around the eyes and a slackness to the mouth—that made her look older than her age was understood to be. This marring of her looks also seemed worse than Mikhail described. Wearing a black suit and white blouse that were probably her office attire, she looked to me like a beautiful woman in her mid-thirties who was grieving over the recent loss of a husband or lover.

"Her demeanor certainly put a lie to that impression. She said, 'Let's start with the drink. How about vodka on the rocks, straight up?' She unbuttoned and removed her suit jacket, throwing it over the back of a recliner chair, and collapsed into the chair. 'God, I'm beat!'

"I was at the bar, fixing her drink. 'Hard day at the office?' I opened a bottle of weak beer for myself and was stingy in pouring vodka on the ice in her drink, not wanting her to get befuddled before we could have a good conversation. I also had to remember at all times that we were being filmed and recorded by the KGB technicians.

" 'God, yes,' she said. 'You sound like an American. Or maybe a Canadian, eh?'

" 'Maybe. Sorry you had such a hard day. Makes me feel guilty. Mikhail invited me because he knew I wanted to see Istanbul. No work today, just visiting some of the wonderful sights here. Today we spent a lot of time at Hagia Sophia and a short while at Topkapi Palace. I'm sure you've been to both. How long have you lived in Istanbul?'

"She said she'd been in Istanbul for just under three years. We went on to discuss the amazing number of things to explore in this city, agreeing that you probably couldn't do justice to them even in three years. By then she was ready for a refill of vodka, 'less ice this time.' Before filling that order, I put out some food Mikhail had made ready for the occasion—assorted Greek olives, cold meatballs, some cheese and crackers. I hoped this would slow her down on the drinking and put something in her stomach to absorb the alcohol.

"I was relieved that she ate quite a lot and drank less. When talk of sightseeing dribbled to an end, I expected Roberta to start questioning me. Was I American, Canadian, what? What kind of work did I do? At least I expected her to ask if I was married. Nothing but silence followed as we munched on the food, drank our drinks, thought our own thoughts. I was especially aware of the long silence because there were cameras and audio recorders running. If I failed to capture the moment, I would have many judges telling me what I should have done. I had to push forward.

" 'Mikhail told me you work in the American Consulate, Roberta. You're a beautiful woman, but frankly you look tired. You must really have had a hard day at the office.'

" 'Not really,' she replied, 'just part of a hard three years at the office.'

"I said that I understood there were many applicants for visas to the U.S., so she and her comrades must work long hours.

" 'It's not exactly that. Could I have a refill on the drink?'

"She had been more careful with drinking than I thought would be the case. I poured a larger portion of vodka this time.

"When I sat down again and looked at her expectantly, she went into the same long story she'd given Mikhail. She was as well educated as people higher in the organization. Roberta was born in New Orleans, and had most of her education there. Even though she had worked hard to lose the southern accent, she was sure that there were many Ivy League professionals in the staff who looked down on her when they learned of her roots.

"It went on and on. By 10:30 in the evening, she was still elaborating the same story we had heard several times from Mikhail, and from the microphones hidden in this very room. If I was going to push forward as I intended, I had to do it very soon. I fixed us both another drink and bit the bullet.

"I pulled an ottoman up close to her recliner so that I could look her straight in the eye. 'It sounds like you need help. Is there anything I can do? You've talked a lot about how you can't afford many of the things you've dreamed about. Have you thought about ways you could earn more money even without a promotion?' This seemed a bold way to begin a pitch for her recruitment, but I didn't know what else to do. I expected her to ask who I was. But she didn't.

" 'I need more money so I can get a promotion.' She turned around to pull her suit jacket off the back of the recliner. 'Look at this. It's a good suit that I bought in Paris, but that was five years ago and I wear it too often because I can't afford more clothes. Look at the elbows on the jacket. Look! They're almost worn through!' She actually had tears in her eyes.

"We went on for another hour without more progress. I escorted her down to the street, found a taxi and paid the driver in advance. I had made little headway beyond adding my own impressions to information about her received from Mikhail and the tapes, and I was even more convinced that money could play in important part in motivating her.

"At this point I was concerned about the operation. There was something wrong with the way our conversation had gone. Primarily I worried about the fact that Roberta never questioned me about my background and employment. All she ostensibly knew about me was that I might be American or Canadian, was a friend of Mikhail's and had an interest in touring Istanbul. Why would she carry on such an extended conversation and agree to another meeting with me two days later?

"Living the cover, I again toured Istanbul with Mikhail the following two days. This gave us a chance to talk more about Roberta, talk that went on incessantly and finally turned into an interrogation on my part. On the second day, driving somewhere with Mikhail in his car, I was able to confirm a suspicion lurking in my mind ever since the meeting with Roberta. Mikhail confessed that he had all but told Roberta who I really was. In effect he had pre-recruited her. He had not reported this to his KGB control officer, nor had he told the handler that he and Roberta had a brief meeting in the early morning after her meeting with me. She was quite surprised, he said, that I hadn't tried a flat-out recruitment pitch then and there. 'It was like,' she told Mikhail, 'a fellow inviting me up to his apartment for obvious reasons, but when I get there all he does is give me a drink and send me home in a taxi. I think your friend must be a slow lover.'

"I had a serious talk with Mikhail about his going far beyond his orders as I understood them. From that conversation it developed that the local control officer had been loose in giving him orders for the operation. 'He never told me not to do that,' was his excuse. I decided not to report this. I liked Mikhail. He was more charming than bright, and in the right position to help if run by a good control officer. Besides, he'd done much of the work for me. If I succeeded in the recruitment I would get the glory. I hoped he would receive some recognition for his part of the operation known to the higher echelons.

"As planned, Roberta came to the safe house late on the second day after our first meeting. The recruitment went as I'd planned. No blackmail with sex tapes. No ideological motivation. She was a linear thinker who cared little about political philosophy but cared a great deal about doing a good job for her employer because that's the way one earns money to buy the good things in life. If one employer was good, two were better. A lot of the frustration she felt in working with the CIA came from what she saw as unrecognized good performance on her part, and the sexist attitudes of the all-male upper-level staff. It was apparent that she took a lot of pride in her work. Whoever failed to see that, to recognize her in appropriate ways, is at least partially responsible for her accepting recruitment as a mole in your agency. Notice that I didn't say 'responsible for there being a mole in your agency.' To this day I don't know for certain that she became a mole, though it's possible. That's why I told you earlier that the operation might have produced a mole.

"I don't see a need to go into the details of that recruitment here. You have enough to identify Roberta and allow your agency to check on her. We met every other day for a week following the recruitment. Most of the time was taken with training. She of course had many of the basics from your own agency. We concentrated on communications: dead drops, some basic secret writing, memorization of contact telephone numbers, etc. One of Sergei's counterintelligence officers flew to Istanbul for our next to last meeting, to brief her on what material would be of interest when she was installed in a new position at CIA Headquarters.

"The doubt I have about Roberta actually becoming a mole came up in our last meeting, which left me unhappy and discouraged. Mikhail and I kept up our tourist activities, and I came to know and love much about Istanbul. I continued to stay away from direct contact with the residency, Mikhail carrying messages for me. The residency had a twenty-four-hour surveillance on Roberta for several days after our second meeting. I had nightmares about this being a dangle operation—the CIA trying to implant her as a double agent—but there was no indication of activity that the residency considered beyond the normal for someone in her cover position.

"The problem came from the fact that at the end of the week she and I spent in training, she learned that the transfer to your Headquarters included a full grade promotion, which would bring her more money. This made her doubtful about the benefits weighed against the risks in working with us. By that time she had accepted all the communication training, contact numbers, dead drop sites and other secret things I'd given her. I was horrified when she stated that she wanted to look at the situation at her Headquarters before deciding if she would actually go ahead with the operation for the KGB. I did my very best to get a positive commitment from her, but she was adamant. Yes, she might activate the operation by calling the initial contact phone number, or she might not. I was sick. The failure would reflect on me, and certainly in the long run would reflect on my friend Sergei, who had recommended me and taken responsibility for the operation.

"Remember that all our meetings were taped and photographed, so anything I said in that apartment would be known up the line. They couldn't, however, tape or photograph us when I followed the custom of walking Roberta down to the street to hail a taxi.

"On the way down to say our last goodbye, I whispered in her ear: 'I care a lot about you Roberta, and because of that I want to warn you of the consequences if you don't activate that contact within a reasonable time. Ninety days would be acceptable. Six months would be way too long. My superiors are prepared to blackmail you with information they have about your sexual affairs, heavy partying and drinking, anything that would embarrass you with your friends and your agency. You don't want that. I don't want to see that. Please, please just go ahead as we agreed. Once you see the benefits you'll be glad you did.'

"After I was sent home from Stockholm to Moscow, I had no further operational contact with Sergei. We did, though, maintain our social and family contacts. At one of the first family gatherings we happened to be getting drinks in our hosts' kitchen at the same time, nobody else around. Sergei grabbed me by the shoulder so I'd be facing him, and said quietly: 'Remember Istanbul?'

"I nodded that I did remember.

"Sergei picked up his full glass in his left hand. He smiled, and with his right hand he gave the thumbs up signal.

"Her name is Roberta Fletcher.

"That's all I know about a mole in the CIA."

✳ ✳ ✳

Two o'clock in the morning, Wednesday, according to Chris and Plotkin's time. Chris had taken detailed notes as Plotkin told the story, not wanting to interrupt the flow with questions or comments. Now, for another half hour, he did ask clarification of some details. Satisfied that Plotkin had given enough for the Agency's counterintelligence people to get started on an investigation, he gathered the notes into a neat pile, paper-clipped them together, folded the results once across and once again, and stuffed the resulting package in a pocket of his blue coveralls. These notes would not be out of his possession until he was at Headquarters.

"It's the middle of the night, Sasha. At least it's the middle of *our* night. Are you ready for some more sleep before we go on with this?"

"Ready for the sleep, yes. To 'go on with this?' I don't know. Does that mean going over the Roberta story again? Or what? When I thought about defecting to the United States, the picture in my mind was cloudy as far as this part of it goes—

which was probably a good thing. I might not have defected if I'd known what I had to go through. The rest of the picture seemed clearer. Some comfortable accommodations in the countryside, friendly debriefers, maybe a month of that and then resettlement in a nice part of the States, a new life. You haven't given me much idea of what will happen when we get there, other than threats if I don't cooperate."

"To tell you the truth, Sasha, I can't give you any details because I just don't know them. I've never been involved Stateside with handling a defector. Of course I hear things about those cases, but don't count on my being accurate. I'd guess—understand this is only a guess—that you're not too far off the mark as far as comfortable surroundings. That is, as long as our people are assured that you're being fully cooperative. You'll probably be guarded for a while, and escorted for any shopping or entertainment trips. The place you're wrong, I suspect, is in how much time it will take. My guess is that it will be six months before you can start looking at resettlement.

"All that is based on getting your full cooperation. If they aren't satisfied, expect much less comfortable surroundings and some heavy interrogation methods. But that would not include torture and beatings. Our people just don't have the stomach for that.

"As we've discussed before, you almost certainly will be polygraphed at the first opportunity. This is where I go out on a limb, most of all because you claim you can beat the polygraph. There's no way I'll accept your doing that in order to give false or misleading information. The situation we have between us, the situation involving Lisa, does not override that. If I hear about even a hint of duplicity in your debriefing—and believe me, I will find out—I'll blow the whistle even if it causes me severe embarrassment or affects my career. I appreciate your cooperation in telling me about Roberta. For the rest of our time together let's hit the highlights—just the highlights—of your 'Ulla' case. And then we can start going over names and details of sources you controlled in England. Most important will be the Illegals you worked with during your tours in Moscow Centre. I'll take the best notes I can and turn them over to our welcoming party when we get to the States."

Plotkin seemed satisfied with all that. Chris stripped down to his skivvies before climbing into the bunk and stuffing his package of notes under the pillow. Tired as he was, sleep eluded him. One hour, two hours passed and he was still awake, the story of Roberta going round and round in his mind. Who was Roberta Fletcher? He was fairly certain they had not met, though the name and description rang a faint bell. Five o'clock in the morning, still no sleep.

Muttering softly to himself, Chris turned on the individual reading light in his bunk space and pulled the notes package from under the pillow. A half hour later he had reviewed it all and come to no new conclusions. Still, the name *Roberta Fletcher* rang its distant chimes in the far reaches of his mind.

Finally, he slept.

CHAPTER THIRTY-SEVEN

Wednesday, November 15, 1972
Edmonds, Washington

Mor was getting more and more excited about Lisa's plan to leave the children with her and fly to the other Washington for a meeting with Chris. At first opportunity she spoke to her husband. "Yah, Herman," she said after he had come home from the Tows office the evening before, "you will be taking Lisa to the airport tomorrow morning."

Never too surprised by his wife's pronouncements, Herman said, "I probably will."

* * *

The three adults in the household were having a pre-dinner glass of sherry in the living room, no children present. "Maybe you, Lisa, could explain why I'm being ordered around like this. Not that I'd mind sharing a ride with a fine young woman like yourself. It would just be nice to know why you're leaving and where you're going."

"You know, Dad, that Chris and I have had been at odds over the demands of his work and his traveling and being away from our family so much of the time. This latest caper was the last straw because it totally changed our plans. Sometimes he seems to forget that our family has needs—for comfortable housing, decent educational opportunities and reasonable stability. I can't provide these things on my own."

"What is this word, 'caper'?" Mor interrupted.

"Quiet, Mor! Let the woman talk." Herman must have had a hard day at work. He seldom spoke sharply to his wife.

"A caper is kind of like an adventure, Mor." Lisa wasn't comfortable with Mor's being shot down for her eccentricities. "The problem, Dad, is that this adventure caused an argument between Chris and me, and nothing was resolved before he left. I'm flying to Washington, DC, at eight fifteen tomorrow morning. I hope to be there when he returns from wherever he is now, and spend some quality time working things out."

"And I offered to watch the children while she's gone." Mor shot a steely glance at her husband. Lisa had no doubt that he would hear later about his manner of speaking to her.

"That's certainly not a problem for me, Lisa, taking you to SeaTac. As long as you don't mind leaving at five forty-five in the morning. I need to be at our offices before seven o'clock, so that'll get you to the airport plenty early."

Seven people were seated at dinner on this evening. Lots of happy chatter and only a few tears from Lisbet, whose insecurities surfaced when she realized that both her mom and dad would be gone at the same time. Lisa spent most of her free time that evening with her littlest girl. Her heartstrings were tugged by this daughter who had played no part in the deceit that had brought her into the world, who deserved every bit as much of her mother's love as her three siblings and yet—as Lisa admitted to herself—had never received it.

When she finally tucked Lisbet into bed, Lisa couldn't hold back the tears that blurred her vision as she bent over to kiss the little girl. A teardrop fell on Lisbet's face. "Are you all right, Mommy?"

"I'm very all right, Sweetheart." As she kissed her other daughter and closed their bedroom door, she knew that to be true.

Lisa's alarm clock had just sounded at five o'clock the next morning when there was a soft rap at the door. "Time to get up," Herman called softly, "you've got forty-five minutes before we leave." There was no problem getting up. She'd been awake for at least half an hour, as excited as on the day of her wedding. That day represented one beginning. This day represented another, a fresh start she was sure would bring lasting happiness into a marriage that had good, solid roots, but a few bugs. If everything went according to plan, they would soon be cleared away.

She had a reservation at the Watergate Hotel in Washington, a small suite overlooking the Potomac, not too far from the White House. She'd already called Kathy Brewer to alert her to the plan and would call her after checking in this evening.

"Coming, Dad." She swung her legs out of the bed, planted her feet on the carpet and stood with arms in the air, stretching, ready for the next leg of this journey.

CHAPTER THIRTY-EIGHT

Thursday, November 16, 1972
Aboard the *Rockfish*

Early morning, according to the time Chris and Plotkin kept on their watches. It should be five o'clock in the morning in Sweden, so wherever they were now—presumably sailing west or south—local time could not be more than an hour's difference. Time became important because they sensed changes in course and a decreased velocity that—together with the forty-eight hours they'd been underway already—indicated they might be entering port.

Since Plotkin's revelations about a possible mole at CIA Headquarters, their debriefing time had been more routine. With no marching orders beyond the note received from Llonis while he was still at Headquarters, Chris was playing it by ear. He had pushed for as much detail as possible on the Roberta Fletcher case for obvious reasons. It was *the* high priority of the mission. The "Ulla" case had occupied more of the debriefing time than he thought it deserved, but it was so important in Plotkin's mind (it did, after all, play a role in his ability to defect) that Chris had gone along with his wishes.

Reasoning that the specialists at Headquarters would have priorities he couldn't guess, Chris approached remaining time aboard the submarine as an opportunity to fashion an outline of information available to Plotkin, filling several sheets of notepaper with dates, names and places that would serve to give those specialists a history of this KGB officer's assignments throughout his service with the Soviet intelligence agency. They could choose their priority interests from those notes and then take all the time they needed to pick the man's brain. These sheets joined the others in the folded papers Chris had put together while on the submarine, a thick wad he guarded at all times. It was kept under his pillow while he slept, and bulged in the pocket of his coveralls during waking hours.

The debriefing sessions had taken place at irregular hours, because the two men had not yet adjusted their biological clocks after the sleep deprivation resulting from what they now jokingly referred to as The Great Escape. After an excellent supper at six o'clock Wednesday evening, they had slept until three a.m. on this Thursday morning, helped themselves to coffee from the wardroom, and were debriefing again when they were interrupted by a soft knock on the stateroom door. The skipper, Ron Smith, entered and closed the door.

"I hope you men have had a good trip." Both nodded vigorously. "And that you've been able to work under these very unusual circumstances." Nods again.

"Thanks, Ron," Chris said. "I can't think of a better way to decompress and get some talking out of the way."

"My thanks, too," Plotkin joined in. "As I told you before, in my next life I'm going to be a submariner."

"I'm glad it worked out. You've been model visitors, but now we're ending this trip. We'll dock in about an hour, and I want to go through some procedures about your transfer to another transport. I can tell you now that we'll be docking in Scotland at Holy Loch, which our navy uses as a submarine repair facility. A message came in a few minutes ago regarding your transfer. You're going to be met by one of Chris's colleagues, who will be waiting in the administration building."

Chris interrupted. "Did they say who?"

The skipper smiled. "No, and I don't suppose it would be a real name anyway, would it? The point of the message was that they want you to look like crew members when you disembark. It's raining hard, and the bad weather is expected to continue. I'm going to have one of my men bring you suitable gear in a few minutes. You'll stay in your coveralls. When you feel the boat docking, put on the enlisted men's hats and the raingear he brings. He'll also provide a couple of duffle bags for your own clothing.

"My Exec will come get you as soon as we're tied up. He'll walk you off the boat and up to the administration building, where your contact will be waiting in the office of the Base Commander. He'll be the only one there. The Exec will wait while you change into your own clothes, and he'll bring our gear back to the boat. My understanding is that your man has made arrangements for you to leave the base and will have a car waiting.

"I don't suppose we'll see each other after this little adventure. I wish you both the very best of everything as you go forward. It's been an honor and a pleasure to help you out." He pumped each man's hand in turn, adding a slap on the back.

The rest of their submarine experience went as Commander Smith described.

When the Executive Officer called the two men from their stateroom, they were joined by several sailors dressed as they were in coveralls and raingear. Together they walked in the pre-dawn darkness to the administration building, where the sailors broke off in different directions and the Exec escorted Chris and Plotkin inside and to the office of the Base Commander. There he waited for them to change clothes before saying goodbye. He then went down the hall to another office, coming back with the CIA officer who would escort them on the rest of the journey to the States. Chris was happy to say hello once again to his old friend, Bob Brewer, though he would not say the name aloud until he learned the identity Bob was using for this mission.

Brewer shook Chris's hand and greeted him solemnly, signaling that he did not want to reveal their friendship to Plotkin. "Nice to see you again, Chris. It's been awhile. And to you, Sir." He shook Plotkin's hand. "I'm Richard. We have a car and driver outside. He'll get us through the checkpoint on the base here and onto the tarmac at Prestwick Airport. Do you know that facility?"

Plotkin smiled. "Very well. I was in England for some years, and took advantage of my time there to make several tourist trips that included Scotland."

Brewer smiled back at him. "I understand. Then you know it's near Glasgow. We should be at the plane within an hour and on our way to the States shortly after that."

Chris broke in. "What about documentation? I don't have an exit stamp from Scandinavia, and Sasha only has his true-name passport."

"Not to worry. Our man at the wheel of the car has it all covered."

Plotkin was worried nevertheless. "Does that mean he's with British Intelligence? Do they already know about my defection?"

"Not at all," Brewer replied, "he's with us. I don't know any details about how the arrangements were made, but it shouldn't have been too hard with our being on the submarine base here and flying out of the military section of Prestwick. Whatever the case, you're in very good hands and will be at the end of this journey before you know it."

Plotkin appeared satisfied. "Before we go in the car, I need to try out a new American phrase. 'I have to hit the head.' "

Brewer turned to Chris. "He's a quick learner. You don't have to go very far. The Base Commander has his own bathroom off the office here, behind that door." He pointed Plotkin to the door and waited with Chris while the KGB man was in there. They talked very quietly, almost in whispers.

"How did it go?"

"Well. Once we were settled on the submarine he seemed to be fully cooperative. I have the name of the only person he thinks could be a mole at Headquarters."

"Fantastic. What's the name?"

"Roberta Fletcher."

The name caused Brewer to stare at Chris, his mouth opening and closing several times before any sound came out.

"You're kidding!"

"Not at all. I've never heard the name. Do you know her?"

"Christ yes. So do you. Remember the woman who brought lunch to you on that day you spent at Headquarters?"

"Barely. I didn't pay much attention. You suggested I ask her to bring some food for me. I asked her, and by the time I was back in your office you were asleep. I remember you woke up when the food was brought in by another woman. You asked her what happened to your secretary, and this woman said she'd gone to lunch. I don't recall her name or much more beyond my putting a notebook over the stack of files so she wouldn't see what they were. I certainly don't remember the name 'Roberta.' "

They could hear the toilet flush, water running. Plotkin was washing his hands. "She goes by the nickname 'Bobby.' That's why you didn't hear 'Roberta.' We need time to talk about this, but I don't want Plotkin to be aware of our knowledge of her at this point."

Plotkin's hand was turning the doorknob on his way out of the bathroom as Chris quickly passed his wad of notes to Brewer, transferring them from an inner pocket of his jacket. "My turn," he said, as he went into the bathroom.

* * *

This moment outside the Base Commander's bathroom was a turning point for the Russian—his first time alone with a CIA officer other than Chris. He and Chris had been joined at the hip, night and day, ever since their rendezvous on the Sunday past. The fact of his defection became more real as he made small talk with this new acquaintance, who seemed a very serious character despite the occasional smile. Much like Chris seemed most of the time. He wondered if any of these men ever let themselves have fun, get drunk, tell dirty stories, chase women, or really live outside their work.

"How was the boat trip?"

"I hate boats. The sailboat was a nightmare, but I was surprised by the comfortable ride in the submarine."

"The weather is sure bad here. What a rain! Does it ever rain this hard in Moscow?"

"Often. And I think even harder."

* * *

Chris saved the pair from further banalities when he came out of the bathroom. "Sasha, before we leave for the airport, Richard and I have some planning to do in private. I'm going to ask you to make yourself comfortable for a few minutes in this office while we stand outside in the hall and talk. You can wait over in that corner with the comfortable chairs and some magazines to read." He hardly thought Plotkin would be a flight risk, and in any event it appeared next to impossible to leave the office any way other than the door to the hall.

"No problem." Sasha settled himself comfortably in one of the overstuffed chairs.

In the hall with the office door closed, Chris talked quietly with his friend from Headquarters. "Sasha begged me not to send anything to Headquarters before our return to the States. He's understandably scared of the consequences of a leak of any kind. I understand his concern, but we have to weigh that against the possibility that Roberta will be alerted somehow and run before we get back to Headquarters. How certain can you be that Bobby is the Roberta Fletcher he described?"

"How did he describe her? Where else has she served?"

"He made a recruitment pitch while she was in Istanbul." Chris went on to tell Brewer how Plotkin had described Roberta physically, and of her interest in material things.

"That's her. I haven't done any work directly with her, but I've been in the lunch room at Headquarters with Bobby and others at the same table, and heard her talk about clothes, cars and men. It's her. No doubt."

"So what do we do about getting word to Gary and the top floor? Do you have any secure communications channel to Headquarters?"

"I could send something from the plane during our flight back, but I'm not sure it's wise. Look at it this way. The KGB is extremely upset about letting Plotkin get away, which means they're more concerned than usual about the information a defector possesses. He ran last Sunday afternoon, less than four days ago. They don't know where he is or what he's doing—or at least we hope they don't. Would they immediately pull back all the agents he ever knew about or take a few days for damage assessment? My guess is that they'd start with the damage assessment. If I'm wrong, and Bobby really is the mole, she's probably hightailed it out of the United States already. If I'm right, she'll still be there and asleep right now. We should be landing at Andrews Air Force Base by mid-morning DC time, when she should be at work. The way I see it, our choices are to call Gary at home right now and double-talk a message about Bobby, send a secure 'Eyes-Only' message from the flight back to DC, or do nothing until we arrive. I'm quite sure Gary will meet us at Andrews, but not expose himself to Plotkin. The last choice means we could brief Gary within a half-hour of landing."

"What's going to be done with Plotkin at that time?"

"We'll turn him over to some people from Security Division. They'll escort him to the safe house where he'll be staying, get him comfortable, see about clothes and reading materials and all that. He'll be in good hands. Gary and I will get the debriefing set up and going, probably by the end of today."

"It's going to be a pretty abrupt ending for Sasha if I'm not part of that."

Brewer put a big hand on his friend's shoulder. "I'm sorry, Chris, but you certainly will not be part of that. Nor will I. Gary and I will supervise the debriefing at a distance. After we land at Andrews and you and I say goodbye to him, Plotkin will not be seeing any of the people he met this week. Considering all you've been through together, I'm sure you and he have a special bond that will be hard to break. You're so close to this operation that it will be hard to see the logic in breaking these ties. Once it's all over and you can take a step back, you'll have better perspective."

A special bond indeed, Chris thought. If Bob and Gary—or anyone else—knew what a *special* bond it was, things might turn out differently from the way they seemed to be heading. "I understand, but it's going to be tough just to shake hands and turn our backs on the adventure of a lifetime. Let's arrange it so that, after landing, I say goodbye first and walk away, leaving you to explain all that to Sasha."

"Agreed. I'll stay on the plane with Plotkin, and you get off first and disappear before I introduce him to our Security people. Now we'd better be on our way to Prestwick. The sooner we arrive, the sooner home, and the sooner we can start getting into this Bobby thing."

Chris later recalled the ensuing events as an anti-climax. The driver of the car taking the three of them to Prestwick said not a word, nor did his passengers talk other than to make remarks on the weather. They passed through checkpoints at the submarine base and the secure military facility at Prestwick with no trouble. The driver presented a document to the guards at each place that caused them to raise the barrier gate immediately and salute as the car passed. "Impressive," Plotkin said quietly to Brewer as they passed through the Prestwick checkpoint.

More impressive yet was the aircraft awaiting them, an upscale business jet with civilian markings and a luxurious interior. The all-male crew was made up of pilot, co-pilot and steward. The latter was the only one of the three to speak to the passengers, introducing himself as Matt and offering drinks even before they took off. All three refused, limiting themselves to coffee with a breakfast served soon after they were in the air.

By tacit agreement, Bob Brewer sat close to Plotkin throughout the flight, while Chris sat by himself, alternately reading magazines, staring at the clouds below the plane, and dozing. After breakfast Brewer smoothed out the wad of notes Chris had given him and reviewed a few details with Plotkin, concentrating on the Roberta Fletcher affair and making notes for himself.

The landing in clear weather at Andrews Airforce Base gave Plotkin an impressive view of his new country of choice. Soon after the aircraft's stairway was lowered, two men came aboard and spoke to Bob Brewer. Judging from their dark blue suits, white shirts, conservative ties, and close-cropped hair, Chris figured they were either the Security Division people Brewer had mentioned or FBI agents playing a similar role. As they spoke with Brewer in the forward section of the cabin, Chris motioned to Plotkin to come aft and join him.

"This is where we say goodbye, Sasha."

Plotkin looked surprised. "Certainly you're going to be part of the debriefing team, aren't you?"

"No," Chris replied, "and it's probably just as well. You and I harbor some biases for good and for ill that could affect a formal debriefing. Even though we're the only ones here who know about that, I've already been informed that this is the last you and I will see of each other. That decision doesn't reflect on either of us. It's just standard procedure." He stared intently into Plotkin's eyes. "I'm sure you can imagine the mixed emotions I have right now. Under other circumstances I might have regretted that decision coming down on us, but I believe it's for the best."

As Chris offered a handshake of farewell, Plotkin grasped his hand in a hard grip. "I'm terribly disappointed, Chris, and I suppose your people will manage it so we don't see each other in the future. But I'm not certain I agree with that, not ever meeting again. I want to know how you and your family are getting along. Can't we—" He was interrupted by the blue-suited men coming aft to escort him off the plane and into the future.

Plotkin said a simple, "Goodbye, Chris," shook hands with Brewer and gave a wave as he headed down the stairway from the plane. Brewer and Chris remained on the plane for another five minutes before Gary Llonis boarded. They sat together talking about the case before leaving for CIA Headquarters to begin a debriefing of Chris and the formation of plans to investigate Roberta Fletcher.

The farewell at Andrews Air Force Base was indeed the last time Plotkin and Chris would ever set eyes on each other.

CHAPTER THIRTY-NINE

Thursday, November 15, 1972
Washington, DC

The United Airlines flight from Seattle arrived at four twenty in the afternoon at Dulles Airport, a few minutes ahead of schedule. Lisa felt relieved as she left the plane's cramped tourist section for the People Mover transfer to the main terminal—excitement as well. She never would have arrived in DC unbeknownst to her husband earlier in her marriage.

She had an outline of what she wanted to accomplish, based on her belief that Chris would be coming back to Headquarters within a very few days. It would take a lot of research and imagination, but she was sure she could meet her goals in time for his arrival.

There was no sparing of expenses on this all-important mission to save her marriage. Tourist class air, yes, but the nightly rate for a suite at the Watergate was high compared to what she and Chris usually paid at hotels. So be it. From Dulles Airport she took a taxi to the hotel at twice the cost of a shuttle bus. Tomorrow she'd be using cabs for most of her research, relatively cheap compared to Seattle but still a luxury she would usually do without. It would be worth it. She just wished she could see Chris's face when he received the first note.

Her splurge on travel included overweight charges for luggage on the flight. Lisa had brought more clothing than ever before when traveling, more than she'd ever use, but she wanted to be flexible, to be able to change her appearance as necessary, and—above all—to be so attractive when the time came that a man would trip over himself trying to get to her.

Her third-floor hotel suite was even nicer than she'd imagined. The balcony seemed to hang right over the Potomac, high enough to provide a good view of the river but low enough to smell the water, to feel the atmosphere of an eastern river that played such a large part in the history of the States.

Though tired after the long flight, Lisa wanted to get to her evening tasks right away. First, the two phone calls. One to the Edmonds home to let the family know she had arrived safely. Mor must have been sitting next to the phone, she snatched it up so quickly. She sounded relieved to hear that Lisa was safe; she must have been imagining all manner of disaster scenarios; she was already filled with foreboding about the fate of her son's marriage. Lisbet was the only one of the children at home. Lisa spoke with her for several minutes, enchanted all over again by what she could learn when truly listening to the little girl.

It took Lisa several minutes to control her emotions before she could make the second call, to Kathy Brewer. Now it was almost six thirty in the evening, local time.

"Kathy? How good to hear your voice! It's Lisa Holbeck. I just arrived here. I'm staying at the Watergate. Have you heard from Bob yet? Does he know when Chris might return? Nothing yet?

"I'm making some plans to surprise Chris. If it's okay with you, I'd like to come by your house tomorrow or the next day and leave a note for you to get to Chris somehow. I'm just sure that Bob either is with him or will know where he is. That would be okay? Great, you're the best, Kathy. And Kathy ...? Thanks so much. We've never had a chance to get to know each other well, but I'm finding you're a great friend."

Next on the agenda after the calls was to stoke up her furnace with a good meal, ordered from room service. She'd need the energy for the final item on tonight's agenda—driving around in a taxi to locate the first site for the other notes to Chris. Outside it was cold and raining, but she had two raincoats and an assortment of hats in her luggage.

A shower and a good meal restored her energy. At eight o'clock that evening Lisa stood in the entry of the hotel, waiting for a taxi. Dressed in a pants suit, a long pale-blue raincoat and sensible rain hat of the same color, and wearing walking shoes, she felt ready to tackle any challenge the evening might bring. The bellhop who opened the taxi door for her was less certain.

"Where to, Ma'am?"

"I'm just going to be driving around for a while. I'll tell the driver."

The bellhop wasn't satisfied with the answer. "It's not a good idea for a single woman to be wandering around by herself late at night, even in a taxi. You best give the driver a destination."

"Okay, okay. How about Union Station?" She handed a dollar to the bellhop before he closed the door and slapped the top of the taxi to send it on the way.

The driver asked "You going someplace by train, Ma'am?"

"No, I just want to look at something there."

There was little talk on the trip to Union Station, Lisa keeping her focus on the matter at hand: to find a news vendor willing to pass a message from one stranger to another. Arriving at the station, she found lots of construction in progress with many scaffolds and cranes and little of the foot traffic one would expect at a busy railway station.

"There's a big remodel going on," the driver explained, "but they don't seem to be getting anywhere fast."

Lisa directed him to drive the length of the station, not saying what she was hoping to find. At last, there it was. A news vendor stand at the west entrance. Closed, of course. Damn! She'd have to come back tomorrow. Nothing more to be done tonight. On to the Jefferson Memorial.

"The Jefferson Memorial? You sure it'll be open on a winter night like this?"

"I read in a brochure at the hotel that it's open until midnight."

"If you say so, Ma'am." Lisa's relief was great when they arrived at the memorial, lit beautifully as the brochure advertised. A few people were wandering around the entrance.

She had visited this and all the other great monuments in the nation's capitol many times. Jefferson was one of her most admired historic figures. The monument was beautiful in its own way, although in her opinion it was eclipsed by the nearby Lincoln Memorial. She studied the figure inside the monument with a sense of pride in her country and awe for the artisans who could craft such wonders. Then she went to work outside, looking carefully at the steps up to the entrance and the bordering foliage, seeking a crack, a niche, a hole in a tree, anyplace where a message could be left safely for a few hours. Satisfied that she had found what was needed, Lisa returned to the taxi and asked to be driven to the hotel.

Nine thirty in the evening, and she was back in her room at the Watergate with nothing left to do until tomorrow. Only six thirty in Edmonds, the time clock she was running on. Not sleepy yet, she tried watching TV but found nothing interesting. Next was the book she'd bought at SeaTac airport. A quarter of the way in when she arrived at Dulles, it now held her attention even less than it had on the plane. What to do, what to do? Thoughts of going down to the bar were quickly rejected. She had never enjoyed the bar scene, even with Chris, and couldn't imagine sitting by herself with a drink in hand, people staring at her.

It was a long night. Her wake-up call came right at seven thirty in the morning, as promised. She ordered a hearty breakfast, donned the luxurious white robe offered as a hotel amenity, and read the *Washington Post* that was left outside her door while waiting for breakfast. Now this was living!

Lisa was surprised to find that it was already ten o'clock in the morning by the time she finished luxuriating in her suite and went downstairs, waiting only a moment for another taxi. The driver was a turbaned Indian with excellent English skills and a manner that gave her the impression he would cater to her every whim. Her first whim was to return to Union Station and the news vendor stand. The driver, who introduced himself as Wellington, showed no surprise when she asked him to wait long enough for her to talk briefly with the news vendor. The weather on this mid-November day had taken an unusual turn for the better, so warm and sunny that Lisa left her raincoat and hat in the taxi. Wellington held the door for her, eyes twinkling with admiration as she walked toward the kiosk. Today she was wearing her green plaid skirt and a brown suede jacket over a snug-fitting blouse, with the sturdy walking shoes that would serve well for the planned program.

The planned program. She already knew that plans don't always work out, but was learning that plans for this kind of program would prove more fragile than she expected. As she approached the vendor she saw that he was blind. That could be an advantage. It was also a boon that nobody else was at his stand just now.

"Excuse me, Sir, may I ask you a question?"

"You can ask me anything you want, Lady, but I can't promise to answer it." Dark sunglasses hid whatever was wrong with his eyes, but his mouth was smiling.

"I'm taking a train to New York. Somehow I've lost track of my husband. Is there any way I could leave a message for him with you?"

The question wiped the smile from the man's face.

"There's no way in hell I'd do that. If you know what's good for you, I'd skedaddle to that train right now and never come back here. I memorize voices, so I'd know you tomorrow or next year. Git! Scat!"

Shocked, Lisa took a step back. "I'm sorry. I didn't mean to offend you."

"You didn't offend me, Lady, you scared the shit out of me. A couple of years ago I accepted a message left for somebody. The guy who left it hadn't been gone five minutes before a couple of FBI agents showed up, made me close the stand and took me down to the FBI Building. I was there about three hours with them shooting questions at me. The one good thing that came out of it was that they had me listen to a bunch of voices on tape, and I was able to identify the guy who left the message. Those agents were nice enough, but I don't want to go through that again. Skedaddle before I give them a call."

"I'm terribly sorry I disturbed you. It wasn't anything like that, but I respect your privacy and I'll be on my way."

"You sound like a nice person, so let's just forget it. Can I sell you something? A paper? A magazine? Candy bar?"

"Nothing, thanks. I'll just leave." Lisa skedaddled back to the waiting taxi. She must have appeared stricken by the encounter with the news vendor.

"Anything I can do, Ma'am? Did that chap say something? Do something?"

Lisa knew she'd botched this thing something awful. Damned U.S. Government had its nose in everything, even a newspaper stand. Wellington, who remained concerned despite her protestations that nothing was wrong, suggested a small café on Pennsylvania Avenue as a spot where she could spend a half hour planning the rest of the day. He happily agreed to wait.

Lisa ordered a cup of coffee and a Danish and laid out her notes for the original plan and the tourist brochures. She crossed out Union Station as one of the sites. The plan for hiding her notes to Chris was now:

1. Jefferson Memorial
2. Lincoln Memorial
3. Smithsonian Institute ("The Castle")
4. L'Enfant Plaza Hotel

Her immediate tasks were to locate hiding places at the Lincoln Memorial and The Castle.

Back in the taxi, Wellington was all smiles, so she must have appeared more relaxed. Off they went to the Lincoln Memorial, where an unexpected number of people were on the steps and in the rotunda, brought out by the unseasonable warm weather. Within fifteen minutes she had located a niche similar to the one found at Jefferson's memorial.

They went on to The Castle, where she came up empty in her search for a suitable place for her note. Not that there weren't plenty of hiding spots. The problem was that the huge old pile of bricks, with its extensive landscaping, had so many possibilities that it would be hard to write an understandable, brief description. Wellington was concerned once again when she dragged back to the taxi.

"Madam didn't have success here?" he asked.

"Madam sure didn't," she replied. "Let's swing by L'Enfant Hotel for a minute, and then I want to go home. Back to the Watergate."

At L'Enfant she went into the lobby just long enough to pick up a couple of tourist brochures as a cover for casing out the concierge desk. Nothing unusual. Perhaps a bit more formal than some of the other hotels, but no reason to think her plan wouldn't work there.

Back at the Watergate she paid Wellington and added a generous tip, then went to her room to make some telephone calls, celebrate the small successes of the day, and mourn the big failures. Two of the sites for hiding notes—places she had known as a younger woman working there for the U.S. Navy—proved impractical. Back to the drawing board.

But first the calls. Phoning Edmonds, Lisa was startled to learn that Mor had received a call from Chris only an hour before her own call. Mor reported that he was very upset when she would not tell her son where Lisa might be, only that she had asked for some time away from family and children to consider the state of her marriage. Thank Heaven Mor had gone along with Lisa's request not to reveal her presence in the nation's capitol. Reassured that everything was fine with the children, she rang off and made the next call—to Kathy Brewer. With even more startling results.

"It's a good thing you phoned now, Lisa, because both of our men spent the night here. They arrived together yesterday morning, worked all day and didn't get here until about nine o'clock last night. Both of them looked exhausted. They ate the soup I fixed, crashed into bed right afterwards, and were up early this morning. I think it was about seven o'clock when they left. I asked Chris if he'd talked with you. He said he hadn't but would try to call you in Edmonds today."

"I just learned that he did call at his parents' home, but he still doesn't know I'm in town. Is it going to be possible for me to visit you briefly without Chris's knowledge?"

"What time would it be?"

"Probably sometime between three and four o'clock this afternoon."

"That should be okay. Our husbands seem to be deep into some all-important operation, so they probably won't come back until late tonight." The two women agreed that Lisa would come to the Brewer home no later than four o'clock in the afternoon, and in the meantime she would not leave her hotel room in case Kathy had any news for her. She ordered lunch from room service and went to work.

For Lisa, this was more fun than work. She had already written a poem for the occasion, even before arriving in Washington. She planned to use a stanza from the poem as a lead-off to each note. Through reading spy novels and hearing Chris and his Agency friends talk, she knew something about these things they called drops, though she was no expert on the terminology. She smiled to herself as she sat down at the mahogany desk in her suite, ready to finish the details. The smile came from the fact that she was probably better at that game than any of them.

Her memory of the techniques went way back to the days when her parents were still alive, when she was a little girl. On every one of her birthdays after she learned how to read, her mother hid Lisa's most exciting present and gave her a note to start her off on the treasure hunt. There were several hidden notes leading to the present itself. Each one rhymed cleverly and gave the location of the next note. The final one led to the treasure. She had resurrected the practice with her own family once her children came along and began to read. When she played the game with Chris on his birthdays, he seemed to take longer even than the children in figuring out from a note where to go next. It made her feel superior.

Now for the details. Her first note would be handed to Chris by Kathy Brewer at a time agreed on by Lisa and Kathy. This was the tricky part. Presumably Chris and Bob were working today and would be back at the Brewer home rather late, too late to set the gears in motion. Tomorrow being Saturday, Lisa hoped that the two men would not be working over the weekend or on Sunday. Thus Saturday would be the target date to get things going, with Sunday the backup. For want of a better plan, she thought it would be best to trust Kathy's judgment in choosing a time to pass the note, a time when Chris had a few unplanned hours ahead of him. Once he had the note in hand she'd alert Lisa through a call to her room at the Watergate, triggering Lisa's own part in the operation.

And now for the notes themselves. She brought out the poem she had written at the Holbeck home in Edmonds after the cathartic session with Elle. Could it have been just three days ago? Yes, it was on Tuesday, the day after her let-it-all-hang-out session with Elle. Feeling the effects of that and the earlier session when Elle lectured her on forgiveness, alone in the house with the children in school and Mor off shopping, she sat down to work on an old manual typewriter in the room where she slept. In two hours she pecked out a poem of six stanzas. It was a plea for the salvation of a marriage, a message of understanding for the other's pain, a promise of undying, unconditional love.

Lisa had been so taken up with details for her trip that she never looked at the poem again after finishing the last stanza in Edmonds and folding it into her purse. Reading it now, she was struck by the depth of feeling poured into those lines and a little nervous about the sentimentality. She didn't consider herself especially romantic; the hard knocks of losing her parents and going through the betrayal of a foster parent had mostly hardened her against such emotions. Re-reading the poem, she wondered if her capacity for romance, for sentimentality, was returning.

How would Chris view these lines? Men were generally held to be less sentimental than women. Throughout their marriage Lisa had concluded that her husband was an exception to the rule, a different class of male, one who—according to pop science—"was in touch with his feminine side." He could shed copious tears at a romantic movie, mourn a death in a distant friend's family, even cry at a beautiful wedding (although he'd joke about "regrets for the poor groom"). His rude, sudden departure from Edmonds had left her feeling misunderstood and unloved, in doubt about his present frame of mind.

By two o'clock she had made her final decision: the plan would go forward as outlined. She wrote the first note, struggling over a description of the hiding place at the Jefferson Memorial. Halfway through composing the note, it hit her: she was writing on Watergate Hotel stationery! How dumb was that? She hurried down to the gift shop in the lobby, but found no plain writing paper of the kind she wanted—only packages combining fancy paper and envelopes with various Washington DC themes. Not exactly what she wanted. She chose the least fancy of the lot.

Back in her room, Lisa copied what she had already written, completed the note and sealed it. She donned the raincoat she would use in the operation, a light fabric item that was reversible, blue on one side and beige on the other. There was a matching, broad-brimmed hat, but she didn't want to use that in today's beautiful weather. Several taxis were waiting at the hotel entrance when she went downstairs.

Her taxi waited outside the Brewer home while Lisa stepped inside and spoke with Kathy for a few minutes. Kathy had no more information about their husbands' plans. She agreed with Lisa's proposal that she make a call to Lisa at the Watergate as soon as possible after passing the note to Chris. There wasn't much more to be said. Not wanting to be caught at the Brewer home in case Bob or Chris should show up unexpectedly, Lisa excused herself with many thanks.

She was shocked at the fare charged by the taxi driver when they returned to the Watergate. It wasn't that she doubted his honesty, but rather that she realized for the first time how much money she had already spent since arriving in the capitol. As Lisa rode the elevator to the third floor, she estimated the hotel bill if she stayed through Monday, added up other expected expenses, and guessed that by then she would have spent every last penny of money saved from her living allowance while Chris was in Vietnam. When the elevator stopped at her floor, she pushed the down button, going to the lobby and the concierge desk. "Is there a market nearby where I might buy fresh fruit?" She was pointed in the direction of an all-night market, where she bought nutritious snacks, some fruit of questionable quality, and a bottle of cheap champagne, all at outrageous prices at least double those she paid in supermarkets at home in Edmonds. By the time she arrived back at the Watergate with two heavy sacks, she was exhausted. A bellhop rushed to help, but she shook him off with a grim, "Thanks anyway," not wanting to pay another tip.

In her suite at last, Lisa tucked away the groceries, slipped out of her clothes and into a nightgown topped by the hotel robe, and settled down to wait. Twenty-four hours? Forty-eight hours? It might be that long, though she hoped not. With any luck she would receive the call from Kathy before noon tomorrow and all would be resolved. Anything beyond that, and Chris would be coming back to a crazy woman.

✲ ✲ ✲

Kathy was still up and about when Bob and Chris arrived home Friday evening, somewhat worse for wear. It wasn't just that they were tired; they had obviously been drinking when they blew in close to ten o'clock, blustery and full of a good cheer fueled by alcohol, judging from the fumes. When she met them at the door in her wheelchair, Bob stooped down to give her such a gently loving kiss that she forgave him all present and past sins. Chris, on the other hand, was so exuberant that he half lifted her out of the wheelchair with a bear hug that bordered on dangerous, letting go only after Bob offered a nightcap.

Kathy had to laugh at their antics, which were unusual for both these rather conservative men. "What in the name of Heaven have you two been up to, besides trying to drink all the alcohol between here and Headquarters?"

"We weren't able to drink it all," Bob said, "but we gave it a good try." Her remark did nothing to deflate his good mood. "Chris and I had a lot to celebrate, didn't we, Chris? Better said, don't we? I'm going to get the stuff for celebrating while you two talk. Do you want anything to drink, Kathy?"

"No, Dear, I'm going to bed soon." She wheeled into the living room and motioned Chris to sit in one of the easy chairs where she could face him from the wheelchair. "What have you been up to that's got you so full of it?"

"You mean besides saving the Western World?"

Kathy couldn't help but smile at all this silliness. "I know you do that every day. What else?"

Chris put a finger to his lips and leaned toward Kathy to speak very solemnly, very quietly. "Nobody outside the Agency knows this. Do you swear not to tell anybody? And that means my wife if you ever see her or talk to her again." He followed with a mumbled after-thought. "In case I ever see her or talk to her again."

"I don't want to be told any state secrets."

Chris's laugh was exaggerated by the alcohol. "It's not a state secret! It's just that I quit the Agency. Left them for good. No more sneaking around. From now on I'm an honest man. No lies. No shit."

"Watch how you talk in front of my wife, friend." Bob entered with a tray carrying a bottle of Johnny Walker Black Label, an ice bucket and a couple of tumblers. It was a friendly warning.

"You mean to tell me you're retiring at such a young age?" Kathy was truly surprised by this news.

"He doesn't have to retire, Sweetheart; he's one of these rich guys who can go home and clip coupons." Kathy decided she would have a short drink. Bedtime could wait until she had the real news. Bob fixed the drinks and passed them out.

"Not quite that rich," Chris clarified for Kathy, "it's just that my family has a successful tugboat company headquartered in Seattle. My parents have wanted me back there for years, eventually to run the company. It's a job that pays so well that I don't have to worry about a retirement annuity, so I'm just drawing out the money I've put into the retirement system and going home. I have a couple of last minute things to do on Monday, clearing out of the Agency, and then I'll catch the first flight to Seattle."

"Are you in trouble with the Agency, or are the people there unhappy with you?" Kathy felt she had to obtain all the information possible in order to pass it on to Lisa.

Both men laughed. "He's a goddamn hero, Kathy. It's nothing like that. He has a wife and lots of kids to worry about. Not like us." As he said it, Bob realized the hurt those words had inflicted on Kathy, who had always wanted children but was unable to become pregnant after her diagnosis. He reached for her hand, giving it a squeeze.

Chris sipped his drink slowly, coming down from the highs of the day and the drinks he and Bob had enjoyed earlier. He was saddened by the little scene before him and reminded of his own family challenges. "Speaking of my family, do you suppose I could use your phone to call home? I haven't been able to talk with Lisa since we came back here."

With permission granted, he went into the kitchen to use a telephone extension located there. The Brewers watched him return soon after with a long face. "She's away from Edmonds. My mother won't tell me anything. It sounds as if Lisa doesn't want to talk to me." He had lost his taste for hilarity and nonsense. "Sorry, Bob, but I don't feel much like celebrating anymore. I'm going to go to bed. Thanks to you two wonderful people for putting me up here and putting up with me. See you in the morning." With that he was off to the Brewer's spare bedroom.

The next morning Chris dragged out of bed, as tired as he'd felt on the submarine after all the stresses of getting out of Sweden. This weariness was also due to stress, but stress of a different kind. As he sat on the edge of the bed in the Brewer's guest room holding his aching head, he admitted to himself that the intemperance of Friday night had not helped either his mood or the dull pounding behind his eyes. He decided to wash it all away with a long shower and a change into new clothes purchased the previous afternoon. He was grateful that the Agency had provided an allowance to cover the loss of his effects in The Great Escape.

At nine o'clock Saturday morning he appeared in the Brewer kitchen, showered, shaved, and feeling much better. Kathy was awake and bustling around the kitchen in her wheelchair, preparing a full-scale breakfast of eggs, bacon, hash browns and toast. Thirty minutes earlier Chris would not have been able to face all that food, but now it smelled delicious.

"Don't we look spiffy," Kathy teased. "Where did you get the new duds? You look great."

He felt better still. "I only had the clothes I was wearing when we got in on Thursday, so with a little help from my friends at the Agency I bought a few things to last until I get home." A nice pair of tan slacks, shiny new brown loafers, a light-green shirt and a casual tweed jacket. He felt as much like a new man as possible under the circumstances.

Dropping the teasing manner, Kathy said, "You really do look nice in that outfit. What are your plans for the day? Bob tells me that you're not going to work over the weekend. That's good news."

"Speaking of Bob, is he out of bed yet?"

Kathy laughed. "Out of bed? You must know he never stays in bed late. He's already down at the auto shop, buying stuff so he can work on the other love of his life—his Thunderbird. He tries to reassure me by insisting that I'm the first love of his life, that the Thunderbird comes second. He promised to be back in time for breakfast. You still haven't told me your plans."

Bob came through a door from the garage into the kitchen. "Somebody talking about me? When's breakfast?"

Kathy was giving the scrambled eggs a final stir. "It'll be ready in about two minutes. I was just asking Chris what he planned to do over the weekend."

Chris broke in. "I don't feel I want to do much planning until I've eaten that wonderful breakfast you're fixing there."

Most of the talk as they ate was between Bob and Chris, reminiscing about cars they had owned. Bob went on at such length about his Thunderbird that Kathy finally declared she didn't want to hear another word about cars, only about plans for the weekend.

"What's all this interest in weekend plans?" Bob asked. "Chris and I have had enough excitement in our lives to last awhile. Maybe he just wants to relax, do some reading, visit some friends. What do you say, Chris?"

Before Chris could answer, Kathy jumped into the conversation. "Since you don't seem to have any real plans, I have something that might keep you occupied." She drew an envelope from a pocket on the side of her wheelchair and handed it to Chris. He opened it, glanced at the contents and, without a word, walked out of the kitchen and to the spare bedroom, where he could hide the emotional impact of the message he held in his hand.

> Years are like clouds, scudding across the sky
> Some white and fluffy, filled with the promise of a sunny day,
> Others dark and storm-filled, pouring down their rain of despair—
> Those days are gray.

If you, like me, seek to end gray days
And renew our future together,
Look for clues—your personal strength—
And hunt for romantic treasure.

Think of a man, a talented man,
Once an owner of slave and plantation,
Revered then and now for his many gifts
A founder of this great nation.

Now cast in bronze at a nearby shrine,
He guards a hidden message
It's up three steps and to the right
In a crack 'neath the wall's top ledge.

The next thing Kathy and Bob saw of Chris was when he walked rapidly through the kitchen. With a "See you later," he was out the front door, trotting in the direction of the Vienna town center. Kathy never thought he would bolt so quickly after reading the message. It was a good thing she had called Lisa when Chris went back to the bedroom to read her note.

"What the hell was that all about?" Bob was miffed that he seemed to be the only one out of the picture. She explained the contacts with Lisa and what little she knew of Lisa's plans to lure Chris to the Watergate.

* * *

Lisa was thrilled when Kathy called to alert her that the note had been passed to Chris. Even more so when a second call informed her that he seemed to be running for a taxi. She'd have to hurry. In order to look like a tourist, she dressed in a plain pair of dark-brown slacks and beige sweater. Her sturdy brown shoes were perfect for the walking parts of her mission. The reversible raincoat and broad-brimmed hat would help her follow Chris undetected. She found it satisfying to be involved in one of Chris's activities. He'd spot her in a minute if her disguise wasn't right. But it was. It was perfect for the circumstances she'd arranged.

With everything set out the night before, it took no more than five minutes to get into this outfit and downstairs to the lobby, where luck held and she was able to hail a taxi right away. There was little traffic on this Saturday morning, so she was able to arrive at the Jefferson Memorial in another five minutes, certainly before Chris would be able to get there. If he figured out the clues. If he really wanted to see her. Doubts started to mount as she paid the taxi driver and walked to the Tidal Basin side of the memorial, but another day of sunshine boosted her spirits.

Her first task was to load the drop. She leaned with her backside against the low masonry rail bordering steps up to the monument and slipped the second envelope into the niche. Many people were nearby, but none paid any attention to her. Next, Lisa decided that her best bet for avoiding exposure to Chris was to associate herself with one of the groups listening to a tour guide. A couple of tries brought unfriendly stares from tourists who paid good money for their guide and attracted more attention than wanted. Finally she spotted a row of trees near the waters of the Tidal Basin. Standing close to the end of the row, in the shadow cast by a sun low in the sky at this time of year, she thought herself invisible to someone bound on a mission to find a hidden note.

Ten minutes passed before she saw Chris trotting around the monument, aiming for steps to the entrance on the Tidal Basin side. He was wearing clothes she hadn't seen before, but even at a distance she recognized his movements and the fierce determination that seemed to flow from him. He headed for the right side of the steps, stopped, made a full turn and looked again.

Oh no! Lisa realized that the letter was hidden on a second set of stairs. The bottom set described in her note had no wall. Her impulse was to run over and lead him to the note. But as she watched and worried, Chris turned, went to the second set of stairs, and spotted the envelope. Just as she had done in placing the envelope, he leaned against the wall to withdraw it. That was enough.

Lisa walked first, then ran to the parking lot at the back of the monument, intending to walk-run to the Lincoln Memorial. But her luck held, and she spotted a taxi dropping tourists off for a visit. The driver was disappointed that this next fare would only take him a half-mile distance, but minimum was better than nothing. She was away and certain that Chris hadn't spotted her.

☼ ☼ ☼

For his part, Chris smiled to himself over the description of the drop. Fortunately he had no trouble in discovering the minor mistake and certainly didn't dwell on it. He was much more interested in the real message of the notes than the mechanics of finding them. As he turned his back to the crowd, drawing the contents from an envelope like the one passed to him by Kathy, his spirits received the same upward bump as when he read that first message:.

> You think we've drifted far apart and long for something new
> To bring back the wonder and love of youth—of peace long overdue,
> You want the warmth of empathy, the cloudless skies of blue,
> How can I say, "I understand," "I care," "I hurt for you."

Go half a mile north to a marble man,
Beloved for setting slaves free,
Take five steps up, find this niche on the left,
And you'll be much closer to me.

Chris was so touched by the poem that he stood still for a few moments, directing his gaze at the Tidal Basin. Hope was burning brightly in his heart as he took off, walking quickly, toward the next of Lisa's drops. He knew exactly where to go.

Arriving at the Lincoln Memorial he paused before going up the steps to retrieve the next message, taking time to admire the memorial he treasured most among all those in Washington. On such a beautiful day as this, with the exciting possibility of reconciliation with Lisa, the huge marble statue spoke to him as never before. With a gladdening spirit he mounted the steps and found the next message.

I've hit the depths of despair, come face to face with me,
No lying or evading here, and no hypocrisy,
Like cosmic bullets pelting, the answers seem so clear,
I love you and adore you, every inch of you is dear.

You speak Russian, Swedish and even some French
It's the latter you'll need to get there.
Look around for a person who knows tourists' sights
At a hotel called "Child on the Square."

Getting closer! This must be it! Chris took no time to muse over the message, but tucked it in his pocket as he started down the memorial steps, on his way to flagging down a taxi. Feeling that Lisa might be watching, just as she did when playing the birthday game at home, he scanned the territory in front of him and saw a woman about her size break away from a knot of tourists, walking rapidly toward a part of the memorial circle where it was possible to flag down a taxi. Just where he was headed.

Keeping her in sight, he was about to start running forward when she did something that brought him to a full stop. She took off the raincoat she was wearing, turned the sleeves inside out, reversing the coat so that it was now brown rather than blue. And then she did the same thing with her hat. There was no way that he could see the woman's face with such a distance between them, but all the evidence pointed at one person. It had to be Lisa. He held back until she found a taxi and left, then found a taxi for himself.

* * *

Lisa was in a high state of elation as her taxi approached L'Enfant Hotel. Her scheme had worked like a dream, and watching Chris as he eagerly followed her trail had renewed her faith that he truly wanted to put their differences aside. She paid the taxi driver at the hotel entrance and dashed into the lobby to leave her last note with the concierge. Then she walked a hundred yards up the street to a place where she could observe the entrance but stay hidden herself.

Judging from Chris's quick movements at the other sites, he would arrive momentarily. When five minutes passed without seeing him, she started to worry. After ten minutes she was filled with negative speculation. He'd had enough of the game and given it up. The taxi he'd taken from the Lincoln Memorial had crashed, killing or maiming him. He'd entered and exited the hotel from another entrance. There just was no way he could have interpreted that last message incorrectly. Something awful must have kept him from showing up here.

Lisa was inventing still more morbid excuses when something round and hard was pushed between her shoulder blades.

"This is a gun in your back, Lady. Do not scream. Do only what I tell you." It was a low voice, like none she'd heard before.

Lisa swore later that her heart stopped completely for five full seconds. She knew because she counted each of them. When the blood finally started flowing again she was able to squeak out a timid few words. "What do you want me to do?"

The gun was still in her back. The voice came again. "I want you to lie down. I'm going to ravish you right here."

Lisa's heart stopped again, but only momentarily. There was a chuckle in the voice of the speaker who uttered these last words. It seemed impossible, but she was going to take a chance and act on her instinct. She whirled around quickly to find just what she suspected: her husband Chris, holding a blunt-ended pen.

"Oh, you, you!" She pounded him on the chest with her fists. "Damn you. How could you know? I was sure you would complete my game!"

Chris grabbed her wrists to stop her pummeling. "This isn't a birthday party in Edmonds, Love of My Life." He forced her hands behind her back and gave her a lingering kiss. "You were playing with someone who's had lots of experience. You shouldn't change your disguise while there's any chance of your mark seeing you."

Tears were streaming down Lisa's face.

"Are you crying because you're mad, sad, or glad to see me?"

She let go his hands and backed off a little to get a good look at him. "All of the above. I'm mad because you caught me, sad because we've wasted so much precious time, and glad as anything to see you, Mr. Smarty Pants. You look wonderful! Why haven't I seen the outfit you're wearing before this?"

"I lost all my belongings except the cruddy clothes I was wearing when I returned. The Agency treated me to this." He turned around as if modeling, which earned a laugh from Lisa.

"But first things first," he said. "How about that ravishing bit? Want to do it right here, or go up to your hotel room?"

"Oh no! I'm no exhibitionist. And what makes you think I have a hotel room here?"

"It's only logical, after all the hoops you've made me jump through to get here. So where do we go to get this done?"

Lisa took him by the arm and started walking toward the hotel entrance. "It's not where do *we* go, but where do *you* go. You teased me about my finders game for birthday gifts. Nobody gets the gift unless they complete the game, and you haven't finished this one. I'm pretty sure I know what you want your gift to be. If you really want it, you'd better read that last note again. After you've gone into the hotel I want a half-hour head start before you follow the last directions." She reached up to give Chris an even more lingering kiss and pushed him toward the lobby, past a grinning doorman. "Promise!"

Chris went into the hotel in a state of wonderment over all that had happened in less than two hours of a Saturday morning. He fished the last note out of his pocket and re-read it as he looked around the lobby. Ah yes, the gentleman "who knows tourist sights." He walked up to the concierge desk, where a friendly man asked if he could help. "Do you have a message for Chris Holbeck?"

He did. "Your wife left this note just minutes ago, Mr. Holbeck. She seemed in quite a hurry to leave. You might even catch her outside if she's waiting to be picked up."

Chris was so grateful that he gave the concierge a tip, not knowing that Lisa had been even more generous when she left her envelope at the desk. Checking his watch with the intention of waiting half an hour before moving out on the final leg of the search, he sat down to read the note.

> I've put away false weapons of anger and regret,
> The past is dead and buried ... the future unclear as yet,
> But now I stand before you as I never have before ...
> Naked, open, loving, before another door.
>
> And so my gift for you today is just a promise true,
> To love you as I never have—to devote my life to you.
> I love you and I want you, and I've put away my pride.
> To think of life without you is to cease to live inside.

Now on to another fancy hotel,
A president's recent waterloo.
Ask for a key to Lisa Holbeck's room,
Where I'll be waiting for you.

Delaying half an hour was sheer agony. He paced around the hotel lobby, admiring the art work. Read some of the brochures near the concierge desk, reminding himself of sights that he already knew well. Checked his watch. When the time came he hurried to the hotel entrance, happy to be ushered into a taxi so quickly,

* * *

Back in her room at the Watergate, Lisa took a quick shower to wash away the perspiration generated from trying to stay ahead of Chris. A look in the mirror as she toweled herself off helped her decide against any makeup but lipstick. A few dabs of scent in the appropriate places, and she slipped into a white blouse, a plain blue skirt and some dressy sandals. In the few minutes remaining before Chris was expected, she brushed her hair until it gleamed, knowing that Chris considered it her crowning glory. She was still brushing when the lock on the hallway door clicked.

He came to the bathroom where she was still working the brush, stood there with a hand high up on the doorjamb and a lopsided grin on his face, handsome in his new clothes, watching as she brushed, meeting her eyes in the mirror over the sink. The sexual tension between them was as vibrant as the air just before lightning strikes.

"You'd make a pretty good spy." Chris said.

"Thanks, but you caught me. I was disappointed."

"A little training is all you need. Just a little training."

"Maybe you could be my teacher."

"Maybe."

The awkward silence that followed reflected the insulation that kept the spark from firing—doubt. Lisa continued her mindless brushing.

He followed my directions like a Bloodhound on a scent trail, but why? Because he truly loves me? Because he wants a reconciliation of our differences for the sake of the children? Or because he's missed having sex for a couple of weeks? How can I tell him what I want, what I'm willing to do, beyond what I already said in the poem? Did he really understand it, or did he just skip the poetry and follow the directions?

* * *

"It's hot in here." Chris removed his jacket and walked into the sitting room of the suite, where he hung it over a chair pulled up to the desk. He returned to the open bathroom door, stood with hands in his pockets and stared at Lisa, who was still brushing.

How do I tell her I'm leaving the Agency without its seeming to be total capitulation on my part? Her poetry was touching, but did she really mean all those things? I want to believe her.

"I've got a bottle of champagne on ice." Lisa put the hairbrush down on the bathroom counter and signaled for Chris to go into the sitting room, still not touching him. "I'm running out of the money I saved while you were in Vietnam, so it's not a vintage of any sort. Kind of a cheap imitation champagne that cost a lot at a market up the street."

"Should I open it for you?" He moved toward the ice bucket that was sitting with drink glasses on the credenza holding a large TV set.

"It would be better if you opened it for us."

"Touché ."

✳ ✳ ✳

Lisa watched as he neatly removed the foil and wire keeper from the top of the bottle, smiling inwardly as he looked for a wastebasket to dispose of them. Always orderly, Chris. He had some trouble at first with removing the cork, which she knew he would find embarrassing. He fetched a hand towel from the bathroom for a better grip. The cork popped satisfactorily and Chris poured champagne for each of them in the regular drink glasses provided by the hotel. She should have thought of getting some goblets for their celebration, or what she hoped would be a celebration. Oh, well, she couldn't think of everything. Or afford everything.

Chris handed one of the glasses to Lisa, who was sitting at one end of a small sofa. He looked around for a seat, finally settling on the desk chair, which he dragged comfortably close but not too close. Lisa noted his efforts not to invade her space. Perhaps the invasion would come later.

They raised their glasses and said "Skål!" in such perfect unison that they were both smiling as they took the ritual sips of the drink.

"Well, we at least can still do that together," Lisa said as she put her glass on the end table next to the sofa.

Chris kept his drink in hand as he leaned toward his wife and looked earnestly into her eyes. "With the sentiments in your poetry, I thought we might be doing something else together by now, something I've always thought we did well."

"Those sentiments are very true, Chris, but all things in their time. I bared my soul in those lines I wrote. I truly love you and am willing now to follow wherever you go. But before we go any further, I want to hear about your meeting with Sasha, or at least the part that bears on our situation. Where do we stand?" She took another drink of the champagne, making a face at its cloying sweetness.

"I don't want to insult your taste, Lisa," Chris said, rising to his feet, "but this stuff would make horse piss taste good." He took the glass from her hands and together with his own poured the so-called champagne into the toilet, followed by what was left in the bottle. Next he called room service, ordering a bottle of Dom Perignon.

Lisa was aghast. "Chris! We can't afford that. A bottle of Dom Perignon through room service is going to add a hundred dollars to my bill!"

"Not your bill, my love, *our* bill. I'm moving in as of now. And yes, we can afford it."

"Not so fast, Buster. I want to know more before I let myself be invaded just like that, and before I agree that we can afford it. Besides, you still haven't answered my question about Sasha."

* * *

Chris pushed the desk chair back where it belonged and sat down where he belonged, next to Lisa on the sofa. Looking into her eyes, he said, "I don't believe Sasha will be a problem. He's here now, and we made a side deal that he will never, ever, reveal anything that went on privately between us."

"Don't you think the interrogators will be able to get that out of him?"

"I honestly believe that they won't. He's extremely well trained to hold up against interrogation on matters he doesn't want to discuss."

"But how can he be valuable to your people if he will only talk about whatever he wants to talk about?"

"We had quite an adventure together, Sasha and I, and I got to know him very well. I'm still angry, disappointed, hurt, and ... lots more emotions I can't even name. But I have to say that despite that one personal lapse, he's a man of honor. He made no bones about loving the United States. He's here because his other life became intolerable. I believe that he'll do what he promised—give us all the information of intelligence value learned in his former life—but he hasn't pledged to put his life on the line working for us."

Lisa started to ask something. Before she could speak, Chris held up his hand. "Just let me finish. I'm sure I know what you want to hear. Sasha said more than once how sorry he was about luring you down to Gamlastan. He went to great lengths to explain that it was his feelings for us as a family, and of course his strong feelings for you, that motivated the actions that eventually brought him here to the States."

"But supposing he can't hold out, that he does reveal it, how about your career?"

There was a knock on the door before he could answer. "Room service!"

"Great timing." Chris pushed up from the sofa and admitted the waiter, a very polite older man who smiled throughout the ceremony of presenting a bottle of premium champagne. It came nestled in a silver ice bucket and accompanied by chocolate truffles.

"Shall I open it for you, Sir?"

Chris looked over at Lisa, who was hiding a smile behind her hand. "Yes, why don't you."

The waiter, who had no trouble with the foil, the wire or the cork, received an appropriately large tip before he wheeled his cart out of the room.

After allowing Chris to taste a sip of the champagne, he had poured for both in the proper crystal goblets brought for the occasion. Chris took his position back on the sofa, sitting next to Lisa.

"Skål again." Their eyes lit up when they tasted the Dom Perignon. "Now you know why it costs so much," Chris told Lisa. "It's worth it."

"It's wonderful, but I'm not sure it's worth that much." She took another taste. "Well, maybe. But you still haven't told me how all this is going to affect your career."

"Even if it all came out, it wouldn't be revealed outside the Agency. And as far as my career goes, I no longer have one, at least not with the Agency."

Lisa was so shocked by the news that she leaned away from Chris, against the armrest of the sofa, in order to get a better view of her husband.

"No! Are you in trouble?"

Chris smiled. "In all modesty, I'll quote Bob Brewer answering Kathy when she asked the same question, 'He's a goddamn hero.' No, I'm not in trouble. For all the pain it cost us—and it was a lot of trouble getting Sasha here to the States— the operation turned out to be a real coup because he provided badly needed information."

"Then why are you leaving? Seems like you're at the peak of your career."

Chris reached across Lisa to place his glass of champagne on the end table next to her, then put his arm around his wife and pulled her to him so that her head rested on his shoulder. "As you said before, all things in their time. I've put in twenty years with the Agency, and I believe I contributed a lot. While I was in Sweden I had a chance to sail on the *Valhalla*, Nils Schmidt's big boat, and realized once again how much I miss being on the water."

Lisa gently pushed away from him to get more Dom Perignon. She filled their glasses before sitting next to him again. Both sipped at the champagne as they talked, the tenseness visibly draining out of Lisa as she heard her husband talk of joining the family towboat company.

Chris said, "I might want to spend some time on the tugs, getting my licenses to run them. I know I'll be in management, but I really believe that managers should be able to do the jobs of the people they manage."

Lisa said, "I want to get a house in Edmonds and be close to your folks, but not so close that Mor could just walk next door to see her grandchildren. A couple of miles away, at least."

Chris laughed. "Five miles might be better. How would you feel about my being away for a couple of weeks on a towing job?"

Lisa smiled and shook her head. "As long as I knew where you were and what you were doing, I wouldn't mind."

And so they talked of their plans and dreams, sipping their expensive wine. Finally Chris asked the last question on his mind. "I've shared why I'm leaving the Agency and your poetry went a long way in convincing me that your love is strong as ever. I'm grateful, but curious about what inspired your change of heart."

"It's a long story, Chris, too long to tell tonight. While you were away I was counseling with an old friend from college days. She's a wonderful person, a clinical psychologist who works only with women. Elle taught me how to be forgiving, not only of other people but of myself. My guilt about being with Sasha has held me back in many ways, probably the most important being in how I've acted toward Lisbet. I was not able to love and treat her as I should because of that guilt. Now I believe I've conquered those feelings."

Chris drew her to him, overcome by emotion. "I'm so glad." was all he could say.

"There's one final thing, Chris. I need your permission to love her unconditionally."

"You know you have my permission."

"No, I need you to say it." She pushed away again to be able to look at him directly.

"Lisa, Love of My Life, you truly have my permission to love our daughter unconditionally." With that, their eyes brimming with joyful tears, they put down their glasses and turned to each other.

Scientists have argued about the lightning strike that finally comes when tension between the dark cloud and tall tree is too great. When it strikes, does the lightning travel down from cloud to tree, or travel up from tree to cloud? Whatever the proper answer, the energy released that evening in the third floor Watergate suite traveled both ways, and there were many strikes.

❊ ❊ ❊

A maid cleaning the suite the following morning found a bottle of Dom Perignon with still a third of the expensive wine remaining. She shook her head at the waste, wadded some foil into a ball, stuffed it in the neck of the bottle and placed it in her large purse to take home that evening. Such a gift to her husband would bring good loving.

Love and good wine were too precious to waste.

EPILOGUE

By the time Chris Holbeck and Bob Brewer arrived back at CIA Headquarters on the Thursday of their flying into Andrews Air Force Base, Roberta Fletcher was no longer at work. She had been at her desk at eight thirty that morning, but pleaded illness shortly after their flight from Prestwick landed, saying she would be at home. A check of her home found neither Roberta nor her car, and none of her neighbors had seen her return that morning.

The FBI was notified and a nationwide search set in motion. Roberta's car was found in long-term parking at National Airport. It was impounded and thoroughly searched, as was her home. While the car yielded nothing incriminating, a small room in the basement of her Virginia home was found to have many items commonly used by intelligence operatives, including one-time code pads and secret writing materials. These were carelessly hidden in a room ostensibly used for storage.

A full-scale check of all public modes of transportation out of Washington and nearby cities found no trace of Roberta Fletcher. U.S. authorities involved in the search were more and more pessimistic about her ever being captured. And Gary Llonis suffered more than any of them, at times venting his rage on Bob Brewer and Chris Holbeck for not having reported their discovery of Roberta before leaving Scotland, at other times going into a deep funk when he admitted that he would have made the same choice under the circumstances. The discovery of Roberta as the mole would stop the flow of information from his division to the KGB, but there was much information she could have provided on materials she had made available to the Soviets and KGB modus operandi in the United States. Most of all, Llonis wanted desperately to know how Roberta was alerted to the threat. Was it a coincidence that the warning came soon after Plotkin arrived in the U.S.? Had the KGB delayed alerting her to danger in the vain hope that Plotkin wasn't under U.S. control or through some snafu in communications?

A break in the case came on the following Tuesday, November 21st, when Roberta attempted to enter Canada from the U.S. at the International Bridge crossing between Sault Ste. Marie, Michigan, and the town of the same name on the Ontario side of the border. She had every reason to believe she could cross safely into Canada and find whatever transport the KGB had waiting for her there. Her U.S. passport in a false name seemed genuine in every respect, as did documentation on the car. But human failing was her undoing.

A female border officer on the Canadian side, dealing with heavy traffic at this time of day, asked Roberta only a couple of perfunctory questions and was ready to motion her on. But there was something about the way Roberta answered the questions that bothered the Canadian officer, so she asked her to pull into the side parking by the border authorities' office. Roberta was tense after more than five days of running, and a bit high from some drinks she'd taken for courage before attempting the border crossing. She panicked. First she put the car in gear and hit the accelerator. She had driven no more than a hundred yards when she remembered that the Canadian officer still had her passport, so she slammed on the brakes. Only then did she realize what she was doing. In full panic mode she stopped the engine, grabbed the keys from the ignition, and started running in the direction of Canada. Border officers ran her down in another hundred yards. After a brief conference with the female officer who was the first to question Roberta, and finding that she was an American citizen, she and her car were taken back to the U.S. border station. In less than an hour fingerprints revealed her true identity as Roberta Fletcher.

Unfortunately, Roberta proved nearly useless as a source of information. The stresses of clandestine work and the terror suffered at the Canadian border drove her into a nervous breakdown that never fully responded to Agency attempts at healing. After a year of treatment she was found to be stable enough to stand trial for treason, but was still not a reliable source for the kind of information the Agency hoped to get from her.

Roberta Fletcher is currently serving a life sentence in a Federal prison, with no possibility of parole. The location of that prison has not been made public.

* * *

Aleksandr Elyovitch Plotkin was true to his word. He answered all the questions posed by Agency interrogators factually and with satisfactory detail, but elaborated as little as possible and rarely volunteered information. He felt he was holding up his end of the bargain.

At the beginning of the relationship with this source the interrogators believed they would have a full year of work before getting all the information possible. As it turned out they discovered nothing new after a mere five months of dealing with Plotkin. After six months he was prepared for resettlement in the United States under an assumed identity as a Swedish immigrant—a photographer specializing in family portraits, weddings, pets and the like. The place chosen was one where research showed that a popular family photographer had announced his retirement and planned to sell the business. The price was right, and the city was big enough to absorb another resident without a lot of excitement but small enough that Sasha would be able to establish new relationships more easily.

Moscow, Idaho, a city of some 200,000 people, is located in the northwestern part of the state, just across the border from Pullman, Washington. Moscow is the seat of the University of Idaho; Pullman is home to Washington State University.

In September 1974, Sasha Plotkin drove to Pullman in answer to an invitation from the university there, to attend a show featuring art produced by faculty members. While at the show he met Mary Gilmore, a fellow photographer and an art faculty member. Mary was in her late thirties, single and attractive, and seemed interested in Plotkin, who was interested in return. They made a date for the following weekend, when Plotkin would come to Pullman to meet Gilmore for dinner. There was no talk of after dinner plans. Plotkin toyed with the idea of bedding Mary, but found her so attractive that he was willing to take it slow in hopes that the relationship would turn into a long-term friendship and perhaps more.

The dinner proved to be everything Plotkin had hoped. They talked and talked … and talked. Mary Gilmore had an interesting background, and he was so comfortable in his current role that he could talk for hours with no fear of blowing it. They were still not talked out after a wonderful two-hour dinner, so they went on to a hotel bar, where both sipped non-alcoholic drinks as the conversation continued. With all her friendliness, Gilmore made it clear that Plotkin would not be invited to her home that evening. They parted in the hotel parking lot with a hug and a kiss on the cheek, and the promise of another date the following weekend. Gilmore would do the traveling then, first visiting Plotkin's studio, then having dinner. Again, nothing was specified for the rest of the evening. Plotkin was thrilled.

While the cities share higher education as central to their core of activities, they are located in states with an important difference at the time: the minimum drinking age in Washington State was 21 years, while it was 18 years in Idaho. Many young students from Washington State University crossed the state line for a twenty-minute drive to Moscow, where they could legally drink alcoholic beverages.

Plotkin left the hotel in Pullman about half past midnight. Twenty minutes later, on the two-lane asphalt highway between Moscow and Pullman, a car approached from the other direction, driving at high speed. It was driven by a freshman from Washington State University who had passed the evening in Moscow, swilling beer with the three passengers accompanying him on the return trip to Pullman. All were nodding from the effects of the beer and the late hour, including the driver. The eighteen-year-old fought off sleep, but finally succumbed as he neared the car driven by Sasha Plotkin. Just as he fell asleep the car veered sharply to the left, striking Plotkin's car head on before he had time to react.

Sasha Plotkin and the driver of the other car were killed instantly. The student in the front seat of the Washington State car died after a few hours in the hospital, while the two young men in the back seat of that car had injuries that were not serious.

When police searched for Plotkin's identity they found and called an emergency number in his wallet, which brought an immediate response from the Agency. There was a fast reaction. Plotkin's "closest friend" arrived in Moscow the next day, where he spent a week disposing of the assets and arranging an honorable, very quiet burial. Contact with Plotkin's widow was later established through a cutout in Germany, who notified her of the death and delivered to her the many thousands of dollars remaining after the disposal of his estate.

The burial ceremony for Sasha Plotkin was simple, attended only by Plotkin's "friend," the funeral home director and his assistant, and by Mary Gilmore. There was much publicity about the early Sunday morning accident that had taken his life and the lives of two young men. After reading the news, Mary had called Plotkin's studio number repeatedly until the phone was answered by the man disposing of his estate. Others in Plotkin's small group of local friends accepted the news that the burial would be private, but Gilmore refused to take no for an answer.

Fall was in the air on the sunny but cold September morning when Gustav Hinas's crushed body was lowered into that grave. A Lutheran minister read the burial ceremony. The Agency friend stood with an arm held awkwardly around Mary Gilmore. He was uncomfortable in the role of consoling this woman crying so grievously at the loss of a man she had known only a few weeks.

If only he had known the sweet blossoming of a relationship between Mary Gilmore and the man who had inhabited that body nearing its final resting place.

If only she had known the real man who began life in that body in the Soviet Union and ended it in this grave on a cold, sunny day in Moscow. Idaho.

✷ ✷ ✷

For Chris and Lisa, the return to Edmonds in November 1972 was the beginning of the rebirth of their marriage, bringing healing for their children, themselves individually and all their family members. Mor had her grandchildren in the United States, and Herman had a family member in place as a successor to manage Tows, Inc.

The children seemed to have overcome a loss of balance caused first by Chris's long assignment to Vietnam and by the subsequent events. Lisbet was blossoming under the newfound love and attention showered on her by her mother, and Missy was secure enough in her mother's love to understand and appreciate her sister's happiness.

Finishing their final year of high school, Matthew and Mark were able to enjoy a few months with their transformed family, settling into the new home before going off to college. They surprised their parents—pleasantly—by deciding on their own to split up for this stage of their lives, Matthew attending Western Washington University some hundred miles north of Seattle, Mark going to Washington State University in the southeast corner of the state, even farther away.

Their home in Edmonds was too far from the senior Holbecks for a comfortable walk, but close enough to be convenient by car. The families exchanged hosting Sunday dinners, and Mor visited often to spend time with her granddaughters— visits that were always welcomed by the girls and their mother.

As happy as Lisa was with this new life, she had some residual guilt about her stupidity in sleeping with Plotkin. She also feared that he might one day try to contact her or make their brief affair public. As often as Chris tried to allay that fear, she was just as often beset by it. She knew Plotkin was somewhere in the States, and that was enough to tinge all the colors of her happiness with regret.

Chris shared fully in the satisfaction of other family members with this new situation, and to a much lesser extent than Lisa in the fear of Sasha Plotkin's potential for spoiling that happiness. His position at Tows, Inc., was both satisfying and challenging, the only downside being that he had to give up the dream of becoming licensed to run the tugs. Administrative duties simply did not allow for the kind of time required to be fully licensed. Instead he designed an orientation plan that gave him a refresher on tugboat life through short trips of two or three days, shadowing the various positions from deckhand to mate, engineer to skipper. He enjoyed those times and found them useful in learning to manage the company.

And so it was that in late September, 1974, Chris was aboard the *Björn*, anchored off of the Cherry Point oil refinery north of Bellingham, Washington, standing watch with the mate. They were together on the bridge, surveying the astounding scenery of the northern San Juan Islands, waiting for a signal that the tanker needing their escort was ready to depart, when the Tows dispatcher called by radio to alert Chris to a telephone call waiting for him. He would patch the call through to the tug if Chris wanted to accept the call. This was worrisome news. Chris discouraged all but emergency calls while he was sailing.

The call was from Lisa. "What's wrong, Honey?"

"You won't believe this, but I was awakened this morning by a call from the Agency. This time it was Bob Brewer. I told him you might accept a radio call on the tug, but he will talk with you only on a landline. He wants you to contact him as soon as possible."

"That's interesting."

"It's a lot more than interesting. You really are retired, aren't you?"

"Yes, Honey, I'm truly retired. Did Bob say when or where he wanted me to call?"

"At the office now or at home later. You are really, really retired, aren't you?"

"Yes, Dear, I'm really, really retired."

"Good. Call Bob, and then call me with the good news that you're not going off somewhere outlandish. This frightens me, Chris. I thought we were through with all that."

How to find a landline when sitting on a tugboat off the shore of Whatcom County? Posed with this question, the mate said that the refinery dock manager on duty was someone he'd dealt with. He used the marine radio to call the man and confirm that they could slip into the refinery dock and stay for half an hour. The tanker they would be handling was due to depart at the end of that time.

Reaching the operations office after the tug docked, Chris was allowed to make a long-distance call as long as it was collect. He heard Bob Brewer's agreement when the operator asked if he'd accept the call.

"I'm sure you want to know why I called, Chris. I've got some sad news."

Chris felt his stomach churn. "Did you say sad or bad?"

"A bit of both, I suppose. You went to a lot of trouble to help out a fellow a couple of years ago. We both spent some time with him. You remember it?"

"How could I forget?"

"Well, the bad news is that he was killed in a car crash early last Sunday morning, not his fault. The sad news is that he had just started a relationship with a young woman who would have been perfect for him. I've just spoken with the fellow who cleared up matters and handled the burial. He said the woman is distraught because she was certain that each of them had finally found the one person in the universe best suited to a forever relationship. From everything he found and heard, he thought that our friend felt the same way."

"Dear Jesus! Where did this happen?"

"You mean you never heard from him? He wasn't supposed to contact you, but I figured he would anyway since the two of you had such a close friendship."

Chris's grip on the telephone receiver tightened. "I truly believe he was a man of honor, so when he agreed not to contact me, he meant it." He looked around the little operations office from his borrowed desk, finding that nobody was paying attention. "You're right about it beginning as a friendship, but that part never seemed to get back on track after he disappeared the first time around. Anyway, I do appreciate your letting me know."

Brewer promised to send newspaper clippings that would give more detailed information. When the call ended Chris sat for a time, staring at a framed picture on the borrowed desk—a man, a woman and two children, boy and girl, all nice looking and seeming to radiate good health and cheer. Presumably the family of whoever used this desk. He reflected on his own family and what effect this news might have on them, how he and Lisa, two boys and two girls, would look just as healthy and happy in a picture seen by an outsider. He placed another collect call, this one to Lisa, who was eager to hear what the call was all about.

"The fellow I met in Europe a couple of years ago."

"What about him?"

"He's dead. Killed in a car crash last Sunday morning."

"Really? Are you sure?" When Chris assured her that it was true, she said, "I have to be sorry in a way, but I'm relieved, too." The news removed much of the tension in Lisa's voice, softening the edge in her speaking that had been there too long. "How do you feel, Chris? Aren't you relieved, at least a little bit?"

"In the sense you're talking about, yes, but I feel something deeper than that, too. After all, he did start out wanting our friendship, but then a lot of things got in the way. You should know that he's been just a couple-hundred miles away all this time, but he stuck by an agreement that he would never contact us. He was a straight-shooter in many ways."

"I'm really surprised, Chris. After all that's happened, especially considering how you felt, it sounds like you're defending him. Explain that to me if you can. Do you think he ever ... ever ..."

"Knew about that little girl?"

A pause, and then a small voice, "Yes."

"I really don't believe he ever knew about that. If he did, he never discussed it with anyone as far as I can tell. It would be another example of his being a straight shooter. I'm at the refinery now and on one of their phones. I really don't want to talk more about this until I get home. I should be back day after tomorrow. Let's go out to a nice dinner, park the car somewhere with a good view, and talk it out then."

"That sounds good, but it's too long to wait. You can't just leave me hanging that way. This has been too important to our lives. How do you feel? Is this the ending we've been waiting for?" There was a silence on the phone, stretching so long that Lisa thought the connection had been broken.

Finally her husband replied. "Even though we never said as much to each other, this is probably the most satisfactory ending we could have imagined. It makes life better in a way for both of us. But you need to know that I can't help grieving for a friendship that was lost in such a strange way. And most of all, I can't help grieving for that friend's new love, found just a couple of weeks before he was killed. I'll tell you all about it when I get home.

"Most of all, Lisa, this untimely death should remind us to love each other fiercely each day of all those that remain to us. No couple has ever had that lesson more clearly laid out for them."

AUTHOR'S NOTES

This is a work of fiction. The plot is fictional, as are the characters described, although some of them have traits of people I've known and loved. One drawn rather directly from life is a dear aunt who was almost "as Swedish" as the character "Mor" in the book. "Mor," the character, is a bit overdrawn in comparison to my late Aunt Gertrude Bardarson, but however you find her in reading the book, please know that I have tried to sketch Aunt Gertrude lovingly.

Likewise, a few of the incidents other than those involved with the fictional case actually took place. The embarrassment of a senior Swedish official because of his boorishness regarding her maiden name was caused by my late wife, Eunice Sherman.

In regard to historical information I have tried to be as accurate as possible. Gammalsvenskby was a real community, founded as described. The basic idea for the book came from Aunt Gertrude's introducing me to Folke Hedblom, Professor of Linguistics at The Institute for Dialect and Folklore Research at Uppsala, Sweden. I learned of Gammalsvenskby from Professor Hedblom during a visit to Seattle in 1961, and later met him in Stockholm. At that time he gave me a copy of his small book, *The Gammalsvenskby People: Swedish-Canadian Immigrants from South Russia,* which was the basis for much background in the book. I am grateful to a personal friend in Sweden, Anders Eckerström, who many years ago researched newspaper archives that provided additional information on Gammalsvenskby. Anders and his wife, Charlotte, also reviewed portions of the manuscript for accuracy.

Likewise, I am thankful to another Swedish friend, Åke Martinson of Gothenberg, who on two separate occasions took me on tours of the Swedish west coast north of that city in order to choose a port that would reasonably fit the fictional *Valhalla's* winter home. I'm also grateful to Åke and another Swedish friend, Bengt Ekroth, for reviewing the manuscript for accuracy concerning details of the trip between Stockholm and the Swedish west coast described in Chapters 29-31.

Parallels drawn to the Gordon Lonsdale (Konon Molody) case are based on a host of sources available on the Internet and in various books. One of the most useful here was *KGB—The Inside Story*, by Christopher Andrew and Oleg Gordievsky, an excellent history and description of that organization. Labels for various KGB departments follow that description, except for the "special operations group targeted at American intelligence services" described in Chapter Forty-One. While such a group is conceivable, in this case it comes from the author's imagination.

The Internet provided a great deal of information on the German opening offensive in the Soviet Union, Barbarossa; on Russian tank warfare in World War II; on KGB operations; and on the U.S. Sturgeon Class nuclear submarines.

Readers who find inaccuracies may blame this author. I accept full responsibility for factual errors in the text.

I thank my family and friends for their support and in particular my wife, Janice Lind-Sherman, who read the manuscript and gave many useful suggestions. Janice also is the author of a poem titled "Years Without Clouds," from which several stanzas are quoted in Chapter Forty.

My very special thanks go to the three people most responsible for publication of this novel. Jennifer McCord brought *Sasha Plotkin's Deceit* to the attention of Catherine Treadgold, Publisher of Coffeetown Press and its subsidiary, Camel Press, and remained closely involved in every step of the process. I am particularly grateful for the skill and care Catherine devoted to editing this manuscript. I would also like to thank Sabrina Sun for her clever cover design and the rest of the team at Camel Press for their hard work. I truly appreciate these good professional friends.

Vaughn Ashley Sherman
Edmonds, Washington
January, 2012

Photo courtesy of Anna Crowley, www.annaphotography.com

Vaughn Sherman was born and raised in Seattle, Washington, where he attended Roosevelt High School. After an active duty Navy tour late in World War II, he attended and graduated from the University of Washington, working in Alaska for the Fish and Wildlife Service during summer vacations.

The Alaska experience led Vaughn into the career of a fisheries biologist, working for the Washington State Department of Fisheries. That career was cut short when he was recruited by the Central Intelligence Agency. He served long assignments in the Far East and Europe before doing a short tour in Vietnam 1973-74. That assignment ended when his wife became ill and he was needed at home to care for her and three school-age children.

After taking early retirement Vaughn's community activities have mostly involved the governance of non-profit agencies and community colleges. This work includes presentations and retreat leadership all over the country. He has served on the Board of Trustees of Edmonds Community College, as president of Washington State's Trustees Association of Community and Technical Colleges (TACTC), and as president of the national Association of Community College Trustees (ACCT).

Vaughn studied creative writing at the University of Washington, an interest that has resulted in several publications. In addition to *Sasha's Plotkin's Deceit,* he wrote the memoir of a northwest mariner titled *An Uncommon Life* (1988). Two small books dealing with the management of community college boards of trustees have been published by ACCT. *Essentials of Good Board/CEO Relations* was released in 1999 and is now in its second edition. *The Board Chair: A Guide for Leading Community Colleges,* a collaboration with his colleague Dr. Cindra Smith, was published in 2002. A third book will be released in early 2012: *Walking the Board Walk—Secrets of an Enjoyable Nonprofit Board Experience.* This guide shares Vaughn's thirty years of experience both as a member and trainer of nonprofit boards.

A certified mediator, Vaughn is a volunteer with the Dispute Resolution Center of Snohomish, Island and Skagit Counties.

After the passing of his first wife, Vaughn married Jan Lind-Sherman, a teacher who brought her own children into the marriage. Their extended family includes eight children, eleven grandchildren, two great-grandchildren, and assorted siblings, nieces, nephews and daughters-in-law.

You can find Vaughn online at www.vaughnsherman.com.